Kate Hardy has always  read before she went to s... Mills & Boon books when s... decided that this was what she wanted to do. When she isn't writing Kate enjoys reading, cinema, ballroom dancing and the gym. You can contact her via her website: katehardy.com.

Hana Sheik falls in love every day, reading her favourite romances and writing her own happily-ever-afters. She's worked in various jobs—but never for very long, because she's always wanted to be a romance author. Now, happily, she gets to live that dream. Born in Somalia, she moved to Ottawa, Canada, at a very young age, and still resides there with her family.

Also by Kate Hardy

Mills & Boon Love Always
Forbidden Kiss with the Prince

If the Fairy Tale Fits… collection
His Strictly Off-Limits Ballerina

Mills & Boon Medical
Paediatrician's Unexpected Second Chance

Honolulu Medics collection
The Surgeon's Tropical Temptation

Also by Hana Sheik

Mills & Boon Love Always
Forbidden Kisses with Her Millionaire Boss
The Baby Swap That Bound Them

The Abdullahis miniseries
Falling for Her Forbidden Bodyguard
Another Shot at Forever

Discover more at millsandboon.co.uk.

SECOND TIME'S A CHARM

KATE HARDY

HANA SHEIK

MILLS & BOON

All rights reserved including the right of reproduction in whole or in part in any form. This edition is published by arrangement with Harlequin Enterprises ULC.

This is a work of fiction. Names, characters, places, locations and incidents are purely fictional and bear no relationship to any real life individuals, living or dead, or to any actual places, business establishments, locations, events or incidents. Any resemblance is entirely coincidental.

Without limiting the exclusive rights of any author, contributor or the publisher of this publication, any unauthorised use of this publication to train generative artificial intelligence (AI) technologies is expressly prohibited. HarperCollins also exercise their rights under Article 4(3) of the Digital Single Market Directive 2019/790 and expressly reserve this publication from the text and data mining exception.

® and TM are trademarks owned and used by the trademark owner and/or its licensee. Trademarks marked with ® are registered with the United Kingdom Patent Office and/or the Office for Harmonisation in the Internal Market and in other countries.

First published in Great Britain 2026
by Mills & Boon, an imprint of HarperCollins*Publishers* Ltd,
1 London Bridge Street, London, SE1 9GF

www.harpercollins.co.uk

HarperCollins*Publishers*, Macken House, 39/40 Mayor Street Upper, Dublin 1, D01 C9W8, Ireland

Second Time's a Charm © 2026 Harlequin Enterprises ULC

Sweet on the CEO Again © 2026 Pamela Brooks

Their Save-the-Date Charade © 2026 Muna Sheik

ISBN: 978-0-263-41935-1

02/26

Printed and Bound in the UK using 100% Renewable Electricity
at CPI Group (UK) Ltd, Croydon, CR0 4YY

SWEET ON THE CEO AGAIN

KATE HARDY

MILLS & BOON

To Gerard—for sharing Brussels
(and the chocolate!) with me. :) xxx

CHAPTER ONE

'I'VE LEFT THIS pitch until last because I wanted to give the other two a chance to impress us, first,' Michel Lambert said, leaning against the desk in his office at the family's Covent Garden brasserie. Tuesday was usually Livi's day off, but her parents had asked her to swap her shift so she could help with the big project they were working on—bringing the brasserie up to date and expanding the business. Michel had even rearranged the furniture so the office looked more boardroom style, with four chairs around the desk.

'Why would the other agencies need to try harder to impress us, Dad?' Livi asked, not understanding.

'Because we know the CEO of this one,' Sophie said. 'He's your brother's old schoolfriend.'

Even before her mum could say the name, ice slid down Livi's spine.

No.

It couldn't be *him*.

Could it?

She'd spent the last eight years avoiding Joshua Garrett, so she had no idea what he did for a job nowadays. Mutual avoidance, really; the two occasions where they might've been forced together were six years ago at her elder brother Etienne's wedding to Lucy, when Josh had been supposed to be the best man, and two years ago at the christening of Eti and Lucy's daughter Louisa, when she and Josh were both supposed to be godparents. Thankfully, both times, Josh had cancelled very late on, saying that he needed to go into residential therapy for a few days. Livi had been dreading having to face him at the wedding and pretend that everything was perfectly all right between them. It would've been worse still, having the traditional best man and chief bridesmaid dance with him to something smoochy; everyone would still have had their eyes full of metaphorical confetti and started speculating that maybe a romance could blossom between Eti's little sister and his best friend.

When it most definitely couldn't.

Livi had learned that in the harshest possible way, when she was twenty. And she'd kept what happened that night a secret ever since, even from her mum.

'Josh Garrett,' Michel confirmed, making her heart plummet.

When she'd first seen her father's notes, Livi hadn't even considered that 'JGA' might stand for 'Joshua Garrett and Associates.' And right now she was caught between a rock and a hard place. Nobody apart from herself and Josh knew what had really happened between them, that night. If she threw a hissy fit and refused to attend the pitch so she didn't have to face him, her parents would want an explanation—an explanation she wasn't prepared to give. The excuse that it was her day off wouldn't wash, because it was their family business and she'd always been flexible with her time. But if she went to this meeting, how could she possibly behave as if everything was perfectly normal between herself and Josh?

Plus her dad had pretty much hinted just now that he was biased in Josh's favour and was more likely to appoint him than either of the other two agencies.

Livi really didn't want to have to work with the man who'd trampled her heart into tiny pieces.

Though if her father was right and Josh had indeed become a hotshot marketing guru, and his pitch turned out to be the best of three, she couldn't let her heart get in the way of business either. Insisting on hiring someone whom she knew would be second-best at the job simply wouldn't be fair to the brasserie and their staff.

She'd just have to be professional and keep Josh at a distance.

Somehow.

Josh's palms were actually sweating as he walked through Covent Garden towards Lambert's Brasserie, and there were butterflies in his stomach.

Which was utterly ridiculous. Why on earth was he so nervous? He was good at his job, and he'd worked hard on this pitch. Plus it was for his best friend's family—people he thought of practically as his own family. He wanted to do his best by them, and he thought he'd done that with the marketing plan he'd suggested.

Except he knew that Livi would be there. Not just in the building, which would've been tough enough, but at the pitch itself.

His best friend Etienne's little sister. The woman who had always been off limits. He'd known Olivia Lambert since she was a little girl, and he'd always followed Eti's lead and treated Livi as if she were his own little sister.

Until that night, eight years ago.

Josh had been spiralling deeper and deeper into a black hole after the accident that had ripped his music away from him. The accident that he'd wished at the time had taken his life, instead of leaving him with a left hand that would never be the same again. The surgeon had been brutally honest about it. The average person would've been relieved to have a left hand that still functioned reasonably well, but Josh was a virtuoso violinist, whose left hand needed far more dexterity than the average person's. Even after extensive physiotherapy, his hand simply wouldn't be able to cope with the demands of his job. He wouldn't be able to play the pieces he'd become famous for, the pieces that made his blood sing: not Vaughan Williams' *The Lark Ascending*, nor Paganini's *Caprice Number Twenty-four*, nor the *chaconne* in Bach's *Partita Number Two*.

He'd sat there, trying to absorb the news as the surgeon spoke. That he'd never again transport audiences to another plane at a concert. That he'd never again feel as one with his violin. That the life he'd planned and worked so hard for was over.

A second opinion—and a third—had confirmed it.

He'd never play again.

Not to the standard he was used to, the standard he'd spent his entire life striving for. When you'd sailed through all your exams early, won accolades for your playing, were offered the loan of a Stradivarius, and above all knew that you brought the joy of playing into your audience's heart… Anything less than that couldn't ever be enough.

Josh had given the Stradivarius back—the precious ancient violin he'd been trusted to play by its owner, now cherished by another violinist—and it had felt like ripping out his heart.

The only way he'd been able to cope with such a massive change to his life was to shut everyone out.

Livi had been the one to knock at the door of the flat he hadn't left in weeks. Livi, with those big brown eyes and thick dark hair worn in a messy bob that would make any man want to run his fingers through it. No make-up, no fancy clothes: just jeans and a plain T-shirt, and a Tupperware box containing six different types of cake. She'd smiled at him. 'I'm glad you're in, Josh. I need a favour.'

Josh had stared at her, not understanding. What could she possibly need from him? He had nothing to give. Without his music, he was an empty husk.

Taking his silence as a request to know what she wanted, she'd continued, 'I need you to taste-test this cake for me.' She'd lifted up the box. 'Mum, Dad and Eti want me to enter that TV baking competition. But they're my parents and my brother. They're biased, so I can't trust their judgement and I don't want to make a fool of myself. Am I really good enough to make the grade? I know you'll be honest with me, Josh. And—well, the problem is, I've been dragging my feet about it.' She'd given him a shy little smile. 'The application has to be in tomorrow. Do I go for it or not? I need you to taste this and tell me the truth, right now.'

Part of him had wanted to snarl at her and tell her in

very harsh words of one syllable to go away and leave him alone with his despair. Particularly as it was the flimsiest excuse he'd ever heard in his entire life. It was blindingly obvious that his family and friends were so desperate to get him to open up that they'd asked sweet little Livi to try, as a last resort.

Well, tough.

He didn't want to talk.

To anyone.

He just wanted oblivion from the searing loss of his music. Something he'd been lurching towards, hour by aching hour.

But another part of him hadn't been able to resist her request. Something about Olivia Lambert's smile made the world feel brighter—a brightness Josh hadn't been able to see ever since the surgeon had given him the news that had shattered his world and the other doctors had confirmed it. Plus there was always a chance that she might be telling the truth. That she really did need his help. That instead of being Josh the burden, Josh who needed coddling, he could actually do something useful. Something unconnected with music.

He'd caved.

Let her in.

His stomach clenched. Such a wrong move. He should've sent her away. For pity's sake, he'd *known* she'd had a crush on him when she was a teenager. Those puppy-dog eyes, the blush whenever he'd called in to see Eti and she'd been there, the shyness in her smile. He'd always been careful to treat her as Eti's baby sister, even though once or twice he'd glanced in her direction as she laughed and felt a weird zing somewhere in the region of his heart—something he knew he shouldn't act on, so he'd kept his distance.

He should've stuck to his normal resolve, that night, and kept his distance. She should've been *safe* with him.

But he'd been broken, at his lowest ebb. Needy as hell. She'd reached out to him, and he'd reached right back, wanting the comfort she'd offered him. Could she ease the pain in his soul?

He'd taken everything she'd offered, with her full consent.

Afterwards, the enormity of what he'd just done had slammed into him. He'd panicked. And he'd acted atrociously, said cruel things that he knew would make her walk away from him.

They hadn't seen each other since.

He'd apologised to her, a few weeks later, after he'd started therapy. He'd written her a very honest and heartfelt letter, and it had taken him a long time to get the words right; he'd shredded plenty of drafts until he'd finally found the right ones. He'd thanked her for being the catalyst that had finally made him go to therapy and get his head sorted out. And he'd apologised for taking what he shouldn't have taken.

Technically, she'd offered. And she was over the age of consent. They'd both been adults in the eyes of English law.

But he still knew he should've refused. Kindly. He was four years older than her, supposedly more worldly-wise. He should've acted responsibly. Let her down gently. Not taken her to bed. *Definitely not taken her virginity.*

He blew out a breath. She'd never replied to his letter, and he was pretty sure she'd never forgiven him for what he'd said to her that night. In her shoes, he wasn't sure he would've forgiven him, either.

Since then, they'd avoided each other by tacit mutual agreement, somehow without either of their families noticing. Being busy at work was a useful excuse, he'd found—first of all studying for his new career, then going for promotion within the firm, and then finally setting up his own business.

The only sticky bits had been Eti's wedding, six years ago, when things were still so raw, and at Louisa's christening. Of course Josh had said yes when Eti asked him to be the best man. But later that evening Eti had casually mentioned that Livi was going to be the chief bridesmaid. And Josh knew what that meant. A slow dance, in front of everyone. It wouldn't be fair to put her through an ordeal like that. And Josh wasn't selfish enough to make Livi be the one to find an excuse for missing her brother's wedding. It was obvious that he needed to be the one to back out; and it had taken him a while to work out how, without hurting anyone else.

In the end, spending a week in residential rehab—despite not actually having the mental wobble he'd claimed he was having—was the perfect excuse. He'd done the same when Eti had asked him to be godfather. The main thing was that Eti hadn't been hurt; though it had hurt *Josh*. He'd really wanted to be there and share the joy at his best friend's wedding to Lucy and then their daughter's christening instead of being stuck in rehab. Even though Eti had sent him photographs from both celebrations and a slice of wedding cake, it hadn't been the same as actually being there. Being part of the whole thing and making memories together.

Now he had a business meeting with Michel and Sophie Lambert...and with Livi.

Maybe when Michel had asked him to pitch, Josh should've made an excuse. He should've said he was flattered to be asked but he couldn't help the Lamberts because he specialised in other areas. He should've recommended someone else.

But the Lamberts had always been good to him. The way Josh saw it, helping them with their next business move was his chance to pay them back. He wished that Livi wasn't going to be involved with the marketing project, but he needed to be realistic about it. She was their *pâtissière*. If they were going to take some of the options he'd suggested, she'd be in charge of them. So all he could do was be professional, try not to meet her eyes, and do the best he could for the Lamberts.

He came to a halt outside the red-brick building with its Flemish gable, white shuttered windows and discreet gold lettering that proclaimed *Brasserie Lambert*. There were two smart zinc tubs flanking the doorway, each containing a bay tree clipped into a ball; when he went through the door, the interior was all polished cherrywood and chairs upholstered in mulberry-coloured velvet. There were shelves behind the bar showcasing bottles of different Belgian beers along with their specially shaped glasses, and a chalkboard on the wall listed the day's specials. Although it was nearly three o'clock, and the place should've been practically empty, the brasserie still had a few customers who were lingering over coffee and petits fours.

He walked over to where one of the waitresses was cleaning a table. 'Excuse me, please. My name's Josh Garrett, and I have an appointment with Mr and Mrs Lambert in a couple of minutes. Could you let them know I've arrived, please?'

'Sure,' she said, returning his smile and disappearing behind the bar area.

And Josh told himself that his heartbeat was only rocketing because it was adrenalin making him sharp for the pitch. It had nothing to do with the prospect of seeing Livi again for the first time since that night.

He ignored the disappointment flickering through his veins when Michel Lambert was the one to come out to greet him. Of course Livi wouldn't have been the one to collect him.

'Josh! Good to see you,' the older man said with a broad smile. 'Come through to the office.' He shepherded Josh into the small room that held a table and four chairs set out in the style of a boardroom.

Sophie Lambert—an older version of her daughter, with those same dark eyes but with her grey hair tamed into a sleek bob—stood up and greeted him warmly. 'Josh. Thank you for coming. Livi's just sorting out a tray of coffee.'

Livi. His heart skipped a beat.

It was just pre-performance nerves, he told himself, which was a good thing because it meant he wasn't taking anything for granted. Just as, back in the days when he'd been on stage, he'd never taken his audience for granted. He'd always given everything.

He could do this.

He took his laptop from his briefcase, switched it on,

brought up the presentation and turned the laptop so the screen was facing the Lamberts.

When Livi walked through the door a couple of minutes later, carrying a tray with four mugs, a jug of coffee, and a plate of delicious-looking chocolates, he managed to ignore the way his heart skipped a beat and gave her his most professional smile.

She inclined her head. 'Good afternoon, Joshua.'

Ouch.

She'd always called him by the short version of his name that everyone used. Using his full first name was clearly her way of signalling to him that she'd make an effort to sound friendly for her father's sake, but she intended to keep things strictly businesslike and formal between them.

Fair enough. It was more than he deserved. 'Good to see you, Olivia,' he said, using her own full name as a way of telegraphing back that he'd match her professionalism. The tiny nod of her head told him that they had a truce. For now.

She'd changed in the last eight years, he thought. She'd lost her shyness, meeting his gaze with no hint of a blush; she had an aura of calmness and self-containment. And this new, confident Olivia was incredibly attractive. Her dark hair was caught back in a ponytail—clearly for hygiene purposes at work, because she was also wearing a white chef's jacket and black-and-white patterned trousers.

Her eyes were the same, though. So dark he could drown in them.

But he didn't have the right to think of her in those terms. The way he'd treated her had ruined his chances of having any kind of relationship with her. Besides, she was twenty-eight now. The chances were, she was in a long-term relationship with someone. Someone who would treat her a lot better than he had, he thought with a stab of guilt.

He accepted a mug of coffee, added his own milk, and waited for the Lamberts to sit down before he began.

'Thank you for giving JGA the chance to pitch for the business,' he said. 'I've read the brief thoroughly, and the way I see it you have three possibilities for expansion. I'll cover those in my presentation, and then perhaps we can discuss my suggestions and you can ask me any questions the presentation raises for you.'

Joshua Garrett had changed in the last eight years, Livi thought. He'd broadened out, no longer the skinny boy he'd been in his teens and early twenties. He was still as beautiful as ever, though he no longer had the messy dark curls she'd fallen in love with; they'd been tamed into a neat businesslike cut, teamed with a short neat beard. And he was wearing a formal business suit—expensively cut—instead of the black velvet tailcoat, silk bow tie and wing-tip shirt he'd worn while playing at a concert, or the scruffy jeans and worn-into-holes T-shirt with an obscure music reference that he'd been wearing the last time she'd seen him. There were tiny lines fanning from the corners of his cornflower-blue eyes, as if he spent a lot of time laughing or smiling; he'd lost the brooding intensity she remembered.

Which was probably a good thing.

She'd thought of Josh as a fallen angel, when she was sixteen and sitting in the front row of the Royal Albert

Hall, watching him perform. All that beauty, all that talent, the way he'd made her see a skylark soaring up, up, up into the sky as he wielded his bow.

Now, he was just a man.

No. Of course he wasn't. Joshua Garrett could never be *just* a man. Not to her. But he was still easy on the eye. And he had a warmth and professionalism she hadn't quite expected. As he went through the presentation, she could see exactly why Josh's agency had won awards. He'd read the brief thoroughly, and it was clear that he'd asked her parents some supplementary questions before he'd even started working on it, checked out their competition, and seen the gaps in the market that they could fill. He'd looked at the possibility of franchising the brasserie, as well as simply adding new branches in a rolling programme of expansion.

'You have distinct sets of clients at the brasserie: the ones who come for business lunches, the ones who come for pre-theatre dinners, and then those who want a romantic dinner or a family meal later in the evening,' he said. 'You're known for good quality, authentic Belgian food and beer. You could easily turn Lambert's into a chain or a franchise, keeping this brasserie as the flagship, and the other branches would follow the same pattern. Maybe they could offer different specials of the day so your chefs feel they have some creative say in what's produced,' he added.

He'd thought of the staff? Of the fact that a chef needed to feel untrammelled? That was impressive, too, Livi thought. The other agencies hadn't even touched on that.

'But you also have gaps,' he continued. 'As part of

running the restaurant, it makes sense to have quieter times where you can focus on preparation. But I think you could also make those gaps work for you. You could fill them here, or you could do a sideways expansion.'

'What kind of gaps?' Sophie asked.

'Mid-morning coffee and pastries, brunch, and afternoon tea,' he said. 'A sideways expansion would be a café rather than a brasserie, but using the Lambert name and design to make it clear that it's part of the same business and has the same attention to quality. Like the brasserie, the café would do things the Belgian way. Coffee with waffles or pastries in the morning. Tartines—' open-faced sandwiches '—as part of brunch, with options of savoury waffles and maybe a spectacular cake. And afternoon tea with a Belgian twist.'

As Lambert's *pâtissière*, Livi had originally suggested expanding their range of desserts, and she'd wanted to launch a range of handmade chocolates—she'd been testing them out with coffee after meals, and they'd gone down well with customers. She hadn't thought of moving sideways and opening a café, with a completely different menu, where she could offer cakes and patisserie creations... Even though she'd intended to stay professional and cool, she couldn't help sitting a little straighter and asking, 'What do you mean by a Belgian twist?'

'Traditional English afternoon tea is sandwiches, scones, cake and something in a "verre",' he said. 'Swap the sandwiches for mini *croque monsieurs*, and the cakes for mini Belgian specialities—waffles, *speculoos* biscuits, the cake of the day and a fruit tart or a frangipane. Make the "verre" a Belgian chocolate mousse, or swap it for a couple of handmade pralines.'

'And the scones?'

His smile made her heart skip a beat. 'Ah, you need to keep them. We're in England, and an afternoon tea wouldn't be a proper afternoon tea without warm scones. But maybe offer a choice of different jams or spreads—ones that might not usually be offered in England.'

'A Belgian twist. Cherry jam, blueberry, and maybe apricot,' she said thoughtfully.

He held her gaze. 'Your dad said you were thinking about producing a range of chocolates. You could have a takeaway counter in the café, for the pastries and for chocolates. Test what your customers like, and then maybe offer mail order if you want to expand into other items. Chocolates, waffles, and *speculoos* biscuits with the Lambert's logo stamped on them.'

'It's something to think about,' she said coolly, though inside her mind was racing. He'd pretty much nailed the things she'd been thinking about—things that the other two candidates had ignored, focusing solely on turning the brasserie into a chain.

This was something they could test at the brasserie without having the start-up costs of a café. Josh was right about the gaps in their offerings: morning coffee and pastries, and afternoon tea. And brunch would help them blend seamlessly from breakfast into lunch. They'd need to juggle staff rotas a bit, but it was doable. If it was a success, then they could open a café in its own right, which could perhaps double as a bar in the evening and offer a much more casual limited menu of mussels, steak and *frites*.

Her parents had a few more questions, and Josh answered honestly; she appreciated the fact he actually said he didn't know the answer to one of them, but he'd find out and get back to them later that day. She remembered that the other two agencies had bluffed, which had annoyed her.

'Any more questions?' Michel asked his wife and daughter at the end.

Sophie and Livi shook their heads.

'Then if you wouldn't mind waiting a few minutes, Josh, I need a quick confab with my business partners,' Michel said with a smile.

'Shall I see you in the bar, when you're ready?' Josh suggested.

'That'd be great. Do you need Livi to show you out?'

'It's fine. I know my way,' he said, to Livi's relief—or was there a tiny bit of disappointment blurring the edges, too?

She shook herself.

Not now. Wrong time, wrong place, and *definitely* the wrong man.

The second the door had shut behind Josh, Michel said, 'That was the best presentation out of the three, by far.'

'I agree,' Sophie said.

Livi knew that if anyone other than Joshua Garrett had given that presentation, she would've picked the agency. Disagreeing and picking someone who wasn't as good—solely because they weren't Josh—would be the wrong thing to do for the business. It looked as if she would just have to do her best to work with Josh, and somehow try to minimise her interactions with him. 'OK,' she said.

'I know he still has to come back with some figures for us, but I think we should hire him,' Michel said.

'Livi, I think he had a great point about the café. And that would give you room to try new things,' Sophie said. 'If there are any masterclasses you fancy, now's the time to book them.'

That would be a perfect get-out, Livi thought. She could be away on a course any time she had to deal with Josh. 'I'd love that, Mum. Thanks. And I was thinking, maybe I should do a fact-finding mission when I'm in Brussels for the chocolate course. Obviously I can do an internet search, but seeing things for myself means I'll have better ideas about what's on offer, what's popular with customers, and what kind of tweaks I can do here in London.'

Sophie smiled. 'Great idea, darling.'

'I think,' Michel said, 'we should put you in charge of the expansion.'

What? Now that she hadn't expected. In charge in the kitchen for the café expansion, perhaps. But her mum had always done front of house and her dad had always been the main chef, just as her grandmother had been front of house and her grandfather had been the chef before them, and her great-grandparents before *them*. 'But the brasserie's yours and Mum's,' Livi protested. If there were going to be any changes, surely her dad wanted to oversee them?

His next words told her exactly how he felt. 'We're both getting to the point where we think it's time to hand over to the next generation,' Michel said. 'Eti decided to take a different career direction, and he's happy in his work, so I'm not expecting him to drop everything to run Lambert's. Besides, asking him to run the business wouldn't be fair on you; you've worked hard, in every area of the business, and you know inside out how things work. The staff all know that and they respect you. Putting you in charge will be the right choice for everyone.'

On the one hand, this was huge. Everything she'd worked towards. Her parents were trusting her with the family business and letting her choose its direction. She'd be in control, knowing that she'd worked her way up and earned the role. And the bit that really made her feel good was that her dad sounded so proud of her. She knew she'd let her parents down, picking too many Mr Wrong-for-hers and not managing to settle down with anyone the way her brother had with Lucy, but where the business was concerned she could make her family proud of her.

On the other hand, it meant there was no way she could get out of working with Josh.

'Livi?' Sophie's forehead creased with concern.

Livi forced herself to smile. 'Sorry. I wasn't expecting it, that's all.'

'It's your turn to shine, *ma petite*,' Michel said. 'We're not stepping away and abandoning you completely. You'll have our full support in anything you need. But your mum and I have talked about it for a while, now. We think it's time to step back. We talked to Eti about it, and he agrees with us.'

Even though her brother didn't work in the family

business, his support was appreciated. 'Thank you for trusting me,' Livi said.

'You've earned it,' Sophie said.

'Let's go and tell Josh the good news,' Michel said.

CHAPTER TWO

'You really don't need me around for this bit,' Livi said, trying not to panic. 'Anyway, I have things to do in the kitchen.'

'I'll step in for you and keep things ticking over,' Sophie said. 'Your dad's right. This is going to be your show, so you should be the one to tell Josh and brief him for the next stage.'

'I need to pop out and see one of our suppliers,' Michel said, 'so you can use the office.'

From anyone else, Livi would've suspected a set-up. But her parents wouldn't do that to her. They genuinely still thought Josh, as their son's best friend, got on OK with their daughter, and besides this meeting was all about their business.

Livi was relieved they didn't know what had happened between herself and Josh. She still felt a squirm of shame every time she thought of that night. Right now her face felt hot and her skin felt too tight. But what choice did she have? She didn't want to burst her parents' bubble, so she'd have to play along.

'Why don't all three of us tell him?' she suggested. 'And then I can book in a meeting with him to discuss the way forward.' By which time she would've managed to get a smooth, sophisticated mask in place and could deal with the situation.

'All right,' Michel agreed.

But clearly her parents had really meant it about her being in charge of the project, because when they met Josh in the bar area her dad smiled. 'Livi has news for you.'

'You've won the pitch,' she said, hoping she looked and sounded a lot cooler than she felt. 'And I'm the one who'll be taking things forward.'

Livi was going to be in charge? Josh blinked. That was something he hadn't expected. He'd known she'd be part of the project—of course she would, given that she was the brasserie's pastry chef. But her dad had said nothing about stepping down from the helm of the business or taking a lower profile. If Livi was in charge of the project at the brasserie's end, it meant that Josh would be working much more closely with her than he'd anticipated.

How did she feel about it, given that she'd sent him that coded message earlier with the use of his formal name rather than the short version everyone used? Right now, her expression was inscrutable and he didn't have a clue what was going on in her head.

'That's good,' he said carefully. 'Thank you. I look forward to working with you, Olivia.'

'If you wanted to make a start,' Sophie said, 'Michel's about to go out and I can take over from Livi, so the office is free.'

He noticed Livi's eyes widening slightly. She seemed a bit reluctant to be in a meeting with him this afternoon. But maybe this was what they needed. A quiet, private space where they could talk properly and decide how they were going to handle this. And this time he'd say that apology to her face instead of hiding behind a letter.

'We can at least agree the next couple of steps,' he said.

Livi gave a sharp nod of agreement. 'I'll try to be as quick as I can, Mum.'

'Take your time, darling,' Sophie said with a smile. 'See you later, Josh.'

'Thank you again for choosing JGA, Monsieur and Madame Lambert,' Josh said.

'There wasn't any nepotism involved, if that's what you're thinking. Yours was the best pitch.' Michel chuckled. 'And we're still Michel and Sophie, to you. Even if we weren't, I prefer business footings to be on first-name terms, just as Livi does.'

'Michel and Sophie,' Josh echoed with a smile.

He followed Livi in silence back to the office where he'd pitched to all three of the Lamberts, and closed the door behind him. 'I think we need to talk,' he said.

'Yes.' Her face was tight with anxiety, and that made him feel even more guilty.

'We need to clear things up between us,' he said, 'and decide where we want to go from here.' Suddenly, it felt as if there wasn't enough air in the room. But he wasn't a coward. He'd face up to what he'd done. 'Obviously your family knew you were coming to see me, that night—but you didn't tell them what happened between us, did you?' If she had, he was pretty sure that either Eti or Michel would've confronted him at the time.

'I just said you didn't let me in.' She shrugged. 'They assumed that meant not letting me into your flat.'

Whereas she'd actually meant that he hadn't opened up to her. Hadn't talked to her, the way he should've done. Hadn't told her the deep, dark secret he hadn't even told his therapist.

'I didn't deserve that protection,' he said, 'but I appreciate it. And I'm truly sorry for hurting you, that night, Livi.' He swallowed hard. 'I have no excuse, though I do have an explanation. When you came to my flat, I really wasn't in a good place.' Which was the understatement of the century. He'd been shattered, raging at the universe and feeling as if he was right at the bottom of a dark, hopeless well. He hadn't been able to see a future in front of him, not without his music. 'But I still shouldn't have taken out my misery on you. You're Eti's little sister. You should've been perfectly safe with me.'

Colour flared into her face, but she said nothing.

'I apologise for everything,' he said. Everything he'd done. Everything he'd said. 'I did write you a letter of apology, a few weeks later—after I'd had a few sessions of therapy and finally started to get my head round the accident.'

'I got the letter,' she said. 'But I never read it.'

Had she recognised his handwriting and thrown it straight into the bin? Well, he could hardly blame her. If it had been the other way round, he wouldn't have wanted to listen to anything she had to say, either. 'I'm ashamed of the way I treated you,' he said. 'I wasn't coping with the aftermath of the accident. I couldn't handle knowing that everything I'd always wanted to do with my life was over. Permanently.' Her expression was still completely inscrutable. Clearly he'd blown it, so he might as well go the whole way. 'It doesn't excuse what I did to you—there is no excuse for that—but, as I said, it's an explanation. I'd pushed everyone away and managed to keep them at a distance. I'm assuming that's why my parents and Eti were desperate enough to ask you to try using cake to get through to me.'

'Yes,' she confirmed.

She'd agreed to help because she was a decent person, and that made him feel even worse. 'When I saw you on the doorstep, it was the first time I'd felt anything—other than being in a black hole—since the crash. I didn't want to let that feeling go. That's why I kissed you.' She'd offered him cake and he'd kissed her. He swallowed hard. 'I shouldn't have done it. I shouldn't have taken you to bed.'

Taken her to bed, and taken her virginity.

Though it had been with her consent. Livi knew she needed to be fair about that. 'You gave me the chance to say no,' she said. 'I could've said no at any point, and you would've listened.'

'Thank you for that,' he said. 'But I'm still firmly in the wrong. You were vulnerable. You were only twenty, and you'd never even left home,' he said softly. 'I was older than you. I'd lived away from home during my degree course, and I'd travelled the world for my job. I knew you were sheltered. I should've been more responsible. Afterwards, when I realised you were a virgin and I'd taken something precious from you, something I didn't deserve, I panicked. I didn't want anything more than—well, just that night. I was terrified when it occurred to me that you might want more than that. Something I couldn't give you. And I said some unforgiveable things to you.'

Was that what he'd written in his letter?

Livi remembered every searing bit of shame and embarrassment as he'd told her that he didn't want her. How scornful he'd sounded. How stupid she'd felt, thinking that she might be able to be the one to reach him through the wall of his misery and save him from himself—thinking that he might be glad of her help, and then they might become friends in their own right, and then one day he might notice her as more than just his best friend's little sister and realise they were perfect for each other...

Instead, he'd made it very clear that she wasn't what he wanted. At all. She was little more than a schoolgirl, in his eyes.

And maybe he'd had a point. When it boiled down to it, she'd had the equivalent of a teenage crush on a man who wasn't who she thought he was. A selfish, spoiled, entitled manchild. And how stupid had she been not to see that when it was so blindingly obvious?

The humiliation still felt as fresh and stinging now as it had back then. Even though she was nearly a decade older.

'Did you...' Her voice sounded cracked, and she cleared her throat, not wanting him to know how much it still hurt. 'Did you know I had a crush on you?'

'Since we're clearing the air and being honest—yes, I did,' he said, and then Livi *really* wanted the earth to open up and swallow her. 'But I'd also known you for years and years. If I'd been in my right mind at the time,

I would've treated you as I always did: as Eti's little sister. I would've treated you how I would've wanted anyone to treat my own little sister, if I actually had one.' He gave her a rueful smile. 'I would have made it very clear that nothing other than friendship was ever going to happen between you and me. But I wouldn't have been cruel about it.'

That night, he *had* been cruel. He'd sneered at her, asked her why on earth she thought he'd want someone like her.

'I should've treated you with the respect you deserved,' he said quietly. 'Instead, I used you to anaesthetise the feelings I couldn't handle.'

He'd had sex with her. Taken her virginity. Then he'd gone cold on her.

'I felt guilty. I knew I was in the wrong. I said things I didn't actually mean, to stop myself from feeling anything at all. And I'm sorry for hurting you. It was incredibly unkind, and I'll always regret the way I behaved,' he said. 'That's why I didn't go to Eti's wedding or Louisa's christening. It wouldn't have been fair to you, pretending everything was all right between us, when it wasn't.'

She'd always wondered why he'd really called off being the best man, only a couple of weeks before the wedding. 'Did you lie about needing to go to therapy?'

He wrinkled his nose. 'Not completely. I did go to residential therapy, that week, even though strictly speaking I was managing OK at the time. But I knew it was an iron-clad excuse that Eti would accept without digging any deeper, and that would leave you in the clear.'

He'd avoided the wedding and the christening because of her. He'd been sensitive. And that was a shock, because in her head it brought Josh back to being the man she'd always thought he was, rather than the one she'd encountered that night in his flat and considered him to be ever since.

'So that leaves us here,' he said. 'Working together on the future of Lambert's Brasserie.' He looked her straight in the eye. 'I didn't know you were going to be in charge of the project when your dad asked me to pitch. I thought you might be involved, but I also thought we'd manage to find a way round it so we could avoid each other. If you'd rather not work with me, I understand completely. I'll find an excuse to step back from the project and make it clear to your parents that it's my fault, not yours. Or I could delegate almost everything to my team. They're good people and they'll do their best for Lambert's. I'll oversee things my end, but you won't have to deal with me personally.'

'They're the options?' she asked. 'You resign from the project, or you delegate?'

'There is a third option—and I'm well aware that it's asking a lot,' he said.

She folded her arms and waited for him to tell her.

'We could try to put the past behind us,' he said quietly. 'We could work together to make Lambert's have the future you want it to have.'

Put the past behind us.

It had been eight years ago. She'd been young and impossibly naïve. He'd been broken, failing to come to terms with losing the future he'd planned for himself.

They'd been different people. It had been another life. They'd both moved on.

And now he was giving her the choice. No pressure. He'd made it clear that he would accept her decision rather than try to charm his way round her.

She thought about it.

She thought about it for so long that he said softly, 'Livi? I'm not the person I was, that night. Talking therapy has helped me a lot. And I owe you a huge debt for that, because that night was what made me realise I'd hit rock bottom and things wouldn't get better unless I accepted help. I'm only sorry that you were the one who took the brunt of my pain and my anger.' He blew out a breath. 'I was massively unfair to you. Unkind. And I'm truly sorry about it. What I did, what I said—it was all unforgiveable. I wish I could go back in time and change things.'

And give her back her virginity, too? Of course he couldn't, and they both knew it.

'But maybe we can find a way to make the business side of things work, for your parents' sake,' he finished.

She looked him straight in the eyes. That blueness she'd once mooned over was full of sincerity. She could see that he really did regret hurting her, back then. That night, he'd taken everything she'd offered, then thrown it back in her face because he'd been in too much pain to appreciate what she'd given him.

But now he'd owned up to his mistakes. And he'd been honest about the fact that, at the time, he'd been in a bad place, unable to come to terms with losing the career he loved—that he'd put everything into. It hadn't been just a job, had it? Where the arts were concerned, it was a vocation: what you did was who you were. Thanks to the accident, Josh had lost his identity as well. She'd known all that before she'd even knocked on his door. Her beloved older brother had told her how worried everyone was about him, how Josh had gone in on himself and nobody could reach him. And she'd seen herself as the equivalent of a knight in shining armour, armed with cake to chase his demons away…

What would she do, if she couldn't cook anymore? If, say, she lost her sense of taste and smell, and couldn't be certain that even an old recipe that she could virtually make in her sleep had worked properly? How would she react if everything she loved doing was ripped away from her?

She'd always been aware of the age gap between them, but maybe four years wasn't that huge. At the time of his accident, Josh definitely hadn't had the maturity to deal with what had happened to him; but would anyone have been able to cope with that at the age of twenty-four? He'd been heading for the top, tipped as being the best violinist since Paganini. He should've had decades of playing and success in front of him.

It had all been ripped away in a few seconds—because someone in another car had decided to drive after a few drinks, ending up on the wrong side of the road and smashing into the car in which Josh had been a passenger. Irony of horrible ironies, the driver who'd caused the accident had walked away without a scratch. Meanwhile Josh had lost everything. His incredible talent. His music.

'Do you miss it still?' she asked.

'Yes,' he said. 'It's not as raw as it was, but that hole will always be there. A missing piece of me.' He gave her a lopsided smile. 'Sometimes I have incredibly vivid dreams—in colour, with sound—and I think I can play again. Then I wake up, and it takes me a while to adjust. Luckily my therapist gave me some good tools for coping.'

'You don't play at all, now? Not even a little bit?'

'When I'll never be able to play the way I used to?' He shook his head. 'That'd hurt more than not playing at all.' He paused for a moment, clearly thinking about it. 'Say you couldn't make your favourite dishes ever again or learn a new technique. All you could do was boil an egg, and even then you'd need a bit of help to scoop the egg out of the pan. Would you have the heart to do that? Stick to the confines of just one very simple recipe, never again being able to create one of your incredible pastries?'

How did he know her pastries were incredible?

Then again, he'd clearly done his research into the brasserie. Maybe he'd even eaten here without her knowing and sampled one or more of her desserts. But the compliment pleased her, the more because he clearly hadn't been trying to compliment her. He was trying to make her understand how he was dealing with his limitations.

Could she handle the situation he'd just outlined?

She thought about it. 'Not cooking at all would be easier to handle than only having the most limited repertoire,' she admitted. Now she could understand why he avoided what had once been his entire life. 'So you retrained.'

'I found something I could do,' he said. 'I'm lucky. I got a second chance. And even though I admit I'd trade it all in a heartbeat for just one night playing on stage the way I used to...' He shrugged. 'It's not going to happen, so there's no point in breaking my heart over it. And there are bits of my job that keep me going. My team.' He smiled. 'Maybe it's daft, but it makes me feel like a proud mother hen when my babies get a bit more confidence and try new things. And I always encourage them when it comes to job enrichment. It makes everything better for everyone.'

'Mother hen.' She couldn't help chuckling at the idea. Josh was the least hen-like person she'd ever met.

'Seriously. Roosters aren't involved in the care and upbringing of the chicks,' he said. 'Before you ask, I know that because I have a client who runs a farm park. She taught me a lot about her animals. And it's got nothing to do with gender. I'd rather be the mother hen who encourages my babies and notices when they achieve something, than the rooster who's full of noise but doesn't actually do anything for them.'

Which was exactly how she ran her bit of the kitchen. She liked hearing her team's ideas and giving them the chance to practise a new skill. Maybe she and Josh had more in common than she'd thought.

He hadn't mentioned his personal life, she noticed. There was no wedding ring on his left hand—not that *that* meant anything. Not all men wore rings; and you didn't have to be married to be committed to someone. 'I'm glad you've found a way through,' she said.

'I was lucky to find a good therapist who understood what made me tick, and helped me learn to deal with things. The whole process made me realise how close I'd come to...' He broke off, and a muscle flickered in his jaw. 'Well. It is what it is.' He took a deep breath.

'I owe you an apology, Livi,' he said softly. 'And I'm sorry it's taken me so long to face you. I should've had the guts to come and apologise in person, years ago.'

She hadn't read his letter because she hadn't wanted to see in black and white any expression of regret for something that had meant something to her. 'I'm not sure I would've agreed to see you, years ago,' she said. She'd almost backed out of the meeting today.

'I don't blame you,' he said. 'And I hope you've found someone who appreciates you the way you deserve to be appreciated.'

How had he managed to arrow in on the one thing she knew she'd failed at—the one thing where she'd let her family down? Her brother Eti was happily married, with a little girl. Her parents were happily married—they'd been together since they were eighteen. And there she was, with a string of broken relationships behind her and an inability to commit. Most of the time, she'd been the one to call a halt; but sometimes, just when she'd thought she might finally be able to open up and let someone in, her partners had given up waiting for her and dumped her.

She narrowed her eyes at him. 'You don't need to be in a relationship to have a successful life.'

'I know. I didn't mean to imply otherwise.' He raked a hand through his hair, displacing his curls slightly, and that tiny bit of scruffiness made him look much less polished—and dangerously sexy.

Livi had to remind herself that she couldn't afford to let herself think like that about him, ever again.

'I guess what I mean is I hope how I treated you didn't put you off. Relationships, I mean.'

Was he asking if she was single? Hitting on her? Now? Was he being just a little bit patronising, thinking he'd put her off love? Or was she being oversensitive because she knew she was a failure at relationships, and ascribing motives to him that he didn't actually have? 'That's irrelevant to the project,' she muttered.

He winced. 'Sorry. It wasn't my intention to pry.' He lifted his chin. 'And you don't owe me absolution.'

'I'm glad we've got that straight,' she said, doing her best to sound cool and collected and not as if he'd just stoked up an old fire.

He winced again. 'I'm not normally this clueless or inarticulate. Livi, can we maybe start again, please? Even though we've known each other for years, I think we stopped knowing each other eight years ago—which is entirely my fault. But we're both different people now. Older. Wiser. Wanting different things from life.' He held one hand out to her. 'This time round, it'll be strictly business. I want to do my best for Lambert's. You're my client and you're trusting me with your company's future. I want to do my best for you, as a professional.'

She believed him.

And this Joshua Garrett—the thoughtful marketing guru who'd come to terms with his past and who went to bat for his entire team rather than just ordering them around—was a man she thought she might be able to work with.

'I want the best for Lambert's, too. I think we're on the same page,' she said, and took his hand. She shook it firmly. 'It's a truce.'

'Good,' he said. 'I'll look at what your nearest competitors are offering for afternoon tea—and I mean cafés rather than the upmarket hotels. Then perhaps we can sit down and work out what Lambert's can offer to make it different.'

'Actually, I've already suggested that to my parents.' The next words bubbled out before she could stop them. 'Maybe we should do the research together.'

He blinked, and she felt warmth flood into her cheeks. She didn't want him taking this the wrong way, as if she was suggesting a date. Because she absolutely wasn't. Dating Joshua Garrett might have been her absolute dream as a teenager, but it wasn't the case anymore. 'What I mean is, you can learn the basics of what a company offers from their website, but you can only judge their quality and the ambience if you actually visit them and try the product.'

He nodded. 'You're right. And it makes sense to work together. Your view will be that of a service provider, whereas mine would be that of a customer. Between us, we'll cover all the bases.' He paused. 'How about we both make a list of the five strongest competitors, then compare the list tomorrow, put them in order, and work through the list one a day for the next week?'

'Like a late business lunch,' she said. If she said the b-word often enough it might squash any more of these ridiculous thoughts that were threatening to surface. 'Works for me. What about your diary?'

'If necessary, I can move things. I'll send you my list later this afternoon.' He handed her a business card. 'Here's my work phone and email. If you can message me your contact details, that'd be useful. Let me know which competitors you want to start with and which times are good for you, and I'll book something.' He paused. 'Thank you for giving me a second chance.'

Second chance?

Her pulse sped up for a moment.

No, of course he didn't mean that kind of second chance. He meant not letting their past get in the way of their business relationship.

Except then he shook her hand again, and her palm tingled where he'd touched it. Oh, help. She definitely needed to ignore this lingering awareness of him. Nothing, absolutely *nothing*, was going to happen between them, this time around. She wouldn't take that risk again. 'You're welcome,' she said, trying to keep her tone entirely professional. 'Let me see you out.'

'No need. I know my way,' he said. 'I won't take up any of your time unnecessarily.'

She felt a twinge of disappointment. Which was utterly ridiculous, because there was no reason for her to feel disappointed at not being in his company. 'I'll message you later,' she said, as coolly as she could.

And it really didn't help when he smiled at her. A proper, genuine smile. One that made her heart feel as if it had done an award-winning gymnastics routine.

She was going to have to be really, really careful.

CHAPTER THREE

OLIVIA LAMBERT HAD grown up, and Josh really liked the woman she'd become: quiet, thoughtful and honest. She still had that warmth that had attracted him so much on the long dark night of his soul. Until that night, he'd never even really seen her as a woman; she'd simply been Eti's little sister. He'd been focused on his career, not his love life. But now he looked back and remembered times when he *had* noticed her—when she'd been laughing at a joke, or that sweetness in her smile had suddenly pierced his consciousness and he'd felt that weird little throb in the region of his heart.

Livi was obviously still Eti's little sister, but the four-year age gap didn't matter anymore. And she drew him. Every bit of his common sense told him to put this out of his head, because she was off limits, but he couldn't ignore that zing of attraction.

He was still none the wiser about whether she was involved with someone. Not that it was any of his business. He'd more or less asked her outright, and she'd set him straight. *That's irrelevant to the project.*

Of course it was.

But he still wanted to know. Had she found someone to cherish her, treat her the way she deserved and undo the damage he knew he'd done to her all those years ago? Was she happy?

He could hardly ask her parents. Or Eti. They'd want to know why, and he didn't want to tell them the truth.

Maybe the internet would give him a clue, he thought. But her social media profile turned out to be so low-key it was untrue. Livi had clearly had a hand in some of the posts for Lambert's Brasserie, but she wasn't on any social media as herself. That, or she'd locked down her profile details securely so that nosey strangers—such as he was, right now—couldn't find her at all.

She was right about it being irrelevant. Even if she *was* single, nothing was going to happen between himself and Livi. She was his client. End of. And he'd just have to stop thinking about the way his skin had tingled today when she'd shaken his hand.

'She's off limits,' he told himself out loud, earning himself a funny look from the woman sitting next to him on the Tube. He gave her an apologetic smile and resisted the urge to explain. Given that he couldn't work out his feelings himself, he could hardly lay them out for a complete stranger.

No, what he needed was to bury himself in some work. As soon as he was back in the office, he'd brainstorm some ideas with his team. Focus on his job. And he'd definitely stop thinking about Olivia Lambert.

Livi needed to get her game face on before she went back to the kitchen to take over from her mother, because she knew Sophie would have questions. She also knew that her mother was well aware of her old teenage crush on Josh; and that her parents both worried she was too focused on her job and never dated anyone for long. Half the time when her brother invited her for dinner, it wasn't because Eti wanted her to bring dessert. He and Lucy, her sister-in-law, had tried pairing her off with a few of their suitable single male friends until Livi had gently explained that she wasn't desperately looking for Mr Right—or Ms Right, for that matter—and was quite happy with her life as it was.

Just please don't let her parents get the bright idea that Josh would be perfect for her and try to throw them together, she begged silently. She could hardly tell them that she already knew he was Mr Wrong, because then she'd have to explain why. They could all do without that particular grenade being lobbed into the mix.

Josh had actually told her he hoped he hadn't put her off relationships. She'd brushed the comment aside, but now she thought about it, part of her was irritated. Then again, she didn't think he was driven by arrogance or a desire to patronise her. She rather thought it might be guilt that had made him say it, because he knew he'd treated her badly.

And he also had a point. Nobody she'd dated had ever matched up to the Josh of her dreams; ironically, that included Josh himself, and she hadn't even *dated* him. She'd simply had sex with him, which wasn't the same thing at all.

Although Livi had been attracted to a few of her boyfriends enough to spend the night with them, she'd quickly realised she didn't want to spend the rest of her life with them and had broken it off. There hadn't been any depth to her feelings, and it wasn't fair to continue a relationship when she knew it didn't have any kind of future. Others, she hadn't even let close. They'd all been Mr Wrong-for-her. And the ones that maybe could have made it...well, they'd dumped her.

Now she considered all those failed romances. Had she perhaps blocked off her feelings on purpose, so nobody would get the chance to disappoint her the way Josh had? Had she dumped them—with a couple of exceptions—before they'd had a chance to dump her? Was he right, and she'd let her experience with him put her off falling in love with anyone?

She shook herself. This wasn't about her love life, or the lack of it. This was about expanding the family business. Nothing more. And she wasn't going to let Josh unsettle her—even though he might be right when he'd said that they were both very different people from the last time they'd met. She was going to treat him like she would any other business acquaintance: fairly and politely, but staying detached.

Thus determined, she did a mental trawl through the local cafés that would be their nearest competitors and made a quick list. This was the perfect thing to distract her parents, if they asked her about Josh. They could maybe add to her list. She put them in a rough order, added her own contact details, then checked Josh's business card for his email address and sent the list to him along with a note saying that she could be free for an hour after two p.m.

Then—because the business card listed JGA's website—on impulse she looked up his company.

At thirty-two, Josh seemed to be the second oldest in his team. His office manager looked like everyone's favourite aunt; but his social media and SEO manager, the campaigns manager, the research guru and the digital marketing manager all looked almost fresh out of university. He had a designer, a photographer and a wordsmith; and in the candid shots on the website it was clear that they all loved their jobs and the team was closely knit.

His social media outside work was non-existent. Then again, she wasn't surprised. The last thing he needed was for people to work out who he used to be and ask when he was going to start playing again. Unless any of his clients were classical music fans, they probably wouldn't connect him with Joshua Garrett the violinist. She smiled wryly. Not that she was one to talk. She didn't bother with it, either, outside the Lambert's social media accounts. She enjoyed scrolling through certain foodie accounts just for the videos, but she'd rather spend her free time reading—or experimenting in the kitchen in her flat.

She wasn't going to ask her brother about him, either. Lucy would overhear, put two and two together and make five—and then invite both of them round to dinner. Awkward, awkward, awkward. And it wasn't any of her business whether Josh was involved with someone or not.

She'd just logged off the computer and was about to slide her phone back in her pocket when it pinged with a message.

Josh.

The message was a copy of the booking receipt for one of her nearest competitors in Covent Garden; it would be a two-minute walk for her, though he'd need to come in from either the JGA office at King's Cross, or his flat in Bloomsbury—if he still lived there. Not that that was relevant. Or any of her business.

Have booked afternoon tea for two at 2.15 tomorrow. Let me know if not convenient. J.

He'd given her a ready-made excuse to chicken out.
Though she had no intention of using it. It made sense to do this particular research together; it would give her extra feedback from a customer's point of view. And it had been her idea, after all. This was business. What could go wrong?
Is fine. Thank you for booking, she replied. And then, because she really *was* curious about his life now, she added, If your partner wants to join us, that's fine. L.
If he was attached, then that would be yet another good reason to keep her distance and make sure her old feelings for him stayed in the past, where they belonged.
His reply, later that afternoon, didn't give her the answer she'd fished for. I don't have a business partner at JGA. But thank you. J.

Livi managed to keep all thoughts of Josh out of her head until after the lunchtime rush the following day. And then she went up to her flat above the restaurant, changed into a summery dress, and found herself applying make-up.
Oh, for pity's sake. This was a business meeting; she was the client, so it didn't actually matter what she wore. She absolutely didn't need to try to impress Josh Garrett.
Cross with herself, she wiped off the make-up and kept her hair in the ponytail, the way she wore it for

work, rather than taking it down. Josh was already there, sitting at a table waiting for her as she crossed the square and walked into the café at fourteen minutes past two.

He stood up politely and waited for her to take her seat before sitting again.

Those manners would be the death of her. Truly old-fashioned: and so, so sweet.

'Good afternoon, Livi. I took the liberty of doing a spreadsheet,' he said, 'so we can analyse the components more easily.'

Very businesslike. Just what she should've done. 'That's a good idea.' Livi gave him a professional smile. 'Actually, I had a mental checklist.'

'Want to hit me with it, so I can compare it with mine and amend the spreadsheet?' he asked.

She lifted an eyebrow. 'Don't you trust me to amend the spreadsheet?'

'Fair point,' he said, and passed his phone to her.

She scanned what he'd listed: contents of the tea, split by type of food; ratings for quality and quantity; what drinks were on offer; whether refills were offered; if there were options or it was a set menu; price. 'That's fair, from a consumer's point of view,' she said. 'You've listed what you get for afternoon tea and how much choice you have.'

'Anything you'd add?'

'From my point of view, we need to look at presentation,' she said. 'Do they use a cake stand, plates or a slate? Is the tableware matching, vintage or plain? Is everything brought out at once or is it staggered? Are the scones warm or cold? If there's a choice of cake, do customers choose at the counter, from a menu, or is a selection brought over on a trolley?'

'That would obviously affect how things are plated and how much work it makes for the staff,' he said thoughtfully. 'Which I didn't consider. Do you want to add them in?'

'It's your spreadsheet and your tech,' she said, 'so it makes sense for you to do it.'

There was a flicker of amusement in his gorgeous blue eyes as she handed the phone back to him without actually entering anything.

'I learned a long time ago to pick my battles wisely,' she said, steepling her fingers. 'By the way, because this is my idea, it's my bill.'

'It's client research,' he corrected. 'Making it my bill.'

'And then it'll be part of your expenses,' she said, 'meaning the brasserie will be paying VAT twice. No.'

He grinned. 'No flies on you.'

'I'm not just a...' she began, and stopped halfway through the hackneyed phrase. *Not just a pretty face.* She wasn't even that, according to the man sitting opposite her. She was a stupid, spotty-faced schoolgirl playing dress-up. It made her regret wearing a dress now; and she was relieved that she'd wiped off the make-up before she left her flat.

Maybe Josh had become a lot more perceptive, because he seemed to guess the thoughts she hadn't said. 'From what I've seen of you, Olivia Lambert,' he said quietly, 'you're capable of doing anything you put your mind to, whether it's making those amazing desserts or running a business empire. Though personally I think you'd be wise to hire a business manager to handle the stuff you don't enjoy doing as much. It's a better use of your time to do what you love and delegate what you don't.'

Josh had once loved what he did for a living. His music had been his life. And when the accident had taken that away from him, it had broken him.

Not that they were going to discuss that.

She mumbled something anodyne and glanced through the menu. 'So it looks as if we get sandwiches, scones, a savoury, cakes and a verre. Choice of five different types of tea or filter coffee. Set menu. OK.'

When the waitress came over, she ordered a pot of Earl Grey; Josh ordered green tea with lemon.

'Pretty china,' she said approvingly when the teapots arrived. 'And it's looseleaf tea.'

'I need to add that in,' Josh said. 'In case some of them don't offer looseleaf.'

'Some places use silver teapots rather than china,' she said. 'Though I think that would be more the high-end afternoon tea they'd serve at a posh hotel, which isn't the market I'm aiming for.'

'Agreed,' he said, and added in the comments she'd made earlier.

The sandwiches were excellent, and talking about the food meant they didn't touch on anything personal. But then they ran out of business to discuss.

She needed to make small talk. Something not too personal. 'Did you come from the office, or were you working from home this morning?' she asked.

'The office,' he said. 'I don't tend to work from home that often. I focus better with people around me.' He looked at her. 'Do you still live with your parents?'

'I moved out a couple of years ago. There's a flat right above the brasserie,' she said. 'Which means I don't have a commute.' She paused. 'Are you still in Bloomsbury?'

He shook his head. 'I sold the flat and moved back home when I first went to rehab. I stayed with my parents until I'd finished retraining.'

Completely understandable, she thought. There would be too many memories in his old place.

'I live in Bayswater now,' he finished.

'A flashy penthouse in a Georgian building?' she guessed.

'A three-bedroomed mews house, not far from Hyde Park,' he corrected. 'Cobbled street, lots of greenery outside—one of my neighbours is very keen on the Mews In Bloom stuff and nags us all into taking part. I'm not a gardener, so I pay him to do it for me.' He smiled. 'The house has been renovated so it has a modern kitchen-cum-living room, but it still has most of its historic character.'

'There's a lot to be said for historic character,' she said. 'My flat's only a one-bed, but it's full of light and I'm right in the middle of Covent Garden.'

'Just round the corner from St Martin-in-the-Fields.' His voice was soft, but it held a world of pain.

She remembered when he'd played a candlelight concert in the church. She'd gone with Eti to watch Josh as a soloist, and she'd been spellbound. The way Josh had moved as he played had made it look as if the violin was actually part of him.

How much he must still miss it, even though he'd made a new and successful life for himself.

'It's also close to all the big theatres and the National Gallery.' She decided not to mention the Royal Opera House. She was pretty sure Josh had played on that stage, too, and avoided it now. 'And I'm not that far from St James's Park, which is a nice walk in summer.' She looked at him. 'What made you decide to move to Bayswater?' If he was near Hyde Park, that meant he lived within walking distance from the Royal Albert Hall—which he'd once told her was his favourite place in London. Another stage where he'd conquered the world. Surely it was too close for comfort?

'I liked the house,' he said. 'And it's an easy Tube journey to work. A ten-minute walk to Paddington station, and no need to change lines.'

'You didn't fancy a posh warehouse in King's Cross overlooking the canal, then, so you could walk to work?' she asked, striving for lightness.

'No. I did think seriously about Notting Hill,' he said. 'I nearly put an offer on one of the ice-cream-coloured houses. But then the mews house came up. I went for a viewing and it just felt...' He spread his hands. 'As soon as I walked in, I knew I was home.'

'That's how I feel about my flat, too,' she said.

A one-bedroomed flat—one that she'd said was quite small, although it was smack in the middle of Covent Garden and that made it a desirable piece of real estate. If Livi was involved with someone and was thinking about moving in with them, she'd probably need more space. She hadn't mentioned needing more space, so it sounded as if she was single. Josh really hoped that was by her personal choice, and not because he'd put her off relationships. He'd asked her, earlier, and she'd batted it aside. Maybe he needed to be a bit more explicit.

'You mentioned my non-existent business partner joining us for research,' he said. 'Did you want yours to join us?'

'Mum and Dad? No. They're happy to leave this to me,' she said. 'Though they did make a couple of suggestions for places we should check out. I've made a note. I'll send it on to you.'

'Thank you.' He still didn't have the answer he wanted. Obviously he was going to have to be a little bit more explicit. 'And your non-business partner is OK with you more or less having lunch with me exclusively for the next week?'

'Is yours?' she countered.

He should've guessed she'd answer a question with another question, batting it back to him. OK. If she wanted him to answer first, it was the least he could do. He owed her. 'I don't have a non-business partner.' Before the accident, he'd been too focused on his career to think about his love life. Afterwards, following rehab, he'd dated sporadically, but nobody had drawn him enough to make him want to make the relationship last. He'd been careful to end things kindly—he'd learned that much from what had happened with Livi—so he was still on good terms with his exes, but he hadn't let anyone close enough to think about any kind of future with them. 'I've been busy changing my career, studying and getting the media company up and running.' Using work as his excuse to keep his distance from relationships.

'Me, too. Well, I haven't changed careers, but I've

been busy with the restaurant,' she said. 'Everything from shadowing Mum on the admin side through to taking full responsibility for the dessert menu, and teaching my skills to my team.'

So she *was* single. Because of how he'd treated her? Or because she hadn't found the person who lit up her world? Part of him felt guilty, because she deserved more than that. Another part of him was pleased, because if they were both single he could act on that pull he felt towards her. And yet another part of him was worried that this was a really bad idea, because he'd been a failure at relationships these last few years and he didn't want to get involved with her only to let her down again.

As if the questions showed on his face, she said, 'I think we can agree that we're coming from a similar place.'

'Yes,' he said.

Her phone beeped with what sounded like an alarm. 'That's me due back to the brasserie,' she said. 'I could stay out a bit longer, as this technically counts as work, but I don't want to put needless pressure on my team.'

'Of course. I'll fill in my bit of the spreadsheet and send you the link to a shared document. Or you can send me your notes and I'll collate it—whatever works best for you,' he said. 'I'll book somewhere for tomorrow and send you the details. Same time?'

'Same time is good. Thanks. I'll sort the bill on my way out,' she said.

'OK. See you tomorrow,' he replied.

He wasn't sure whether he was more relieved or disappointed when she didn't shake his hand. But he lingered thoughtfully over the remainder of his pot of tea. This was the new start he'd asked her for. The question was, where did they go from here?

CHAPTER FOUR

'I MEANT TO ask you when your days off are, so I don't take up your free time,' Josh said to Livi on Friday, after they'd finished their late lunch and discussed the menu thoroughly.

'Monday and Tuesdays,' she said.

He blinked. 'You work every weekend?'

'Saturdays and Sundays are busy days in restaurant terms,' she said. 'I'll fill in on a Monday or Tuesday if we're short—and obviously there was your pitch on Tuesday, this week—but usually that's my equivalent of a weekend.'

'I need to book our next afternoon tea for Wednesday, then,' he said.

'Actually, I don't mind doing them on Monday and Tuesday,' she said. 'I don't have anything in particular planned next week.'

Her day off. Which meant she would be free to spend a decent part of the day with him, not just a one-hour slot with the occasional messaging flurry in between. An idea bloomed in his head; even though part of him knew he shouldn't be mixing business with pleasure, it was too irresistible to turn down. Because he really wanted to get to know Livi better. 'How about,' he asked carefully, 'we go off-piste?'

Her eyes narrowed. 'How do you mean?'

'There's a new heritage venue just opened not far from me,' he said. 'A Regency house, set up how it would've been back in the day. There's a revolving exhibition of clothes on loan from the V&A. If I remember rightly, you were a bit of a Jane Austen fiend in your teens.'

She looked surprised. 'You remember that?'

He chuckled. 'I remember Eti complaining about your parents' living room being taken over by a posse of teenage girls arguing over which was the best adaptation of *Pride and Prejudice* and watching all of them back to back, the summer you were seventeen.'

'I remember that,' she said, smiling. 'And Mum kept us all going with tea and cake.' She widened her eyes at him. 'Actually, the bank where Austen's brother Henry was a partner is just round the corner from Lambert's. Jane herself stayed at the flat above the bank when she was working on the proofs of *Mansfield Park*.'

'Henrietta Street,' he said. 'She wrote to her sister Cassandra in 1813 that the flat was "all dirt & confusion, but in a very promising way".'

'You know that?' She blinked. 'You're an Austen fan, then?'

'Yes and no,' he said. '*Mansfield Park* was one of my A level texts. I absolutely hated it. But I get Austen's importance, and my mum likes costume dramas. I've kept her company watching some of them.' And he'd had to try very hard to tune out the music. Not that he was going to tell Livi that. He didn't want her sympathy—or, worse, her pity. 'Anyway, I thought it might be interesting to have a look round. Apparently the garden's fabulous. There are guided tours of the house twice a day, and the exhibition and gardens are both open a bit longer. They have a tearoom. It'd be good to see what they do with afternoon tea.'

'You're thinking Regency afternoon tea? Nope. Strictly speaking, afternoon tea wasn't invented until the 1840s,' she pointed out.

'By Anna Maria Russell, the seventh Duchess of Bedford,' he said.

She gave a wry chuckle. 'I should've realised that you'd do your homework.'

'Of course. That's why I also know that in Regency times women were more likely to drink tea than coffee.'

'Hmm,' she said. 'You're edging into show-off territory, now.'

'Thoroughness,' he corrected. And then he thought better of it. What had she said about picking her battles wisely? 'Anyway, I thought maybe we could enjoy an anachronistic afternoon tea after a look round the house and garden.'

It wasn't an official date. It was a continuation of their research, he told himself. And he hoped she'd see it that way, too.

'All right. If nothing else, it'll be a palate cleanser,' she said. 'Something different.'

'Good. And this one's on me—because it's slightly off-piste, and because it's my suggestion.'

For a moment, he thought she was going to argue. But then she smiled. 'Thank you. That'll be lovely. What time?'

'The house tours are at eleven and two,' he said.

'Let's go for the eleven o'clock,' she suggested.

'Paddington's the nearest Tube. Meet you by the Paddington Bear statue on Platform One at ten forty-five?' he asked.

'Perfect,' she said.

Weird how her smile made him feel warm all over. And weirder still how he kept thinking about her all over the weekend.

Apart from the briefing meeting, they'd spent all of three hours together. They'd eaten and discussed three afternoon teas together. Everything had been strictly business.

But he'd also learned a lot about the woman Livi had become during those three meetings. She was kind. Tactful—she'd asked him about his music, but she hadn't pushed. She thought about things before she made a decision, analysing them properly.

Then there was his physical reaction to her. Eti's little sister, all grown up. No longer the awkward, shy twenty-year-old she'd once been; now she was comfortable in her own skin. That confidence alone would make her beautiful; but when you added the warmth of her personality, she *glowed*.

If he had any sense, he'd find an excuse to stay out of her way.

But she drew him. Not like a moth to a flame, because Livi wasn't about pain. More like a butterfly to the sun, he thought, because her warmth made everyone around her feel that the world was a better place.

Maybe their new start could change things between them. Maybe they could get to know each other as they were now. Put the past behind them, where it belonged. And then maybe they could see where things took them...

On Monday morning, Josh walked to Paddington station and stood near the bronze statue of the bear just before quarter to eleven, making sure he wasn't in the way of families wanting to take photographs of their children next to the statue. He saw Livi walking towards him across the platform; she was dressed for sightseeing in comfortable shoes, black trousers, a pretty summer top and a sunhat.

'That was a good suggestion for a meeting point. It was easy to find,' she said, and her smile made his heart squeeze.

He desperately wanted to tell her how lovely she looked, but held it in. 'Thanks for coming,' he said instead, hoping he sounded professional and nothing like the hot mess of his feelings. Part of him knew that he shouldn't be blurring the lines between them—that he should be sticking to a business relationship with her and not thinking about anything else. But he found Livi hard to resist. Her warmth made him feel things he hadn't felt for years, and it made him want to explore that further.

'Well, it was a choice between doing this or doing chores. A nosey round a historic house and garden and the promise of good cake won. Just,' she said, giving him a sidelong look.

He couldn't help smiling at the tease. 'I should hope so.'

The heritage house wasn't far; there was a group of

ten on the tour, and he and Livi were the youngest by a generation. But he enjoyed walking round the house, listening to what the guide had to say.

'Oh, I love this room,' Livi whispered as they went into the library. 'I can really imagine living here. It'd be the perfect place to curl up and read for an hour.'

So she liked reading, still? He wondered what she read, apart from Austen.

Most of the walls in the library were covered by glass-fronted mahogany cabinets full of books; there were drawing room chairs with gilded arms and comfortable red velvet upholstery, and little tables dotted about. Josh could imagine a room like this being updated with modern reading lamps. 'It's easy to imagine living here,' he agreed.

The dining room was very grand, with duck-egg-blue walls, a marble fireplace, an ornate plaster and gilt ceiling and chandeliers. There was a large mahogany table with sixteen chairs in the centre of the room, and there were dishes piled with incredibly realistic-looking replica foods.

'Service *à la Française*,' Livi said. 'The dishes were served all at the same time—more or less like a buffet, and you'd be helped to the dishes nearest you. The first remove was joints and sides, then they'd clear the table completely and bring in the second remove of fish, poultry, pies and puddings. The most important guests would have the fanciest dishes close to them, and the least important would get the poorer dishes to choose from.'

'Didn't the servants do the—well, serving?' Josh asked.

'If they carried the dishes round like they do today,

that was known as service *à la Russe*,' she said. 'But *à la Française* was the usual way. The thing I couldn't get my head round, though, was that if you doubled the number of guests, instead of just doubling the quantity you'd make double the number of different dishes.'

'That sounds like a lot of work,' he said. 'And the potential for a lot of waste.'

'Not necessarily wasteful. They'd reheat the leftovers, the next day,' she said.

'How do you know all this?' he asked. 'Did you study the history of food as part of your training?'

'No. Holly, my best friend, is a history teacher, and she's fascinated by food in history,' Livi said. 'I've been to a few exhibitions with her—including seeing the carbonised bread they found in Pompeii—and we've done a couple of special Jane Austen days where we dressed up in Regency outfits and had dinner and a ball.' She smiled. 'I'm definitely going to send her photos of this place. She'll love it.'

Livi was clearly enjoying their outing, and he was really glad he'd suggested it. Until they went into the next room; he felt himself freeze as he realised that this was the music room. The room itself was gorgeous, with sky blue walls and comfortable sofas; the plasterwork on the fireplace and ceiling was a little plainer than that in the other rooms, as were the chandeliers. There was a piano to one side of the fireplace, and a harp on the other: the perfect space for performing. And on an occasional table there was a violin propped up in its open case. Something that made his fingertips itch and his heart ache.

Josh did his best to keep his expression neutral, but

Livi clearly noticed because she took his hand and squeezed it briefly. Pity? But when he glanced at her, it was empathy he saw in her eyes. He gave her a rueful smile, hoping she'd know he appreciated the support.

He was relieved when they were taken through to the withdrawing room with its crimson silk damask wallpaper, the ballroom, the bedchambers with an extraordinary array of clothes, and finally below stairs to the kitchen and scullery. At least then he didn't have to think about music and the massive hole at the centre of his life.

At the end of the tour, they were able to wander through the gardens at their leisure. It was a beautiful space with a rose arbour and rich herbaceous borders; some of the paths were in bright sunlight, and there were several benches set in shady corners. The orangery at the far side of the garden had been converted into a tearoom, and Josh was delighted to see that among the bistro tables and chairs there were actually a couple of orange trees in large terracotta pots. They ordered afternoon tea for two and found a quiet table.

'That's definitely one of the most liveable period houses I've ever seen,' she said. 'Would you have liked to live during Regency times?'

He thought about it. 'No. If you were poor, you had very few choices and a tough time trying to keep your family alive and fed. If you were at the other end of the social scale, then you were stuck spending your time with the *ton*.' He shook his head. 'I think they would've seriously annoyed me. A bunch of entitled people, bored out of their skulls and spreading vicious gossip because they had nothing else to fill their minds—because of course gentlemen couldn't *possibly* do some work.' He grimaced. 'Can you imagine being forced to put up with people you really didn't like for days on end, just because they were of the same social class as you and you were supposed to invite them to your house party and entertain them?'

'For me, it's all the restrictions on what you were allowed to do, the rules and regulations, that would put me off,' Livi said. 'I would've had no independence. I would've been expected either to marry—meaning the minute I got married, my husband would take ownership of all my possessions and I'd be nothing more than his chattel—or to be a companion to someone who expected me to do everything they wanted and be grateful for the opportunity.' She shuddered. 'And, as you say, the endless house parties. Being forced to sew or draw when you had no talent or interest in it, because that's what women were supposed to do. Listening to people singing out of key and having to be polite about it—or, worse, hearing other people rip them to shreds behind their back.'

'Or listening to someone playing the piano or the harp really badly.' He grimaced. 'Maybe I'm being territorial or over-fussy, but I really wouldn't be happy about someone ham-fisted sitting down at my piano and bashing out a tune. I'd want the instrument respected.'

'No, that's fair,' she said. 'The *ton* were an entitled lot. Pushy parents and desperate debutantes, all chasing the money. I know they were a product of their time, but I think I would rather have stayed on the fringes. I would've preferred to be with the bluestockings.'

'So,' he said, 'would I.' Clever women who thought

about what they said—like the one who was sitting opposite him right now and who tactfully hadn't brought up the way he'd frozen in the music room. And he needed to acknowledge what she'd done. How her warmth had thawed him again. 'And thank you,' he said quietly, 'for understanding what was going through my head in the music room.'

'No problem,' she said.

He almost—*almost*—reached across the table to take her hand.

But this wasn't the time or the place. Even though he wanted to change things between them—to get to know her properly, become friends and maybe then start dating—he'd promised her that their relationship would be strictly professional. It was the least he owed her. He needed to back off and keep things light between them. He went back to their discussion about the Regency. 'All the fussiness around clothes back then would've driven me mad, too. Employing people specifically to dress you, for pity's sake! I can't get my head round that.'

'To be fair, zips hadn't been invented,' she pointed out. 'Women needed someone else to do up those buttons down the back of their dresses.'

Josh wished she hadn't said that. Because even though he was trying to damp down those growing feelings towards her, her words had put a picture in his head and now he was thinking about what it would be like to undo a row of buttons down her spine, kissing every centimetre of skin as he revealed it. And he really hoped she didn't have a clue what was going through his mind. She'd run a mile.

Thankfully, the waitress came over with their afternoon tea at that point and they switched the conversation back to work. But he was still incredibly aware of Livi. The curve of her lower lip. The length of her eyelashes. The way her eyes crinkled at the corners when she laughed. He wanted to walk with her to a quiet spot in the garden. Take her hand. Press a kiss into her palm. Move his mouth upwards and feel the pulse in her wrist beating against his lips...

Focus, Josh. That's not our deal, he reminded himself.

But the more time he spent in Livi's company, the more he realised he liked her. *Really* liked her. Provided she felt the same way as he did, could they make it work? The gap between their ages wasn't an issue any longer; she was a woman in her own right and he should see her as that, rather than just his best friend's little sister.

The sticking point, though, was that night.

How much he'd hurt her, when he'd pushed her away. It would be hard for anyone to forgive that.

But they were both different people now. If he asked her—maybe told her the truth about what almost happened, that night—would she give him a second chance?

Even after they'd left the house and gardens and he'd gone back to work, he couldn't stop thinking about her. His office manager, Shelley, even called him out for daydreaming, and he had to think on his feet to come up with something even vaguely resembling a valid excuse.

At the end of the week, they'd finished working through Livi's list of competitors. All Josh had to do was finish collating their thoughts and write a report. Then he realised that it meant he had no real reason to see Livi, which in turn made him realise how much he *did* want to see her again. He'd enjoyed their lunch dates—well, business meetings, he corrected. He hoped that she had, too. They hadn't found themselves at cross purposes; if anything, he'd felt they'd been in tune with each other.

So maybe, he thought, just maybe, he should talk it over with her. Tell her his feelings had changed. Ask her on a proper date.

And she might even say yes.

Josh was still mulling over what he'd suggest as a first proper date when his phone pinged with a message; and his heart skipped a beat when he realised it was from Livi. Was she thinking about him, too? he wondered. Did she feel this same odd mixture of shyness and wariness and need?

He flicked into the message.

Been thinking. Need guinea pigs.

Not quite following her train of thought, he sent an immediate reply: ??

This time, she responded by calling him. 'Is this an OK time to talk?' she checked.

'Yes. What's the guinea pig stuff about?'

'I've worked out my afternoon tea menu, but I need some people to taste-test it—and not my family or Holly, because they're biased—even if they tried not to be, they wouldn't be able to help themselves. I need someone neutral,' she said. 'I was thinking, maybe I could drop in to your office on Monday lunchtime and your team can give me an honest opinion of the food?'

'That's an excellent idea,' he said. Especially as it gave him a very valid excuse to see her again.

'That's settled, then. I need to know how many people are in your team, any allergies or food intolerances, how many are vegan or veggie, and if there's anything they won't eat,' she said. 'Don't worry, you don't have to remember all that. I'll text you. But would you be able to let me know the answers by, say, the end of play today?'

He smiled. 'I imagine you already know that kind of information about your own team.'

'Well, yes,' she said. 'Of course I do.'

'Snap,' he said. 'So I can give you the answers right now. Nobody in my team has any food allergies or intolerances. There are ten of us, including me. Two are vegans and two are veggies; of the rest, one hates fish and one hates egg sandwiches. They all love chocolate, if you wanted to test your pralines on them.'

'Perfect,' she said. 'Next question. Do you have a staff kitchen?'

'You're planning to cook everything at my office?'

'Possibly some of it,' she said. 'The alternative is using a thermal bag to keep things hot. What facilities do you have?'

'A microwave, an oven with a hob and grill, and an air fryer,' he said. 'We also have a good coffee machine and a kettle.'

'Perfect. I can work with that,' she said. 'What time does everyone break for lunch?'

'Usually it's flexible,' he said. 'Tell me what time you want everyone there, and I'll make sure they are.'

'I'll take over your kitchen at twelve,' she said, 'and serve at one.'

'OK,' he said. 'Do you want me to put together a questionnaire so we can analyse their responses?'

'That's probably quicker than asking them and recording their answers, isn't it?' she asked.

'Yes,' he said. 'I'll draft something and have it with you by tomorrow morning.'

'Great. Thanks,' she said. 'I'll look forward to that—and I'll see you on Monday.'

Monday, Josh thought, was going to be an excellent day.

CHAPTER FIVE

On Monday morning, Josh texted Livi and asked her to call him five minutes before she arrived, so he could meet her at the door and help her bring in the supplies. He had to force himself to focus on the new brief he was working on, because his thoughts kept straying to Livi and how he felt about seeing her again. Which was ridiculous; he was a sensible thirty-two-year-old man with workaholic tendencies. Yet he felt as giddy as a fifteen-year-old boy waiting to meet his new girlfriend after school. Giddier, because at fifteen Josh had been much more focused on his music than on girls.

Finally she called him. 'See you in five.'

'Be right there,' he said, and he was outside the front door of the office when the black cab pulled up.

'What do you need me to carry?' he asked.

'This crate, please,' she said, pointing to one of the two crates in the back of the taxi. 'It's the china, cutlery, skillet and baking trays.'

It was surprisingly heavy, but then again he supposed it was for ten people.

She carried the other crate, which Josh surmised was the food.

'So this is your office,' she said, outside the glass door with 'JGA' written in discreet script.

'It's open plan, with a boardroom and a couple of breakout rooms, plus the kitchen and bathrooms,' Josh said. 'Let me introduce you to everyone.'

He set the crate on his own desk, and his team crowded round.

'Lovely to meet you, Miss Lambert. This is going to be such a treat,' Shelley, the office manager, said. 'I've been to your brasserie a few times with Elinor, my partner, and the food's always amazing.'

'Thank you,' Livi said, smiling. 'We've got a really good team at the brasserie. And we're all excited about the new direction.'

'What can we do to help?' Indira, the designer, asked.

'Nothing. I'm making you all work through your lunchbreak, and that's enough,' Livi said cheerfully.

'Stuffing our faces doesn't feel like work,' Indira said. 'It's going to be a pleasure.'

'I thought we'd eat in the boardroom,' Josh said. 'Do you want us to lay the table?'

'No, it's fine. It'll be quicker for me to do it than to talk you through it,' she said. 'Show me where the boardroom and kitchen are, and you don't have to babysit me. Just all be ready for one o'clock, please. And if someone could do me a list of what drinks everyone wants, I'll bring out the tea and coffee at the start.'

Once Josh had helped her carry the crates to the kitchen and shown her to the boardroom, he followed her instructions and left her to get on with things. Keep it professional and don't get under her feet, he reminded himself.

At five to one, he ushered the team into the boardroom. She'd set up the table with a runner in the centre; the plates were on placemats, and the cups and saucers on coasters. In front of each place setting was the questionnaire he'd designed with her.

A couple of minutes later, she came in with a tray containing a teapot, a coffee-pot, a sugar bowl and a jug of milk. She looked every inch the professional in her dark trousers and double-breasted chef's coat, and her hair was pinned up below a dark red skullcap.

'Thank you all for agreeing to be my guinea pigs today,' she said. 'As I'm sure Josh has already told you, this is a test run for the afternoon tea I'm planning to serve at Lambert's, so it has a Belgian twist. At the brasserie, I'm planning to use tiered servers, but for today I'm using large plates and I'd like you all to try as many of the different options as you can, please. You've probably already looked at the questionnaire by your place setting—Josh and I thought this would help us analyse your responses more quickly—and it's up to you whether you do them as you go or fill them in at the end. I'd like to emphasise that I'd like honest responses, please; I won't be upset or offended if there's something you don't like about the meal. I need to know what works and what needs tweaking.'

She was clear and precise; Josh thoroughly approved of the way she was running this.

'Please help yourself to drinks,' she said. 'I'll be back with the first lot of savouries.'

By the time everyone had filled their cups, she was back with the first two plates. 'Josh suggested that instead of finger sandwiches, I should serve warm Belgian sandwiches. So we're starting with mini *croque monsieurs* and tartines. They're all on sourdough bread, which I made this morning. The standard *croque monsieurs* are cheese and ham, and the vegan ones are smoky aubergine and smoked vegan cheddar. Enjoy, and I'll bring the next plates in.'

It was definitely the best *croque monsieur* Josh had ever eaten, and that included ones in Paris.

When she returned to the boardroom, every scrap of food had been eaten. 'Next up, the tartines. They're basically open-faced sandwiches, on toasted bread. I have a grilled vegetable and hummus version here, and a fig and prosciutto; I'll bring the tomato and vegan Boursin next, plus smoked salmon and pickled cucumber.' She swapped the new plates for the empty ones, then brought the other tartines through.

'Aren't you eating with us?' Pete, the photographer, asked.

'No, I'm fine,' she said with a smile. 'I'm simply here to serve the food and answer any questions.'

But she did at least need a drink. Josh decided to go for the professional approach. 'When I run focus groups, where people will be talking a lot, I always make sure drinks are available—particularly for the group leaders or any presenters,' he said. 'Can I get you a glass of water or a cup of tea?'

'Tea would be lovely, please,' she said.

He poured her a cup of tea the way he'd learned that she liked it. She gave him a warm smile that made his heart do a backflip.

When the savouries were all gone, she brought in warm scones and dishes of butter, cream and jam.

'They're all vegan scones today, and it's vegan butter,' she said, 'simply because that makes everything easy. I plan to offer dairy and non-dairy versions. The coconut cream's in the blue bowl and the clotted cream in the yellow bowl, depending on whether you want dairy or not. The jams are cherry, blueberry and apricot, and the colours make it obvious which one's which.'

'It's all amazing,' Jenna, one of the two vegans, said. 'I'm going to be telling everyone I know about this when you start serving afternoon tea at the brasserie, because they really need to try this. And I run a food blog. I'd love to do a piece on you when you open.'

'That'd be great,' Livi said with a smile. 'And you can perhaps direct me. I do the occasional photo or menu for the brasserie's blog, but I don't do videos.'

'A video of you making the scones would be awesome,' Jenna said. 'But I'll shut up now and make notes on your questionnaire.' She grinned. 'I don't want to miss out on eating time!'

Next, Livi brought in the sweet section. 'This first lot are all vegan, so they're suitable for everyone here. The *speculoos* are traditional Belgian biscuits made with caramelised sugar and Ceylon cinnamon, so they should taste slightly orangey. The waffles have a drizzle of dark Belgian chocolate. The cream-coloured macarons are vanilla, and the green ones are pistachio. Finally, the brownies are made with dark chocolate.'

And every single morsel that Josh tried was delicious.

She followed up with a tray of bite-sized gateaux. 'Mango mousse and passion fruit curd; raspberry mousse and lemon curd; mini salted caramel eclairs,' she said, gesturing to them in turn. 'I'm afraid the only vegan-friendly cakes here are the strawberry tartlets, but I'm going to work on vegan versions of the others.'

'Good,' Jenna said. 'Because they look stunning.'

Josh thought of the cake Livi had offered him, eight years before. If he'd only eaten it and opened up to her, talked properly instead of pushing her away...

He shook himself. Not now.

Finally, she brought in the verres and a plate of pralines. 'This is Belgian chocolate mousse. The vegan ones are made with coconut cream, and they have a solid chocolate V rather than an L on the top,' she said, gesturing to the stylised letters she'd clearly drawn in chocolate.

'L for Livi?' Peter asked.

'L for Lambert,' she said with a smile.

'You can buy letters made out of chocolate?' Indira asked.

'I made them,' Livi explained. 'With melted dark chocolate on a teaspoon. It takes a bit of practice, but once you get the hang of it it's easy. Oh, and the pralines are vegan-friendly. I made them this morning, too.'

'I have never, ever had such good food,' Jenna said. 'I'm not sure whether I want you to marry me or adopt me!'

'Me, too,' Peter said.

'Wait your turn in the queue, you two,' Indira said. 'I think we all feel the same.'

Livi chuckled, clearly enjoying their banter. 'Well, it's good to know you like the food.'

'Love it, more like,' Jamal, Josh's wordsmith, said. 'Any time you need someone to test things for you, I'm more than happy to be there.'

'When you open the café, are you going to offer take-away as well as dining in?' Shelley asked. 'Elinor works at King's College, and she'd definitely buy sandwiches and cake from you.'

'I haven't thought quite that far, yet,' Livi said. 'We're starting with a soft launch at the brasserie so we can gauge the demand. If it goes the way I hope, then we'll open a dedicated café as well as a second branch of the brasserie. And maybe we'll sell ballotins of pralines at the café and the brasseries.'

'I'll make a note,' Josh said.

'Definitely sell the chocolates,' Peter said. 'Add them to the menu so people can order them and take them home after their meal. Mail order via the brasserie website is another possibility we came up with when we were brainstorming ideas. These are seriously good.' He paused. 'If the jam's home-made, you could sell that as well.'

'I hadn't thought about jams,' Livi admitted.

'Another note,' Josh said with a grin.

She accepted a mug of coffee and sat chatting to Josh's team until they'd finished eating the cakes and the mousses. They insisted on doing the washing up, and Josh ordered a taxi back to Covent Garden for her.

'That was a definite success,' he said outside the office as they waited for the cab to turn up. 'I'll analyse the questionnaires, this afternoon, and give you a report first thing tomorrow morning.' He looked at her. 'Actually—maybe we can discuss it over dinner, tomorrow night? I'll cook for you, if you like.'

She widened her eyes at him. 'That's brave. Most people would worry about cooking for a professional chef.'

'I didn't say it was going to be a fancy dinner,' he said. 'And I'm definitely not trying to compete with you. It'll only be something simple.'

She smiled—and he loved the way that smile reached her eyes. 'Simple food is often the best food.'

'And there's no way I'm even going to try impressing you with a dessert. I'm not going to pull the wool over your eyes, either—I can tell you now it'll be fruit and ice cream bought from my local deli,' he added.

'I love fruit and ice cream. There's nothing nicer in the summer,' she said.

'Any allergies or major dislikes I need to know about?' he checked.

'No. What time do you want me to arrive?' she asked.

'Would seven work for you?' he asked.

'That's fine. The only thing I need now is your address,' she said.

'I'll send it over tomorrow with the report,' he said. 'Thanks again for making us part of your research, Livi. The team were blown away by the food—and that includes me.'

He was rewarded by another smile, revealing the cutest dimples. How had he never noticed them before? And how was he going to get the picture of said dimples out of his head and concentrate for the rest of the afternoon?

CHAPTER SIX

JOSH KEPT HIS PROMISE, sending Livi the report and his address on Tuesday morning. His team had come up with a lot of thoughtful comments and suggestions, and Livi started to feel confident that the soft launch was going to work well.

But she was having second thoughts about Josh cooking for her in his home. This was blurring the boundaries. They were supposed to be client and contractor; and this was meant to be a debriefing meeting. Discussing business over dinner in a public place was one thing; talking in the privacy of his home was quite another. It felt more like a date.

Maybe she should suggest meeting at the brasserie, instead.

Or maybe she was overthinking things. She shook herself. Of course it wasn't a date. It was work. It was going to be just fine.

In the evening, she headed for his house. Butterflies were doing a stampede in her stomach by the time she left the Tube station at Paddington. The last time she'd gone to Josh's flat, her world had fallen apart.

She reminded herself that they were both older and wiser, now. Different people. And it wasn't the same situation as before; she wasn't trying to be a knight in shining armour, arriving unannounced on his doorstep. Josh had asked her over for dinner; he was expecting her, and they were planning to discuss business. Everything would be just fine.

And thankfully it wasn't the same place. She didn't think she could've handled meeting him in his Bloomsbury flat. Not with all the memories of that night.

Bayswater was beautiful. When she turned into the cobbled street, she noticed that the mews houses on both sides of the street had terracotta pots and wooden planters stuffed with herbs and flowers outside, everything from geraniums to pansies to bay trees. Some of the houses had wrought-iron Juliet balconies, which were filled with pots of flowers.

There were no cars anywhere; Livi assumed they were parked in the next street at the back of the houses. Some of the houses were painted cream, while others had pale yellow unadorned London brickwork. The ground floors all had the hallmark large double doors of a mews, along with windows containing a dozen smaller panes. The windows were mainly painted white, while the doors were painted heritage colours.

Josh's front door was painted a soft sage green. She rang the doorbell; a few moments later, he opened the door and smiled at her. 'Hello.'

'Your street's so pretty,' she said. 'I totally get why you fell for the location.'

He looked pleased. 'My neighbours are all good sorts. And the local shops are fabulous—everything you could want is within walking distance, and the coffee shop round the corner even roasts its own beans. The only thing missing is a chocolate shop.'

'Hmm. That could be a potential offshoot of Lambert's,' she said with a smile. 'And, speaking of chocolates...' She handed him the bottle of wine she'd bought earlier and a box of chocolates. 'I made them this afternoon.'

'That's very kind, but you really didn't have to bring anything,' he said.

'You know perfectly well that's how Eti and I were brought up,' she said. 'So just shut up and accept everything gracefully, will you?'

'You even sound like your brother,' he teased. 'But thank you. Come in.'

Livi stepped into the small hallway.

'The cloakroom's here, if you need it,' he said, gesturing to a door, then led her through to the doorway opposite into a large all-in-one kitchen, living room and dining room.

The soft sage green of the front door was echoed in the kitchen area, with its sage green cabinets and cream marble worktops. Vegetables were cooking in an electric steamer, and through the glass door of the oven she could see a wrapped foil parcel as well as what looked like vine tomatoes roasting in a tin. The flooring in the kitchen area was terracotta-coloured tile; the rest of the flooring in the room was all polished pale oak, and there was a large cream rug set between the chesterfield sofas in sage green velvet. Clearly that shade of green was one of his favourites, because the curtains were in a pattern she recognised as William Morris's Willow

Bough. There were some abstract prints on the walls, and lots of books on the shelves.

And all of a sudden, Livi was very aware that they were alone. Just the two of them. She'd dressed up a bit, for once, actually wearing a little black dress instead of her favourite black trousers, teaming it with heeled shoes she could walk in. Josh had dressed down from the suit he'd worn in the office: a crisp white shirt and faded jeans. The casual look made him more approachable—worse still, *touchable*. And once that thought was in her head, she couldn't shift it.

Which meant she was in trouble.

She wasn't supposed to let herself feel attracted to Josh again. Even if he *had* changed.

'Can I be nosey?' she asked, indicating his bookshelves. It would be an excuse to put a little distance between them, and perhaps then she could get this sudden surge of desire under control.

'Sure. Let me get you a drink?' he said. 'Glass of wine?'

'That'd be lovely,' she said.

He went over to the fridge while she scanned the shelves. There were a few volumes of poetry and classic novels, plus a complete Terry Pratchett collection that didn't surprise her because her brother loved the author, too; but she was a bit surprised to see that there was nothing remotely connected to music. No biographies, and definitely no music scores. She wondered if he'd left them all with his parents so he didn't have to face the memories, or whether he'd given everything away once he'd decided to cut himself off completely from music.

He came back over carrying two glasses of perfectly

chilled rosé wine and handed one to her. Livi felt a zing of energy as his skin brushed against hers and nearly dropped the glass. Oh, for pity's sake. She wasn't a teenager anymore, or even the naïve twenty-year-old she'd been that night...

And she wished she hadn't thought of that night. The problem was, she could still remember what it felt like when he'd kissed her. And there was a very big bit of her that wanted to feel it again—because the Josh she'd got to know over the last couple of weeks was more like Dream Josh had always been. A decent guy. Funny, clever. Thoughtful. Someone she would enjoy sharing her life with.

Either he was being tactful or—she hoped—the tangled mess of her feelings didn't show in her face, because he clinked his glass against hers. 'Cheers.'

She took a sip to give herself some breathing space. 'This is gorgeous. Very smooth.'

'From the wine shop round the corner,' he said. 'Sancerre rosé. I thought it would go well with the salmon.'

'That's a good pairing,' she said.

'I like it,' he said, 'but obviously you know more than I do about pairings.'

That sounded almost like an admission that he was actually nervous about cooking for her, despite his bravado yesterday. She smiled. 'I'm not going to grade you out of ten, like some snooty TV chef,' she said. 'It's actually quite nice for someone to make the effort of cooking for me and thinking about the wine. I appreciate it.'

He smiled back. 'Did you ever apply for that TV baking show?'

Of course she hadn't. It had been an excuse to come over to see him. Her stupid attempt to try and help him. He'd noticed her, all right, just as she'd hoped he would. He'd kissed her. Made love with her.

And then there had been the fallout.

Unable to push a single word from her suddenly dry mouth, Livi simply shook her head.

'You really should've given it a go,' he said. 'Everyone in the office was raving about your cakes today. Half of them suggested telling you that they couldn't fill in their questionnaire unless you came back with more, to remind them about what they'd tasted. And they didn't mean just once: they wanted every day for the next month!'

'I guess that's a compliment,' she said.

'Yes. And very much deserved,' he said.

'Thank you.' She inclined her head in acknowledgement of the compliment, but she felt awkward. Time to change the subject. Fast. 'What do you do when you're not at work?' she asked.

'I walk—I'm not far from Hyde Park,' he reminded her. He gestured to the shelves. 'And, as you can see, I read.'

'I was surprised not to see anything even vaguely musical on your bookshelves,' she said. 'Have you really cut yourself off from that world completely?'

'Yes. I don't want to think about anything classical,' he said, 'or at least anything that I would've played, either on the violin or on the piano.'

Livi had noticed the absence of musical instruments or any kind of music system, too. She waited, giving him the chance to fill the silence.

Eventually Josh said, 'I know this is going to sound weird, but I think when you play an instrument you listen to music in slightly a different way to someone who doesn't play. You *feel* it as well as hear it. It's muscle memory, I guess—the same way that a ballet dancer would hear *Swan Lake* but they'd know how it feels to perform it. A musician feels music in their hands. You can't detach one from the other.'

'That makes an odd kind of sense,' she said. 'What about the kind of music you didn't play—say, pop and rock? Do you listen to that?'

'Not really. If I listened to anything, it'd probably be the blues,' he said. 'Though I haven't been to a gig in years.'

'There's nothing like singing your head off with fifty thousand people,' she said. 'I've been to a couple of big gigs with friends at Wembley and Hyde Park and loved every second. And to the Pr—' She stopped mid-sentence, aghast at what she'd just been about to blurt out. Although she hadn't meant to be cruel, saying it would definitely hurt him, and that wasn't who she was. 'Sorry. Ignore me.'

'I'm glad people still enjoy the Proms,' he said, clearly picking up what she hadn't said.

Well, she'd brought up the subject and he hadn't shied away from it. Maybe she could push a little more, after all. 'You played a couple of Proms, didn't you?'

He nodded. 'I did the *Lark*, and the Paganini *Caprice*.'

'I saw you play the *Lark*,' she said softly. 'At St Martin's, and at the Royal Albert Hall. The first time, I looked up Meredith's poem when I got home, and what I read…that was exactly what you made me see.'

'"He rises and begins to round, /He drops the silver chain of sound/ Of many links without a break, /In chirrup, whistle, slur and shake,"' Josh quoted. 'Vaughan Williams wrote some of that poem in his score.'

'The bit I remember most is, "And ever winging up and up,/ Our valley is his golden cup, /And he the wine which overflows /To lift us with him as he goes",' she said. 'That's what I saw in my mind's eye when you played. A skylark rising into the air, the melody dropping down to us and taking us up with him.' She looked at him. 'Josh, it must be incredibly tough to know you can't play it anymore. But nobody can deny the joy you've brought to your audiences when you were able to play. The joy you still bring, because there are recordings of your work and people can still play them. That's special. Something to hold on to.'

'Maybe I'm being a bit self-indulgent,' he said.

'No. You're protecting yourself,' she said. 'I get that. But have you ever thought that cutting yourself off from the joy of music might hurt you more? Even though you can't play it, you can still feel it in your heart.'

Josh wasn't sure he even had a heart, these days. He kept it well covered, thinking he was protecting himself; or maybe a closed-up heart just turned to stone from lack of use. 'Maybe,' he said.

She reached out and squeezed his hand briefly. 'You asked me a few days ago what I'd do if I couldn't cook anymore—if the only thing I could do was boil an egg, with a lot of help, would I do that? I told you I wouldn't, because I completely understand why you don't want to play at anything less than the level you played at before. But there's a difference between being a creator and being a consumer. I'd still eat.'

'You kind of *have* to eat, if you want to stay alive,' he pointed out dryly.

'You need to consume enough calories to make your body function and make sure you get all the nutrients you need,' she said, 'but there's a big difference in seeing food solely as fuel, and enjoying what you eat for its own sake—being able to savour the taste and the texture, the scent, the way it looks. If I couldn't cook, I'd still enjoy the food. Maybe I'd find patisserie a bit difficult to manage, but if it was a choice between not having it in my life at all and having it in my life in just a little way…' She spread her hands. 'Well, I'd want to keep it in my life. I'd want to keep at least some of the joy.'

She had a point, but Josh didn't want to think about that. Instead, he switched topic. 'What do you do when you're not working?'

'I work unsocial hours,' she said, 'so it's either the cinema or theatre on my nights off, or maybe a matinée performance. And I like wandering around art galleries.' She smiled. 'Holly, my best friend, is really good at craft stuff. She knits, she sews and she crochets.'

'The history teacher, right?' he asked.

She looked pleased that he'd paid attention. 'Yes. She did try to teach me to knit, because she says it's great for relaxation, but my scarf ended up more holes than knitting, and it was a very peculiar shape.' She chuckled. 'So we gave up. The deal is that she knits me a gorgeous cardigan for winter, and I make her a batch of cake every week when I'm trying new ideas.'

'You bake on your days off?' He'd known Livi was driven, but he hadn't realised how much: that she continued working even when she wasn't in the brasserie.

'It's not really work. I play with recipes,' she said. 'Ideas. Sometimes they work, sometimes they don't. But you never know until you try.' She paused. 'I'm going to Brussels in a couple of weeks, for a chocolatier's course.'

'If you need guinea pigs,' he said, 'I can supply a few.'

She chuckled. 'Speaking of which, I need to earn my supper. I got your report this morning. Shall we sit down and talk about it?'

He glanced at his watch. 'Dinner's just about ready. Let's do it over coffee.'

Do it. He felt colour scorch into his face. Oh, for pity's sake. Way to go, Josh, he thought. How to make her feel uncomfortable around him. 'Analyse the questionnaires, I mean,' he mumbled.

'Anything I can do to help with dinner?'

'No. Come and sit down,' he said, ushering her to the table.

He'd chosen recipes for their simplicity, remembering what she'd said about simple food. Baked salmon, roasted vine tomatoes, steamed Jersey Royal potatoes with a little butter, and asparagus wrapped in prosciutto and baked with a little parmesan scattered on top.

'This,' she said appreciatively, 'goes together really well. And you've plated it very nicely.' She looked up at him, the corners of her eyes crinkling with mischief. 'It'd get you a pretty good mark at chef school.'

He couldn't help laughing, 'Well, you said to keep it simple.'

'It's the principle my dad brought me up on,' she said. 'Good food doesn't need extra complications. Just use good quality ingredients, keep the preparation simple, and let the food shine in its own right.'

'That's a good rule for life,' he said. 'Be honest. Be yourself.' Something he maybe hadn't been since the accident, because he still had that gaping hole in his centre. He'd learned to cover it up, but it was still there. And he hadn't ever told the people closest to him what he'd nearly done, that awful night. He'd wanted to protect them from the knowledge, because he didn't want to hurt them by telling them the truth; but keeping a secret also meant he'd ended up keeping a space between himself and the people he loved. And sometimes he really missed how it felt to be close to someone.

'Be yourself. That works for me,' she said lightly. As if she guessed that he was feeling awkward and a bit out of sorts, she switched the topic of conversation, talking about recent films she'd enjoyed, and Josh found himself relaxing again with her.

Olivia Lambert really was like balm to the soul. Did she realise how special she was? he wondered. And would she give him that second chance, if he asked her to?

Over coffee, they went through the questionnaire results.

'The menu's in the right area,' she said. 'And I like the suggestions of us offering picnic boxes and takeaway lunches. It'd work if we open a café, but I think it would be too much to add it to the brasserie.'

'I'd advise a soft launch in the brasserie,' Josh said. 'Cake of the day on your socials, reviews on the foodie sites—including Jenna's vegan one—film of you making something, and running a competition to see if they can guess the flavour, that sort of thing. Focus on your Belgian heritage, use old family photos of the brasserie when your family first started out in London, and if there's anything of you as a toddler making cakes with your mum or your gran we can use them. Those sort of things, with the personal touch, go down really well. Your brand's all about family, good home cooking and the Belgian twist on things.'

'That's all doable,' she said. 'I've definitely got film of toddler me making cakes with Gran.'

'We can do it as a reel,' he said. 'You as a toddler, you as a teenager, you doing the patisserie course, graduation. We want customers—young and old—talking about their favourite cake and their favourite tartine. Give me the material, and we'll sort it out for you.'

'All right,' she said. 'Let's make a list of what you need.'

When they were done, she sent the list over to him. 'Just in case you have any bright ideas tomorrow,' she said with a smile. 'And I need to be getting back.'

For work. From what she'd told him, he was pretty sure she started early and finished late. 'Of course,' he said. 'I'll walk you back to the Tube.'

'No need. It's still light,' she said. 'I'll be fine. And I'm sure you have things to do. Can I do the washing up, first?'

'No. That's what dishwashers are for,' he said.

'Thank you for dinner,' she said. 'I really enjoyed it.'

'Thank you for the wine and the chocolates,' he said. 'I'm keeping that quiet at work, or they'll all come round to raid my fridge.'

She chuckled. 'I'll drop some of the next batch round.' Then, to his surprise, at his front door, she rose on tiptoes and pressed a kiss on his cheek. 'I'll speak to you soon,' she said, and sashayed out of the door.

He didn't recognise the light scent she wore—oranges and toffee, he thought, and something he couldn't quite work out that felt sparkly—but it put him in a spin. Or maybe that had been the feel of her mouth against his skin. He watched her walking down the cobbled street, hoping she'd look back at him when she reached the corner and feeling ridiculously disappointed when she didn't. He closed the door and touched his cheek, tracing the outline her lips had made. This was crazy. He wasn't supposed to be feeling like this about her. She was his client, which put her off limits; and that night, years ago, put her even more off limits. But, even knowing that, the more time he spent with her, the more he wanted to be with her.

They'd become friends again, of a sort.

He wanted a lot more than friendship from her; but, until he knew how Livi felt, he needed to keep his own feelings under wraps. Rushing things now would ruin everything. He just needed to wait. Be patient. Be professional. And, most of all, keep that need under strict control.

CHAPTER SEVEN

EITHER LIVI WAS rushed off her feet at the brasserie, or she'd decided to put some space between them, Josh thought, because she kept everything strictly on business terms for the next week.

Then, on the Monday morning, she sent him a text. *Wanna be a guinea pig?*

He remembered the afternoon tea she'd brought over, the previous week—the team was still raving about it. *Me, or the team?* he checked.

Just you.

Sure, he said, trying to play it cool. *When were you thinking?*

Dinner tonight at seven, she said. *My place. Make sure you're hungry.*

Oh, dear God, the pictures that put in his head. He rather thought he needed a cold shower. *Look forward to it,* he said. *Flat above the restaurant, yes?*

Red door next to it. Press the intercom for Flat One.

OK. Shall I bring red, white or rosé wine? he asked.
Whatever you'd like to drink with chicken, she replied.

He found it hard to concentrate all afternoon. And clearly it showed, because his team kept making little comments and asking what had put him in such a good mood.

No way could he tell them. He made some bland excuse.

But even the idea of seeing Olivia Lambert again made him feel like a teenager.

This wasn't a proper date. 'Guinea pig' meant that she was testing something out on him. Probably brunch, he thought. He needed to think of this as work.

But he couldn't.

She'd said he could bring wine. And she'd liked the rosé Sancerre. He couldn't take her chocolates—especially as he knew she was going to Brussels on Friday for a chocolatier's course. But he could take flowers.

Roses were too obvious.

And a big flashy bouquet would make her run a mile.

In the end, he went to the florist round the corner at lunchtime and asked for help. 'I need something that isn't too obvious or too flashy, but it's for someone…' He paused. 'Someone special to me.'

'Do they have a favourite flower?' the florist asked.

'Um—I don't know,' he said.

'OK. Let's try a different tack. Do you know what colours they like?' the florist asked.

'No.' And how bad was it that he'd known her for twenty-five years—well, with a bit of a gap, and he'd only got to know the woman she was now over the last three weeks—and he didn't have the faintest clue? 'Sorry. Um, if it helps, she's a pastry chef.'

The florist smiled. 'Actually, that does help. We'll go for a summery scent. Stocks would be good.'

'She likes gardens,' he said, brightening up.

'All right. I can do you a hatbox arrangement, so you won't have to worry about whether she has the right size vase. Stocks, chrysanthemums—the tiny santini ones are really pretty—irises and alstroemeria,' the florist suggested. 'Pink, cream and blue. We can add in some cream roses, too; as part of a mixed bouquet, they add depth and they're not obvious.' She smiled. 'A bit nicer than a dozen red roses, and it'll be special but not completely over the top.'

Which fitted his brief exactly. 'Perfect. Thank you,' Josh said.

He collected the flowers later that afternoon, finished off some work at home, then took a cab to Covent Garden. He went to the red door next to the restaurant and pressed the intercom for Flat One; there was an answering buzz, and a click as the door opened.

On the landing at the top of the first flight of stairs, Livi stood at the open door. 'Good evening. Perfect timing.'

He handed her the wine and the flowers.

'Oh, these are so lovely!' she said. 'How did you know stocks were my favourite flowers?'

'I didn't,' he admitted. 'I asked the florist for something nice that someone who loves gardens would like. I mean—I could hardly bring a box of chocolates to a chocolatier, could I?'

She chuckled. 'You have a point. They're stunning.' She buried her face in the flowers for a moment, inhaling their scent. 'Thank you. Come in and sit down.'

He closed the door behind him, and she indicated the middle doorway. 'The bathroom's there, if you need it.'

He assumed the first door was her bedroom. When he followed her through the third door into the open-plan kitchen-cum-living room, he stopped dead. 'Wow. I wasn't expecting *this*,' he said, glancing round. The walls were painted a deep grey-blue, and the matt colour extended to the kitchen cabinets. The counter-tops and splashback were cream marble, and there was a white marble fireplace surround; there was an ornamental metal basket piled with logs in the fireplace itself. The two sash windows had roman blinds in what looked to him like a Morris pattern; there was a rich crimson-and-white rug in the centre of the polished floorboards, and a comfortable-looking sofa in crimson velvet with matching tub chairs by the windows. There was a brass and crystal chandelier hanging from the ceiling, reflected in the mirror above the fireplace. There were book-shelves—painted in the same matt colour as the kitchen cabinets—and he could see at a glance that they contained mainly classic novels and poetry.

'I'm going to put these here,' she said, placing the flowers on the occasional table between the chairs. 'And how clever of you to get them in a hatbox so I don't have to rummage around for a vase.'

'I can't take credit for that. It was the florist's suggestion,' he admitted.

'But you were sensible enough to take it,' she pointed out.

He didn't feel very sensible, right now. He felt all at sixes and sevens. 'Your flat is amazing,' he said. 'And it's a really bold colour choice. Most heritage places tend to be painted cream, to make the most of the light.'

'Covent Garden deserves something theatrical,' she said with a grin. 'I admit, the flat was painted cream when I moved in—some of the wall in my bedroom is actually bare brick. Holly's cousin was training as an interior designer and asked if she could redesign the flat for me as part of her degree project. I said yes—and I admit, I panicked a bit when she brought the paint round because I thought it'd be way too dark and I'd feel as if I were living in a rabbit warren. But she asked me to trust her, painted the whole flat the same colour—including all the woodwork—and I love it.'

The small round dining table was set for two, with a white damask tablecloth and napkins folded into a rose shape, silver cutlery and plain crystal wine glasses.

And something smelled incredible.

'Anything I can do to help?' he asked.

'You can open the wine and pour two glasses, if you like, then sit down,' she said. 'I'm just about ready to serve up.'

He followed her directions, and she dished up.

'It's chicken breast stuffed with goat's cheese and sundried tomatoes, and wrapped in parma ham, served on a bed of puy lentils and spinach with a pesto dressing,' she said. 'And the bread's sourdough.'

It had taken her seconds to add the little fancy finishing touches that he never even thought about using when he was cooking, but which made the food look special. And the food tasted every bit as good as it looked. Even though she was a pastry specialist, she could hold her own when it came to cooking the other courses.

She wouldn't so much as let him clear the table for her when they'd finished the main course. 'It's fine,' she said with a smile.

And then she brought out the pudding: a small dome with a deep raspberry-coloured mirror glaze, topped with a stylised daisy made from white chocolate.

He'd known she was talented, but this went beyond his expectations.

'That looks incredible.' He blinked. 'I'm almost scared to touch it in case I spoil it.'

She laughed. 'It's not for decoration, it's for eating. It's a white chocolate and raspberry mousse with a raspberry gelée, on an almond sponge, with a raspberry mirror glaze. If you slice through it with your spoon, you'll see the layers properly.'

'Just… I knew you were a proper *pâtissière*, and Eti always raves about your desserts,' he said, 'but I wasn't expecting something like this.'

She chuckled. 'I admit this was a bit time-consuming to make—you have to freeze the layers as you go, and obviously with this being raspberry I needed to do a bit of sieving as well, to take out the pips. I didn't have time to make them when I did the afternoon tea at your office, but here I could take my time. Technically, it's known as an *entremet*.'

He picked up his spoon and sliced into the dome so he could see the layers, the pale sponge and the dark gelée and the fluffy pale pink mousse and the glaze. And then he hesitated. 'This is going to be part of the afternoon tea?'

'Some days,' she said. 'I've done a blueberry version

before now, and a passion fruit and orange one which looks almost fluorescent.'

He narrowed his eyes at her. 'This isn't greed speaking—well, it might be that as well—but did you only make two of them?'

She smiled. 'No. I have several more in the fridge.'

'Good. If you don't mind, I'll ask Pete to nip round to the brasserie and photograph them tomorrow,' he said. 'Because I guarantee that pictures of this pudding alone will get people to queue up in the brasserie for your afternoon tea.'

She looked pleased. 'Good. But the proof of the pudding is meant to be in the *eating*.'

He took the hint and tried the first spoonful, then closed his eyes in bliss. And all the common sense went flying out of his head, because he found himself saying, 'I think you should call this First Kiss. That's what it's like—light and sweet, but not cloying, and it makes you want more.'

First kiss.

Their own first kiss hadn't been light or sweet, Livi thought. It had been hot and needy and desperate. And it had led to disaster. To recriminations and misery.

But maybe, just maybe, this was a second chance.

A first kiss that was light and sweet...

She'd impulsively kissed Josh on the cheek, last week, but he hadn't mentioned it again. She'd thought he was being polite and ignoring the subject to avoid embarrassment, so she'd backed off. But the way he'd blurted out the words, just now, made her wonder if he'd been thinking the same thing that she had, all along.

His eyes were still closed, and his lips were very slightly parted—just a tiny, tiny gap in the centre. A wave of sheer heat throbbed through her. Right at that second, he looked as sexy as sin. Irresistible.

Before she knew what she was doing, she stood up, closed the gap between them in two steps, bent down and brushed her mouth against his.

First kiss.

Light and sweet, but not cloying.

Makes you want more.

And that tiny contact between them, that gossamer whisper of a kiss, had made her lips tingle. She wanted more.

He opened his eyes, then; they were like deep blue pools, reflecting the same need and longing that burned through her.

'Livi,' he whispered, and reached up to brush her cheek with the backs of his fingers. And then he shifted and scooped her onto his lap, holding her close. She slid her arms round his neck to balance herself, and he reached up so his mouth just brushed hers. Tiny, tiny kisses, little butterfly movements, and it felt like fireworks going off in her head. All she could see was glittering stars.

This was the kiss she'd wanted all those years ago. The kiss in her head that nobody had ever matched up to, before. Yet Josh was kissing her now, kissing her properly, and it was perfect. It was *everything*.

Josh.

Josh, who'd pushed her away and stomped on her heart.

Josh.

She couldn't do this. Panic flooded through her. Last time, it had all gone wrong. And OK, now it was years later and they'd both grown up and changed, but what was to say that this time wasn't a mistake, too? What was to say that he wouldn't let her down again?

Clearly he felt the tension that had made her freeze, because he stopped kissing her.

'Livi,' he said softly.

How could she face him?

What if she saw rejection in his eyes again?

How could she have been so *stupid*, when they were supposed to be working together and being professional and, and, and...

'Breathe, Livi,' he said quietly, taking her hand and squeezing it.

Oh, God. She'd panicked so much that she'd actually stopped breathing. 'I...'

'Don't talk. Breathe with me. In for four,' he said softly. 'Out for four.'

It was easier to give in and follow his directions. Though even after several breaths she still felt light-headed, and she thought that was more than just down to breathing: it was his nearness. The fact his arms were still round her. The fact those blue eyes were filled with concern. And oh, dear God, he was so damned sexy and she wanted him so much, she didn't know what to do with herself.

'Livi.' He kissed the tip of her nose. 'We need to talk. Properly. But I think you need some space, first, so I'm going to leave now. I'll call you tomorrow.'

Meaning he'd talk to her later, after he'd found a kind way to tell her he wasn't interested—that as far as he was concerned she was still Eti's baby sister? Which meant that this *was* just the same as the last time he'd rejected her, except this time he'd have a veneer of kindness instead of bitter scornfulness when he told her that he didn't want her—that he couldn't want someone like her, and she'd never be what he wanted.

Misery welled up in her heart.

'Tomorrow,' he said softly. He stood up, still holding her, then settled her gently into the chair he'd just vacated. The chair that was still warm with his body heat. Ridiculously, she felt freezing cold.

He pressed the backs of his fingers briefly against her cheek in a gesture of affection, then left the room. She heard the click of her front door as it closed behind him.

What the hell was she going to do now?

CHAPTER EIGHT

Time seemed to stop. Livi wasn't sure if it was seconds or minutes or even longer until she finally forced herself to move and clear up in the kitchen.

A warm shower did nothing to relax her. Neither did listening to music, because music made her think of Josh. And she couldn't concentrate enough to read or even watch a re-run of an old favourite sitcom.

What was she going to do?

She didn't want to fall for Josh and for him to let her down again.

Kissing him had been a huge mistake. A whim she should never, ever have acted upon. Maybe it had been a mixture of proximity and unfinished business; but she couldn't get it out of her head, and it rattled her. Over the last three weeks, she'd discovered that she really liked the man Josh had become. Was she still in love with Josh, after all these years? Was that the real reason why she'd never managed to get a relationship to work—because the men she'd dated hadn't been *him*?

She spent a sleepless night and was seriously out of sorts, the next morning. Josh had said he'd talk to her later today, but she didn't have a clue what she was going to say to him. Worst of all, she still had some of the raspberry *entremets* in her fridge—the 'first kiss', as Josh had dubbed them—and she knew he was planning to send his photographer over to shoot them.

Livi really couldn't face dealing with that, pretending that everything was fine when it wasn't.

Even though Tuesday was usually her day off, she boxed up the desserts and headed down to the brasserie. Maybe the photographer could shoot the *entremets* in the kitchen, rather than in her flat. And maybe doing an extra shift, keeping herself too busy to think about what had happened with Josh, would help to clear her head. At least it would be doing something practical instead of moping around her flat, full of angst.

'Hello, sweetheart. I wasn't expecting to see you today,' Sophie said, when Livi walked into the kitchen.

'Josh is sending a photographer over, this morning, to shoot these for some social media posts,' Livi said, gesturing to the box.

Sophie took a look inside. 'That mirror glaze looks amazing—and I like that chocolate daisy. Raspberry, I'd guess?'

'Raspberry and white chocolate layers, on a bed of almond sponge,' Livi confirmed. 'Once they've been photographed, they're up for grabs if you and Dad want to try one.'

Sophie's eyes narrowed and Livi knew that her mum had picked up on the flatness of her voice, even though she'd tried to hide it.

'Is everything all right, darling?' Sophie asked quietly.

'Yes,' Livi said. Then, knowing that her mum would

see straight through the fib, she admitted, 'No.' She sighed. 'I don't know, Mum.'

'That sounds...complicated.'

Sophie sounded warm and non-judgemental, and Livi wanted to throw herself into her mum's arms and burst into tears. Except that wasn't who she was. Olivia Lambert was cool, calm and sensible...or she had been, until Josh Garrett had come back into her life. Right now, she was a hot mess, and she hated feeling so out of control. 'It is.'

'Talk to me, sweetheart,' Sophie said. 'Whatever it is, we can sort it out.'

'I'm not sure we can.' Livi bit her lip. 'I've made a really stupid mistake.'

Sophie waited, giving her space, and eventually Livi burst out, 'I kissed Josh, last night.'

'I think that was rather a long time coming,' Sophie said neutrally.

Livi laughed wryly. 'Mum, if you only knew.'

'Tell me,' Sophie said gently.

Livi glanced round the busy kitchen. Much as she liked her team, she didn't want to bare her soul in front of them. 'Not here.'

'The office, then. Your dad's out at a supplier's.' Sophie deftly grabbed two mugs on the way out of the kitchen, filled them with filter coffee and thrust one into Livi's hands when they reached the office and Livi sat down. 'Take a big gulp, then talk.'

The coffee didn't help at all, but Livi supposed at least the mug gave her something to do with her hands. 'It started years ago.' She told Sophie what had happened the night she'd gone to rescue Josh.

Sophie leaned over, took the mug from her daughter's hand and placed it on the desk next to her own, and held Livi close. 'Oh, darling. I'm so sorry I didn't know any of this, back then. And you've been carrying the burden ever since? I wish you'd told me. I could've helped you deal with it.'

Livi shook her head. 'I couldn't tell you, Mum. I was just so *ashamed*.'

'You did nothing wrong. Josh, on the other hand, most definitely did,' Sophie said grimly.

Livi winced. 'He was in a pretty bad place at the time.'

'You're protecting him, after what he said?' Sophie looked shocked.

'It did hurt me, the way he pushed me away afterwards. How he dismissed me as a stupid, spotty-faced schoolgirl.' She took a deep breath. 'It hurt so much.' And the comment about her skin had stung viciously. Like anyone else who'd ever suffered from teenage spots that hung around a bit longer than the teens, she'd been sensitive about the way she looked.

'Of course it hurt. It was a horrible thing to do. And you were never a stupid schoolgirl. Even when you were at school, you were never immature. And as for that thing about your skin, I could punch him for being so tactless. You were still growing up, for pity's sake.' Sophie looked furious. 'I know he'd just had a life-altering injury, but it sounds to me as if he knew you had a crush on him and he deliberately broke your heart, so someone else would feel as bad as he did.' Sophie hadn't taken her arms from round her daughter, and Livi could feel the tension in her mum's body. 'Right now, I could happily break every bone in that man's body.'

Sophie looked at her sweet, lovely mother—the woman who made people feel the brightness in life—and shook her head. 'That's not who you are, Mum. And I rather think he's beaten himself up about it enough ever since.' She rested her forehead against her mum's shoulder. 'He wrote to me, a few weeks afterwards.'

'And he apologised?'

'So he says. I never actually read the letter.' She took a deep breath. 'I didn't throw it away, either.' Though she wasn't sure why. She should have shredded it. Burned it. Done something with it, instead of leaving it as a ticking time-bomb. 'It's upstairs at the back of a drawer somewhere.' That wasn't quite true; she knew exactly where the letter was. She just hadn't had the courage to read it. Even now. Because giving her virginity to Joshua Garrett had *meant* something to her; she didn't want to read something that dismissed it as a mistake.

'Maybe it's time you did read it,' Sophie said.

'I don't think I'm ready for that,' Livi admitted. She raked a hand through her hair. 'I don't know what to do, Mum. Right now, I just want to run away, but that's not fair to you.'

'You're on that chocolatier course in Brussels in two days' time,' Sophie said. 'Why don't you go early and give yourself a bit of space? And don't worry about cover here. It's only a couple of days. I'll sort it out.' She paused. 'Do you want me to come with you?'

Yes, but Livi knew that would put the rest of the team under too much pressure and that wouldn't be fair. She couldn't even ask Holly to come with her for a couple of days, because she was in Greece with her boyfriend. 'I think I need to be alone,' she fibbed. 'Like you say, I need some space. To think.'

'All right, but you know you can call me any time. And you can change your mind. Text me if you need me there, and I'll be on the next train or plane to Brussels.' Sophie stroked her hair. 'I'd even drive over through the Channel Tunnel, if I had to.' Which Livi knew was a huge ask, because her mum hated driving abroad.

Livi believed her. Sophie had always had her back, and Eti's. 'I love you, Mum.'

'I love you, too, my precious girl.' Sophie hugged her.

'Don't break Josh's bones,' Livi said.

'I'll hold off until you're back home and you've sorted your head out,' Sophie said. 'That's as far as I'm prepared to promise. Now, go upstairs and finish packing. I'll change your hotel booking and your train tickets.'

'And don't tell Dad?'

Sophie looked troubled. 'I've never kept anything from your dad.'

'Please. Just until I'm back,' Livi said. 'I'd rather tell him myself. But I can't face doing that today.'

'All right,' Sophie said. 'As long as you promise me you'll call if you need me.'

'I will,' Livi promised. 'And thank you. For understanding.'

'Of course I understand. You were twenty years old. It didn't feel like a crush. You were in love with him, and he took advantage of that. And then he broke your heart.'

'I was the one who kissed him, last night.' Hot shame flooded through Livi's veins. 'Then he left.'

'Oh, darling.' Sophie stroked her hair. 'You can't help who you fall for. But if he doesn't treat you the way you deserve to be treated, you're better off without him. And if it's too difficult for you to work with him, then we'll pay off the contract and use someone else.'

'He said he'd talk to me today. But I can't face him.' Livi grimaced. 'Right now, I feel embarrassed and stupid and clumsy.'

'You're neither stupid nor clumsy,' Sophie said briskly. 'Or you wouldn't be about to take over the reins of the brasserie and move the business forward. But maybe it's a little tricky to mix business and…well, emotional stuff. Try not to worry. It'll all come out in the wash, as my gran used to say.'

Livi smiled wryly. 'I guess.'

Sophie gave her a last squeeze. 'Go and pack. A bit of distance will give you some perspective. And this is about what *you* want. Whatever you decide that is, you have my full backing.'

'Even if I decide I want Josh?' Livi tested.

'Whatever you decide. Just know that your father and I love you very much, and we're hugely proud of you,' Sophie said.

'I love you both, too,' Livi said.

And that chat with her mum made her feel better enough that she could pack swiftly.

She glanced at the flowers in her living room before she left her flat, and on impulse grabbed them and took them down to the brasserie.

'Darling, they're utterly gorgeous, but I'm your mum and it's my job to be there for you and listen when you're having a tough time. You really didn't need to rush out and get me flowers,' Sophie said.

'I didn't,' Livi admitted. 'Actually, Josh brought me these, last night. And they're so lovely. I'd rather give them to you so you can enjoy them than leave them in my flat and let them shrivel unseen while I'm away.'

'Then I'm the lucky one,' Sophie said lightly. She paused. 'They really are gorgeous.'

'He said he couldn't bring chocolates to a chocolatier,' Livi said. 'But these...'

'...are quite a bit more special than the average supermarket bouquet,' Sophie finished. 'And they're not the sort of flowers you give to any old someone. It looks to me as if Josh might have feelings for you.'

Livi had thought that, too. But had she been deluding herself, seeing something that wasn't really there? 'What if he changes his mind? What if he thinks it's a mistake? I mean, *I* worry it might have been a mistake.'

'Distance and perspective—that's what you need,' Sophie said. 'Think about what *you* want. Then you'll be in a place to have a proper conversation with him.'

Livi smiled wryly. 'That's common sense, and I should've worked that out for myself.'

'It's a lot easier to do from the outside, when you're not the one tying yourself in knots,' Sophie said. 'Go to Brussels. Make chocolate. Sit in the sun drinking good coffee and eating waffles. Go to art galleries. Let your subconscious work it out for you.' She glanced at her watch. 'You have a train to catch. Go. Safe journey. I love you.'

'Love you, too, Mum,' Livi said. 'I'll ring you when I get to the hotel.'

* * *

Josh frowned. Livi wasn't responding to emails or texts, and when he rang her phone it went straight to voicemail.

Had she had second thoughts after he'd left her flat last night, and was trying to avoid him now? Or maybe he was being paranoid. Hadn't she said that she sometimes swapped her shifts if they were short-staffed at the brasserie? If she was working, then she probably wouldn't have her phone with her.

He still needed the photographs of her amazing desserts as part of the social media campaign. He probably should've taken the shots last night, instead of kissing her back. That had been mistake number one. Mistake number two had been kissing her back.

And mistake number three had been leaving.

Or had it?

The very first time he'd kissed her, he'd rushed her. He'd taken everything she'd offered. And then he'd panicked, and said things that he knew would push her away. Things that had hurt her badly, and even now it made him feel ashamed.

This time round, he'd wanted to get it right. He'd wanted to give her space, to make sure this was really what she wanted and he wasn't railroading her into anything. That was definitely the right thing to do, he was sure.

But it felt as if it had backfired. Had she thought he was walking away from her again, instead of trying to be honourable and letting her dictate the pace rather than his own need?

They needed to talk. He'd been clear about that, last

night. He'd told her he'd call her this morning. And surely she'd learned over the last few weeks that she could trust him—that if she could trust him with her family's business, she could trust him with herself?

The quickest way round this, he thought, was go to the brasserie and talk to her. They'd arranged for him to photograph the raspberry *entremets*; instead of sending Peter, he'd do it himself.

At Covent Garden, he rang the intercom for Livi's flat, but there was no answer. That had to mean she was at the brasserie, he decided.

When he walked into Lambert's, Sophie was on front of house. She greeted him with folded arms, a narrow stare and a very cool voice. 'Joshua. Good morning.'

Uh-oh. This didn't sound good.

'Good morning, Sophie,' he said politely. 'I was hoping to talk to Livi and sort out some photographs of her amazing desserts for social media, but I can't get hold of her.'

'She said you were sending a photographer over.'

'I was,' he said, 'but I'm doing it myself so I can talk to her. I assume she's in the kitchen?'

And just like that the curvy, smiling woman he'd known and liked for years turned into a forbidding, granite crag. 'I'm afraid not.'

Sudden fear flooded through him. 'Is she all right?'

'I rather think you should've asked that question eight years ago,' she said quietly and very, very coldly.

Josh stared at her in shock, understanding now why she'd turned glacial on him. 'You *know* about that?'

'I do now,' Sophie said. 'Livi told me this morning.' She narrowed her eyes even further at him. 'My little girl's been hurting all these years, and I didn't have a clue.'

'Sophie, that wasn't your fault. It was mine. And Livi's not a little girl. She's the most amazing woman I've ever met,' Josh said. 'Eight years ago, I was in a bad place—and that's an explanation, not an excuse. I said things I know I shouldn't have said, and I've always regretted hurting her. I've apologised. Since we've been working together recently, I've realised...' He stopped abruptly. 'Actually, with the greatest respect, I need to discuss that with her, not with you.'

'Perhaps,' Sophie said, still unbending. 'I'll let you get on with taking your photographs. Let me show you through to the kitchen.'

Josh wasn't used to his best friend's mother being so cool with him, though he could understand why; now she knew how badly he'd treated Livi, of course she was angry with him.

He needed Sophie on his side, not against him. He didn't want to tell her how he felt about Livi because, although he knew his feelings for Livi were deepening, he wasn't entirely clear yet where this thing between them was going. And although he knew he could tell Sophie Lambert something that would shock her into being on his side, he wasn't ready to open up about *that*, either. To anyone.

Without arguing, he followed Sophie into the kitchen. And he tried not to be disappointed when he discovered that Livi's mum hadn't just been trying to protect her; Livi really wasn't in the kitchen. Then again, if Livi had guessed that he might come to take the photographs himself, she was probably avoiding him.

Even looking at the desserts made him remember the previous night. The way Livi had walked round the table to him and kissed him. How he'd scooped her into his lap and kissed her back. Her warmth. How the world had finally felt as if it had fallen into place instead of being slightly off kilter the whole time.

And he had a pretty good idea of why she'd fled. She didn't trust him not to let her down again. He could hardly blame her for that. She might even be right, and that was a terrifying proposition.

Planning and strategy were two of his key skills at work, but they completely deserted him where Livi was concerned. How was he going to convince her that he was no longer the broken young violin prodigy who'd let her down so badly? That he'd moved on, sorted himself out, and this time she could rely on him?

Brooding wasn't going to help. He forced himself to be professional and take the photographs of the raspberry *entremets*, firstly the complete dome with its immaculate mirror shine reflecting the white chocolate daisy, and then the cross-section with the utterly precise layers.

'That mirror glaze is incredible,' one of the sous-chefs said as Josh zoomed the camera in and took a shot. 'Our Livi's a marvel.'

'Yes, she is,' Josh agreed.

'I can't wait to see the ideas she'll come back with from Brussels.'

'Her chocolatier course is later this week, isn't it?' Josh asked.

'Yes, but she's gone a couple of days early to check out desserts, brunch and afternoon tea,' the sous-chef said.

Livi had gone to Brussels already?

That made sense. It would give her some space and time to think.

And maybe Brussels would be a good place for them to talk. Somewhere neutral. No memories, no misunderstandings, no mess of the past.

Which meant he needed to know where she was staying; he could probably find out where the course was, especially as he knew the dates, but it wouldn't be fair to Livi to turn up there.

The one person who could tell him the details probably wouldn't want to help him. But he could try.

Once he'd thanked the kitchen team for letting him sort out the photographs, he went in search of Sophie again.

'Finished?' she asked.

'Almost,' he said. 'Sophie, about that night. I was still coming to terms with things, and not doing a very good job of it.' He'd almost taken a step that would've shattered his family. Not that he was going to open up to Sophie about *that*. 'When I realised what I'd done, and how Livi really felt about me—that she wanted a proper relationship, and my head was in way too much of a mess at the time to even consider doing anything like that—I panicked. That's why I said what I did. To push her away.'

'So I gather,' Sophie said grimly.

'But because I realised how much I'd hurt her, I finally started to sort my life out. I went to therapy. I wrote to Livi, apologising and explaining I didn't actually mean what I'd said to her. When she didn't reply, I assumed she didn't want anything to do with me. I tried to stay out of her way so I wouldn't make life harder for her. If you remember, I ducked out of Eti's wedding and Louisa's christening.' And he would have been so thrilled to be Eti's best man and Louisa's godfather, even though he felt he hadn't deserved that privilege.

'Eti said you'd gone somewhere for residential therapy.'

'I did,' Josh said. 'Strictly speaking, I was managing OK at the time without it, but I needed an excuse that nobody would question and meant that nobody would connect Livi to my absence. I didn't want anyone to blame her or give her a hard time, because none of it was her fault.'

Sophie gave a single nod, signalling that she understood.

'When you gave me the brasserie project and I realised I was going to have to work with Livi, I asked her if she wanted me to back off,' Josh said. 'I said I'd be guided by her. I could turn down the project, or get one of my team to stand in for me, or we could agree to put the past behind us and work together.' He blew out a breath. 'She decided she could trust me to be professional.'

'And she was wrong.'

'No, she wasn't,' Josh said. 'Livi and I need to talk. I know she's in Brussels, and maybe that'd be a good place to meet. Somewhere neutral, away from London and away from the past.' He looked at Sophie. 'Can you tell me which hotel she's staying at, please?'

'Maybe you should give her space,' Sophie said.

'Maybe giving her space means she'll think too much and it'll get blown out of proportion,' he countered. 'I promise you, I'm not going to hurt her again. I just want to talk to her. Face to face—it's too easy to miss things in a video call, and even easier to misinterpret things in a phone call or text messages. But, more than talking to her, I want to listen to her.'

Sophie was silent, as if weighing things up.

He waited rather than rushing her. He needed her to be sure he wasn't going to bulldoze her daughter's feelings—and being patient now would prove to her that she could trust him to be patient with Livi, too.

'If I tell you her hotel details,' Sophie said, 'I expect you to book a room somewhere else.'

'Of course,' he agreed. 'I won't crowd her.'

'All right,' she said. 'But I'm telling her that you're heading to Brussels, so she can prepare herself for seeing you again. And if she decides she's not ready to talk to you, Joshua, I expect you to abide by that and wait until she *is* ready.'

Let Livi be the one to decide the pace. Josh didn't even need to think about it before he answered. 'Yes. That's fair,' he said. 'Thank you.'

She took her phone from her pocket. 'It's probably quickest if I email you the booking confirmation.'

'Thank you, Sophie,' he said. 'I won't let you down.'

'I don't care about me,' Sophie said. 'Just don't let Livi down.'

'I won't,' he promised.

He took a black cab from Covent Garden; on the way back to Bayswater, he emailed the photographs to Shelley, and advised her he was going to be working remotely for the rest of the week. He also checked Livi's hotel and booked his train ticket and a hotel—one that wasn't too far from Livi's, but far enough away so she wouldn't feel that he was crowding her—and then texted the details to Sophie, to keep her in the loop.

It didn't take him long to pack a small case, or to get to St Pancras and catch the Eurostar to Brussels.

Hopefully the city was far enough away from London—and, more importantly, from their shared pasts—for Livi to be comfortable sitting down and having a serious talk with him. Did she feel the same way about him as he did about her? He hoped so; all he needed to do now was persuade her that she could trust him.

All, he thought wryly.

CHAPTER NINE

LIVI HAD ALREADY worked out which tram she needed to catch from the station to get to her hotel. When she went up to street level, she discovered that the weather was glorious: blue skies, with just enough of a breeze to stop the air feeling sticky. A perfect summer day. Just what she needed, right now.

It was a while since she'd last travelled to Brussels, and she'd forgotten how pretty the city was, with its gorgeous historic buildings surrounding cobbled squares dotted with fountains, from ancient sculptures to modern steel spheres. Her hotel was in one of the grand old buildings, only a few minutes' walk from the tram stop; she checked in at the reception and made her way up to her room. As soon as she'd made herself a cup of coffee, she sat in the easy chair next to the bed and rang her mum.

'Just to let you know I'm here safely,' she said. 'And I had a really good journey. No delays, and it was easy to find the hotel. I'm just having a coffee while I unpack, then I'm going out to do a bit of exploring.'

'That's great,' Sophie said. 'Um—I need to tell you something, sweetheart. Josh is on his way to Brussels.'

Livi felt her jaw drop. 'Sorry?'

'Josh is on his way,' her mum repeated. 'To see you.'

'How? He doesn't know where I am.'

'I told him,' Sophie said. 'Though he's not going to stay at your hotel.'

'What? But—why is he coming to Brussels? Why did you tell him where I was?' Livi asked, horrified. Her mother had encouraged her to put some distance between them; why had she changed her mind and practically allowed him to hijack her escape to Brussels?

'Livi, I think you both need to talk. And a neutral place would be good for both of you. Better than London. There's nothing to get in the way.'

'So you're taking his side, now?'

'No,' Sophie said. 'But I believe he intends to listen more than he talks. Which is quite rare, in men, in my experience. Including your father.'

'Mum, that's pretty sexist,' Livi said, with a shocked giggle.

'It's also true. Give him a chance, Livi. For both of your sakes.'

When Livi ended the call, she drummed her fingers on the table. So Josh was planning to come and see her? Well, she didn't want to meet him at her hotel. Neutral ground would be better. And he must be at least two hours behind her own departure, she calculated.

At least they wouldn't be staying at the same hotel, so if things went badly it wouldn't be quite so awkward.

She checked out local cafés on the internet, then texted him. *Mum tells me you want to talk and you're coming to Brussels. Perhaps you'd like to meet for coffee. There's a nice café not far from my hotel, in the*

Galeries Hubert. Can check out their waffles at the same time. Assume 4.30 works for you? L.

Keeping it polite and almost businesslike: that was the best way forward, she thought. Meet him in public, and mix it with a bit of work so she could focus on that. Keep all the emotions out of it.

As he arrived at the train station in Brussels, Josh steeled himself not to think of the last time he'd travelled to Brussels, as part of the orchestra. The last six months of his career. He'd played the Bach *chaconne* in the elegant Art Deco hall at the Palais des Beaux-Arts. But that was another world and another life, he reminded himself. He'd made his peace with it, for the most part, but every so often that empty space inside him seemed to gape a little wider—now being one of those times, when the memories seemed to mock him.

He pulled himself together. Just. When he made his way outside the station, a driver was waiting next to a limousine, holding a card saying *Mr Garrett*.

Josh walked over and made himself known, and the chauffeur drove him into the city centre. The hotel was nothing like the one Josh had stayed in, last time he'd been in Brussels; rather than being a modern-built economy-class hotel on the outskirts of the city, this was an ancient red-brick building with stone quoins, in keeping with the historic buildings around it. Wrought-iron balconies sat at the bottom of every tall window, filled with clusters of pots stuffed with bright red geraniums. The marble-floored reception was light and airy, with sparkling chandeliers, and Josh was delighted to discover that his suite was on the top floor. Not only did it have fabulous views over the rooftops of Brussels and plenty of space, the suite also had its own private roof garden, with comfortable chairs set round a table and roses climbing round the willow screens surrounding the terrace, perfuming the air.

Before he unpacked, he unlocked his phone, intending to check in with the office back in London. Then he saw the notification of the text from Livi.

He read it, to discover that Sophie had told her he was on his way, and she'd pre-empted him. Well, OK. At least it seemed she was prepared to talk. That had to be a good thing. He glanced at the time. He had twenty minutes to get to the café. A quick check on his maps app told him it was less than a ten-minute walk from his hotel to the meeting spot.

Then again, would she really open her heart to him in a public place? Maybe here might be a better place to talk. Just the two of them in this lovely roof garden.

4.30 fine, he messaged back. *Unless you'd rather come and sit on the roof terrace with me here. Is private and has good views.* He took a snap of the terrace, making sure the ornate gothic spire of the town hall with its pinnacles and turrets was in the background, and sent it to her.

Looks nice, but I think neutral ground would be more sensible, she messaged back.

Josh understood where she was coming from; she was clearly trying to set boundaries. It was a valid point. But the kind of conversation they were going to have really needed a more private space than a popular tourist spot.

Agreed, but harder to talk openly in a public space

with lots of people around. Bit noisy. Easy to miss things, he messaged.

She rang him. 'Are you trying to call the shots and make me come to you because you have a flashy hotel with a roof garden?'

'No. I'm just thinking it's difficult to have a private conversation in a busy, noisy café stuffed full of people, and here it's quiet,' he said. 'I want to listen to you, Livi, but I also want to say some things I'd be uncomfortable sharing in a public space. Not because I think anyone might recognise me and go running to the press with what they think is gossip—those days are long gone—but because...' He blew out a breath. 'It's just not the kind of thing that's easy to talk about. Especially with people chattering around you.'

'Hmm,' she said. 'Where are you?'

'Just off Grand-Place. Overlooking the town hall.'

'It's less businesslike, meeting at your hotel, but you have a point about privacy,' she said.

'I'll order us something from room service. What would you like? Tea, coffee, a glass of wine?' he asked.

'Tea, please,' she said. 'I'll walk over to you.'

'I'll text you the hotel details and my room number. I'll keep an ear out for you knocking,' he said.

'All right,' she said.

She didn't reply to his text. Then again, he reminded himself, there was no need. He'd given her all the necessary information. What else was there to say?

The waitress had literally just delivered a tray of tea and biscuits and he'd taken it to the table on the terrace when there was a knock on his door. Heart pounding, he opened the door to face Livi.

She looked amazing in jeans, comfortable shoes, a pretty top and a sunhat, and his heart squeezed. He really needed to get this right because, even though he wasn't entirely sure where this was going, he knew he wanted her in his life.

'Well, Mr Garrett. This is a bit flashy. The penthouse suite?' she commented.

'It wasn't *intentionally* flashy. It was the only room they had left, and your mum told me not to book a room at your hotel,' he said.

'I came to Brussels to get some distance and some perspective,' she said. 'I wasn't expecting you to follow me here.'

He could see the tightness in her expression. And he could understand it now: she thought he was intruding on her private space to think. 'I didn't mean to steamroller you or act like a stalker,' he said. 'That honestly wasn't my intention. I just think we need to talk. Face to face. And I thought—hoped—maybe being out of London would make it easier for both of us.'

'Maybe,' she said. 'And this terrace is quiet, you say? You didn't want to meet in a café, but what if other hotel guests want to use the roof terrace?'

'They, um, don't have access to this particular bit,' he said. 'It's part of the suite.'

She blinked. 'You have your *own private roof terrace*?'

'A small one. But yes,' he said, squirming slightly. 'I didn't realise when I booked the room. As I said, this wasn't intentionally flashy. I'm not trying to impress you.' He gave her a wry smile. 'When I saw the terrace I thought it might be a good place to talk, because we're not going to be interrupted by anyone and we'll have some privacy. I'm not trying to take over.'

She didn't look as if she quite believed him, but she let him usher her into the living room area and through the French doors to the roof terrace.

'It's pretty,' she said, walking round the terrace so she could admire all the views, then bending to smell the roses. 'These are proper scented roses, too. And fairy lights.'

Which would make the terrace look incredibly romantic when it was dark. Not that he was going to be stupid enough to say so. Instead, he kept it neutral and asked, 'Can I pour you some tea?'

'Thank you.' There was still that tightness around her eyes as she pulled out the chair opposite the one he was standing behind and sat down. The fact she sat opposite him rather than next to him, with the barrier of a table between them, was telling.

Hopefully she'd relax a bit before they started talking. He knew how to make a client relax, but this wasn't a business discussion. It was a lot more personal than he usually got, and a business technique simply wouldn't work here. He was beginning to think that her tension was affecting him, too. Addling his brain. Because suddenly he felt really out of his depth.

He poured out two cups of tea, leaving her to add her own milk.

'Help yourself,' he said, gesturing to the plate of tiny buttery biscuits.

For a moment, he thought she was going to refuse.

But then she nibbled one and looked critically at it.

'Shortbread thins with salted caramel nuggets. These are seriously good.'

It wasn't the sugar rush that had relaxed her a little bit, he realised; it was seeing things from a business angle.

'I need to up my biscuit game,' she said.

'If your biscuits are the same standard as your raspberry—' Then he stopped dead, remembering what he'd said when he'd tried the *entremet*. About first kisses. And how she'd kissed him. How he'd kissed her back. Everything had gone weirdly skewed after that.

And reminding her of that would be the quickest way to put up another barrier between them. He felt the colour flooding into his face. 'Um, I apologise. That wasn't meant to be…'

'I know.' But she was blushing, too, clearly thinking of exactly the same moments as he was.

He sighed and rested his elbows on the table, linking his fingers into a bridge and resting his chin on it. He looked levelly at her. There was no point in trying to pussyfoot round it anymore. 'We have unfinished business, Livi.'

'We do.' She sighed. 'And it's complicated.'

'I'm listening,' he said.

She raised an eyebrow. 'You're expecting *me* to be the one to sort it out?'

'No,' he said. 'Sorting it out is something we need to do together. But I want to listen to you first, rather than talk over you. Especially as I've already pretty much wrecked your thinking time away—even though that wasn't what I intended.'

She looked serious, clearly digesting what he meant:

that he didn't plan to railroad her into doing whatever he wanted. That her views were just as important to him as his own. That he wanted them to work as a team—personally, not just in business. 'I'm not sure where to start,' she said.

'Neither am I,' he said. 'I guess it probably ought to be *that* night—' the momentous one all those years ago, that had had such a big impact on both their lives '—but that feels…' He shook his head. 'I don't know. Huge. I think that's too much to handle in a single conversation.' Especially with what he wanted to tell her.

'I think it goes back before then, even,' she said. 'I had a crush on you for years and years and years. All the way through my teens. All my mates were drooling over actors and pop stars they'd never get to meet in a million years, and I just wanted you. My big brother's best mate. The epitome of tall, dark and handsome.' She gave him a rueful smile. 'I convinced myself that you were within reach. Except you never were. Because you were just as famous as the actors and pop stars, and just as far away from me as they were from my friends. The fact I knew you in real life didn't make any difference.'

'I saw you as my best friend's little sister. A bit shy, blushed a lot, very sweet, and completely off limits. When I was eighteen, you were still only fourteen,' he reminded her.

A muscle twitched in her jaw. 'A stupid, spotty-faced schoolgirl.'

He flinched, remembering the words he'd thrown at her. 'It was a horrible thing to say, and it wasn't true.' She hadn't even been a schoolgirl; she'd been twenty, working full time in her family's business. But he'd deliberately said it to make her feel young and small.

'To be fair, I did have terrible skin,' she admitted.

'Lots of people do at that age,' he said. 'And they're often sensitive about it. I was deliberately mean, because I knew it would push you away. I apologise for being so...' He shook his head, unable to think of the right word to describe his behaviour. 'Cruel and horrible, basically. I'm sorry I hurt you.'

She gave a single nod of acknowledgement.

'Plus you've never been stupid, Livi. You're bright. You could've got in to any university you chose, if that was what you'd wanted. But Eti said you wanted to work in the family business.'

'I did. I love what we do at the brasserie,' she said. 'People come to Lambert's for family celebrations, for birthdays and anniversaries and engagements, because they know the food is excellent and there's a good atmosphere. They come to us for first dates, because we have quieter tables where people can talk and get to know each other over good food. They come to us because maybe they've had a bit of a rough week and they're a bit too tired to cook; all they want is to eat some Belgian comfort food or a really fancy dessert, and to have a bit of a fuss made over them. And I love that we're part of people's lives like that, through the good times and the bad. I love that my great-granddad came over from Belgium to London and started it all off; our restaurant's been part of Covent Garden for decades, and I'm part of that tradition. I love that I can produce a dessert that makes people feel special even before I stick a celebratory indoor sparkler in it. It feels as if I'm doing something that actually has meaning.'

'There's no "as if",' he said. 'You *are* doing something that has meaning.' Like he'd once been able to do, with his violin: he'd been able to transport people away from a tricky bit of their lives to a place of joy. What he did nowadays felt as if it was all surface and meaningless. He knew it was important to his clients, because it helped them; but it wasn't the same. It didn't have that personal connection, the way music did.

'Thank you,' she said. 'Anyway. That night happened. And I hated you for a bit, afterwards. But you did at least stay away from me.' She ate another biscuit. 'I dated other guys.' She didn't say it in so many words, but her eyes told him it had been more than just dating. 'It never worked out, but I assumed it was just because I was rubbish at relationships.'

Because what he'd said to her had trashed her confidence and she hadn't let them close in case they hurt her the same way that he had? Guilt pinched him. Hard.

'I really thought I was over you, Josh. When Dad said your agency was the third one pitching, I was a bit shocked, but I honestly thought I'd manage to be all cool and calm—sophisticated was probably a step too far,' she added ruefully, 'but I was managing.' She dragged in a breath. 'Until I kissed you, last night.'

Her eyes went wide, as if she were reliving the kiss, and she suddenly looked lost. He wanted to wrap his arms round her and tell her that everything would be all right, but it wouldn't be. Words just weren't enough to fix this. He didn't know how to fix this, but talking was a start.

'You changed everything for me,' he said. 'Because of you, I went to therapy instead of…' The words stuck in his throat. He couldn't tell her everything just now. It would feel like blackmail. He wanted her to focus on now, not then. Instead, he mumbled, 'I'm sorry I hurt you. I felt horrible when I realised I'd taken your virginity. I didn't have anything to give you back, except the empty shell of who I used to be. I guessed you hoped for more, and I couldn't deliver. That's why I pushed you away.' He shook his head. 'I guess it was a mix of guilt and self-loathing. And I still felt so bad about it, the next morning, that I made the decision to go to therapy and sort my head out. Something I'd been resisting.'

'Why did you resist it?'

'Because I didn't think I was fixable,' he said. 'But my therapist was good. I pretty much came to terms with losing my music and I found something else that I could do. Yes, the empty space inside me is still there, but I can manage it.' Most of the time, but he wasn't going to tell her about the moments when he couldn't. Right now, this wasn't about him and his demons; it was about her. 'And I've never forgiven myself for the way I treated you. That's why I stayed out of your way. I thought if you didn't see me, it would make things easier for you.' He looked at her. 'We didn't really know each other properly, back then. You were my best friend's little sister, and I was focused on my violin. When we started working together on the project, it made me realise things weren't the same. You still have that kindness, that sweetness I remember—but I'm seeing a different side of you, now. The grown-up, professional you. Your cooking blows me away.'

She went pink. 'Thank you.'

'It's not a compliment. It's a statement of fact,' he said. 'This isn't like when I first met you, when I was a snotty-nosed kid and you weren't much more than a toddler. Or when you were a shy teenager and I was focused on my music to the exclusion of everything and everyone else. Or when my life imploded and...' He stopped, still unable to voice what he'd nearly done. If he ever told her about that, he'd need to choose his words very carefully. 'When I was incredibly unfair to you,' he said instead, his voice thick with emotion. 'Now, the four years between us don't matter anymore. And I like the woman you've become, Livi. I really, *really* like you. I want to reset our relationship. And I'm not talking about our business relationship—I mean you and me. I want to start again, get to know each other properly outside work.'

She swallowed hard. 'I don't know if I can do that, Josh.'

'Maybe we can start as friends,' he said. 'Though I'd like it to become more than that.'

'It's all...a bit overwhelming,' she said. 'That's why I came here a couple of days early for my course. To put some space between us and think about how to deal with things between you and me.'

'And I've trashed that by following you here. I don't mean to crowd you,' he said. 'But I do need you to know I'm sincere. I'm so sorry about the way I treated you, back then. I'd like to think that if I hadn't been in such a bad place, I would've been kinder to you. Even so, I know I've changed over the last eight years. Will you let me prove myself to you? Here, where we don't have any memories to get in the way. Where it's just you and me. Obviously you're here to do your course, and I'm not going to interfere with that—I can work remotely when you're busy. But when you're not in class, I'd like to spend some time with you. Take you to dinner somewhere the food's really good, talk with you, maybe hold your hand.' He gave her a wry smile. 'And I promise I won't kiss you again until you ask me to.'

'Time together. Just getting to know each other again,' she said.

He nodded. 'Will you give me a second chance?'

CHAPTER TEN

A SECOND CHANCE. Get to know each other again. Reset their relationship.

It was oh, so tempting. And he made it sound oh, so easy.

But Livi had cried an ocean over Josh, eight years ago. She didn't want to repeat her mistake and end up with that kind of misery filling her heart again. How could she be sure a relationship would work between them, this time round?

And was that what she wanted? Was Josh who she wanted?

Josh had apologised for what had happened. Sincerely. She understood why he'd lashed out at her, back then, and she could even forgive it.

The problem was, she couldn't forget it. And part of her wondered if it would happen again. Life didn't tend to run smoothly. The next time things became tricky for Josh, would he push her away again rather than talk it through with her? Would he see her as his equal, now, or would he be stubborn and feel he had to protect her out of some misplaced sense of chivalry?

She took a sip of tea and thought about it.

Brussels wasn't London. Here, there were no memories. At least, not for her; she suspected that Josh had probably played the violin in a concert hall somewhere here, along with stages in many other European cities. But, together, they could make this a fresh start for both of them.

And she noticed that he was being patient. Sipping tea, relaxing on the terrace, not pressuring her to make a decision or to talk until she was ready. He meant it about giving her space.

OK.

If he could do this, so could she.

'We could,' she said carefully, 'give it a try. See how it goes.'

'Thank you,' he said. 'I'd really like that.' He paused. 'Perhaps we can go for a walk, when we've finished the tea. Take in some of the sights of the city, see if we can spot any of the Tintin cartoons on the walls of buildings.'

'OK,' she said. 'Actually, I spent most of the journey from St Pancras looking up places to go.'

'Did you make a list of things you wanted to do?' he asked.

She nodded. 'There are some cafés and chocolate shops I really want to visit, partly to see what's on offer for afternoon tea and if there are any ideas that I could tweak a bit to suit me. And the art galleries.'

'Sounds good,' he said. 'And if the weather's nice maybe we can go for a walk through one of the parks.'

'That sounds good, too,' she said.

'And maybe we can have dinner tonight? We could find a place that takes our fancy, while we're out; or if you'd like to see what this roof terrace looks like after dark, the hotel has a menu that looks pretty good.'

'Just so you know, I judge menus by the desserts,' she said.

He took out his phone, went into the hotel's website and found the dessert menu, then handed his phone to her. 'Does it pass your test?'

She looked through it and smiled. 'Waffles. Well, I think any place should offer them for dessert in Brussels,' she said. 'And *merveilleux*.'

'Wonderful?' he translated.

She chuckled. 'Meringue. With cherries and white chocolate, in this case. Hmm. Ice cream and sorbets, served with *speculoos* biscuits. Or *pain perdu*—French toast, with salted caramel and apples. And obviously a *dame blanche*—vanilla ice cream sundae with warm chocolate sauce.' She spotted the last item on the menu. 'Oh, now this has my name on it. Almond semifreddo with blueberry compote. Thank you, dinner here will be lovely. With the fairy lights.'

He grinned. 'I love your enthusiasm. And I'll make a special request for them to save you a piece of the semifreddo in case they run out.'

'I appreciate that,' she said. 'That's kind.'

'I want you to enjoy dinner—which is my treat, by the way.'

'Only if you let me buy you dinner tomorrow,' she warned. 'Because if we're going to have any kind of relationship—whether it's business, friendship or something more—we're going to do it as equals.'

'I accept with pleasure,' he said, smiling.

And just like that it was easy.

Josh had a quiet word at the reception desk before they went exploring; he booked dinner and made sure that Livi's chosen dessert would be available, and then they wandered through the narrow street into the cobbled square of Grand-Place. The architecture was really stunning; the buildings all had fancy gables and lead roofs. Some had gold details over windows and on pillars; one had a gold statue of a man on a horse on the roof, while another had a gold plaque of a peacock, and others had statues in niches.

'According to this,' she said, reading from the guidebook on her phone, 'most of the buildings were for different guilds, and each house has its own name.' She pointed out one of the houses. 'That one, *Le Pigeon*, was for the city's painters, and it's where Victor Hugo lived when he was first exiled from France. And Marx and Engels wrote their manifesto over there in *Le Cygne*.' A sculpture of a swan, framed by greenery and his wings highlighted with gilding, stood above the doorway. 'The guilds were abolished at the end of the eighteenth century, but if my hunch is right and my forebears all followed the same trade as my great-grandfather, working in a kitchen in an inn, then they would probably have been associated with either the brewers' guild or the bakers' guild.' She pointed out a building with gilded hop plants twining round its columns. '*L'Arbre D'Or* was the brewers; and the one over there with the dome, *Le Roy d'Espagne*, was the bakers.'

'*Le Roy d'Espagne*. The King of Spain,' he translated.

'It says here the building was named after Charles II, who was the King of Spain when it was built in 1697, and he was also the king of the southern Netherlands—which included Belgium,' she said. 'All the statues on the balustrade are about baking—Hercules having the strength you need to be a baker, Ceres obviously as the goddess of agriculture being linked to wheat, Mercury for the fire in the oven, Neptune for the water in the dough, Minerva with her hourglass for timing the length of the bake, and a woman with a windmill—not a goddess, but she probably should be. Oh, and Saint-Aubert, the patron saint of bakers, is above the door.'

They spent a while with her guidebook, enjoying picking out which house had belonged to which guild.

'Do you know where your great-grandfather lived or worked?' he asked.

'As it happens, I do. Jean Lambert was born in 1907, and he worked in an auberge called *Le Cheval Rouge* in the old part of town, not that far from here—a street off a street off Grand-Place,' she said. 'The family didn't actually own the auberge, but they ran it. It changed hands a few times, and then it became a chocolate shop for a while and then a boutique selling handbags, but now it's a bar again and they've resurrected the old name, which is lovely.' She smiled. 'I've got the address; I was going to check it out and take some photos of what it looks like now for Dad, and maybe have a chat with whoever runs it now and show them the photos we have of my great-granddad when he worked here. With any luck, they might even have photos of the inn from further back that they can share with me.'

'You've got the photos with you?' Josh asked.

'They're on my phone,' she said, and picked out an album from her photos app to show him. 'That's Jean Lambert, in the bar at *Le Cheval Rouge*, in the late 1920s. It's a bit blurry, but he's the one with the beard wearing a white apron and a chef's cap.'

'What made him move to London?' Josh asked.

'My great-grandmother, Elsie,' she said. 'Her dad was in the rag trade. When he came on a business trip to Brussels, Elsie accompanied him. Her dad bought lace from several people, including from Jean Lambert's mum, Marie-Thérèse. Marie-Thérèse told them *Le Cheval Rouge* was a good place to have dinner, and said to mention her name at the bar as her son would give them a discount. Family legend is that it was love at first sight between Jean and Elsie. When Elsie's dad had finished his business dealings and they went back to London, Jean followed them to London and persuaded her dad to let her marry him.'

'And that's their wedding photo?' he asked, turning to the next shot.

'In April 1934,' she said. 'Christ Church, in Spitalfields.'

'Look at all that lace,' he said. 'Her dress and her veil.'

She nodded. 'Isn't it gorgeous? The lace was made by Jean's mum, and Elsie's dad made the wedding dress. My grandparents donated it to the V&A museum so other people could enjoy it, too—it's a part of East End history.'

'So you could've ended up being a dress designer instead of a *pâtissière*,' he said.

'In theory, perhaps, but in practice I'm hopeless at crafts apart from sugar-craft,' she said with a smile. 'It was the cooking side that seemed to stick in the family. Elsie's family lived in Spitalfields, and there were a lot of Huguenots working in the rag trade there. Jean set up a stall selling Belgian comfort food—*stoemp*, sausages, *moules-frites* and carbonnade Flamande.'

'All things that are still on your menu today,' he said.

She was glad he got it. 'Yes. The stall was really popular, and did well enough that when a local café came up for sale Jean could afford to buy it and expand the business. Things were a bit tricky during the war—luckily as a Belgian, Jean wasn't treated as an enemy alien and stuck in an internment camp, but he went off to fight with the English troops. The clothing factory took a direct hit, so Elsie took over the café and ran it until Jean came home.' She gave a rueful smile. 'Sadly, Elsie and Jean both died before I was born, so I never got to know them. But I do remember my granddad. He joined his mum and dad in running the café in Spitalfields, and he moved it to Covent Garden back in the 1960s, just before my dad was born. Back then, his customers were mainly the market workers, so he opened early to get the breakfast trade, and finished when they finished. When the fruit and veg market moved to Nine Elms in the 1970s, Dad was in charge and he turned Lambert's into the brasserie it is now, serving dinner rather than breakfast. And now it's my turn to mix things up a bit.'

'This would all be a great social media story,' Josh said. 'We definitely need to do a page on your website showing how everything changed over the years and what's remained constant. Four generations of Lamberts cooking for their customers and changing to meet their needs. We can drip-feed the story, telling a little bit more each week and including a new photo, so people come back for the next instalment.'

'Dad's got a lot more photos. I'm sure he'd be happy to go through them with you,' Livi said.

'And a link to your own speciality would be good. Maybe we could run a story on the wedding cakes?' he suggested. 'I know you don't make wedding cakes—'

'Actually, I made Eti and Lucy's,' she corrected. 'But you're right in that I don't make occasion cakes as a rule.'

He looked thoughtful. 'I wonder if all the wedding cakes in your family over the years were made by someone in the family? If so, there might even be a link back to the lace, with maybe the patterns on the wedding cake being inspired by the patterns of the lace in the bride's veil.'

'I never even thought of that,' Livi said. 'I wish I had. Lucy had a lace veil. I could've made the cake decorations in matching sugar paste and it would've looked amazing.'

'Eti and Lucy's cake looked amazing in the photographs,' Josh said, and she remembered that he'd deliberately given her space so she wouldn't feel awkward at the wedding. 'He sent me a bit, too. Best wedding cake I've ever tasted, and I'm not just saying that.'

She dipped her head to acknowledge the compliment. 'I'm pretty sure my granddad made Mum and Dad's wedding cake, so Dad can tell us about that,' she said. 'I'm not sure about the generations before, but Dad might know. I'm guessing at the very least he has the wedding photos somewhere, so we can enlarge the cakes and the veil to take a closer look.'

Josh made a note. 'This is going to be fun,' he said. 'Shall we go and find the auberge?'

Livi had already been looking forward to doing the little bit of family history research, but Josh's enthusiasm made her enjoy it even more. They made their way down one of the side streets from Grand-Place, noting the cobbles on the streets and the old-fashioned streetlamps, then turned down another street, and from there took another turning.

'Here it is,' she said. 'Dad's going to love the bar's sign.' It was a very modern stylised horse's head, entirely in red, with a flying mane.

'Let me take a picture of you under it,' Josh suggested. 'My phone or yours?'

'Mine, please—then I can send the photos to Dad, later,' she said.

She posed for the photograph, then Josh took a shot of the bar's sign before they went in and ordered two beers. Luckily the owner was actually working behind the bar, and when Livi told him about their quest he joined them at their table and was thrilled to see the photographs of her great-grandfather working at the old auberge. 'What a fantastic link to the past. Would you be kind enough to send me a copy so I can print them out and put them in a frame on the wall with the ones I already have?' he asked. 'My customers would love to see them.'

He showed them the history wall, with pictures of the auberge from the middle of the last century, the shops that had taken its place, and even woodcuts of the inn as it had been a century before Jean Lambert and his family had run it. 'I've got copies of all of these on my laptop. I'll send them to you,' he promised, and they exchanged business cards along with a promise that he'd come and have dinner with them, next time he was in London.

'That was a good result,' Josh said as they headed back to his hotel.

'Agreed,' she said.

And then she tripped on the cobbles.

'Whoa,' Josh said, catching her arm so she didn't fall flat on her face. 'Are you OK, Livi?'

'I'm fine. Thanks for rescuing me,' she said.

'No problem,' he said with a smile that made her feel all gooey inside.

She was disappointed when he let her arm go, missing the warmth of his skin against hers.

But as they walked on, their hands brushed against each other. She wasn't sure whose fingers clung to whose, but suddenly they were holding hands. Properly. As if they were dating for real.

Her heart rate went up a notch. Was this what it would be like, dating Josh? As a teenager, she'd dreamed of walking along a beach with him, holding hands. Teenage Livi would've been beside herself to think this was actually happening.

She stole a glance at him. He looked utterly insouciant—or did he? Was there a slight wariness in his face, as if he too couldn't quite believe they were walking together, holding hands?

Well, OK. She wasn't going to break the bubble by commenting on it. And they were supposed to be seeing how things went. 'I was thinking, there are a few lace shops in the city that have historic collections. Maybe we can drop in to a couple tomorrow and see if they have any information about Jean's mum, or know where we might be able to find out?'

'That's a good idea,' he said.

When they reached the hotel, he stopped holding her hand so he could open the door for her. She smiled her thanks, then let him usher her into the lift and up to his penthouse apartment.

It was still too early for the fairy lights to have come on, but she enjoyed the late evening sun on the roof terrace. Particularly after they'd ordered dinner and a bottle of wine: white asparagus with truffle vinaigrette, ravioli with burrata, and scallops with a saffron beurre blanc served with sweet potato puree and tenderstem broccoli. Josh ordered cheese where she'd opted for the almond semifreddo with blueberry sauce.

'Would you like an aperitif?' he asked.

'Europe and summer always says Aperol spritz to me,' she said.

'Perfect. I'll join you,' he said.

While they were waiting for their drinks to arrive, Livi sent her father the photographs of *Le Cheval Rouge* and asked him for the photographs she and Josh had discussed earlier.

'This feels like a proper holiday,' she said when their spritzes arrived on a silver salver, in gorgeous glassware and garnished with a twist of blood orange. 'Sitting on a terrace in the sun, sipping a cocktail.'

'Is that your normal kind of holiday?' he asked. 'Or do you like relaxing on a beach?'

'Beach holidays aren't my kind of thing. I'd get twitchy after a day of sitting doing nothing,' she said. 'I prefer city breaks, where I can explore somewhere.

Art galleries, culture and food, that's what I like best.' She looked at him. 'What about you?'

He winced. 'I've never been very good at holidays. In my younger days, obviously I travelled a lot for work and didn't get to see very much of the places I visited; and then I kind of didn't really want to go back and see what I'd missed.'

'So what do you do for holidays now?' she asked.

'I don't really take them,' he said. 'Maybe a few odd days here and there. I might go to an exhibition at a museum. I like Bath.'

'For Austen?' she asked.

'Herschel,' he said, surprising her. 'And the curse tablets at the Roman baths.' He smiled and took a sip of his spritz. 'This is much, much nicer than lukewarm sulphurous spring water.'

'The Austen side of things is fun,' she said. 'Dressing up to go to a proper Regency ball, especially when the dance floor's been chalked with some gorgeous pattern.'

'You like dancing?' he asked.

'I do,' she said. 'But I'm guessing that's something you'd rather avoid.'

'Yeah,' he admitted. He lifted one shoulder in a half-shrug. 'My parents have nagged me into joining them when they've hired a little cottage on the North Norfolk coast. I like taking the dog for a walk on the beach to watch the sun rise and set, or staying out late in the middle of summer to watch for meteors.'

'You're not tempted to get a dog yourself?' she asked.

'I've thought about it,' he admitted. 'A big soppy golden retriever who'd be the office mascot, sitting under my desk and taking a nap with his head on my feet, then getting his share of the sofa back at the house.'

He sounded a bit wistful. Was he lonely? Livi wondered. Because, apart from his team at work, he seemed to keep at a distance from people. Eti was probably the closest one to him, but her brother had mentioned that it was hard to pin Josh down. Because he'd been trying to avoid her? Or did seeing Eti remind him too much of what he'd lost? Not that she could ask without being pushy, and she didn't want him to back away.

'How about you?' he asked.

Of course he wasn't asking if she was lonely. She was probably reading too much into it. He probably wanted to know if she wanted a dog. 'It wouldn't be fair to keep a dog, working restaurant hours,' she said. And her hours weren't really going to change, were they?

Just as it was starting to feel a tiny bit awkward, there was a knock at the door and their first course arrived.

'It's beautifully plated,' Livi said, looking critically at the white asparagus with truffle vinaigrette. 'It looks like a work of art.'

'And it tastes even better,' Josh said, after his first mouthful.

'Is everything OK in the office?' she asked.

'It's fine. I know if there's a problem my team will get in touch,' he said. 'And it does them good to know I trust them to get on with things rather than micromanaging.' He looked wistful. 'I quite envy you the fact you're the fourth generation in the family business. All that history.'

'Would you have wanted to follow your father into stockbroking or your mum into teaching?' she asked.

'No,' he admitted. 'I knew what I wanted to do really early on, even though nobody in the family had ever gone past grade five piano. I just loved the feeling music gave me—as if I was fully alive, right in the moment, whether it was learning to shriek my way through *Three Blind Mice* on the recorder at infant school, or doing endless scales and arpeggios on the piano. The first piece I learned on the piano was Bach's *Minuet in G*—though actually it was written by Christian Petzold, and it was attributed to JS Bach because Anna Magdalena, his wife, copied it into her notebook. I liked the *Minuet in G minor* more, though. That always felt like sunshine falling across a garden on a late winter afternoon.'

'I don't know the pieces,' she said.

'You would if you heard them,' he said. 'Definitely the G major.'

She almost asked him to hum them for her, but maybe that would be pushing him too far.

'I'll send you a link, later,' he said.

He clearly missed music, Livi thought, noting that he hadn't mentioned the moment he'd first picked up a violin; clearly that was too much for him to bear remembering. Though she was sure if he allowed himself to listen to music, he'd get the joy back that he'd first experienced as a small child. Not as much as if he could still play, admittedly, but surely it would be better for him than denying himself that pleasure for the rest of his life?

The waitress came to collect their plates and deliver the next course—ravioli with the creamiest, wobbliest burrata, followed by tender scallops in the most delicious saffron beurre blanc, nestled on a bed of sweet potato puree and tenderstem purple broccoli.

Livi kept the conversation light for the rest of the meal.

The semifreddo was as wonderful as she'd hoped, and so were the salted caramel pralines that came with the exceptionally good coffee.

'Thank you for dinner,' she said when she'd finished the last sip of coffee.

'My pleasure,' he said. 'It was good to spend time with you today.'

'I really enjoyed it, too,' she admitted. 'I'll see you tomorrow, then.'

'I'll walk you back to your hotel,' he said.

'It's only a few minutes away,' she said. 'I think I can manage.'

'You're an adult, and you can look after yourself,' he said. 'I know. But humour me?'

'All right,' she said.

He took her hand again as they walked through Grand-Place again. What could be more romantic, she thought, than wandering through ancient cobbled streets, hand in hand? It was a moment to savour and enjoy.

Josh saw her safely to the door of her hotel. 'See you tomorrow,' he said. 'Shall I call for you?'

'Lovely. About ten?' she suggested. 'Then maybe we can go looking for the lacemakers.'

'It's a date,' he said softly.

And, even though he didn't actually kiss her goodnight—he'd said earlier that he wouldn't kiss her again until she asked him to—the warmth in his eyes felt like a hug.

'It's a date,' she agreed.

In some ways, it'd be their first real date. Their first *official* date, at least. And it was weird how the idea made her blood feel fizzy.

A few minutes later, he texted her the links to the piano pieces he'd talked about. She recognised the first one immediately, but not the second. Like sunshine on a winter afternoon, he'd said: and she could hear what he meant.

Ten points to you, she texted back. You're right, I did recognise the first one. I didn't know the second, but I prefer it. I see what you mean about winter sunshine.

Sweet dreams, he texted back. Try this one to fall asleep to. It's the musical equivalent of Monet's garden.

He'd sent her a link to Debussy's *Rêverie*, another piece she didn't really know but liked instantly.

If sharing music with her would help to give him his music back, then maybe dating him properly would help her to get her trust in relationships back, she thought.

Maybe they could fix each other.

Maybe.

CHAPTER ELEVEN

Josh woke on Wednesday morning feeling happier than he could remember feeling in years. Which was ridiculous. Just because Livi had agreed to spend the day with him, he really shouldn't get carried away.

Even so, he almost started singing in the shower—something he hadn't been minded to do for a very long time. Not since before the accident.

And he couldn't wait to see her.

He caught up with his work while he ate breakfast; then the alarm on his phone pinged to let him know that it was time to go and meet Livi. He texted her to let her know that he was on his way, and she texted straight back. *See you in the foyer.*

He walked into the hotel reception and saw her straightaway. Today she was wearing a pretty summer dress, teamed with comfortable canvas shoes; she was carrying her floppy sunhat and her sunglasses were perched on the top of her head. He raised his hand in acknowledgement, and she stood up.

'Hi,' he said. And then he felt like a prize fool. 'This is kind of ridiculous, but I'm not sure how to greet you today,' he said. 'Shaking your hand would be too formal, but I can't...' He might as well be honest. 'It doesn't feel right to give you a hug and kiss your cheek yet, either. Not when we agreed to take it slowly.'

'It's been a while since I last dated and I've forgotten the etiquette, too,' she admitted ruefully. 'Shall we just pretend we've greeted each other, for now?'

'Good idea,' he said. Better than feeling awkward. 'You look lovely, by the way.'

'Thank you.' She smiled at him, and his heart skipped a beat. 'You look nice, too.'

He'd thought ridiculously hard about what to wear, not wanting to be too casual but not wanting to look stuffy, either; in the end he'd picked dark tailored trousers and a white collarless linen shirt teamed with black suede lace-up shoes, and added sunglasses and an olive-green bucket hat as a nod to the sunshine.

'Thank you,' he said. 'So we're starting at the Galeries Hubert?'

'We are,' she confirmed. 'And then we're going in search of antique Belgian lace and Marie-Thérèse Lambert.'

The Galeries Hubert turned out to be a beautiful arcade with a covered glass roof.

'I checked the guidebook this morning,' she said. 'It was built nearly two hundred years ago, and apparently it was once known as the Umbrella of Brussels, because you could go to all the different shops without getting wet when it was raining.'

It was a gorgeously light and airy space, Josh thought, filled with a mixture of shops and cafés and high-end jewellers. The large square windows of the shops and cafés were topped by graceful arched fanlight windows, separated by marble pilasters; the upper floors had niches displaying statues and gorgeous plasterwork. The cafés all had small bistro tables and chairs outside, and patrons were enjoying coffee and delicate pastries.

'This is lovely,' he said. 'I assume there are lace shops in the Galeries?'

'There are,' she said.

As they walked along the Galeries, window-shopping, their hands brushed against each other. Even though they'd held hands yesterday, Josh reminded himself that Livi needed to make the first move, not him. To his delight, the next time their hands brushed, her fingers caught his.

Exactly what he'd hoped would happen.

Without comment, he let her link her fingers properly with his. And how lovely it was to just walk with her through the arcades, holding hands: another cautious step closer to each other.

They went into one of the lace shops, and spent a while browsing some of the antique pieces on display, before chatting to one of the assistants about Livi's great-great-grandmother Marie-Thérèse and the lace she'd made.

'There was a lace centre at Brugge as well as at Bruxelles,' the assistant said. 'The *béguinages*—not quite convents, because the religious women who lived in the community didn't take nun's vows—ran lace schools to teach the local girls a trade. The girls would sit in rows with a stand holding a pillow in front of them, which had pins pricking the pattern out. They'd wind the flax round wooden bobbins, and they'd use the bobbins to weave the lace. Belgian flax gives the finest strands in the world, and makes the most delicate lace.' She smiled.

'I can show you pictures of the girls back at the same kind of time that Marie-Thérèse was working, and I can show you a video of someone making lace in the city more recently.'

'I'd love to see that, please, if you have the time,' Livi said.

Josh, too, was fascinated by the way the lace was woven, the wooden bobbins clattering and then the lace-maker stopping to move a pin before swiftly moving the bobbins again. 'How do they know which bobbin to move where?' he asked.

'Practice,' the assistant said with a smile. 'They actually only work with two pairs of bobbins at a time. They're either making a cross movement, when the left bobbin moves over the right—or a twist movement, when the right bobbin moves over the left. But in a complex pattern, you just see the lace-worker's fingers flying between what looks like a hundred bobbins, and the lace gradually taking shape.'

'There's no way I'd ever be able to do that,' Livi said, sounding awestruck. 'I can do sugar-craft, but I can't even crochet. I could see Holly taking this up, though.'

Josh bought a delicate lace square for his mother, and Livi bought a similar one. 'I'm going to have this framed with a photograph of Marie-Thérèse, and put it up in the brasserie,' she said. 'I'd like to do a history wall like the one in *Le Cheval Rouge*.'

When they'd finished wandering through the galleries—again holding hands as they walked, to Josh's pleasure—they stopped at one of the little cafés for coffee and *speculoos* biscuits that had been stamped with the maker's logo.

'I think your idea of a Lambert's stamp for the biscuits is a good one,' Livi said to Josh. 'Something simple. Maybe just the name embossed across the top, with a rose from an old-fashioned lace design underneath?'

'I can ask Indira, our designer, to mock up some ideas for you,' Josh said. 'If you can find some examples online as a kind of mood board for the brief, send them over to me and I'll get it sorted.'

'All right,' she said with a smile.

They spent the rest of the morning in the old part of the city, window-shopping. In the afternoon, they headed up to the royal quarter; the palace was closed so they couldn't visit the state rooms, but they enjoyed strolling through the formal gardens at the front of the palace and the beautiful park.

Once they'd had their fill in the art galleries, they walked back to Grand-Place via the garden on the Mont des Arts with its beautiful flower beds, clipped topiary, roses and fountains and amazing view of the city. They found a restaurant in a beautiful Art Deco building, with stunning floral stained-glass windows, and the food was presented exquisitely: a starter of a Belgian specialty of smoked salmon croquettes, followed by grilled sea bass with fresh herb mousseline and exquisitely cooked vegetables, and finally a vacherin.

'This is the sort of dessert you make, isn't it?' Josh asked.

Livi nodded. 'The vacherin goes back a couple of centuries; originally, it was a cake, and then a French pastry chef invented the meringue version, layering fruit and ice cream and whipped cream with meringue. It's crisper than a pavlova, though.' She tasted a mouthful.

'Oh, I like their take on it. They've soaked the strawberries in limoncello, and flavoured the whipped cream with it as well. And that's seriously good vanilla ice cream in the layers.'

'The top looks really pretty,' Josh said. 'Are those crystallised violets?'

'And tiny wild strawberries,' she confirmed.

'I like that meringue swan.'

She looked thoughtful. 'We could have a lace swan instead of a lace rose on the *speculoos* biscuits. I'll take a look at the lace patterns and see what would work best.'

'What would you like to do tomorrow?' he asked.

'I'd quite like to go to Bruges for the day, especially after the assistant said it was an important lacemaking centre,' she admitted. 'Holly went there, a couple of years ago, and she says it's so pretty with all the canals. The Venice of the North.'

He checked his phone. 'It's two hours from here by car, or an hour by train.'

'Much quicker by train. The train's greener, too,' she said.

'If we go early, to make the most of our time, I could ask my hotel to make us a picnic breakfast for the journey,' he suggested.

'That'd be lovely,' she said.

After dinner, he walked her back to her hotel. 'Good night, Livi. I'll text you to confirm the train times and tickets,' he promised.

'Good night, Josh. And thank you for a lovely day,' she said.

He looked at her. 'I didn't know how to greet you,

this morning,' he said. 'And I don't know how to say good night.' He badly wanted to kiss her, but he absolutely wouldn't do that unless she asked. He'd made a promise and he intended to stick to it.

'This, I think, is appropriate,' she said, and stood on tiptoe to kiss him on the cheek.

Every nerve-end tingled where her lips had brushed against his skin.

'May I?' he asked, hoping she hadn't noticed how croaky his voice sounded. 'Kiss your cheek, I mean?'

She nodded, blushing, and he did so.

Crazy.

This felt more as if they were teenagers rather than being twenty-eight and thirty-two, respectively. But, at the same time, taking things this slowly took all the pressure off and left just the sweetness—and in a world where everything was so fast-paced and urgent, that was refreshing.

'Sweet dreams,' he said.

And he smiled all the way back to the hotel.

On Thursday morning, Livi headed for the tram stop where she was meeting Josh to go to the train station, and they arrived at almost the same time. The journey to Bruges was comfortable—he'd bought first-class seats, giving them more room, and his hotel had made them a wonderful breakfast of pastries, fruit and freshly squeezed orange juice. Better still, all the packaging was recyclable.

They spent the morning strolling through the narrow streets, enjoying the architecture; the gothic city hall was stunning, with its tall arched windows, turrets and spires. There were lots of colourfully painted buildings with Flemish stepped gables, and Livi couldn't resist taking several snaps of their reflections in the canals. The market square was dominated by its enormous thirteenth-century belfry tower; they climbed the 366 steps to the top for an amazing view over the city, and also spotted the wooden keyboard and foot pedals used to ring the carillon in the belfry floor above.

Livi's 'must see' guidebook directed them to Minnewater Park. 'It's named after the water nymphs—the *minnen*, in Dutch—that were believed to live there in medieval times,' she said. 'Though it's also known as the Lake of Love. So the story goes, a girl called Minna fell in love with a warrior called Stromberg, but her father wanted her to marry a rich nobleman. She ran away and was found perished on the shores of the lake. Stromberg buried her beneath the lake and said their love would last for ever.'

'That's a very sad story,' Josh said, 'for such a pretty park.'

And it really was gorgeous; the bridge across the lake, the lock-house with its stepped gables and ornate turrets, the willow trees and the swans swimming majestically across the water.

'On a more prosaic note,' she said, 'it was also once the docks for Bruges; merchants would bring in spices, silk, wool and wine, and leave with Flemish cloth and lace. Speaking of lace, the Béguinage is near here.'

'Where the nuns taught local girls to make lace,' he said, clearly remembering what the assistant in the lace shop had told them, the previous day.

To Livi's pleasure, the complex—with its beautiful

white buildings and courtyard gardens—was open and they were able to look round. One of the assistants also directed them to the lace museum, based in the renovated building of the lacemaking school, and she was fascinated to see a live demonstration of lacemaking. The lacemaker had been plying her craft for more than sixty years, and when Livi showed her the picture of Marie-Thérèse and explained that her great-great-grandmother had been a lacemaker, she guided Livi through how to manipulate the bobbins and then move the pins to their next position.

'I have even more respect now for my great-great-grandma,' Livi said after a couple of minutes. 'Because it would take me at least ten times as long as it takes you to make the lace, and I think mine would come out with holes in the wrong places.'

The elderly lacemaker smiled. 'It comes with practice, my dear. But I'm glad it's given you an idea of what she did for a living.'

They stopped for lunch in a pretty little bistro off one of the little squares. 'These have to be the best *frites* I've ever eaten,' Livi said with a contented sigh.

In the afternoon, they wandered through art galleries and took a boat trip along the canal, and Livi was thrilled to photograph a bevy of swans gliding together under a bridge near the Béguinage, as well as more of the gorgeous architecture. Best of all, Josh sat with his arm round her through the whole trip, making her feel cherished.

Their second official date.

Maybe tonight they might kiss—she remembered he'd told her that he wouldn't kiss her again unless she asked. Maybe tonight she'd ask him; and this time she wouldn't panic.

'Your course is tomorrow,' Josh said eventually. 'It wouldn't be fair to make you stay up late when you're going to be busy. Let's go back now, and have dinner on my roof terrace. We can chill out in the last of the sunshine with a glass of wine.'

'That sounds wonderful,' she said.

They bought coffee to keep them going on the return train journey, then walked slowly back to his hotel off Grand-Place. The menu had changed again that evening; Livi chose violet artichokes, served with a lemon dressing and burrata and garnished with capers and a twist of frisée, followed by chicken with tarragon sauce on a bed of potato puree with snow peas and baby carrots, and finally a tarte tatin flambéed with Calvados and served with ice cream flecked with vanilla seeds.

'That was wonderful,' Livi said when she'd eaten the praline that came with the coffee. She gave a sigh of contentment. 'I'd better head back, because I want to re-read a few things before tomorrow.'

'I'll walk you back,' Josh said.

When they reached the street outside her hotel, he asked, 'Obviously you have your course tomorrow, but what are your plans for the evening?'

'I'd originally thought to have dinner with the others on the course,' she said. 'But that was before I knew you were going to be here.'

'Don't change your plans for me. Mixing with the other course delegates is half the fun,' he said with a smile. 'But maybe we can meet afterwards for a cocktail or something, if you're free?'

'That'd be lovely. I'll text you when we're done and let you know where we are,' she said.

'OK. I'm going to have a day thinking about a new project,' he said, 'so I'll find a nice park to walk through while I'm thinking, and then I'm going to catch up with paperwork—and brief Indira, if you have time to send me the kind of lace patterns you want.'

'I'll take a look before I do my reading,' she promised. 'See you tomorrow night.'

'Enjoy your class,' he said. 'See you tomorrow.'

Was he really going to leave without kissing her goodnight? 'This is our second date. I think a kiss goodnight is just about allowable,' she said lightly.

'A kiss goodnight,' he repeated, his voice satisfyingly husky.

And it would be relatively chaste, given that they were in public. *Safe*.

He closed the gap between them, and stroked her cheek with the backs of his fingers. She tilted her head towards him, and he bent to brush his lips against hers—the softest, sweetest kiss.

The last time he'd kissed her, fireworks had gone off in her head.

This time, it felt like walking through an orchard on soft clouds of apple blossom: warm and sweet and promising.

'Good night,' he said softly when he broke the kiss. 'Sweet dreams.'

And she rather thought they would be.

CHAPTER TWELVE

ALTHOUGH JOSH HAD planned to find a little park to walk through in the morning while he thought about his new project, he spent his time catching up with work on his quiet roof terrace instead, finding the little garden just as inspiring as a park; he ordered lunch and dinner through room service, and he'd just shut down his laptop and was about to chill out with a book when his phone pinged with a text from Livi. Finished dinner. Meet you outside your hotel in fifteen minutes?

Which gave him enough time for a quick shower and change. See you then, he messaged back.

Just as he walked through the front door of the hotel, he saw Livi walking towards him, and raised a hand in acknowledgement.

'How was your course?' he asked.

'Fabulous. We spent the morning working on tempering chocolate.'

'Which is?'

'Melting, cooling and reheating the chocolate so it has a stable structure,' she said. 'If you do it properly, the chocolate will have the right kind of "snap" when it's broken, it'll be smooth rather than grainy, and you'll get that lovely glossy finish. If you don't,' she added, 'the chocolate will go crumbly, it'll look dull or streaky or have a white bloom on it, it might crack when you take it out of the mould, and the mouthfeel won't be good. And you need different kinds of chocolate for moulds and enrobing.'

'Got it,' he said.

'We made pralines in the afternoon,' she said. 'Which was noisy and fun.'

'Noisy?' he asked.

She grinned. 'Once you've tempered your chocolate, you fill the moulds, scrape the chocolate off the top, then rattle the mould against the worktop to get rid of air bubbles—we sounded like a class of tap-dancers! There's a bit more rattling later, after you've filled the praline.'

'And did you eat them all in class, or did you take some home?' he asked.

'Both,' she said.

He coughed. 'That *was* a hint.'

'What, you were expecting a sample of my work?' She chuckled. 'Well, now. That depends. Have you been a good boy, Mr Garrett?'

He pantomimed offence. 'That makes me sound like a Labrador.'

She pretended to consider the idea. 'No. Your ears aren't floppy enough.'

He couldn't help laughing. When was the last time he'd had this kind of fun, stretching a silly joke with someone?

'So have you been a good boy?' she asked again.

Teasing, huh? Two could play at that game. He lowered his voice to a purr. 'Oh, yes. I've been *very* good.'

She went deliciously pink, and he laughed. 'Hey. You started it, Ms Lambert.'

'Hmm, well.' She batted her eyelashes at him. 'There's a bench over there, next to the fountain. Let's go and sit down.'

He was happy enough to hold her hand and stroll across the square to the bench. She delved into her handbag and brought out a small red cardboard box tied with a matching ribbon. 'I brought these for you. Only a couple, as they're quite rich,' she said.

He opened the box to discover two perfect heart-shaped chocolates. The outer shell was perfectly glossy. 'They look fabulous. So the chocolate shell should be crisp to the bite, and the centre should be soft and rich?' he checked.

She nodded.

He took a bite, examined the centre, then finished the chocolate. He knew she was waiting to hear his response, so he left it until he could see she was practically wriggling with impatience. And then he said, 'Best chocolate ever. I'm going to save the other one until tomorrow—so I can savour it with a cup of coffee in my morning break.'

'Do you want me to put the box back in my handbag?' she asked.

'Thanks—that'd be great,' he said. 'Then it won't get squished in my pocket.' He looked at her. 'Did you enjoy the course?'

'Very much. Tomorrow, we're making ganache fillings and caramels, and working with finishes for hand-dipped chocolates—structure sheets for embossing the tops, transfers—they're made with coloured cocoa butter on acetate—gold lustre, piping with coloured cocoa butter, and textured inclusions.' She smiled. 'The course is definitely helping me to up my chocolate game.'

'That's great,' he said. 'Let's go and find a bar, and I'd love to hear all about your favourite bits of the day and what you're planning to try on your customers when we're back in London.'

'And what about you? What have you been doing today?' she asked.

'Catching up with work, mainly. Sketching out a few ideas for a new client.'

'Obviously that's all confidential,' she said, 'but would I be right in thinking that's your favourite bit of your job?'

'One of them,' he said. 'It's looking at something and seeing all the possibilities, without any limits. Even crazy ideas you know would be completely impractical are useful, at this stage, because they might spark off something else.'

'Blue-sky thinking,' she said. 'Looking at something, deconstructing it, working out how it can become something else. It sounds a lot like what I do when I'm playing with a new dessert.'

He nodded. 'What if you change one element for another? What does the end customer really want and what's the best way of showing them what your client can offer?' He looked at her. 'I always believed I did my best thinking either walking in a park, or in the office, with everyone around me and their energy gelling with mine. But with video-conferencing you can have that feeling anywhere. And I discovered I like working in a sunny corner of a garden. Well, the roof terrace.'

'You don't have a garden, do you?' she asked.

'Usually I go for a walk in Hyde Park. But maybe,' he said, 'having my own green space, even if it's a roof terrace, is something I need to look at for the future.' And how crazy was it that all of a sudden he could see himself in a garden, with a dog stretched out on the patio in the sunshine, while he was pushing a small child on a swing? A small child with dark messy hair and huge brown eyes...

He shook himself.

He'd never thought about having a family of his own before. Why here? Why now?

Well, he knew some of the answers to that. Being here with Livi, seeing the genuine joy her family brought her—it made him want that sort of thing, too. That closeness. The connection that stretched from the past to the future.

Not that he intended to tell her that. Not yet, anyway. He needed to be careful not to scare her off, especially as he was halfway to scaring himself off.

They made their way through the streets of the old town and found a square with a large rectangular pond in the centre, with giant waterlilies floating in the centre.

'This must be some kind of art installation,' Livi said. She checked in her online guidebook. 'It is. Apparently they're made from mineral fibres which contain solar lighting.'

'They'll look pretty after dark, then,' Josh said.

She took a photograph. 'Even as they are now, they're pretty. And I could make a dessert based on that. Raspberry and lime,' she said. 'Maybe piped Italian meringue for the petals, and I'd be tempted to spray them.'

'It's fascinating, seeing the way your mind works,' Josh said. 'I look at those waterlilies and I think flowers: maybe Monet, maybe nice lighting. But you not only visualise the dessert, you know the flavours you want to use, too. That's amazing.'

'I guess it's just part of being a pastry chef,' she said. 'You get inspiration from all over the place. I might try a cocktail, and I'll deconstruct it into colours and flavours, and from there I'd think about what textures would work with those flavours to make a good dessert.'

'It's still an amazing skill,' he said.

They walked through the square, hand in hand, and then he spotted a bar with flower garlands outside; they took a peek inside, and discovered an enormous chalkboard with the cocktail menu, shelves containing beer bottles next to the specially shaped glasses matching the beer, and a selection of draught beer from a microbrewery which was apparently just round the corner.

'This looks fabulous,' she said.

'It does,' he agreed. 'What would you like?'

It took her a while to choose, but eventually she picked an espresso martini. 'It's an old favourite,' she said.

'I'll join you.'

They found a quiet table with comfortable bar stools, and she was thrilled when the waiter brought over what looked like two vintage martini glasses. 'And it's garnished properly, with three beans,' she said in satisfaction. 'The perfect presentation.'

He was enjoying talking through the menu with her, challenging her to make desserts out of the cocktails on the list, when he suddenly glimpsed something he hadn't noticed when they first came into the bar.

There was a stage at the back of the room.

A stage which now held a drum kit, amplifiers, a keyboard and a microphone.

He took a large gulp of his cocktail, but it wasn't enough to stop the darkness uncurling inside him. Particularly as there were four people walking onto the stage, two of them holding guitars.

'Josh?' One moment, he'd been laughing and joking with her, teasing her about how many different desserts she could possibly create out of any one given cocktail. And now his face was ashen. He seemed to be looking at something behind her. Frowning, she glanced round, and then she saw the band.

Oh, no.

She should've thought. It was Friday night. A lot of bars offered live music for their customers at the weekend. It was something she loved, but she also knew this had to be a nightmare for Josh.

She reached out to take his hand and squeeze it. 'Let's go.'

'I'm fine,' he said, though she could tell he was speaking through gritted teeth and he was very far from fine. 'We can stay. You've barely touched your drink.'

'That's not important,' she said gently. 'But you are. And this is too much for you, isn't it?'

He closed his eyes briefly and nodded.

'Then we'll go back to your hotel. Back to your lovely roof garden. Come on.'

They left their unfinished drinks and walked out of

the bar just as the band started tuning up. The square was filled with people sitting at bistro tables on the little patios outside the various bars and restaurants, eating and drinking and chatting. She didn't bother trying to make a conversation with Josh because she felt that he needed the endorphins from walking more than anything else. He'd talk when he was ready. But she kept holding his hand, just so he'd know she wasn't deserting him.

Once they'd turned off the square into a quiet road, he said, 'I'm sorry. I've ruined the evening.'

'No, you haven't,' she reassured him. 'I get that it's hard for you.'

'I can tune out recorded stuff, most of the time,' he said. 'But not live music. Not when there are musicians working only a few metres away from me.'

'Doing what you used to do. Doing what you loved most in the world,' she said gently. 'It's like a hollow inside you, missing music, isn't it?'

'Yeah.' He looked at her. 'You're about the first person apart from my therapist who's ever really got that.'

But did that empty space also mean he was always going to protect his heart, keep people at a distance? He'd talked about getting to know her better, getting closer to her, but she remembered the last time they'd been really close. That night. He'd rejected her then; what was to stop him rejecting her again? Maybe she was the one who needed to be more careful of her heart.

Yet, at the same time, she couldn't just abandon him while he was hurting.

Maybe she needed to try telling him straight.

Back at his hotel, they took the lift up to his penthouse suite. There was a coffee machine with a selection of pods and a kettle with a range of teabags; she was pleased to note that they included her favourite blends.

'Go and sit on the terrace,' she said. 'I'm going to make us a mug of chamomile tea.' Once she'd brewed the tea, she carried the mugs out to the roof garden. Josh was sitting at the table, his face drawn with misery. Clearly the scent of the flowers and the prettiness of the fairy lights had done nothing to make him feel better.

He looked up as she approached. 'Thank you,' he said.

'No problem.' She set the mugs on the table and sat down opposite him. 'Josh, I'm going to give you some tough love. I think you need to get music back into your life. It's part of who you are and, even when you're putting on a smiling face to the world, you're so unhappy without it.' She reached over to take both his hands in hers. 'OK, the classical stuff might always be too hard. But there has to be a way. Music brought you so much joy. Could you do something without having to play? I guess that would rule out teaching, but could you produce, maybe? Compose?' She shook her head. 'I dunno—conduct, even?'

'I don't know,' he said. 'Where music's concerned…'

He'd built a wall between himself and what he'd loved most in the world, in an attempt to stop his heart breaking, Livi thought. And instead it had meant that his heart had been shut away. Was it to the point where he was unreachable?

'I get that,' she said, seeing the unhappiness etched into his face. 'But look at the life you've built outside music. You're good at your job. You're good at seeing what's missing, what needs to happen to make something work more effectively. Maybe you need to knock that brick wall down and combine your life now with music. Maybe you could help arts centres that are struggling?'

He made a noncommittal noise, and she knew he wasn't even going to consider it. As far as he was concerned, he'd bricked off the heart of his life, surrounded it in barbed wire, and he was always going to pretend things were fine when they weren't.

Even as she thought it, he straightened up a little. 'I'm sorry. This wasn't how this evening was meant to go. You were all bubbly about your course, and I loved listening to you. I wanted tonight to be all about cocktails and enjoying the crowds on a summer Friday evening.' He grimaced. 'If I'd spotted the stage, we could've had a drink somewhere else. Somewhere without live music. But I just saw a pretty little bar and I wanted to share it with you.'

'Maybe another night,' she said.

But he could see the disappointment in her face. And she'd had a point about getting music back into his life. It *was* part of who he was. He was utterly miserable without it. There was a yawning abyss inside him, as if he were hollowed out, and keeping that hidden from everyone else was wearing him out.

'You like dancing,' he said.

'Ye-es.' She looked wary.

Even though the idea made him feel almost sick with nerves, Livi was the one person who might understand. And here, on this quiet roof terrace, filled with roses and fairy lights, he could maybe be the person she needed him to be, too. 'Dance with me now?' he asked.

'Hang on. You're asking me to dance with you?' She blinked.

He had enough doubts of his own, but he was going to try. 'I'm assuming you have an app. A playlist of some sort. Something soft and slow. Something you love listening to.'

'Well, yes.' She'd obviously worked out that he was trying to follow her suggestion, because her face brightened with hope. 'There's a singer my mum and I really love—Mum used to play him all the time when Eti and I were small, and ever since I've been old enough to go to gigs I always get tickets to see him with Mum for his UK tour. He always does a couple of acoustic numbers in a gig—minimal guitar or piano. Could we dance to that?'

He appreciated that she was trying her best to minimise the instruments. For her, he was going to try his hardest to make this work. Not trusting himself to speak, he nodded.

She quickly found the playlist on her phone, slipped one earbud into her ear and handed him the other. He stared at the earbud as if it were a poisonous asp she'd asked him to put into his ear, but then he gritted his teeth and did it.

'Are you sure about this?' she checked.

No. 'Yes,' he fibbed. 'I'm a bit out of practice.' If he was honest with himself, he could barely ever remember dancing with a girlfriend. He'd never been one for clubbing, even before the accident. People didn't really dance to the kind of music he played. They listened to it. *Felt* it.

He forced himself not to think about that. This was different. This was for Livi.

'No need for fancy steps,' she said. 'Just hold me and sway.' She started the track and slipped the phone into her pocket, then stepped close to him, sliding her arms round his neck.

He remained frozen for a few more moments—but then he wrapped his arms round her waist, drawing her closer, and finally, finally, he swayed to the rhythm of the song with her.

He held her as if he were drowning and she were his lifeline.

Slowly, her warmth relaxed him enough to unstiffen his shoulders and release his grip so he was cradling her.

He could feel the rhythm of the dance, the slow, gentle softness of it, and it felt as if something was cracking inside him. Breaking through all the barriers he'd put up over the last eight years, letting his heart out of the confines where he'd tried to keep it safe but had only succeeded in imprisoning himself.

She sang softly along with the track, and it felt as if she was singing to him. Words of love and comfort and desire and promise. And after all the years of keeping himself rigidly away from music, everything was fluid and strange, spinning a whirlpool of emotions round him.

He desperately wanted to kiss her, but they were supposed to be taking things slowly and he didn't want to push her away. His voice felt rusty; he couldn't even remember the last time he'd sung anything, but he'd picked up the structure of the tune—it always had been like that for him with music, and he had an almost photographic memory for it—and he remembered the words of the chorus. When the second verse ended, he sang the chorus to her.

This time it was Livi's turn to freeze for a moment. Josh was pretty sure she was panicking that she'd pushed him too far, so he held her close and kept swaying with her in time to the music.

A tear trickled down her cheek and he kissed it away. 'It's OK, Livi. It's all going to be OK.'

And then somehow his mouth had moved from her cheek to the corner of her mouth, and then to a proper kiss; she was kissing him back, and everything felt very all right with the world.

He kissed her through another track, feeling as if his heart was breaking out of the darkness at last.

But then the next track started, and after the first few seconds of acoustic guitar a string quartet started playing.

It felt as if the glass wall round his heart had suddenly shattered and the shards embedded deeply. Too deeply for him to be able to do this.

He broke the kiss. Stopped holding her. Stood there, frozen.

'I can't do this, Livi,' he whispered. 'I *can't*.'

Her face was filled with anguish, and she switched off the music. 'I'm so sorry, Josh. I forgot this one had the v—' She broke off the word, biting her lip. 'Josh.'

'I can't do this.' He shook his head, trying to clear it, but he couldn't. And he knew what the problem was. Him. He couldn't offer her what she needed, his whole heart. The black hole was still inside him and it was never going away. And it wouldn't be fair to pull her into this misery with him.

Maybe he should tell her what nearly happened, the night she knocked on the door of his flat. But then she'd pity him. And, worse, she might feel obliged to stay with him in case that particular darkness threatened to overwhelm him again. He didn't want her to be with him out of pity.

So he kept the words inside. Even though they were trying to burst out.

'I'm sorry, Livi,' he said. 'This isn't working. And it's not you—it's me.'

It's not you—it's me.

The ultimate break-up phrase, Livi thought.

It was supposed to soften the blow and make the dumpee feel better—but it didn't. All it really meant was that the person doing the dumping didn't want to explain their real reasons.

So much for thinking all her dreams were finally coming true—that Josh was prepared to make the effort and they actually had a real shot at a future, at being together.

Though maybe he had a point. Maybe she should stop harking back to that old teenage dream. Because what sort of life would they have if she had to spend all her time treading on eggshells, worrying that something would remind him of what he'd lost and drive him back into despair—and knowing that she wasn't enough to fill the empty spaces inside him?

'I'd better go,' she said dully.

'I'll walk you back,' he said.

She shook her head. 'No need. It's not far, and it's on the main streets.'

'I'm sorry,' he said. 'I...' He blew out a breath. 'I'm still a mess. It's not your fault, and it's not your responsibility to fix me. I'm the one who needs to sort it out.'

That was all true; but she wished he hadn't drawn her close again, only to back away.

Last time, she felt that he'd blamed her.

This time, he was at least accepting the fault was his; but he'd still hurt her. Led her to believe in a dream that had burst at the first stroke of a bow across a violin string.

'Good night, Josh,' she said. Though it felt much more final than that. It felt like *goodbye*.

She picked up her handbag. Then she quietly walked away from him through the French doors to his hotel suite, through the front door, and she let it click quietly closed behind her before trudging across Grand-Place to her hotel. She didn't notice the beautifully lit buildings, the crowds of people chatting and drinking and dancing. All she could see was Josh standing there, drowning in misery—and there was nothing, *nothing* she could do to fix it.

He'd said it wasn't her responsibility to fix him. But oh, how she'd wanted to fix him.

He'd wanted to dance with her—for her sake, knowing she loved it. He'd tried to share her kind of music. And, for those first few moments of dancing together, she'd really thought he'd felt the joy and not the pain. He'd let the music flow over him and he'd reacted. He'd held her, danced with her, sung to her, kissed her...

And then the whole thing had imploded.

If only it had been another song playing next, one without the romantic addition of a string quartet. But she had to be honest: if it hadn't happened tonight, it would've happened some time soon. And it would've hurt more, having what she truly believed was their future snatched away again.

They didn't have a future. She had to face it: Josh wasn't ready to start a proper relationship. Not with her—not with anyone. He'd locked his heart back up again. Pushed her away. Told her it wasn't going to work between them. This time, he hadn't been cruel; but this time, his rejection felt final. There was no coming back.

Back at the hotel, she went through the motions of showering and making herself a mug of chamomile tea. She barely tasted it, and it did nothing to help her sleep. She lay awake, too miserable to cry, going over and over in her head what she could've said or done to make a difference.

And the truth was, there was nothing she could've said. Nothing she could've done. Josh was implacable.

She had no idea how the brasserie project was going to work, now. Would he back out of it completely, or would he do what he'd suggested to her weeks ago and hand it over to one of his team? She'd been so looking forward to this: working with him, starting a new chapter in the history of Lambert's—a new chapter in her life, perhaps.

But now she knew it wasn't going to happen.

It was over.

CHAPTER THIRTEEN

When the front door clicked quietly behind her, it felt like the worst day of Josh's life, all over again. Last time, he'd lost what he lived for doing. This time, he'd lost the woman he fallen in love with: but he knew it was all his own fault. He'd pushed her away. She'd given him a second chance, but he'd blown it.

Because he'd rushed things.

Because he wasn't truly ready to move on.

Because locking the pain away inside him wasn't the same as dealing with it. Instead, he'd made himself more vulnerable when he'd finally had to face music, and Livi had been the collateral damage. He'd been unfair to her—and he needed to do something about it. It was too late to ring London now, but luckily he'd bought an open return and could take the first train back tomorrow. And on the train he'd start to make the arrangements he needed.

In the morning, he packed, not bothering with breakfast beyond a mug of coffee, checked out of the hotel, and headed for London. He made the phone call that he hoped would start to change everything; then, once the week in rehab was arranged, he let Shelley know that he needed to be away for a week and arranged for one of his colleagues to handle the Lambert account in his absence.

Next, he messaged Sophie and Michel, to let them know that he was stepping back from the project for personal reasons but his colleague would look after them.

Back at the mews house, he packed, then rang his parents to let them know what he was doing.

Even though part of him desperately wanted to contact Livi, he didn't. Until he'd got through the next week and could be sure that things were changing—that he really could handle this—it wouldn't be fair to keep her hanging on.

And then he put his case in the car. This wasn't going to be a quick fix. But he hoped he'd make enough progress this week to prove to himself—and Livi—that he was going to give it his best shot.

Somehow, Livi managed to concentrate on the final day of her course. Josh didn't contact her. He didn't answer his phone when she called him at the end of the course, but she didn't leave a message—because what, just *what*, could she say? This was something that would definitely be better in person. She walked to his hotel, only to find that he'd checked out.

Well, that was pretty final. Not only had he rejected her, he'd left the city without saying anything to her. He really couldn't make it any clearer that he didn't want her.

Brussels had lost its sparkle for her without Josh. She couldn't even finish the comfort food of a sausage and *stoemp* in the nice little bar round the corner from her hotel. It seemed pointless staying in the city tomorrow just for the sake of it, so she changed her train ticket for an earlier departure, and left for London on Sunday morning.

She'd just unpacked and set a load of laundry going when her door intercom buzzed. For a moment, she wondered if it was Josh—if the almost two days they'd spent apart had given him enough space to change his mind. But when she answered, she recognised her mother's voice instantly.

'Hey, Mum. Come up,' she said, and pressed the intercom to release the door.

'How was Brussels?' Sophie asked.

'I really enjoyed the course,' Livi said, 'and I went to the bar where great-granddad Jean worked. I sent Dad the photographs. And I bought a square of lace very like the kind of thing great-great-grandma Marie-Thérèse would've made.' She took the large gold ballotin box from her kitchen worktop and gave it to her mother. 'These are for you and Dad. Made by me, from scratch, with love. Pralines, ganaches and caramels.'

'Thank you, darling.' Sophie hugged her. 'Do you want to talk about it?'

'The course?' Livi asked, deliberately misunderstanding her. 'Sure. Though maybe I should wait until Dad's free, as well.'

Sophie coughed. 'You know perfectly well I don't mean the course.'

Livi sighed. 'Mum, there's nothing to tell. Josh has made up his mind. It's over.'

'He messaged us yesterday,' Sophie said. 'He's stepping back from the brasserie project and one of his team is taking over.'

Livi closed her eyes for a moment. 'I had a feeling he might do that. OK. I guess it's easier that way.' For both of them.

'So what happened?'

Livi swallowed hard. 'He's still broken, Mum. Without his music, he's not fully himself, and I don't think he can really give his heart to anyone until he's whole.' She told her mum what had happened, her voice catching as she struggled to hold back her emotion. 'I thought he'd be able to cope with an acoustic set. Just a voice and a guitar. The recording from the show we went to at the Royal Albert Hall, last year. But I forgot one of the songs had a string quartet playing. And he...' She dragged in a breath. 'Then he said he couldn't do this. That it was his fault, not mine.'

Sophie winced. 'Oh, darling.'

'I left. I wouldn't even let him walk me back to the hotel. It's over.' She blinked back the tears. 'I really thought we had something, Mum. I liked who he'd become. He liked me. I thought we...' She shook her head. 'Well, I was wrong.'

'I'm sorry,' Sophie said. 'I shouldn't have interfered and told him where you were.'

'If it hadn't happened then,' Livi said, 'it would've happened another time. It's not your fault. It's not anyone's, really,' she added, 'because Josh can't help how he feels.'

'That,' Sophie said, 'is incredibly generous of you.'

'There's no point in being bitter about it,' Livi said. 'I'm going to pick myself up, dust myself down, and—well, just carry on. Moping isn't going to make me feel better. I'd rather keep myself busy.'

'Just remember I'm always here,' Sophie said, and hugged her. 'Come down for dinner. Or I can bring something up to you.'

Livi smiled. 'I'm fine, Mum. I promise.'

After Sophie had gone back to the restaurant, Livi finished unpacking. But, while she was putting things away, she came across the letter Josh had written her all those years ago. The letter she'd never opened.

Maybe it was time she read it.

She slit the envelope, then sat on the end of her bed and read what he had to say.

Things he'd actually said to her, face to face, over the last couple of weeks. That he was truly sorry for the unkind things he'd said. They weren't true and he'd lashed out at her from a place of darkness. But he was truly grateful to her, because without her he wouldn't be here now.

She frowned. What did he mean by that?

Not that there was any point in asking him. She was pretty sure he wouldn't answer.

She turned back to the letter. Thanks to her, he said, he was going to get some proper help. And he hoped she'd be happy in the future, surrounded by people who loved her.

The words were sincere, and the heartbreak was visible in every stroke of the pen. He'd got some help, yes, but it hadn't been enough. Because he was still too damaged to offer her what she needed—his heart.

A week later, Josh walked into Covent Garden, wondering if he was doing the right thing. Should he just let Livi go, and hope she'd find the happiness he hadn't been able to give her?

Then again, faint heart never won fair lady. And the whole point of the last week had been to stop being a coward. To face things. To get himself on a path where he'd deserve all the love Livi had to give, and give her all the love she deserved in return.

Maybe he should've told her what he was doing. Texted her, called her. Except this was something he wanted to tell her face to face. He wanted her to be able to look him in the eye and see that he was sincere.

If she'd let him.

He took a deep breath, walked up to the door at Lambert's Brasserie, and pushed it open. It was still relatively early, but there were several tables of people eating breakfast. Clearly the new brunch menu was a hit. Good. At least he'd helped her to achieve one of her dreams. Even if he had managed to break her heart in the meantime.

Sophie was on front of house. She narrowed her eyes at him. This was starting to be a pattern, he thought. One he needed to break.

'Joshua,' she said, her voice very cool. 'What can we do for you?'

'A very, very big ask,' he said. 'I'd like to talk to Livi.'

'If you're going to let her down yet again,' Sophie said, 'then I'd prefer you not to.'

'I'm not going to let her down,' Josh said. 'I owe her another apology—but I also owe her an explanation. All I want to do is talk.'

'Wait here, and I'll ask her,' Sophie said with a sigh. 'Though I expect you to abide by her decision.'

'That's fair,' Josh said.

He waited.

And waited some more.

And just when he thought that Sophie was about to come back and tell him that Livi didn't want anything to do with him, Livi herself walked out into the restaurant.

She looked tired and a little bit sad, and his heart ached.

'You wanted to see me,' she said, and her voice was completely expressionless. Which he knew he deserved, because hadn't he rejected her twice, now?

'Yes. Would you walk with me?' he asked.

'Fifteen minutes,' she warned.

'Thank you,' he said.

Stallholders were still setting up in the market, but he had somewhere quiet in mind, only a couple of minutes from the restaurant: the small gardens behind St Paul's church, which weren't really on tourists' radar and at this time of year they were the kind of place he thought Livi would like, filled with roses and hollyhocks.

Just as he'd hoped, most of the wooden benches lining the path were empty.

He chose the one furthest from anyone else. 'Shall we sit?'

'What's this about, Josh?' she asked, but to his relief she sat on the bench and he joined her.

'An apology,' he said. 'An explanation. And...' He shook his head. 'No, I'm getting ahead of myself. First off, I want to apologise. Sincerely. You're right. I was still broken, and I was lying to myself as well as everyone else. I thought I could just wall off that bit of me and carry on. But I can't—and it's up to me to fix that, nobody else.'

She looked wary, but at least she was listening.

'I've spent the last week away in rehab,' he said. 'I've done a lot of talking—to a therapist—and a lot of thinking. I'm not there, yet, but I'm in a much better place than I was.'

'That's why you left Brussels? To go to therapy?'

The hurt was obvious in her voice. 'I should've told you I was going,' he said. 'I'm sorry for that, too. But I felt I'd already done you enough damage. I didn't want to give you false hope. I went to start fixing myself. Which is *my* responsibility, nobody else's,' he added. 'It's going to take a while, but I'm working on it and I can see I've made progress. I intend to keep going.'

She gave a single brief nod.

'And I owe you an explanation. One that stems right back to *that* night,' he said. 'Apart from telling my therapist last week, I haven't talked to anyone else about it. Ever. My parents and your brother don't know, so I'd appreciate it if you kept this confidential—I don't want them to be hurt.'

She was silent for a moment, but finally said, 'All right.'

'And I apologise in advance,' he said, 'because I know this is going to be difficult to hear. It's difficult to say out loud, or write, or even admit in my head. But I need to be honest and open with you, Livi. I need to stop hiding.'

'I'm listening,' she said.

'I'd hit rock bottom, back then. Everything I'd always wanted was gone. I didn't have any hope left. I was miserable, and I just wanted the pain to stop,' he said. 'I had a bottle of sleeping tablets. I was psyching myself up to take them.'

Her face lost all its colour. 'You were going to…?'

Clearly she couldn't face saying the words. He understood that feeling. It had been so hard to say it out loud; but telling her had been easier. 'Yes, I was,' he said, and his voice shook slightly as he remembered the despair he'd felt. How close he'd been. 'But then you knocked on my door. And I kissed you. And that kiss made me remember that there was stuff in the world that was good—that life wasn't just unending pain.'

'Oh, my God. I didn't have a…' She shook her head. 'I don't know what to say. Except I'm glad you didn't take the sleeping tablets. And that also explains what you said in your letter.'

He blinked. 'You read it?'

'Last week. It was about time.' She paused. 'You said without me, you wouldn't be here now, and I didn't understand what you meant.' Her eyes glistened with unshed tears. 'Now, I think I do.'

'I didn't tell you about it to make you have sympathy for me or pity me,' he said. 'I told you because I owe it to you to be honest. Last time I did therapy, I still kept too much back. I thought I could manage it on my own, and all I did was block it off instead of dealing with it. And my arrogance meant that you got hurt. For that, I'm truly sorry.'

Again, she didn't speak, just nodded.

'I want to change,' he said. 'You're right. Without music in my life, there's always going to be an empty space inside me. And it's not fair to make everyone else in my life feel they have to be super-cautious all the time in case they do or say something that reminds me.' He swallowed hard. 'I'm not sure if I'm ever going to get to the point where I can see someone else perform the three solos that were my signature, but I can do the rest of it. I'm getting the help I need. I want to dance with you, Livi, in a moonlit garden or on the beach. I want to feel the joy of music again, with you right by my side. But most of all I want you by my side. I know I've treated you badly, and I wouldn't blame you for refusing to give me another chance. But I'm trying to open my heart to you, and I'm really hoping that you have room in your heart to forgive me.' And now was when he really needed to tell her everything. 'But music isn't the love of my life anymore.'

'It's not?'

'It's not,' he said gently. 'It's you.'

She blinked. 'You love me?'

'I think I've loved you for a long time,' he said. 'I always saw you as Eti's little sister, and I knew you were too young for anything to happen between us—but I kind of always knew you were there.'

'With my stupid schoolgirl crush.'

The words he'd used as a weapon, all those years ago. He really *had* hurt her. He winced. 'That was unfair of me.'

'You were right, actually. It *was* a schoolgirl crush,' she said. 'I didn't really know you. And I got over it. But then you walked back into my life, and I discovered I liked the man you'd become. You weren't this slightly-out-of-reach superstar anymore. I thought we had a real chance for a future—but then you rejected me again.'

'I think,' he said, 'I was rejecting *me* rather than rejecting you. I didn't feel I could offer you what you needed. And that in itself was arrogant and stupid, because I should've asked you what you wanted, and whether you'd maybe be prepared to settle for me as a compromise.'

'Settle? For you?' She rolled her eyes. 'Do you not see the way women look at you, Josh?'

'No,' he said honestly. 'And I don't actually care how women look at me. I do care about how you look at me, though. And I'm sorry I let the stuff in my head get in the way of us.' This time, he had the courage to reach out and take her hand. 'I'm not perfect, Livi. I'm a work in progress—but I really do mean to work on my issues and get better. Because I want everything, and I want to give you everything. I want all of you.'

'That's a mite greedy,' she said.

But then he noticed that the corners of her eyes had crinkled, and realised she was teasing him. Pricking his pomposity.

'Yeah, it is,' he agreed. 'But I want to be with you, Livi. I want a family. I never even knew that until we were in Brussels, and we talked about me not having a garden—but I had this clear vision of pushing a little girl on a swing, and a dog on the patio. A little girl who looked like you.'

'You want children?'

He couldn't quite read what she wanted. He could see doubts, but he wasn't sure why. 'If we're lucky, and only if you want that, too,' he said. Just so she'd know he wasn't taking her for granted. 'I see four generations of talent with food stretching over the years in your family. I'd like to see that continue to the next generation, and the next.'

'What if,' she asked, 'we have children and they inherit *your* talent instead of mine? What if they're a classical musical prodigy? Are you going to shut down their talent, or refuse to go to a single performance?'

It was a fair question, and now he understood her doubts. He'd known other musicians who hadn't had family support. Nobody there to catch their eye and give them a smile to push the stage nerves away. It wouldn't be quite like that for his own child—for a start, Livi would be there, plus her entire family and his parents.

But he wanted to be there, too. To give his child the same unwavering love and support he'd had. And to teach them to have a better balance in their life so they never put their talent above true love.

'No,' he said. 'I'd want to be there.' He took a deep breath. 'But more importantly I want to be right by your side.'

'So how do we do this?' she asked.

'Together,' he said. 'We take the rough with the smooth. I'm afraid there's probably going to be a bit more rough than smooth until I've done some more work with the therapist,' he admitted, 'but I truly believe I can do it, with you by my side.' He paused. 'But that's only if you want to be there.'

'Are you asking me?'

'I'm asking you,' he said. 'Will you give me a second chance to put you first?'

'I don't actually want you to put me first,' she said. 'Just as I don't want to put you first, either. I want us to be *together*. As equals.'

'That,' he said, 'sounds perfect.'

And at long, long last, he kissed her.

EPILOGUE

Two years later

JOSH SAT IN the back of the black cab with Livi, on their way from the mews house in Bayswater to St Martin-in-the-Fields. The classical concert tonight contained some of his favourite pieces, Bach's *Concerto for two violins* and the *Air on a G string*. Pieces he'd once enjoyed playing and had shut out of his life for years, but now he could enjoy listening to them again.

Livi had been right. Having his music back had given him his heart back, too. To the point where he could give his whole heart to her.

They'd both blossomed, over the last two years. Lambert's Brasserie had expanded to two more restaurants and a thriving café; and Livi had won awards for her chocolates, exquisite flavour paired with exquisite artistry. JGA had taken on new clients in the music business, including a music therapy charity; working with them had helped Josh solidify his progress in bringing music back to his life.

They'd got married a year ago—with Livi wearing a lace veil based on her great-grandmother's wedding veil and their wedding cake's design echoing the lace—and the photograph was still the one on the Lambert's social media with the most hits.

Josh couldn't imagine being any happier than he was right now. He particularly cherished their once-a-month family Sunday lunches where both sets of parents came over, as well as Etienne, Lucy and little Louisa; he cooked the mains and Livi produced the showstopping desserts. And everyone talked until they were hoarse, played games and just enjoyed spending time together. Two years ago, he wouldn't have even dreamed of this perfect life. This perfect team.

She squeezed his hand. 'OK?' she checked.

'Yes.' He wasn't going to admit to the slight twitchiness he felt before the concert, because he knew he could cope with anything with Livi by his side. 'You?'

'I've been thinking about expanding,' she said.

'A second café? Or do you have your eyes on that vacant shop round the corner?'

'Chocolate shop? We could,' she said. 'But I have something slightly different in mind.' She gave him the sweetest, sweetest smile, and took a box from her handbag.

It was the size and shape of a small chocolate bar, and it was secured with a ribbon tied in a bow. She sometimes left chocolate experiments on his desk, wrapped like this. But what did it have to do with expanding?

'What's this?' he asked.

'Open it,' she said.

He untied the ribbon, then opened the box.

And then he simply stared.

It was a bar of glossy milk chocolate. But not just any old bar: this one had a sketch drawn in white chocolate. A sketch of what looked like a pregnancy test. In the little flat section that would show the test result, there was writing in ruby chocolate piping. The words were very distinct and clear.

Pregnant 3

Was she telling him…?

He stared at her. 'Livi?'

She nodded. 'I did it this morning. The kit's at home, and I took a picture. But I thought this might be a nicer way to tell you. A one-off design,' she added casually.

'You're pregnant. We're having a baby.' He was almost too stunned to take it in. Gently, wanting to protect the chocolate from snapping in half accidentally, he slid it back into the box, then slid the box into his pocket. And then he wrapped his arms round her and kissed her. 'We're having a baby,' he said in wonder. 'You and me. That's amazing.'

'Boy or girl, single or twins, cook or musician or marketing CEO—or something we haven't even thought about yet,' she said.

'Whoever they are, they'll be loved more than any baby's been loved before,' Josh said, meaning every word. 'This is the icing on the cake.'

'Icing on the chocolate bar,' she corrected with a grin.

He laughed. Livi's puns were terrible, but since she'd been back in his life the laughter had been back, too.

And most definitely the love. 'I love you,' he said softly. 'You and our baby-to-be. You're the world to me.'

She kissed him back. 'You're the world to me, too.'

And Josh knew that everything was going to be just fine.

*****

If you enjoyed this story, check out these other great reads from Kate Hardy

The Surgeon's Tropical Temptation
His Strictly Off-Limits Ballerina
Paediatrician's Unexpected Second Chance
A Fake Bride's Guide to Forever

All available now!

THEIR SAVE-THE-DATE CHARADE

HANA SHEIK

MILLS & BOON

To my hooyo and my big sister,
two of the strongest women I know.
Love you both!

CHAPTER ONE

"All right, walk me through your logic again, just one more time." At the exasperated, sleep-roughened voice of his cousin, Alwan Eltahir tightened his hands on the steering wheel and snapped his narrowing eyes from the long, lonely stretch of country road ahead of him to the car's infotainment system.

Glaring at the glowing monitor as if his cousin Malek was right in front of him, he gritted out, "It's simple. I'm taking some time off to clear my head, and I can't do that right now in the city. So, if my parents call—"

"You mean *when* they do," Malek interjected with a long yawn. "Because they always do, Al. No one helicopter-parents like your mom and dad."

Alwan set his teeth but bit his tongue. There was no arguing that point.

"Fine. *When* they do, tell them I'm over at yours."

"So I'm your cover story. What's new?"

"I'm being serious. I don't need them calling me right now, so are you willing to help or not?"

"Give me a second," Malek told him, followed by the faint, muffled sound of voices and then rustling sheets, as though his cousin was rousing from bed, which made sense given the early hour.

While he waited for Malek, Alwan drummed his fingers

over the steering wheel, impatience priming his every muscle. Malek finally yawned, "All right, I'm back. Rima says hello, by the way. She was wondering why this phone call of ours couldn't have waited another two or three hours."

Malek's wife, Rima, was a night-shift nurse.

Softly cursing, Alwan said, "Tell her I said I'm sorry for waking her. I wouldn't have called if I'd known she had the night off."

"Why *did* you call now? You know, besides wanting me to lie to Aami Omer and Khalti Ayaan for you?"

Hearing his parents' names reminded Alwan of everything that had led up to this very point, prompting a groan.

"This wouldn't have anything to do with what happened—"

"Don't. Just, please don't," Alwan cut Malek off, his cousin's chuckle destroying what little calm and peace of mind he had left. Like water through a crack in a dam, the memories first trickled warningly before spewing forth and sweeping him under.

It started a little more than two weeks ago—sixteen days to be precise, not that Alwan would ever admit to marking the hours and minutes, heck *each god-awful second*, as they sped by. No, on the outside he had held on to his usual cool facade, not giving away for a moment that he might not have everything under control.

That his world was possibly a breath away from implosion.

Oh, like that hasn't happened already...

The sarcastic thought had him wringing the steering wheel and pressing his foot down on the accelerator, pushing the small car's engine. Anyone would think he was running away from his problems, and, in a way, he already had. Fleeing everything and everyone he'd known in Toronto, Alwan skulked out of his condo and the city late last night without notifying his family…and the few friends who hadn't yet abandoned him after his so-called villainy was caught in 4K.

The video that had made him an internet villain had been uploaded and *re*-uploaded so many times that he couldn't close his eyes without clearly visualizing it. The seven-minute clip of his confrontation with an angry, now former, client who hadn't liked the way Alwan had handled his defense was branded into his brain. It had taken place in the busy coffee shop on the first floor of his law firm's office building, in the middle of the day, where naturally it had been caught on a phone camera.

Although Alwan could be seen having an assortment of pastries lobbed at him while his client loudly and indiscriminately aired his grievances, it apparently hadn't mattered that *he* had actually been the victim of the altercation.

The video went viral overnight and the internet had held court and swiftly deemed him as the aggressor. All because he was the fancy-schmancy lawyer. Meanwhile, his ex-client, a widower suburban dad of two who had "just been trying to make ends meet" and was "counting on the disputed family inheritance to support his children," had garnered the hearts and sympathies of the public.

It wasn't even the public's opinion he cared about. Alwan's problem was that his law firm had taken one look at the impact his negative image was having on them, and decided he was a liability. They hadn't exactly framed it like that, but how else was he supposed to interpret his bosses foisting a sudden paid leave on him and practically pushing him out the front door?

"It's not fair," Alwan grumbled.

"Yeah, well, it's already happened. No point in sulking

now. The question is, what are you going to do about it?" Malek pressed.

"I have a plan."

For a beat, the silence on Malek's end was punctuated by the distinct sounds of clinking tableware and whirring from a coffee machine. Then he sighed. "Okay, I'll bite. Does this plan happen to involve you getting married to please your parents?"

Alwan scowled immediately, flustered and annoyed. "They told you. When?"

"A couple days ago, and your parents didn't tell me. Mine did."

"Of course they did."

"Did you really think your mom and dad were going to keep it a secret? They've been trying to get you married off for *years*." His cousin chuckled.

Alwan figured his days at his firm were numbered, so he'd had to think outside the box. Starting his own practice had always felt like an out-of-reach dream, mainly because it required the kind of singular focus he didn't have around his high-demand work schedule. But now that he had been temporarily benched, the idea of being his own boss had firmly taken root and wouldn't budge.

That was where his parents and their bargain came in.

Because despite not wanting to accept their help, this time he saw no other option than to throw himself at their mercy in order to get access to their network of high-net-worth contacts.

"I get potential clients and they see me get married. We're all happy," Alwan said, sounding decidedly very *un*happy.

"You're doing this for clients?" Malek tsked. "Man, cuz, that's cold. Even a little sad. Have you considered what your future wife might think?"

"It will be mutually beneficial and she'll be free to leave the marriage…just as soon as my firm is up and running."

"Seems like you have it all worked out. I guess the big question that's left is why do you need me to cover for you?"

Because I feel like I'm going to have a breakdown at any moment, was what Alwan would have said if he hadn't cared about worrying his cousin. As annoying as Malek could be though, he didn't deserve the kind of burden that came with the fear churning away in Alwan's gut. Fear of what the future held in store for him, and fear that he couldn't escape his past mistakes.

Giving his head a shake, he cleared his suddenly hoarse throat.

"I just need to clear my head, that's it. A few days is all I'm asking. Hold them off that long, and I'll owe you one."

"Fine, I'll try to keep your parents from finding you. Speaking of, where are you anyways?"

"Alberta."

Malek's spit take was loud. "Alberta! What's in Alberta?"

Not what. *Who*.

Alwan had lied to his parents about having a fiancée the day before, and now he needed to make it true—and preferably before they discovered his deception.

But rather than divulge his problem to Malek and endure more questions and opinions, he quickly thanked his cousin and ended the call before setting his phone on silent.

Noticing that the sky was even brighter now, the warm golden rays of dawn peeking above the snowcapped mountains in the far horizon gave him an unexpected burst of hope that Alwan hadn't felt for a long time. Hope that he hadn't made a mistake in venturing so far away from home, and that everything—

Everything would be all right after all.

* * *

"Don't worry, Blue, everything's going to be fine." Lulu Sadiq wished she felt more confident as she looked from the inquisitive blue eyes of her cat up at the gathering storm clouds above the treetops.

When she and Blue had left for their early morning hike, the sky had been clear and filled with brilliant sunlight, but now that pleasant mid-April weather was being chased away by brisk, bone-chilling winds.

A shiver rippled through her in spite of all the layers she wore.

Somehow Lulu didn't think that the weather could be entirely blamed. Since waking, she hadn't been able to shake a sense of impending dread.

At first she presumed it might be the worrying sounds coming from her RV lately. Sounds that predicted repair bills in her near future.

No, that's not why. She shivered again when a new wave of agitation ghosted over her.

Spring frost crunched under her hiking boots as she slowly resumed her trek down the path that would take her and Blue back to their warm, cozy four-wheel shelter. Lulu smiled down at her furry companion in his cat carrier. He had his wet pink nose and a paw pressed to the clear bubble window, like he was telling her to hurry up before the storm decided to unleash its wrath.

"Don't worry. We'll be home soon." She grinned when Blue meowed impatiently and pawed at the window, his way of telling her to leg it and quickly. "Okay, okay, I hear you. I'm moving." She hitched the cat carrier over her shoulders and set off at a steadier clip.

She huffed and puffed, the exertion taking away any lingering foreboding thoughts. Before long the shadowy tree line broke up ahead and she smiled to herself.

"We're home, Blue," she called back to her cat, not caring if another hiker caught her talking to her four-legged friend.

Smiling widely, Lulu crossed the wooden markers indicating the end of the footpath and walking trail—

And stopped in her tracks, her widening eyes flitting from the welcome sight of her RV to the small two-door car parked beside it.

She wasn't expecting any visitors.

In fact, avoiding the people in her life was why Lulu had been on the road for a year now. After her divorce it had been hard to pretend that she was doing all right. Harder because she hadn't shared with her family what had led to the end of her marriage.

Unconsciously, she slid her hand down from her chest to her lower belly.

Losing a baby wasn't an experience she'd wish on even the worst of her enemies.

It had felt like someone had reached in and ripped out a vital part of her and left a gaping hole in its place. And, in a way, that was exactly what had happened. On the outside she'd long healed, but inside there were these floating fragments, tiny shards that sliced at her when she so much as thought of everything that could've been and everything that wasn't meant to be.

Was *this* what she'd been feeling was coming for her?

Knowing that she wouldn't get answers standing there, she stiffened her upper lip and drew her shoulders down from where they were brushing her earlobes. She tightened her grip on the straps of her kitty carrier and reminded herself that she wasn't alone. Blueberry was with her, and her Birman cat was her fiercest protector. If anything, she should feel sorry for whoever had decided to come searching for her.

Marching toward the intruder in the small car, Lulu willed a courage she didn't entirely feel right then. She squinted at the darkly tinted car windows and barely made out that no one was behind the wheel. Perplexed, she ground to a halt beside the driver's window and looked around yet again.

The reserved sites of the RV park and campground were at the base of a double-peak mountain in the Canadian Rockies. But no one was driving a small car like the one in front of her. Around these parts, where the wilderness could sometimes deter a smaller vehicle from full exploration, it would've already stood out even if the owner hadn't chosen to invade her reserved spot. She wondered if it was a tourist who had come from the campground nearby. Someone who was new to the area and had accidentally made a mistake and encroached in her space.

A glance at the license plate revealed nothing except that the plate was Alberta-issued.

So, who, then? Tourist, local… Murderer.

Lulu gave her head a shake, the last possibility chilling her more than the winds that were gusting now. She'd been listening to too many true crime podcasts. Still, she couldn't see the harm in erring on the side of caution. Pulling out her phone from her coat pocket, Lulu muttered, "I'll just call the park authorities, then."

But something kept her from pressing their number in her contact list.

That same something had her tucking her phone away, leaning forward and cupping her hands around her squinched eyes to peer through the tinted car window.

Lulu yelped and launched back.

The driver was in the car after all.

Heart racing and mouth quickly drying, she scrambled back out of reach as the driver opened the car door. She watched, wide-eyed, as a man stepped out.

"Alwan!"

Lulu looked him up and down, from his short, curly black hair and handsome brown face to his stylish overcoat, casual dress shirt, slim fit trousers and shiny leather boots, her brain still struggling to reconcile that he was standing before her.

"The beard's new," she blurted before snapping her lips together in embarrassment.

Raising his brows, he lifted a hand and scrubbed his bearded cheek. "Not really. I've been growing it for a while now."

"Oh?" she said, "I guess it's just a testament to how long it's been since I've seen you."

He simply nodded and stared at her sharply.

So sharply it had Lulu shuffling awkwardly in place, gazing back at him like a deer transfixed by headlights. The apprehension she'd been carrying around since the morning crept over her again. Only this time it wasn't this amorphous fear floating around just out of reach. Right in that moment Lulu could affix her uneasiness to the way Alwan was staring at her with a hawkish glint to his eyes.

He was the last person she ever thought she'd see in this secluded part of Alberta.

As far back as Lulu could remember, she and Alwan had shared something of a rivalry.

Born the same year, their unspoken childhood friction could be blamed on their parents constantly comparing the two of them. Lulu had grown up having to listen to her father and mother *sing* Alwan's praises all while pointing out *her* flaws and mistakes. She knew the same thing had to be happening to Alwan to some degree because he always looked as miserable as she did at their families' friendly gatherings.

The way Alwan was looking at her in that very instant had her recalling all the sullen glares he'd cast her way back in the past.

Only this time he isn't really glaring...

Rather, his intense stare had her stomach churning anxiously, her chest squeezing with a confusingly unfamiliar sensation and her heart beating faster than it should. Not liking the feelings he'd engendered in her one bit, and taking the rolling sounds of thunder above as a sign, Lulu opened her mouth to get some answers. And maybe, hopefully, get Alwan away from her.

"What are you doing here?" she asked with a frown. "Did my parents send you? Ladna?"

"No, your parents and sister didn't."

Perplexed, Lulu racked her brain and snapped her fingers when she landed on an answer. "It was Liban, wasn't it?" Her younger brother had always looked up to Alwan, so much so that he followed in his career footsteps and was currently studying away from home at a highly ranked law school in Chicago. If anyone had sent Alwan to her, there was a strong likelihood the culprit was Liban.

Sure enough, Alwan nodded, explaining, "Yes and no. Liban told me you were traveling someplace in Alberta last he spoke to you, but he didn't say where exactly. He *did* mention you posted on your socials regularly from the places you visited. From there it wasn't too hard to track you down."

Lulu blinked, a little astonished and unnerved that he'd gone to such lengths to find her. Whatever Alwan was after had to be important…and possibly dangerous to her. Even more wary now, she drawled, "Okay, Mr. Internet Sleuth, now you've found me, why are you here?"

"I came to ask you…"

Hesitation gripped his features, his full lips slashing into a scowl and his face darkening more than the stormy gray clouds overtaking the sky.

"Ask me what, Alwan? If you haven't noticed, we're about to be rained on, and I'd really like for that not to happen—"

"Ask you to marry me."

Right as he spoke, thunder rumbled loudly over their heads, a warning of the downpour that would follow shortly. Only now the threat of rain soaking them was so far from her mind. Pushed out instead by what Alwan had just said.

Wondering if she'd heard him correctly, Lulu stammered, "S-s-sorry? *Marry?*"

Alwan shut his car door and sealed the short space to her. Now close enough to touch, he filled her vision and commanded her full attention with that intense gaze of his. So much so that she hadn't registered the cold drop of rain splashing onto her cheek. Not until Alwan reached out and swiped the wetness away with his thumb.

Then, shocking her anew, he said, "I want you to be my wife, Lulu."

CHAPTER TWO

"Luula, did you hear me?"

Alwan's hand brushed her cheek again, his thumb caressing her, his touch so gentle it had her heart quivering. She heard him speak her full name, but the rest of what he said was coming down a long fuzzy tunnel at her, slowly drifting past the stupor immobilizing her limbs and rendering her speechless. The only thing that burst through was the irrationally strong urge to lean into the solid warmth of his palm—

He feels so nice... So safe.

Startled by that thought, Lulu quickly pushed his hand away and reared back.

Just like that, whatever spell he cast over her was broken.

"Wh-what are you d-doing?" She almost groaned aloud at her stammering. Revealing that he'd affected her was the last thing she wished to do, particularly when it felt like he had the upper hand right then.

"You had a raindrop, right there." He pointed a finger at her face, those dark eyes of his vigilant in a way that had her body heating up and not so unpleasantly. "It was distracting."

"You know that's not what I mean. You *proposed* to me just now!"

Alwan's brows snapped up and, frowning, he clarified, "I wasn't proposing a *real* marriage. Just a fake engagement."

Her eyes bugged out at him. "Sorry? And how is that any better?"

He winced, though she wasn't sure if it was because of her shrill tone or whether he was finally cluing in to how appalling his words really were.

"Can I at least explain myself? I promise I'm not losing my mind," he said, his tone as even-keeled and serious as his now grave expression.

It was almost as worrying as how comfortable she'd felt being touched by him.

The rain pelting down a little harder and faster, Lulu flipped her coat hood over her head, wrapped her arms around herself and narrowed her eyes. Sure, he looked *and* sounded sincere...but she was still reluctant to believe that this wasn't all some elaborate, twisted joke. Of course, she then had to wonder—

Who is he trying to fool, and why?

They barely knew each other and, at least in the past, barely cared to get to know one another. Why marriage of all things, and why her? Because although they didn't know each other all too well, Alwan had to have known about her divorce, making what he'd just asked of her cruel.

Lulu bit the inside of her cheek, trying to ignore the way her eyes suddenly smarted. She told herself it wasn't tears blurring her vision, rather the rain coming down in sheets now and shrouding the world in a gray mist.

I should turn around, ignore him and walk away.

Meowing from inside his carrier over her back, Blue certainly thought they should take cover from the heavy rainfall and rumbling thunder.

But instead she stayed rooted to her spot and demanded, "I need you to explain yourself."

"Sure, okay." His tweed overcoat was now darker around

his shoulders, his hair curling more from the extra moisture, and he blinked fast to keep rainwater from his eyes. "But can I do the explaining inside my car or your motor home?"

No sooner had he asked then a bolt of lightning briefly illuminated the churning sky. Unsurprisingly, this lightshow was then followed by a loud crack of thunder. Only now the thunder sounded ominously close to where they were standing.

"Fine," she agreed, backing toward her RV and giving his cramped-looking car the briefest of glances. "But I'd prefer my motor home."

"Let me just grab my things."

"Things?" Lulu began to ask, but he moved toward the back of his car and pulled a black travel bag from his trunk.

Locking up his car, Alwan hauled the duffel over his head as a makeshift umbrella.

Lulu unlocked the door to her RV and impatiently waved him in.

Ignoring the inexplicable heat blazing through her as he brushed past her, Lulu closed the door and turned to find Alwan surveying her home.

He was completely oblivious to her rising ire until she sharply cleared her throat.

Of course, now that she had his complete attention, his stare was just as intense and unreadable as ever. Unbidden, her stomach did a little shimmy on her. And it wasn't the only body part acting up. Her heart thumped a little louder in her ears and her urge to fidget was only growing the longer his eyes bore into her.

She gulped quietly. She needed to get ahold of the situation.

"Okay, let's get some rules down first." Rules would keep them on the same level of understanding.

Alwan nodded. "It's your home."

"Good. Shoes off, then," she remarked dryly, watching

him glance down at the puddle forming on the vinyl flooring under his dressy boots.

He stepped forward, drawing to a halt when Lulu kissed her teeth.

Slowly, while maintaining eye contact, Alwan slipped off his boots.

Satisfied that he wouldn't track the mess all over her motor home now, she gestured at him. "You're dripping everywhere."

"You want me to take my clothes off too?"

"I didn't say that," Lulu snapped, cheeks flushed warm as she shuffled from foot to foot.

His lips twitched in a clear effort to hold back his humor, but wisely he just gave a nod and stood there silently awaiting her next instruction.

"My second rule is that you dry off. The bathroom is over there." She pointed behind him to a sliding door. "I'll just grab you a towel."

Once he was ensconced in the bathroom she blew a sigh. Inviting him inside her home might not have been her brightest idea, but she couldn't exactly toss him out now either. Not when rain hammered the roof and sides of the RV.

Freeing Blue from his carrier, he immediately crept over to sniff around the trail of water and Alwan's boots.

"We have a guest," she told him when he looked up and meowed at her for answers.

Not seeming to like that response, he hightailed it to the bedroom.

Lulu sighed again, wishing she could hide too, and wait out the storm and Alwan's temporary stay from the solitary safety of her bed. Instead of giving in to that thought, she rooted around her small linen cupboard for that towel she'd promised him.

Once she found it, Lulu rapped lightly on the bathroom door, called, "Hey, the towel's on the floor outside the door," and started crouching to set the towel down.

When she'd installed the barn door on the bathroom, she never once thought that she would come to regret it even slightly. But that was only because she hadn't ever imagined Alwan would be there with her. That he would slide open the door so fast and catch her mid-crouch, her face level with his lower half. Thankfully for her, he was still dressed in his wet clothes.

But being up close now, Lulu noticed how tightly his soaked trousers clung to his lean legs and his wet shirt suctioned to his abs and pecs and—

Snapping upright, towel still grasped in her hands, she gawped at him.

Knowing that she should look away, that she shouldn't be fixated on the water pooling at the base of his throat or be curious about the droplets trailing down past the open collar of his button-down shirt, Lulu gulped hard.

"Thanks." Alwan reached for the towel.

Loosening her grip, she held it out slowly. Their fingers brushed and she instantly recalled the feel of his long, thick fingers swiping at her cheek and his warm palm framing her face, making her feel secure, protected. All at once the flutters from her stomach swept up into her rib cage, whipped against her racing heart and raged into a windstorm when he huskily said her name.

"Luula? Anything else?"

"Just the third rule," she gritted, annoyed at her reaction to him and grasping for an excuse as to why she was still standing there. "Don't mess up my bathroom."

"Noted," he said and gave her a final piercing look before sliding the door close between them.

A heartbeat later the shower switched on, and her mouth dried at the image of him standing under the new high-pressure showerhead she'd installed, luxuriating in it the way she did regularly. Only now whenever Lulu used her shower, she would always remember Alwan and this moment.

Stop it. Stop thinking about him like this.

Confused by the way he had her feeling, Lulu compelled her stiff limbs to move away. Her eyes landed on the puddle around his boots and the tracks he'd made from her front entrance. She rolled up her sleeves and fetched her mop, suddenly all too glad for the chore.

Once she'd finished cleaning, she started a pot of coffee and hurried past the bathroom and into her bedroom. Drawing the ceiling-mounted privacy curtain closed, she rushed through changing into dry clothes, all the while keeping an ear open to any sounds of Alwan having finished with his shower.

From his resting place in the center of the bed, Blue gave her another of his mystified looks.

Her face was still a little hot when Alwan finally joined her.

"Coffee," he said with a smile, perking up instantly the way she often did at the promise of caffeine. "You shouldn't have."

"Well, I haven't had breakfast yet, and I thought it would have been rude if I didn't offer a cup to my *guest*." She stressed the last part on purpose, eyeing the duffel he'd carried over to the dinette as he pulled out one of the two chairs at the table.

Sitting, Alwan followed her gaze to the travel bag at his feet.

"It's as if you planned a longer stay," she said suspiciously. "Were you just *that* confident that I would agree to your bizarre idea of us getting engaged?"

He smiled, full lips slowly tugging up at the corners, his

eyes squinting and his husky chuckle rolling through her not unlike the thunder rumbling outside the motor home.

"Don't worry. Once the storm clears, I'll leave," he reassured her, reaching for the mug she'd set down on the table between them. "And speaking of shelter, I appreciate you offering a place."

Returning his smile, Lulu hovered her hand over his cup at the last moment and bit the inside of her cheek when he scowled and looked between her and the coffee she was withholding. "Not so fast. You can thank me with an explanation."

He owed her that much after his bombshell proposal.

Though as much as she wanted answers, it didn't bode well that Alwan sighed and scrubbed at his bearded jaw.

"Okay, then." Heaving another long breath, he settled his palms on the table and leaned back in his chair. "Where do I start?" he said before launching into his explanation.

"That's a lot," Lulu said once he finished rehashing the tale of his professional downfall. Taking pity on him, she moved away the hand blocking his access to the coffee mug and even smiled when he took his first sip and sighed with a blissful look on his handsome face.

"I'm just surprised you hadn't heard about it already, or even seen the video."

"I've been living a little off-grid, if you haven't noticed." She waved at their setting before sobering up. "I am sorry that happened to you. It doesn't seem very fair."

"It isn't," he echoed, his hands squeezing the heated ceramic cup in his grasp as angry helplessness furrowed his brow and twisted his mouth into a scowl. "It didn't matter that my client cooled down eventually, gave me a sincere apology and requested that I appeal his case. Because by that point the video had millions of views, and my firm was being targeted by online trolls.

"Naturally my bosses asked me to drop the appeal and let my client go quietly."

"But you didn't drop it," Lulu said, having connected the dots herself.

He shook his head. "I couldn't. And when they found out, they benched me. It's reinforced for me that I should be running my own legal practice. Helping whomever I want to help without having anyone looking over my shoulder. Sadly though, I'm not entirely in a position to do that at the moment. I need influence and wealth from the kind of high-net-worth clients that have both.

"On top of that, with everything that's happened online, my image isn't very polished right now and clients might not trust me."

"And getting engaged would help fix your professional reputation, is that it?"

"Not exactly, but some of the wealthy clients I'm targeting are older, therefore more traditional-minded. To them, marriage equals respectability. Besides, having a fiancée would also ease my parents' worries for me. *Hopefully...*"

She recognized that look on his face from having stared at her own reflection in the past, when she'd felt helpless in her own body. Useless and out of control...

Powerless to stop her baby from dying.

Lulu squeezed her eyes closed, breathed slowly and methodically through her nose before opening her eyes just as the lights flickered.

Thankfully Alwan hadn't noticed her reaction. Preoccupied with the electrical hiccup that lasted a few short flickers, he had his head raised to the pendant light above the dinette.

"Uh, should we be concerned? I didn't exactly pack a flashlight."

"The lights do that sometimes, especially during bad

weather like this. I already unplugged from the shore power and lowered the antenna, so there's no risk of the storm frying the electrical system," she assured him, not certain it was working since he grimaced at the thunder cracking noisily outside.

"So that means no chance of *us* getting fried either, right?" he hedged.

"I promise I won't let you get electrocuted... At least not until you've answered all my questions." She smirked when he gave her another of his pleasant-sounding chuckles. Just like that the anxiety that had reared out of nowhere was gone as quickly as it had manifested. Lulu couldn't shake the feeling that Alwan had helped with that somehow, even if it felt like all he'd done since he'd shown up out of the blue was throw her off-kilter, annoy her and ruin her morning.

Although right now he seemed to be cooperative, even asking, "What do you want to know next?" as if he didn't mind being interrogated.

Not that this is an interrogation.

Since he offered though, Lulu wondered, "I understand why you feel you have to get engaged for your career, but surely you could propose to any other woman?" She blushed with him gazing intently at her again. "Why me?"

What does any of this have to do with me?

It was the question she'd wanted to ask all along.

Before Alwan could answer her, the lights winked again. Once, twice. And then they were gone altogether, plunging them into darkness.

"Nope. The lights are still out," Alwan called out to Lulu after pulling open the door to her RV and taking a peek into the darkness inside.

The electricity to her motor home had gone out half an

hour ago, and once the rain had slowed and the thunder seemed to have rolled past them, Lulu insisted on taking a look at the generator. Even though Alwan hadn't wanted to venture out into the wet, chilly world outside, he also couldn't in good conscience lounge around while she attempted to restore their lost power.

But since he didn't know the first thing about RV maintenance, all he ended up doing was holding a flashlight steady for her to work the circuit breakers. That and occasionally jogging back to check whether any of the lights had come back on.

This was the third time he'd investigated with no change in their lightless situation.

It was also when the rain picked up again and Lulu threw up her hands and called, "I give up."

Already warmer and dryer, Alwan was all too happy to be indoors again. But when Lulu set up a couple more camping lights to cast off the dark, his spirits dampened the second he saw her frown illuminated by the lantern she set down on the table.

Concerned, he asked, "What's wrong?"

"It's nothing." If she was trying to sound convincing, she failed the instant she sighed softly. Barely sparing him a glance, Lulu sat back at the table and, grabbing her mug, took a big gulp of her coffee.

Following her lead, he sat too and gave her a pressing look. "It doesn't sound like nothing."

Lulu lowered her cup slowly.

"Do you want to talk about whatever it is? I'm a good listener, or so I've been told."

"Oh, are you?" She smiled suddenly and it tripped his alarms.

"It kind of comes with my profession."

"I bet it does," she said with a breezy laugh.

Those alarms were now blaring for him to zip his lips, but even if he had, it was too late.

Lulu's smile disappeared in a blink.

"Strange," she said. "You're a good listener, but you still haven't managed to listen and answer my question. Why propose to me?"

Alwan clenched his jaw. It wasn't Lulu's fault for being curious. In fact, he'd anticipated she would have questions. Any normal person would.

She wants answers. Give them to her.

At least this way he possibly stood a chance at turning her around on the admittedly outlandish idea of her playing his fake fiancée.

"I told you my parents want to see me married, and I need their connections to gain new clients and eventually, that is hopefully sooner rather than later, open my private practice. It's our quid pro quo agreement. Doesn't that explain everything?"

She rolled her eyes. "Everything *but* why you chose me. Like I said, I'm sure you have plenty of options available to you."

"Is that a compliment on my good looks?"

He braced himself for a tongue-lashing. As young children forced to grow up in each other's company, she'd often made a point of calling out his ego. Just as he'd rarely passed up a chance at riling her up. And when they hadn't been taking passive-aggressive digs at each other, Lulu avoided Alwan and he steered clear of her.

Now Alwan sought her out purposefully. *Because I need her.*

It was unlike him to depend on others—to *trust* them. He didn't give his confidence away easily. After all, trusting the wrong people was what created this mess for him in the first place.

Trusting his bosses to have his back no matter what, considering all the years he'd toiled away like a model soldier ant on behalf of the firm.

Then he'd trusted his parents to support him no strings attached, but they had bargained with him instead…almost as if they didn't trust *him*.

Why would they after what happened with Hashim?

He froze, muscles tensing at that thought.

It wasn't often that Alwan allowed his mind to drift to his older brother. At least not anymore, not after he had taught himself to repress any recollections of him. And now was the last place he wanted that bleak stroll down memory lane.

He was grateful then when Lulu murmured, "You're incorrigible."

Instead of biting his head off, she turned her head away and gave him a different view of her beauty.

Shoulder-length, wavy black hair framing a heart-shaped face, beautiful russet red-brown skin, deep soulful-brown eyes ringed by naturally long black lashes and those lushly full lips of hers had him a little weak at the knees.

"I heard about your plan to return home soon."

Eyes saucer-wide, Lulu snapped her head back to him, any signs of her adorable bashfulness gone.

He couldn't explain it, but it felt like the rest of the world blinked out of existence, the darkness sucking everything else away and leaving just him and Lulu. Gazing into her eyes, losing himself in the depth of her stare, he dragged a tongue over his dry lips and breathed through the anxiety pressing down over his chest. "That's why I *need* you."

"Alwan…"

Steeling himself against the tantalizing shiver the sound of his name in her soft, breathy voice elicited, Alwan pressed his palms closer together, his short nails digging into the backs of his hands. Like a punch to the gut, desire for her caught him unawares, the heat of it more potent than anything he'd experienced before.

But he wouldn't let it control this moment. Couldn't trust it not to ruin his careful planning.

"You need me?" Lulu repeated quietly.

Plucking open his collar did little to cool the fire in his blood, but at least he managed to untangle his tongue and said, "I... I meant that I require your help."

"Oh" was all she said in turn. And was it his imagination, or did she sound disappointed?

Not wanting to analyze that any closer, Alwan moved on. "There's a reason why I chose you. It's because unlike other women I've met, I know you won't complicate any of this with emotion."

"Why do you think that?"

"Your divorce."

Any hint that she might desire him too disappeared in a flash. Lulu's face grew stony, her eyes two chips of ice freezing him where he sat.

"What about my divorce?"

He wasn't deceived by the calm she portrayed.

"The women I've met expect marriage, but they also want love. And it's only made me realize that love... Love isn't something I desire."

"You think because I'm divorced, I wouldn't want love either," she said, an arctic chill creeping into her voice.

"No. That's not—" He cut himself off, took a breath and recognized that he had one shot at not bungling this and losing her completely. Taking a moment, he gathered his courage. "What I'm trying to say, without sticking my foot in my mouth, is that I think that you'd understand what this could be and not confuse it with anything else."

"And what could it be?"

"A partnership," Alwan said confidently.

"Partners. Us?"

"Yes. And we'd both benefit. For instance, I'd be more than willing to negotiate reimbursement."

"You'd *pay* me to be your bride?"

"My *fake fiancée*, yes."

Lulu pressed her lips together and, still looking wary, she finally asked, "How much are we talking?"

Alwan fought back the urge to triumphantly pump his fist. "Does that mean you're interested?"

"It means that I'm questioning my sanity for even thinking about it." Closing her eyes, she rubbed her temple with two fingers. After a little while she fixed him with a glare. "Let's be clear though, I haven't agreed to anything. Not yet."

This time he couldn't contain his excitement. Grinning, he said, "So, not a complete 'no,' and just not yet a 'yes.' That's still promising."

"Don't push it," she cautioned with a frown.

Alwan laughed. "Fine. But can I suggest a better location while you do your thinking? I could book us a hotel. A really nice one."

"You're trying to bribe me."

"Is it working?"

Lulu flung up her hands and huffed her exasperation. "Like I said, incorrigible. You know what? Do whatever you want, Alwan. I have to feed my cat." As annoyed as she sounded, Alwan could've sworn her lips switched up into a smile as she stood. It was hard to tell with it being so dark, and even harder when she breezed away without a look backward. But he took it as a promising sign.

One, he hoped, that would fix all his problems.

CHAPTER THREE

Alwan couldn't help the spring in his step as he led Lulu into their luxury hotel suite. He had good cause to be happy. The first phase of overturning his recent bad luck was well underway now, and it was starting to look like he hadn't clung on to hope for nothing.

Eyes wide and mouth open, Lulu trailed slowly after him. Almost as though she was afraid she'd break one of the many fragile vases or ornate chandeliers they passed in the castle-like, historic grand railway hotel.

Alwan hid his smile when he heard her soft gasp as they strolled past the rooms, the long winding hallway with its highly polished dark hardwood flooring ending in a grand living room. The room's primary feature was the panoramic view: the surrounding forest, the snowcapped mountains this area of Alberta was known for, and the nearby sweeping green valleys.

Like she was drawn in by a magnet, Lulu drifted to one of the tall, wide windows.

"What do you think?" Alwan asked, coming up behind her.

Startling, Lulu half turned to him and pressed a hand to her chest.

"Are you trying to give me a heart attack? Need I remind you that you might want me alive and well for this plan of yours."

Laughter bubbled out of him like fizz out of a shaken soda bottle. It was instantaneous and seemingly infectious by the way Lulu sucked in her lips and looked away quickly, almost like she was not only holding in her laugh but hiding it from him too.

"I'll take your distraction as a sign that you approve of the hotel," Alwan practically purred, a little too pleased with himself.

With a little huff, she fully turned away and folded her arms, forcing him to step up beside her and gaze down at her instead.

"But if you don't like it, we can always see about an upgrade."

"An upgrade?" Lulu looked around them, surveying the whole room before her eyes landed squarely back on him. "To what exactly? This place is already bonkers-level luxurious." Under her breath she muttered, "Are you going to buy the whole castle next?"

Alwan threw back his head and laughed.

"I would if I could, especially if I knew it would win you over on my plan," he said, wiping the tears of laughter from his eyes and chuckling again.

She sniffed and punched her nose up into the air. "Well, maybe I'm not a castle kind of girl."

"Then *maybe* you need to be convinced." As he spoke, Alwan pulled in closer, amused when her nonchalant facade broke and she sharply turned her head from him. He would've teased her more had her cat not chosen that moment to interrupt, meowing incessantly from its carrier.

Lulu unzipped the bag and pulled the little furry beast

out into the open. Instantly locking those luminescent blue eyes on Alwan, her cat hissed at him.

"He doesn't seem to like me."

"Blue's a good judge of people."

Alwan shook his head at her barb, laughing again. "Are you sure you and the cat don't want separate suites?"

"And be more indebted to you? No thanks. Besides, there's plenty of room for all of us, and our bedrooms are on opposite ends of this massive suite."

"Touché," he said with a grin.

"Now if you don't mind, Blue and I are going to explore the rest of this place." Not waiting for a response, she flitted off.

He had every mind to pursue, especially with the way her sweet, floral-scented perfume lingered in the air like a lure he knew would lead right to her. But not knowing what he would do or say when he caught up to Lulu held him back. Clenching his fists, he stared after her until she was out of sight and only then did he breathe slowly out through his nose, the tension gripping his muscles not fully expelled with the breath.

And it was because he'd felt his phone vibrate in his inner jacket pocket again.

The missed calls—seven in total—were all from his mom and dad.

There were also a few texts from his cousin explaining that Alwan's parents had already tried calling Malek to check on him, and Malek had convinced them that Alwan was currently crashing on his couch.

After sending his cousin a quick grateful text, he sighed wearily.

Alwan knew that this brief peace wouldn't last, and that his parents would show up on Malek's doorstep eventually if they didn't hear from him. And when they didn't find him there, they would send out search parties.

Closing his eyes, Alwan could just imagine what their faces would look like once he confessed that he had no prospective bride. That he had only lied because he'd had his back to a wall and it seemed the easiest thing to do at the time.

Instead, it was looking like all he'd ended up doing was delaying their inevitable disappointment with him.

Unless...

Unless Lulu helped him.

Alwan looked toward the empty corridor in the direction she'd gone, a curious longing to go to her stirring in his breast. The sensation, new and disconcerting, was not like anything he'd ever felt before.

It was nearly as worrying as the possibility that Lulu wouldn't agree to his fake engagement.

"Either you're having trouble deciding on what lunch will be, or something's bothering you."

Alwan's deep voice carried over to her from across the table they shared. Lulu shook her head, lowered the menu and met his inquisitive gaze.

"Does your distraction have anything to do with a repair quote for your RV that hasn't come in yet?"

She bit her lip, masking her surprise that he'd clocked her concern. Was she that easy to read, or was her stress over her nearly depleted bank account and the possibly exorbitant cost to fix her motor home just that obvious? After the storm had cleared up a few hours ago, they'd dropped the RV off at a repair shop on their way to the hotel and ever since then Lulu had been worrying nonstop.

Seeming to take her silence as an affirmative, Alwan

moved on and asked, "Is that why you were preparing to wrap up your travels?"

"Yes…and no," she said, knowing the RV wasn't the only reason she was heading home.

After not having seen them for a year—the longest she'd gone without having any of them for company—Lulu missed her family greatly, and she knew they were worried about her still. So, it seemed a perfect time to let them see that she was doing all right. Show them that she'd long since recovered from the shock of her sudden divorce. And even though she wasn't ready to share her pregnancy loss with them, hopefully she could still give them some peace of mind.

At least that *had* been her plan before Alwan showed up with his outrageous proposal for them to pretend to be engaged.

Outrageous, but you're still considering it, aren't you?

Lulu curled her fingers tighter around the menu, the plastic covering creasing under the press of her fingernails.

If Alwan noticed the rising tension in her, he didn't show it when he asked, "By the looks of it, your motor home seems like an older model. When you purchased it, did you consider you might need to repair it more?"

She glared at him for his insinuation that she hadn't properly planned for contingencies. "I *had* set appropriate funds aside for such an emergency, but I've also been renovating. Some of those costs may have gone beyond my budget."

"Then why not just ask your parents for the money?"

"I can't do that," she said sharply, her temper flaring up. "They have their shop to worry about, and our economy of late hasn't exactly been kind to small businesses. Not everyone is as lucky as your parents."

As soon as the words were out of her mouth, Lulu wanted to swallow them back. Alwan's parents had always been nothing but kind and generous to her and her family. They'd never treated her any different than their sons.

She stumbled through an apology.

"You don't have to apologize. Not when it's true that my parents are blessed with a successful business. I forget that not everyone has the same fortune." Alwan paused before wondering, "Are your parents not doing okay?"

"They're fine." She sighed. "I didn't mean to imply that their business is doing bad or anything, it's just I know the hard work they've put into the convenience store. I couldn't bother them with something as trivial as repairs on my motor home."

"Is it trivial though?"

Not knowing how to answer him, Lulu lowered her eyes back to her menu. She wasn't shocked by the expensive prices attached to the many different options of French Canadian cuisine, having gotten a clue of what the price range would be the instant she had set foot into the moody but elegant dining establishment.

Everything, including the exposed brick walls softened by gleaming dark wood accents in the tables, the vaulted ceiling's wooden beams, and the restaurant's golden lighting from drum chandeliers and wall sconces, added a warmth to the hushed, darkly intimate setting. It was the kind of restaurant that oozed fine dining.

"I think I'll butcher half these dishes names if I try to pronounce them. Also, is there nothing on here that's sensibly priced?"

Alwan's husky laughter had a sultry edge to it.

"Can't say I'll be of much help with the French pronunciation, but lunch will be charged to the suite."

"You'll be paying for me. Again." Lulu compressed her lips, still unsure of how she felt about that. He'd been paying for everything. Their luxurious suite, the hotel's pet-sitting service to mind Blue while they were lunching, and now lunch itself. Knowing that he could likely afford it and then some didn't ease her troubled thoughts.

She knew what Alwan was up to. Softening her up with his lavish gifts was just a way to get her to sign on to his fake engagement ruse. But she hadn't made up her mind on whether she would just yet. And she didn't want him getting the wrong idea before she fully decided on what to do.

After they ordered she squared her shoulders and faced him. "Just so we're clear, I don't want you thinking that I've made a decision because you've been paying for everything. And I plan to pay you back for all of it, eventually."

"I know. Anything I can do to help you make up your mind?"

"Not really, though I do have a question."

"Ask away," he prompted.

"You know why I'm even entertaining this bizarre idea of yours, but I still don't understand why you have to go through all this? I can't imagine why your parents wouldn't just help you. Why the condition that you have to be engaged?"

"Besides wanting grandchildren." He rubbed his bearded jaw thoughtfully and smiled, only she sensed it was more forced than before. And she understood why when he said, "The only other reason I can fathom is they're worried about me."

"Because of that viral video?"

He gave her another tense smile. "Yes, there's that, but I get the feeling they think I'm lonely. And that they believe by getting me married, that I'll have someone by my side."

"You're clearly not happy about it though. Why not just tell them that?"

"Simple. I don't want to disappoint them. You should've seen the way their eyes lit up when I told them I had a fiancée. They haven't been that happy in a long while, and it feels cruel to snatch it away from them."

She swallowed around the lump in her throat, relating more to what he'd said than she'd anticipated.

"Does that answer your question?" he asked.

Lulu nodded slowly. "I… I actually think I understand what you mean. After my divorce, I found the hardest thing to do wasn't filing papers and packing my things and moving out of the home I shared with my ex. It was telling my parents, my family that my marriage had ended.

"All I could think about was having to face their disappointment when I'd moved back in with them."

"And were they disappointed?" he asked, his attention completely riveted on her.

So much that he didn't acknowledge the waiter who set down plates of amuse-bouches on their table. After filling their glasses with water, the waiter made himself scarce and, swallowing thickly, Lulu continued.

"They weren't. It was actually the opposite—they were just really concerned. I didn't mind it at first. But then, it got hard to be around them. No matter what I said, they worried about me. And it wasn't just my mom and dad, but my brother and sister too."

"Seems to be a shared trait of families. At least loving ones."

"Yeah, I suppose," she said softly and cast her eyes down at the artfully plated appetizer in front of them. "It's just, I couldn't take it anymore…"

"That's why you've been traveling for the past year."

She raised her head. "Is that what you're doing too?"

"Which do you mean, hiding or running? Because it feels like I'm doing both right now."

"So, what happens if I don't agree to your proposal?" she asked. "Will you run and hide forever?"

"I could ask the same of you. What will you do if you don't have enough funds for your repairs? Will you go back home and stay there, maybe pick up where you left off a year ago?"

"I don't know. At least not yet. But I know what you're still trying to do."

"And what is it that I'm *still* doing exactly?"

"You want me to agree, but as I've told you I haven't decided what I'll do."

He popped a small bite of flaky pastry in his mouth and chewed slowly and thoughtfully, swallowing before speaking. "I'd be lying if I said I didn't want your agreement. But I'd rather you do it of your own volition. Fake bride or not, your consent is the only nonnegotiable factor here."

Rendered speechless for a moment, Lulu watched him slice and spear a couple more bites of his profiterole. He ate neatly, all except for a small, mesmerizing spot of creamy goat cheese at the corner of his mouth. Though he wiped it away, she kept staring at where it had been, her own mouth going dry.

She knew she should stop, and that any second he would realize that she was looking at him weirdly, but she couldn't.

At least not until he caught her.

Alwan lifted a thick, black brow and an amused sparkle glimmered in his eyes.

Feeling her face heat up, Lulu bowed her head, mumbled, "Well, thank you, I guess," and picked up her knife and fork to try her own appetizer.

They lapsed into silence after that. And only once their

plates were cleared and replaced with their entrées did Alwan speak up.

"So, how do you plan to spend the rest of your day?"

It reminded her that they were sharing a room. Even though the suite was expansive, far bigger than any hotel room she'd ever been in, Lulu knew it would still be hard to be near Alwan. Her body warmed all over at the mere thought of spending time in close quarters with him.

A part of her was regretting not taking Alwan up on his offer of a second suite.

"I'll probably go for a hike now that the weather is better," she said. "Take in the local sights and, um, clear my head."

"I'm guessing you don't want company?"

She shook her head and he smiled, his eyes crinkling with his genuine humor.

"What about you?" she asked quietly, her hand wrapping around her glass of ice water.

"Worried I'll be bored without you?"

And just like that, the tension was broken. Lulu scowled, the prick of guilt she was feeling about not offering him to join her on her hike evaporating into a puff of smoke.

"Not really. I'm sure your ego will keep you busy."

Alwan's low laugh was husky, the sound of it revitalizing her blushing cheeks, raising gooseflesh over her arms and unspooling an illicit heat in her lower belly.

It made her want to skip their meal altogether and fast forward to the part where they went their separate ways for a little while.

Restraint didn't come easily to Alwan, but he had mastered it.

And yet all his practice in patience escaped him when Lulu left for her hike after their lunch together. He might have been all right with it had she not looked relieved when they parted ways. *Like she couldn't wait to be rid of me.*

In fairness, she'd asked for the time alone to think over the fake engagement, and not wanting to force her into agreeing, Alwan had let her go.

The first hour had been a brutal test in self-control. He'd paced like a caged animal in their hotel suite, hovering near the entrance.

When his legs finally tired of that, he briefly entertained the idea of heading out and trying to find her.

But one look out the window, at the immense sweeping landscape of forest, and he knew finding Lulu wouldn't be easy.

Once he put that idea to rest, he'd grabbed his tablet from his duffel bag and stalked out of their suite to find somewhere to work.

That was two hours ago.

Now he opened the door to their suite and walked in, tablet tucked under his arm, key card in his hand. At first nothing but the faint hum of the central heating greeted him. *She's still not back...* That realization tightened his muscles and had his thoughts racing to worrying scenarios, all of them centered around Lulu being injured.

What if she's hurt and can't get help?

Panic, hot and bilious, scorched up his throat.

Placing his tablet down on the entryway table, Alwan tightened his hand around the key card and was about to turn for the door and head to Reception to see if they could help when a flash of snow-white popped up in his peripheral.

Lulu's cat stared back at him from around the corner of the hall.

As soon as Alwan made eye contact, the furry beast gave a warning growl and shot off deeper into the hotel suite.

Realizing that Lulu wouldn't have left her cat alone, as per the hotel's rules on pets, he understood it could only mean one thing. *She's here.*

Stuffing down the odd excitement surging up through him, he followed the direction her cat had gone.

It led him to the living-slash-dining room.

Striding in, he stopped short, a few things popping out at him immediately.

First, it was raining heavily again. Wind-driven rain splattered the windows, the sky full of dark, dense gray clouds now when it had been clear blue not too long ago. Second, the only other light source besides the pale natural light coming through the windows was the fiery glow of the electric fireplace. Finally, Lulu herself.

Curled up under a throw on the chaise lounge, and with a mug in her hands, she stared into the flames, either oblivious to him gazing at her or uncaring of his presence.

He had his answer when she said, "Are you just going to stand there and stare at me?"

"When did you get back?"

"Half an hour ago, just before it started pouring outside." She turned her head to him then, the glow of the firelight casting off her lustrous dark hair and reflecting in her eyes as she looked him over. "Where were you?"

"Down at the bar, drinking my weight in drip coffee and working."

Lulu hummed noncommittally before looking back at the fireplace.

"What about you? How was your trek into the great outdoors?"

"Okay" was her only response, and he got the distinct impression she was preoccupied.

He walked toward her, his glance flicking over to where

her cat lounged on the armchair directly opposite where Lulu sat. The little beast growled low when Alwan passed a little too closely.

Safely crossing her feline guard, he gestured to the end of the chaise lounge and asked, "May I?"

Lulu pulled her legs up in silent invitation.

Alwan sat and only then noticed the paper between them on the chair. He picked it up and squinted, the darkness making it hard to read.

Before he had a chance to ascertain what it was, Lulu said, "It's the repair quote."

"Where did you print it?"

"I used the hotel's printing service. I figured it would be easier to read than on my phone. Not that it changes the cost estimate."

Alwan saw what she meant immediately. Though it wasn't anything he couldn't afford, the high four-figure estimate for her repairs garnered a low whistle from him. "That is a hefty sum."

"Apparently, beyond the generator I'll need to buy, there's also an issue with the engine. I was expecting for it to be costly, but it's even worse than I imagined." She laughed bitterly and looked away, back at the realistic flames crackling and snapping in the fireplace.

He knew what was coming, sensed where the conversation was headed, but he needed to hear her say it.

"If…if I agree to your fake engagement, I need you to agree to some stipulations."

Keeping a lid on his joy was challenging, but Alwan schooled his features into neutral as he said, "Anything to make you more comfortable."

"I don't think anything could make me *comfortable* with this," Lulu said dryly.

"And yet still, your comfort matters to me." Because it did.

Despite knowing each other most of their lives, for the first time Alwan felt like he knew her better after learning a bit more about how her divorce had worried her family and eventually led to her solo-traveling in her RV through the Canadian wilderness. Her motor home was clearly important to her in the same way this next step of his career was for him.

For that reason alone, her comfort was now his utmost priority. He would do whatever he could to alleviate any concerns she had before they embarked on this ruse together.

"Shoot. What are your stipulations?"

Lulu took a sip from her mug before she said, "First, to be clear, we can't actually get married. I'm okay with an engagement, but it can't go beyond that."

What she said made perfect sense to him. Alwan didn't actually want to be tied down, and he was betting that after her divorce neither did she. Besides, his parents never specified that he had to be *married*. In this case, a bride-to-be should suffice for all his intents and purposes and satisfy their clause to see him blissfully and—unbeknownst to them—momentarily engaged.

"Deal. There'll be no official papers, and no wedding party as part of our agreement. Is that all?"

"No, we should also have a timeline for when we want to end things. I'm thinking a year. Is that enough time for you to open your practice?"

"A year should be plenty of time, so I'm all right with that."

"Good. Also, when this ends, we let our families down gently together. We'll simply tell them that it just didn't work between us and that we're on the same page with a mutual, amicable breakup."

He cocked his head to the side, studying her for a quiet moment. "Does that part worry you?"

"Doesn't it worry you?" She lifted her brows at him, frowning her incredulity. "I don't want to hurt my family or yours. Even if *we* know this engagement won't be real, it doesn't mean they will. Besides, our parents are friends. This shouldn't cause a rift between them."

"Agreed. Anything else?"

Lulu wrung her hands around her mug, the nervous tell setting off alarms in him, and when she didn't respond immediately his anxiety only shot up higher.

Finally, after a long pause, she said, "Since none of this is real, there shouldn't be any…intimacy." She avoided direct eye contact when she spoke, her shyness more than apparent now.

His relief quickly switched to amusement. Feeling impish suddenly, Alwan teased, "Intimacy?"

"You know what I mean," she said, glancing at him before bowing her head and staring down at her mug as though its contents were fascinating.

"But just so we're clear though, what are we talking is off-limits exactly? Hand-holding, hugging, and kissing—"

"Alwan!"

He held out his hands placatingly and laughed. "All right, I hear you. No PDA of any kind." But not even a few seconds later, he drawled, "So…does that mean no late-night phone calls too?"

Her disapproving glower was swift, and he had to bite the inside of his cheek to keep from laughing.

"Okay, fine. No intimacy, period. Is that it?"

"That's all," she said.

"Good. I have something I'd like to add, then. A final rule we both can probably agree to, but one that still needs to be said, we can't confuse or complicate this with any kind of emotional entanglement."

"You think I'm going to fall in love with you?" Lulu's laughter was loud and unabashed. He should've been offended, but instead, he smiled.

Face glowing from her mirth, she wiped her eyes and laughed again. "Don't worry. That won't be a problem."

He laughed too. "Then we have a deal." Holding up her repair bill, he said, "And as per our agreement, I'll handle this. The only thing left to ask is, when would you like to go ring shopping?"

"Don't worry," Lulu said, looking down at her hand. "I'll have that covered."

Baffled by his disappointment at that news, he tucked aside his strange upset and said, "I guess there are no more roadblocks. We're officially engaged."

"*Fake* engaged."

Alwan simply grinned and said, "Whatever you say, my fake fiancée."

CHAPTER FOUR

Lulu had always known she'd return home to Toronto someday.

She just hadn't ever pictured that when she did, it would be with a fiancé.

Before they'd left Alberta, Alwan had done as he'd promised and paid the deposit on her repair bill for her RV to the mechanic. The remaining cost for the repairs he'd then transferred to her bank account. And with that he'd honored his part of their fake engagement deal.

Now it was her turn to uphold her end of their partnership.

Be his perfect pretend bride-to-be.

On the four-hour flight home, they'd hashed out their approach and gotten their stories straight. They'd decided to tell their families separately, but that had led to three days of nonstop questions, so she was grateful they'd be together with both sets of parents today so that answers could be given and worries soothed.

"Do you love our Luula?" her father asked the moment Alwan's Maybach pulled away from the curb. He turned in the passenger seat to pin Alwan with a stern look.

Lulu groaned in Somali, "Aabo, please! Stop embarrassing me…"

Her mother swatted her leg and hushed her. "Aamus! Aabahaa dhegayso."

"How can I listen to him when he's being so humiliating, Hooyo?" Lulu complained, crossing her arms and flopping against the back seat only to gasp and jolt upright a second later when her mother gave her a pinch on the thigh. Seeing the warning in her mother's eyes, Lulu rubbed her leg and clamped her lips together.

"We've known you since you were young, son, but still, we have to ask. Don't be offended and please understand that we only want what's best for Lulu."

At a red light, Alwan looked at her father and, in fluent Somali, said, "I understand fully, and I'm not offended at all, adeer." He turned his head forward and his gaze met hers in the rearview mirror, searing through her. "But your concern is unfounded as I respect and care for your daughter."

She didn't know how long he stared at her, but it was long enough for drivers to begin blaring their horns behind them. If Alwan heard the angry honking, he wasn't doing anything about it.

Finally, just when she thought her lungs would burst from holding her breath, he looked away. Lulu let out a soft, shuddery breath and blinked furiously, her eyes dry from their staring match.

That was the state she was in when they arrived at Alwan's parents' restaurant. Dropping them off first, he peeled off in search of parking in the busy neighborhood. She watched his taillights disappear before turning to find her parents studying her.

"He'll catch up. We should go inside," Lulu announced and, hoping they'd follow, headed briskly for the entrance to the restaurant, a two-story sleek, steel, glass and black marble building. But not soon enough to miss their exchange of silent looks and secretive smiles.

Inside, the restaurant was quiet and warm. Too quiet. Confused, Lulu looked beyond the empty host podium facing the entrance to the open space of empty tables on the first floor. Alwan had said his parents were expecting them, and it was their restaurant, but they weren't anywhere to be seen.

Soft music played on the speakers, so she figured someone had to be in the building, and she soon heard the sound of heels clacking over the colorfully vibrant Moroccan tiles toward them.

A smiling young woman was tying on a half apron as she walked, smoothing her hands over the front of it where the restaurant's name, Al-Nuri, was printed in yellow-gold lettering.

"Ms. Sadiq?" she asked, her cheeks dimpling when Lulu nodded. "You and your parents are expected upstairs. If you'll follow me." Leading them deeper into the restaurant, she directed them into an elevator but didn't follow them in.

Alwan's parents were waiting as soon as the lift doors opened, and the second Lulu stepped out, she found herself wrapped in his mother's perfumed embrace while his father smiled broadly at her.

It was a warmer reception than the one Alwan had gotten from her parents. But her stomach still swooped nervously when Alwan's parents ushered them to a table in the far corner with views of Lake Ontario from the window walls. And once they were all seated, Alwan's mother, Ayaan, and father, Omer, on one end and Lulu tucked between her parents on the U-shaped majlis sofa on the other side, she tensed as all their focus landed on her.

Meeting each of their intent gazes, she smiled weakly, suddenly struck by the realization she was all alone.

So she was on her own when his mother, hand keenly outstretched, asked, "Oh! Is that the engagement ring?"

Embarrassed, Lulu had no choice but to flash her new accessory to everyone. While they showered her with compliments, she cast a furtive glance at the elevator, her hope flagging when Alwan was still nowhere in sight. She quietly despaired, figuring no one had noticed.

But Ayaan squeezed her hand with a silvery laugh and smile. "Don't worry, Luula. He texted a minute ago that he found a parking spot farther away and that he'd be with us any moment."

Lulu blushed and bowed her head when all the parents laughed then.

And her cheeks still felt hot to the touch when Alwan finally made his reappearance.

Never had Lulu been more relieved to hear the sound of an elevator ding. Her relief was quickly undercut by her annoyance with him for leaving her in the first place. She glared as he strode over in his gleaming Italian leather shoes, his charcoal-gray suit jacket hooked over one of his arms, his hands adjusting his tie before smoothing over the front of his white-and-gray-striped dress shirt. It only irritated her more that he looked so breathtakingly handsome and impeccably put-together.

"Sorry, I'm late," he panted softly when he reached their table, his tawny brown cheeks flushed red.

Hearing his breathlessness sanded off Lulu's frustration with him. It was difficult to hold on to her irritation when she envisioned him running here from wherever he'd parked his car.

Greeting his parents, Alwan gripped his dad on the shoulder and touched his lips to his mother's forehead. "Salaam, Abu. Yumma. I hope I didn't miss anything," he said before squeezing in between his folks and catching Lulu's eyes across the table.

They were now facing each other, and beneath the table she felt the toe of his shoes bump her low, slingback heels. At first she didn't think anything of it, but then he did it again.

Above the table, his lips tilted up in a small smile and he raised an eyebrow at her in silent question.

Touched that he was checking in on her, she smiled back, mollified for the time being.

"You haven't missed anything, Alwan," her mother said and wrapped an arm around Lulu's shoulders. "We have just been wondering how this happened, and since Luula won't tell us, maybe you can. How did you and our Luula fall in love?"

Love? If only they knew...

The only commonality to love that she shared with Alwan was his love for his career and hers for her RV and the solace and peace it had given her during a rough patch in her life. There wouldn't be—*couldn't be*—anything else between them. Not simply because it would ruin their plans, but also because romance and a happy-ever-after were crossed out of her heart and head forever. And even if she was interested, which Lulu most certainly was not, Alwan, with his big ego and fixation on his profession, appeared to be the last person who would have time for a relationship.

Naturally, she had a visceral reaction at the word *love* used in the same sentence with her and Alwan.

Lulu cringed audibly enough for her mom to kiss her teeth.

"What?" her mother asked sharply. "We can't be curious?"

"I know I am!" his mother chimed in with another warm, tinkling laugh.

Their fathers were more silent, but they too nodded in agreement with their wives.

Since the question wasn't posed to her, Lulu sat back and watched Alwan like everyone else. She already knew what he would say, having rehearsed their story enough times over the past few days. All she had to do was nod and smile at the appropriate times, which was an easy enough task.

At least it *was* easy until Alwan said, "I knew Luula had been *wanting* me to propose, so I figured it was time. Why make either of us wait? I didn't want her pining for me anymore…"

Wanting? Pining!

Since *when* did they agree on that narrative?

Shock wearing away quickly, Lulu nudged his foot under the table. Okay, maybe *nudged* wasn't the right verb. More like she stepped on him. Hard. Right on those stupid toes of his in those stupid expensive shoes and watched him jolt in his seat mid-explanation and bite his lip and stifle a pained grunt.

"Alwan, are you all right, habibi?" his mother wondered.

Quietly, he waved off the concern both sets of parents showed.

Serves him right.

But not fully satisfied, and still out for blood, she grabbed the opening to speak her mind. "But that was *after* Alwan cried and told me he couldn't live without me—"

Alwan's hissing intake of air cut her off, but his wide, shocked eyes gave her an unexpected thrill. Childish though it was, and perhaps a little dangerous when he narrowed his eyes at her, Lulu couldn't help goading him with a grin. She held back the urge to stick her tongue out at him. *Two can play at that game.*

"Cried? Really?" his mom repeated softly, touching his arm.

Alwan smiled down at his mother, but his stare bored through Lulu as he gruffly said, "I forgot that part, but if Luula says it happened—"

"It did," she interjected.

"Then I suppose it did," he assented, his eyes unreadable but his mouth lifting with a smile. He could've outed her. But then, she knew, that he'd be outing himself.

After that Alwan answered more faithfully to their practiced script, leaving Lulu with the impression that he'd learned his lesson and wouldn't play with her like that again. Brunch was eventually served, and Alwan's parents helped their staff with the setup, which thankfully pressed Pause on the questioning. Meanwhile Lulu noted her mother and father were chatting more amiably with Alwan. From the look of things, no one suspected they were lying, so she and Alwan were in the clear.

But just when she thought she could let down her guard, a sudden clenching sensation seized her lower belly. It felt like a fist was slowly but firmly squeezing her insides. Lulu tightened her lips on a pained moan and pressed her hands just below her stomach, where the dull ache was centered.

She hoped it was hunger.

Unfortunately, after an hour flew by and most their plates were cleared, Lulu was still quietly suffering, only now the gnawing discomfort dropped lower and seemed more familiar. Not that knowing it was her period made it any better. Her cycles were never regular, so she wasn't surprised that she was caught off guard now.

Her parents were busy chatting with Alwan's mother and

father, and Alwan himself was distracted scrolling through his phone. It was the perfect time to excuse herself without an awkward explanation, and having visited his parents' restaurant before, she knew where to find the restroom.

On the way there, and desperate to get her mind off her pain, Lulu admired the African-inspired touches to the restaurant's interior design. Woven shades covered the pendant lights hanging over the gleaming handcrafted wooden tables and chairs, the walls were painted a soft, earthy beige, and colorfully vibrant rugs hung in recessed alcoves. The cultural touches in the decor were as well-thought-out as the flavorful Sudanese and Somali dishes they'd just enjoyed.

It was easy to see that his parents had poured their love into making this restaurant feel like a second home.

Her smile turned into a grimace when another pulsating wave of torment struck.

Hurrying into the washroom, Lulu discovered that she'd forgotten to toss painkillers in her tiny, decorative handheld purse. She set her teeth against the now-nauseating waves of pain and shuffled out into the well-lit hallway. How was it that even walking was hurting her?

God.

She'd barely taken two steps back the way she had come when Alwan's low drawl came from behind her.

"There you are."

Letting out a short squeal, Lulu spun around and gasped, "Alwan!" Irritation surging through her almost immediately, she snapped, "Why do you keep scaring me like that? I'm seriously going to strap a bell to you if you don't stop. Honestly, you're worse than my cat. Even he has the decency to meow and let me know he's there."

He chuckled and slid his hands in his trouser pockets.

"Hey, don't blame me if you were too distracted to hear *or* see me. This isn't exactly an ideal hiding spot."

Not ready to admit that she was preoccupied, Lulu settled on quietly glaring at his smiling features. "I'm leaving," she said, but before she could turn away, yet another cresting pain gripped her insides. It was like a white-hot band of agony constricting her middle. And it wouldn't let her go. She hunched over slightly, her arms instinctively wrapping over the front of her. Lulu might've been humiliated that Alwan was still with her, but she was hurting far too much to care.

"Lulu, are you okay?" he asked, his warm, solid presence by her side in a flash.

She shook her head jerkily, focusing on deep breathing through the physical assault on her body.

Hearing Alwan curse under his breath, she closed her eyes and waited for him to panic and rush off to get help from his mother or hers. If he was anything like her ex-husband, Mohamed, that was what he'd have done.

So she was taken aback then when Alwan not only stuck with her but even crouched down low so she could see him.

Once he made eye contact, he asked, "Can you walk?"

Still busy with her belly-breathing exercise, Lulu gave him a curt nod.

The furrows in his brow lessened, his relief sweeping over his handsome face in a bright smile. "All right. That's good news. Though, just so you know, I was fully prepared to carry you if it came down to that."

Lulu snorted. "Duly noted."

Eyes twinkling merrily, Alwan moved toward the end of the hall and stopped when she didn't follow.

"I don't want to go out there yet." She leaned her head back against the wall, straightening her posture and feeling a reprieve from the shooting pain. Worrying everybody else wouldn't make her feel better. "I just need time. Oh, and ibuprofen."

Alwan looked long and hard at her for a beat before he nodded in understanding. "Then we'll go to the office."

"Why the office?" Lulu asked him.

"If I know my parents, they should have some pain reliever there," Alwan explained, looking back to make sure she was following him.

Leading her down the hall past the restrooms for their guests and beyond the Employees Only sign, Alwan stopped at the door at the end that read Office.

He pulled his keys out of his pocket to unlock the door.

"You carry a key to your parents' office?"

Alwan laughed at the unconcealed suspicion in her tone. "Normally I wouldn't, but my father misplaced his spare once. My parents decided that, given I don't live with them, it was best that I keep the extra key."

"I suppose," she said, rousing another amused chuckle from him.

Inside the small but neatly maintained office, Alwan headed straight for the nondescript desk in the middle and opened its drawers. "The first aid kit should be here somewhere," he mumbled to himself. After opening the first two drawers, he finally struck gold. "Aha. I knew it was here."

Eagerly retrieving the pain reliever from the first aid kit, he raised his head to find Lulu still standing closer to the door. She faced the wall and stared at the few framed photos of his family and his parents' staff members hanging there.

Closing his fist around the bottle in his grasp, Alwan walked over with leaden limbs, keeping his eyes on her.

Knowing what the photos already showed, he didn't regard them.

"Luula?"

At the sound of her name, she turned her head to him and noted the bottle in his open palm.

"Let me get you water."

He strode over to the corner of the office where a watercooler was stationed. Filling a small paper cup for her, Alwan walked it back to where she stood. Murmuring her gratitude, her features momentarily twisted into a pained grimace before she opened the bottle, took a pill and washed it down.

"Did you want to sit down?" he asked her when she compressed her lips and squeezed her eyes closed in quiet suffering.

A feeling of helplessness crept over him. He didn't know why he did it, but he flung a glance at the photos on the wall, one in particular sticking out from the collection. Looking away before the darkness clawed into him, Alwan looked back at Lulu and gave her his full attention.

"Actually, I could use fresh air more."

He tossed another quick look at the framed photos. Fresh air sounded good to him right about then too.

Locking up the office, they walked back to where their parents were seated. Before they reached the table, Lulu tapped his arm.

It was a light touch. There and gone. Certainly nothing that should have had him responding instantly by stiffening all over, his body wired tight, his attention at her command.

"Can you not tell them I'm not feeling well?" She looked from their table back to him, rewarding him with a smile when he nodded.

"Where did you two go?" his mother asked him as soon as they were within earshot.

"I was showing Luula around the restaurant, and now we're just going out for some air."

His father pulled his glasses off and furrowed his bushy brows. "It isn't the first time she's been here, Alwan. What were you showing her exactly?"

"Uh, just some family photos in the office."

"Let them go," Lulu's mother, Huda, said kindly. "They're young, in love—"

"And hopefully soon-to-be-wedded," Mahad, Lulu's father, finished with a stern look at Alwan in particular.

Since he wasn't about to argue with her father, Alwan promised, "We'll be right out there on the balcony," and pointed to the long wall of windows letting in a wash of natural light into the restaurant.

With their blessing, Alwan led Lulu away, and folding open the glass doors, he walked her outdoors.

"How are you not dying of embarrassment?" Lulu groaned the instant they were alone.

He grinned and walked with her to the edge of the balcony. "Who says I'm not?"

She appraised him with a sniff. "You look pretty calm to me."

"It's practice," he said, spinning around and leaning against the balcony's guardrail. "When I'm in the courtroom, I have to put on a poker face, even if I know my chances of winning for my client are not in my favor." Alwan nudged his chin toward where their parents were sneaking peeks at them. "It doesn't mean I'm not more than a little worried that they'll try and marry us off sooner."

"Great. Now you're scaring me too," Lulu griped, making him laugh.

Grasping the balcony handrail, she looked out at the shimmering lake and the Toronto Islands, the chain of well-frequented islands near the city's shores.

"Wow," she uttered quietly.

Having seen it so many times wore off the charm, but he tried to place himself in her shoes and turned back around to cast his gaze over the rippling lake glimmering with the bright white sunlight. The longer he stared the more Alwan began to feel the stirring of a lost appreciation for the cloudless blue sky, the nippy lake-scented breeze brushing his face, and the steady drone of the city he loved all around them.

"I know I've been here before, but I always forget how peaceful it is."

He hummed his agreement, knowing he couldn't add anything since she'd said it so perfectly.

"This is where you and your family took that picture together, isn't it?"

Any serenity Alwan had felt blasted away. Just like that he was back in the office, the photo he'd avoided in there filtering into his mind.

Not now. Not here with her.

He clamped his hands around the railing and, feeling Lulu's eyes on him, forced himself to grit out, "Yeah."

"You all looked so happy. When was it taken?"

Alwan clenched his teeth and a muscle leaped along his jaw.

He knew it wasn't her fault for asking innocent questions. It wasn't like Lulu understood that she was poking at a wound and peeling back a scab that had never fully healed despite years having passed since he'd first gotten the injury. *Since Hashim left.*

Since his big brother walked out of the reputable, private

rehabilitation facility their parents had shelled out big money to send him to receive the help he wasn't getting anywhere else. Not the hospitals, self-help groups or the interventions they'd tried staging as a family. Rehab had been their last-ditch effort to drag Hashim out of what they believed was a deep, dark pit of his own making.

What his parents didn't know, what he hadn't told anyone, was that he'd helped Hashim escape. At the time Alwan had thought he had been *saving* his brother, but all he had done was more harm than good.

It secretly made up a big reason why he wanted the fake relationship with Lulu now. Disappointing his parents *again* after everything they'd gone through was all he wanted to avoid.

With great difficulty, he said, "Eighteen summers ago. The day before Hashim left to go to the States for college on a rugby scholarship."

"Right. I almost forgot you had a brother," Lulu said and looked back out at the lake.

Me too. Alwan squeezed the balcony railing tighter, hating that he had that thought but knowing it was true. Because just as there were moments where all he could think about was where Hashim could be and what his brother could have been possibly up to all this time, there were days that went by where Alwan had gotten caught up in his own life and hadn't spared one moment for his runaway brother. Guiltily he admitted that he liked the times where he forgot more and more. But it was exhausting thinking of his brother, knowing possibly that Hashim might not ever have spared a thought for him in return.

Of course, it would be easier to forget him if Lulu hadn't reminded him now.

"I haven't seen Hashim around in a while," she observed. "He's still in Sudan, isn't he? Has he visited you since then?"

That lie about his brother being with extended family in Sudan was concocted by his parents right after Hashim had disappeared sixteen years ago. Rather than letting everyone know what truly had happened, they'd crafted another narrative. One that they'd kept going for a decade and a half now, but it did the trick and spared them the grief of gossipmongers.

Alwan hadn't agreed with their decision.

Why should they cover for Hashim all this time when he'd made the unusually cruel choice to abandon them? It wasn't fair that he'd shattered their trust and broken their hearts and left them to pick up the pieces. *Why should we be the ones hurting and hiding how we feel?*

Fueled by that thought, Alwan toyed with the idea of revealing his family's long-guarded secret to Lulu. This way he could finally unburden himself, though only at the cost of betraying his parents.

Is it worth hurting Abu and Yumma?

Picturing their heartbreak when they learned he divulged the truth cooled his blood. And, in the end, he decided to keep quiet...as always.

"He hasn't visited, and I don't really know what he's been doing. He actually hasn't spoken to any of us in a while. We had a falling-out...of sorts."

Alwan waited for Lulu to ask more questions, or at the very least offer her condolences.

She surprised him when instead she said, "Well, at least you don't have to worry about lying to him."

He blinked his confusion.

"It wasn't hard to lie to my parents," she explained, "but

when I told Ladna and Liban, I could almost sense them feel that I was lying my face off."

Hearing that about her sister and brother pulled a small smile from him.

"Why do I get the feeling you're jealous that I'm not speaking with my brother?"

She shrugged. "I'm probably a terrible person, but yes. I kinda am."

Shaking his head, Alwan let out a soft laugh. *Unbelievable.* He didn't know what shocked him more: that Lulu had made light of what he had told her, or that he was struck by the oddest urge to pull her in and hug her for it. Because the darkness that always seemed to crowd in with thoughts of his brother scuttled back at the first sound of his laughter.

Because of her.

Again, he fought the instinct to embrace her, the immense relief and gratitude he felt lodging in his throat. But he couldn't say more without risking her finding out the truth about Hashim, so he looked away and hooked his arms over the guardrail beside her.

"It goes without saying that I hope you and your brother work it out."

Her kind words made it that much more of a challenge to bite his tongue. Needing them to move past this, he hoarsely thanked her and said, "Don't be too jealous of me. I had my own problems lying to Malek."

"I thought you said your cousin knew about you going to Alberta. That he helped cover for you with your parents."

"He did," Alwan said, his elbow brushing her hand on the railing as he leaned in closer to her and whispered the rest, in case their parents were eavesdropping. "I just don't want him knowing any of this is fake. Malek and I, we're close. Because of that, like your brother and sister, it was hard getting him to even believe in all of this."

"It's hard, isn't it? Lying to them," Lulu said with a fluttery, tired-sounding sigh.

"It is, but it's best that we keep this between us. Remember, this is how we get what we want. Your RV. My business."

She frowned but nodded, now anxiously twisting the ring on her left finger.

"Speaking of keeping things between us, is that the engagement ring I'm supposed to have given you?"

Lulu stopped fidgeting immediately and, covering a hand over the ring, looked down, mumbling, "Maybe."

"May I?" He held out his hand.

"Are you going to break one of our conditions already? No unnecessary physical contact, remember?"

Alwan felt his lips kick up, amusement coursing warmly through him. "That won't be a problem if you allow me." And then because he sensed she'd approve, he added, "Please."

That appeared to do the trick because Lulu slowly, cautiously placed her hand in his upturned palm. Though she held her fingers still in his grasp, her nervousness was apparent. She had her glossy bottom lip tucked between her teeth and her head turned to the side, though Alwan didn't miss her peeks every now and again when she thought he wasn't looking.

Curling his fingers gently around her hand, he lifted her ring up closer to the light, the sun glinting off the larger cubic zirconia in the center of a circle of similar but far smaller stones. Not that he was a jeweler, but as pretty as the silver band was around her finger, Alwan knew he could've given her something far less…simple. *Cheap.*

A ring that better matched her beauty.

With Lulu looking away, he found a rare opportunity to study her and he didn't squander it, drinking her in shamelessly.

She'd dressed up for the meeting between their parents. Her shoulder-length dark hair drawn up into a tidy bun with two thick tendrils coiling down from her temples, her makeup only enhancing her glowing, warm reddish-brown skin. The long-sleeved black jumpsuit she wore was as sparkly as her gold chandelier earrings, and gone were her hiking boots, replaced by a pair of kitten heels that weren't as dainty as their suede appearance belied. His poor toes could attest to it.

She looked different, but not in the way that made her unrecognizable. Still enticingly pretty to him no matter how she appeared or what she wore.

And the ring was her choice, so he'd respect it.

She must have felt his stare because Lulu turned her head back to him and asked, "Do you not like it?"

"Would you change it if I said so?"

Without missing a beat, she breathed, "No."

"Then," he rasped, "it's perfect."

Just like this arrangement could be for them, so long as Alwan kept his emotions in check and Lulu did the same.

CHAPTER FIVE

ALWAN WAS BEGINNING to believe that the reason he wasn't already married was because he'd suspected just how exhausting wedding planning could be. And even though he wasn't really getting married, that fact didn't exempt him from the tortuous activity of venue searching with his parents and Lulu's.

It had all started when the subject of not finding a suitable venue in time came up in conversation.

What if all the good places are booked up? his mother had said.

We should help them look, Lulu's mother had then suggested.

To keep up appearances, he and Lulu had no choice but to agree and be hauled along for the search.

The only upside was that he had her to commiserate with.

And from the amount of times Lulu flung him comical looks that said she'd rather be anywhere else as they strolled the newly blooming garden grounds of the famed, historic Casa Loma, Alwan safely guessed that she wasn't happy either.

Unlike him though, she was faking her good mood far easier than he ever could.

"I thought the library and conservatory were beautiful, but this pavilion is lovely," she gushed at one point when her parents and his looked to them for their opinions. Despite the grand Gothic Revival castle being the third venue that they'd visited already that day alone, and all by noon, Lulu smiled brilliantly and said all the right things to please his parents and her mother and father.

With her doing all the heavy lifting, all he had to do was trail closely by her side and nod and beam on cue.

When the tour finally, joyfully, came to an end, the venue staff member showing them around guided them to the pavilion's exit. Their parents followed, chattering excitedly, and as Alwan began to stalk after them, already dreading the next venue they likely planned to drag him and Lulu to, he noticed that his bride-to-be wasn't by his side any longer.

Looking back, he didn't have to search far for her.

Bathed in the sunlight pouring in from the pavilion's glass roof, Lulu stood still and stared up transfixed at the mansion's towering turret and stony exterior.

"Luula, everyone's left," he said, walking up to her.

She blinked over at him as though she'd lost track of time.

But that wasn't what robbed him of his breath temporarily. With the light outdoors brightening her brown eyes, he saw clear as the sunny day outside a longing in her gaze that went beyond the power of any words in any language on this planet. So palpable was that yearning, it eked a shiver out of him before a strange pining to give her what she quietly desired squeezed his chest.

"You like this place." He knew he didn't have to say it, but she confirmed it when she looked back up at the castle.

"It's stunning, how could I not?"

Alwan surveyed the impressive pavilion, seeing exactly why she was taken with the naturally lit space with its touches of indoor greenery, all glass walls and roof, charcoal-stained cedar flooring and sparkling crystal chandeliers hanging from the metal rafters. Still, it wasn't anything he hadn't seen before. Though he couldn't recall specifics from having attended countless work-related gatherings, Alwan swore he'd dined in a similar pavilion. *Maybe even this very one*, he mused. Not to mention he had lost track of the times his parents had dragged him to one of their boring business networking soirees, from silent dinner auctions to ballroom charity galas, and all hosted in elegant venues just like this one.

Of course *now* in hindsight he wished he'd hobnobbed more with Toronto's upper-crust, networked on his own without his parents' intervention, and spared both him and Lulu this marriage charade. Still, as hard as it was for him to smile and lie while looking his family and hers in the eye, Alwan could only imagine what it was like for her.

All of this had to be reminding her of her divorce.

And that knowledge made him feel like a heel. *She's getting something out of this deal too.* But even though she'd benefited by taking his money, it didn't make him feel any better.

Rather than pretend like he was thinking about anything else, he asked, "Is this the kind of venue you had for your first marriage?"

She gave a light snort. "Hardly. Our budget was modest, so the event space was smaller. Weren't you there? I certainly recall seeing your parents—they gave generously to my wedding money box."

"No, sorry, I missed out. And yeah, that sounds like them." He said the last part with a proud smile. The one trait he'd always admired was how readily his mother and father swooped to the aid of others, whether it was for extended family or a stranger they had met only once, they were openhanded to a fault. But that was where the power of their compassion ended because even with their millions, his parents couldn't prevent Hashim from running away and leaving them—

Leaving me *behind*.

But this wasn't about his brother, and training his sights back on Lulu, he smiled to mask the darker path his thoughts had taken.

"Were you happy with your wedding? I know little girls dream of their big day, so the expectation had to be set high."

"Oh, and little boys don't?" she taunted with a quick smile.

He grinned and shrugged. "Hey, blame society's gender stereotyping. But if you're asking me specifically, no, I never really dreamed about getting married."

"Not even a little bit?"

"Not in the least. Always seemed like a lot of pressure, and after today, I know my gut instinct's proven. Weddings are a lot of work and certainly not for the faint of heart." And that was saying plenty given he'd sat through his rigorous bar exam and the grueling hours of studying and prep work required for it. Still, he would rather do that all over again than plan a wedding anytime soon. Lucky for him, all of this with Lulu was make-believe.

Alwan didn't know what he'd do if it were actually real.

If we were really getting married.

Staring down at her lovely side profile, he blinked out of his momentary stupor when Lulu suddenly strolled away from him, through the open doors of the pavilion and into the estate gardens.

"Where are you going?" he called after her before hurrying to catch up.

"For a walk," she replied, her strides slow and carefree

as she walked the cobbled path from the pavilion onto the green, well-kept lawn. Drawing her wavy dark hair from her face, she looked back over her shoulder at him and asked, "Are you coming?" Even though she extended the invitation, he had the feeling that either way Lulu seemed determined to take a stroll with or without him.

Glancing around, Alwan followed.

As soon as he fell into step with her, she said, "One thing I've discovered is that a happy wedding doesn't guarantee a happy marriage. Sometimes a fairy tale is just meant for a storybook."

"Was it that bad? Your divorce?" Normally he wouldn't have dared to be so nosy, but there was something about the way she looked just then—sad yet resigned to the fate of her previous relationship—that hooked its claws into him. But considering it wasn't any of his business, Alwan was prepared for her to ignore him, possibly even snap his head off.

Instead of doing either of those things, she bowed her head. "It was…tough. I think it ending was the best for both of us, but obviously most people marry thinking it'll be for a lifetime. At least that's the hope, and we trust it, but sometimes that trust is misplaced."

"That's why I haven't married yet," he said.

Alwan swallowed when her eyes locked onto his. This wasn't where he envisioned their once-harmless conversation heading, but after witnessing her unexpected vulnerability, it not only seemed fair to reciprocate—it felt oddly *right* to do.

"I find it hard to trust others easily, and before you ask, it isn't because a woman tore my heart out and ripped it to shreds. I've been this way for as long as I can remember." He could've left it there. Possibly *should* have, but under

Lulu's watchful gaze, the urge to tell her more pressed in on him, squeezed in from all sides until he burst.

"I told you about how my brother cut communication off with my parents and me. What I didn't tell you is that his silence has made it harder for me to trust others and I resent him for it," he said, speaking so fast, his tongue tripped over some of the words. Breathing deeply, he tried and failed to ease the anxiety tightening his muscles and adrenaline priming him to flee.

Rather than running though, Alwan glanced away from Lulu to the fountain they were standing beside and waited for the regret to slam into him.

For his brain to scream that he'd made a big mistake, and then push him to retract everything he'd just said. *Lie to her. Tell her that none of what I said is true. That I'm not as pathetic as I just made myself out to be.*

"Alwan?" Lulu called to him, her voice rising above his nagging thoughts.

He forced himself to turn his head back to her. And what he expected he didn't see. The pity that he'd been so sure would be present wasn't there. She had nothing but a smile for him, small but full of compassion and sympathy.

"Trust isn't an easy thing to hold, and it's even harder to give away," she said softly, soothing his soul in a way she'd never know...not unless he told her, and he'd said enough today.

Curiously, the weight in his chest he'd grown accustomed to for so long had shifted. *Shrunk*, he realized in shock.

He was lighter. Not entirely freed of the burden tied to the memories of his brother, but no longer shackled all over either. He had Lulu to thank for it.

The irony that he'd *trusted* her with his feelings wasn't lost on him.

Alwan had always thought Lulu was the best option for a fake fiancée for the sole reason that she'd never get swept up in their lies and fall in love with him. But now he was wondering if there was more to his selecting her...

Don't go there.

None of this was real, and pretending otherwise would only end in the kind of trouble and grief he was trying to avoid all along by choosing Lulu.

Needing more of a reminder, he gazed up at the gushing waters of the fountain and said, "I'm doing this because I don't want to hurt my parents too. Everything I'm doing is just to make all of us happy. I don't want them to worry about me..."

"But they *will* be worried, even if we do our best to reassure them that neither of us holds hurt feelings and the decision to end things was mutual. It's just what parents do," she said quietly.

Steel shooting through his jaw, Alwan lowered his head and leveled his eyes on her. "That may be true, but hopefully by that point I should have a successful legal practice. Then I'll tell them the truth, that I have no interest in marriage. At least that way their disappointment might be mitigated."

"Why do I get the feeling that you've thought all of this out from the beginning, even before you considered coming to me with your plan," she observed and raised her brows expectantly.

He flashed her a smile. "Perhaps I did." Before he could say more, his phone buzzed in his pocket. Excusing himself, he regarded the incoming notification and smiled wider, the news in his inbox timely.

"You look pleased," she said, walking away from the fountain to a bench nearby, the blossoming cherry tree beside it offering shady shelter from the midday early May sun. Brushing the pale pink petals off the bench, she sat down and smoothed her hands over her sleeveless white blouse and down the front of her long, belted, denim skirt.

Taking the seat beside her, Alwan said, "Definitely pleased. I'm officially a free agent as of this very moment. Which means that nothing's holding me back from moving forward with my business plans." Quitting his job had been the last obstacle over the past couple weeks since he and Lulu had returned to Toronto, and now that he'd cleared his exit interview with HR, he could put all his drive and passion into opening the doors on his own practice.

Just another thing he owed to Lulu. If she hadn't agreed to this fake engagement, he'd never have considered quitting so soon and so confidently.

And he was beyond appreciative.

Maybe that explained what he was feeling now. Because the longer he stared at her, the more a new kind of heat trickled through his bloodstream. He was already leaning in when he stopped himself forcibly, fastening his fingers around the seat of the bench and using it to ground him, his mind reeling from the powerful, mind-numbing instinct to *kiss* her.

He didn't even want to think about what would've happened had he not gotten control of himself at the last moment.

Mistake narrowly averted, and feeling Lulu's curious eyes on him, Alwan cleared his throat and pasted on a confident smile. He needed to remember that this was temporary. All of it, but most especially his confusing attraction to her. And what better way to remind himself then by diving headlong into the very reason he sought her out.

"Now that my schedule is freer, how would you like to help me find an office for my new business?"

* * *

Lulu was tired and annoyed of being carted all over Toronto to different buildings and venues for a wedding that wouldn't ever be happening. But she wasn't upset at all when Alwan had asked for her assistance in scouting an office for his business venture, even though their search entailed much the same thing.

She supposed the difference was that his goal to establish a business was real.

Our engagement isn't.

It was why she reasoned it was in her best interest to help him. The sooner he set up his practice, the quicker they could end their relationship ruse and move on. Closing this weird, wild ride of a chapter of her life was her sole motivation—

Or that was what Lulu had tried to convince herself all of this was really.

If she was being honest though, deep down she'd just wanted to help Alwan. His professionalism was admirable. His passion for his career inspiring. The fact he had left a prestigious law firm and what was likely a fat paycheck spoke to her on a level most people might not have understood and certainly couldn't appreciate. That *she* might not have gotten until she'd completely flipped her own life a year ago.

He was taking a big risk. The kind that could hurt him… and not just his pocketbook.

Despite their past, and the annoyance that she'd been roped into his engagement scheme, Lulu wasn't heartless enough to let him flounder on his own. By lending a hand, helping out even in this small way, she could be evening out his odds in his business crashing and burning before it even took flight.

Don't lie. You liked him asking for your help.

Lulu quietly admitted that there was that too. Given their not-so-friendly history and past childhood rivalry, she wouldn't have ever imagined that Alwan would value her opinion let alone request it for something that he'd made clear was important to him.

She was still surprised and touched that he had three days and a dozen properties later.

"Now, I know I said this about *all* the other places we've looked at, but I promise this is the one!" the real estate agent announced cheerfully as he walked them down the short hall to the latest space that he was showing them.

"Let's hope it is," Alwan whispered to her, his fatigue unmistakable.

She couldn't blame him. They'd been run off their feet pretend-wedding-planning ever since they'd arrived back to the city together. And if that wasn't enough, Lulu had returned to her job as a staffing consultant at her old recruitment agency. It was her first time working since her yearlong personal leave.

Alwan, on the other hand, had picked up work as a volunteer lawyer for a local youth-serving nonprofit associated with their community masjid. He'd had plenty on his plate, and the fact that he was also generously donating his time, knowledge and skills not only impressed her—it *left* an impression on her. The kind that had her wanting to step up and help him scratch finding an office off his to-do list.

"Isn't it something?" the agent asked, all smiles, before launching into his pitch for the space.

As the agent pointed out key selling points, Lulu admired the large windows and glass partitions on all the three smaller offices, which allowed an uninterrupted flood of natural light into the space. The sunlight was bright on the plain white walls and light gray vinyl flooring, the ceilings high and with exposed ductwork that gave it an industrial feel. The top-notch air-conditioning allayed the heat from the sun's bright rays.

If it had been her choice she would've signed the lease on the space right then and there.

Turning his head this way and that, Alwan surveyed the office space slowly, methodically. Until he finally looked back at her with an unreadable expression and then over at the agent.

"Do you mind giving us a moment to speak?"

Once the agent's shiny leather loafers clacked to the exit and the door closed behind him, Alwan asked her, "Well, what's your honest opinion?"

"I could ask you the same question," she said. "It's not like what *I* think is the deciding factor."

He frowned, looking adorably perplexed. "But it is. That's why I wanted your help."

He stared at her with large, dark eyes, and she was struck by how lost and overwhelmed he appeared.

Sympathy moved her into gently saying, "Alwan, I can't make the decision for you. It...it wouldn't be right. Trust me, you want to be the one choosing where you'll be working from to get your clients the justice they're seeking. Not anybody else. *You*."

"It sounds like you're talking from experience." He crossed his arms, his eyes piercing through the normal shields she held up to the world.

Lulu pulled in a slow breath, anxiety clanging loudly in her head as the conversation turned back on her. Her initial thought was to shut it down and move them back onto the subject of Alwan making his own decisions. But instead of doing that, she said, "When I first considered traveling, it was more of a fantasy I'd play in my head every now and again. A fun daydream to get me through the day.

"After my divorce, the fantasy played nonstop on loop, and that was when I finally decided I'd have to do something about it."

"You bought the motor home," he said with an understanding nod.

"I'd taken half my savings out to do it, then used the rest to budget my expenses on the road."

Lulu swallowed dryly, recalling that nerve-racking moment of her life when she'd put not only money on the line, but all of her hope. It had been one of her toughest choices to leave her work, her friends and family, and everything else she knew and loved in Toronto in the rearview mirror. And she'd had good cause to be concerned because it hadn't been easy being a traveler. There were skills, like doing light maintenance work on her RV, that she had to learn on the go. Terrifying moments like being caught in a powerful storm current in the wilderness that had her questioning her sanity in choosing that path. And then there was the doubt… That small but loud part of her that wondered whether the RV and road-tripping wasn't all just an excuse for her to run away from her real-world problems.

Problems like her failed marriage…

And any chance of starting my own family.

Lulu hugged her arms around her middle, her heart as heavy as the thoughts packed in her head. She shook most of them away when Alwan spoke up, pretended like her mind hadn't been steeped in dark sorrow for a minute there.

"It must have lived up to the fantasy though, otherwise you wouldn't have been gone for a year, and you wouldn't be thinking of going back. You *are* still going back?"

Funny. Now that he asked, she wasn't so sure about her

plans moving forward when her motor home was repaired. And considering she'd only signed up to this engagement charade of his to secure the money for repairs, it made that revelation all the more ground-shaking.

But reminding herself that they weren't standing around there for her, Lulu forced a smile and nodded, hoping that was enough since she didn't think she could lie to his face right then.

"So, the moral is I should trust my gut and go with the choice that's best for me at this moment?"

"Pretty much," she said with feigned cheer.

Lowering his arms from where they were crossed over his chest, Alwan blew a loud breath, his frustration turning down his mouth and etching frown lines over his brow. Swiping his face with both his palms, he groaned, "I wish it made this easier." He heaved another long sigh. "I guess the only way over is straight through. I'm just worried about…" He trailed off, turning his head to the windows and the flood of sunlight streaming into the office space. Stroking at his short beard thoughtfully now, he continued, his voice lower, hoarser, "To be honest, I sometimes wonder if I might not have made a mistake. What if nothing comes from any of this, quitting my job, striking it out on my own…even this ruse with you."

Lulu's breath hitched when he looked back at her.

"What if it amounts to absolutely nothing? What then? Not only will I have let myself down, I'll have disappointed my family, and…and wasted your time with this partnership."

"I can't make you feel better about anything else, but I *can* say that not once have I considered our arrangement a 'waste of my time.'"

He raised his brows and his smile made a reappearance. "You're not just saying that to make me feel better?"

"When have I *ever* gone out of my way to make you feel better?"

"Good point," he laughed, the gusty, unfettered sound of it filling the whole room and fizzing through her. Unable to fight it any longer, Lulu joined in his laughter until his phone interrupted them.

"It's my mom," Alwan said with a small frown. "She and my dad are usually busy with the restaurant this time of day. I hope nothing's wrong."

"The only way you'll find out is by answering," Lulu encouraged.

With a short nod, he did just that. "Salaam, Yumma."

The conversation was short, and mostly in Arabic, but Lulu sensed a friction from the one side she could hear. It only grew more pronounced by the end of the conversation when Alwan grunted, "Yeah, okay. Salaams to you and Abu both. Yes, I'll tell her you said hello."

"What happened?" she blurted, too intrigued to even pretend like she wasn't invested in whatever had transpired between Alwan and his mother.

"Nothing good," he muttered.

Lulu's chest squeezed, her curiosity morphing into apprehension.

"First off, my mom says 'hi,'" Alwan informed her, sighing sharply. "And the reason she called was because tomorrow she'd like us to visit a venue that a friend of hers owns and rents out for events. Apparently, this friend of hers has had a date suddenly open up and is desperate to fill it."

"What's so bad about that?"

"That date that's opened up? It's just about four months from now, on Labour Day."

"Oh, I see." That explained why he'd gotten so worked up about it.

"Don't worry," Alwan assured her. "I already told her we won't do it."

"Why not?"

Eyes widening and his brows snapping up, Alwan said, "Because four months isn't anywhere near the one-year timeline we agreed on to do *this*." He pointed to the cheap but pretty ring on her finger, prompting her to toy with it.

"I know that, and I get at the time that it seemed like a year was what we needed, but do we feel that way now?"

It wasn't like there were very many obstacles in their path. He had quit his job, and they had spent the last few days searching the city high and low for a suitable workspace for him to run his business from. At this rate, it wouldn't be long before he opened the doors on his practice. And by that point, their fake relationship would've come to a natural end. So if that end happened earlier than planned, wouldn't that be even better?

Only Alwan didn't look like he was happy at all.

His scowl darkened his brooding features, his voice a rumble like warning thunder when he said, "It's too soon."

"Four months is quick, yes," she conceded, hastening to add, "*but* hear me out, what if you had your practice ready to go by then?" When she saw his brows knit together, she was hopeful he was considering it.

That hope died when Alwan suddenly sealed the distance between them in a few short strides. Evidently, he had something else on his mind now.

With no time to back away, she stood her ground and peered up at him, his sun-bright brown eyes drowning her in their beauty. Every part of her attuned to his larger-than-life presence, only made more prominent now that he'd gotten up close and personal with her. There wasn't a part of Lulu that Alwan didn't affect. His musky, spicy cologne poured into her lungs and his body heat had her wondering where the AC that had been working just fine up until that point had gone.

She stood motionless when Alwan raised his hand and held it hovering by her cheek, the question in his narrowed eyes clear.

She shouldn't even be thinking it.

Should definitely be walking—no, *running* away from the electrified chemistry sparking between them. A chemistry that absolutely shouldn't exist, and shouldn't be wreaking havoc on her senses and driving out all sensibility from her brain.

We can't.

We really, really *shouldn't.*

But she was, swaying into him, following her instincts completely just like she had when she'd impulsively purchased her RV and then again when she had agreed to Alwan's proposal to be fake lovers. This didn't have to be any different…

Not when all the things in her life that had been carefully thought-out decisions—her marriage and dream to have children—had never panned out the way she had hoped.

If she'd learned anything from her reckless choices, it was that they had worked best for her and ultimately given her the most joy in her life.

And why should it be different with Alwan?

So, without a thought or care for anything but wanting to feel him, Lulu leaned into his big palm and closed her eyes, her face as warm as his hand. And when a sigh fluttered from her lips, she opened her eyes and found him staring at her with heated approval, his thumb caressing her cheek, his smile slow and seductive.

"We're breaking our no-touching rule again, but it feels good, doesn't it?"

She rolled her eyes and mumbled, "Don't ruin it," smiling when Alwan's throaty chuckle set her pulse racing.

"Fine. Let's move up the timeline." He stroked her cheek gently. "But only on the condition that you'll keep helping me."

"All right," she said, eyes closed again, experiencing his soft caresses more viscerally that way, as if his touch was everywhere at once. Lulu could've snuggled her cheek into his hand forever.

Unfortunately, she only had another few minutes before the door to the room clicked open and familiar-sounding clacking shoes came down the short hall. By the time the agent was in view, the only evidence that anything had happened between them was Alwan's toothy grin and her sudden fascination with her shoes.

None the wiser, the agent launched into trying to close them on the property. "The final decision is yours, of course, but I strongly advise that you might not find a better price or a better office—"

"You're right," Alwan cut in, looking toward Lulu and flashing her another sultry smile. "I'll take it."

CHAPTER SIX

As displeased as Alwan was about his parents pushing for the wedding date to be moved up, he was far unhappier that he had to yet again endure a venue tour.

Going to one more of these will kill me, he thought, not certain if he was being serious or not.

But with the way his feet ached in his new slip-on leather loafers, and the summerlike temperature baked him in his lightweight polo shirt, pale blue blazer and tan-colored chinos, Alwan had to assume he might not have been exaggerating completely. Especially when the unseasonably hot wind picked up and it started lightly raining.

The threat of a storm was all the more reason for him to end the tour of the multi-acreage country estate as soon as he was able.

"We'll take it," he announced to Hawa, their tour guide and the owner's twentysomething daughter from what he'd gathered at the beginning of the little excursion.

Recovering from her shock quickly, she smiled brightly and looked between him and Lulu. "Wonderful! If you're decided on a Labour Day wedding, then I'll just have you follow me to the back where we'll fill out some paperwork and accept your deposit."

As Hawa forged ahead, likely moving fast so as they didn't change their minds, Alwan heeded Lulu's pointedly judgy stare.

"What? I didn't see a point of wasting any of our time. It's not like we're actually getting married."

She sucked her teeth. "That's my whole point. We're not getting married, so you could've waited for the tour to end. Now it looks suspicious that you agreed to a venue that neither of us have seen fully. Let's just hope your mother's friend doesn't suspect anything." Then lowering her voice, she grumbled, "I already feel bad about booking a venue for a wedding that won't ever happen."

Alwan smiled sheepishly, though the damage was already done. Hawa ushered them into her office and handed them a couple different forms to read through and fill out together to secure their reception at the venue. Lulu took charge of that, but her irritation with him was palpable.

After the paperwork was done, all that was left was for Alwan to pay the deposit.

Once the payment went through, Hawa beamed and bounced up out of her chair, telling them that her mother would love to congratulate them personally and that she'd fetch her.

"I can see why she's so happy, that deposit had a lot more zeroes than I expected it to. I'll pay you back half of it," Lulu said when they were alone.

He shook his head immediately. "No, you won't. It's the least I can do for rushing through the tour…and I'm not above using the money as a bribe to get you not to be upset with me anymore. So, did it work?"

Alwan only relaxed when Lulu gave him one of her patented eye rolls and finally smiled, her rosy brown cheeks lifting with the gesture, her deep berry purple lip stain popping up against her white teeth and complimenting the warm undertone of her gleaming skin. She'd dressed in a dark tan tunic and trendy mom jeans, the choice of loose-fitting clothing doing little to hide her naturally curvy figure from his suddenly hungry gaze. He raked his eyes over her from her plain white tennis shoes to the top of her curly ponytail, realizing that standing side by side, it almost looked as if they'd purposefully matched outfits...

...like a real couple might have done.

A week ago, that thought might have freaked him out. Now Alwan simply let it sit and marinate in his mind quietly. Before he could make heads or tails of how he felt, Hawa returned with her mother.

"Mr. Eltahir, Ms. Sadiq," she said, "this is my mother, Gisma."

Stylishly dressed in a colorful thobe complete with a matching scarf, and speaking a torrent of arabiyyah with a sprinkling of English here and there, the older Sudani woman embraced them both and every so often would pinch their cheeks affectionately with her henna-tipped fingers.

And that wasn't even the most embarrassing part. He was glad Lulu only understood a handful of Arabic words. It spared him some humiliation.

Smiling and nodding his way through the conversation, he breathed a sigh of relief when Hawa intervened by reminding her mother they had other appointments.

Outside, the weather had taken a turn for the worse, the rain now pouring. Since Alwan had parked his car a little farther down the long drive, Gisma and Hawa offered to fetch umbrellas and wouldn't take a refusal of their hospitality.

Alone once more, Lulu rubbed the cheek Gisma had squeezed and asked, "What were they saying? You looked like you wanted the ground to swallow you whole."

He tipped his head at her amusedly. "Are you sure you want to know?"

"Would I have asked if I didn't?"

"Okay, just don't say I didn't warn you," he cautioned before translating, his face heating up as he did. "Gisma was offering us a blessing, wishing us many grandchildren—'enough to fill a whole house,' specifically." Alwan laughed nervously and avoided looking at Lulu directly as he spoke. Though when she remained silent, he glanced over at her and swore ice pooled into his veins despite the oppressive humidity in the air.

Standing still, Lulu gazed through him, her eyes on him but he could tell she wasn't seeing him. She probably wasn't even *with* him mentally.

"Lulu, what's wrong?" he called, raising his voice to be heard over the rain pounding the pavement.

When she didn't respond, Alwan waved his hand before her face.

She blinked, visibly startling, but the glassiness to her stare was, thankfully, gone.

"Hey, are you okay?"

She didn't answer, just gazed ahead at the long driveway with that distant look in her eyes and bit her lip. Just as he noticed her chin trembling, Lulu started forward, stepping out from under the cover of the porch and striding into the heavy rainfall.

"Lulu!"

He pursued, the whole world fading away as he locked his sights on her fleeing form.

Nothing else mattered to him right then.

Nothing but her.

His heart pounding, Alwan saw Lulu heading for his car and he unlocked the doors so neither of them had to be caught out in the rain for any longer than they'd already been. Not that it mattered. They were both soaking. And normally he'd have cared about what that would mean for his car's premium leather seats, but right then what concerned him more was what happened to have made Lulu take off the way she'd just had. *Was it something I said?*

Knowing that he wouldn't get the answer any other way, Alwan shifted in his seat to look at her fully. He was stung when Lulu quickly turned her head away and looked out through her window, her arms folded over her chest, her body language closed off.

Fine, he thought petulantly, *if she wants to be like that...*

With a hardened jaw, he asked, "Why'd you run, Luula?" When she didn't respond, he curled his hands into fists atop his thighs and forced himself to breathe until he was calmer. Whatever was going on with her wouldn't be helped by his anger. Especially not if he wanted to get her to relax and trust him enough to open up.

And though Alwan didn't understand why, he wanted her trust.

He could *feel* her emotional pain. Recognized it in the way her shoulders hunched and she banded her arms tighter around herself.

He had a flash of a similar scenario, only instead of Lulu seated beside him, it was Hashim.

Rankled by the comparison, Alwan shook that memory out of his head as fast as it resurfaced and before it played fully.

"I can't help you if you don't tell me what's wrong," he softly reasoned with her.

Lulu turned her head slowly back to him.

After staring at him for a while, she murmured, "If you want to help me, then drive. Please."

Shoulders sagging from the letdown, he clenched his teeth and forced an exhale out through his nose. But he did as she asked, started the engine, set the wipers on high and drove away from the picturesque country estate.

Driving through the storm required all his concentration, which, lucky for Lulu, meant that he was too preoccupied keeping them safely on the freeway to grill her on her odd behavior. Though Alwan planned to as soon as he was able. Until then, all he could do was eagerly anticipate that moment as they sat in silence through the first half of the two-hour drive back to Toronto.

When the rain finally did let up, the sun even breaking through the gray clouds, Alwan flung her a quick look and broached the subject again.

"I want to know what happened." No asking this time. No more pleading with her. He deserved an answer, even a vague one. Anything to plug up his worry for her and keep it from spilling out and causing him trouble. Again, he had a flash of his brother's face. Wringing his hands over the smooth leather of the steering wheel, he kept his eyes forward and waited for her to speak.

And waited.

It was only when Alwan had finally accepted that she might not respond, that Lulu whispered, "I'm sorry."

He snapped his head to her, brows raised and voice gruff with confusion. "For?"

"It's not...*easy* for me."

He pressed his lips tightly together and forced himself to simply listen. He sensed Lulu had more to say.

Sure enough, she sighed a soft, shaky note and, for a brief moment, their eyes collided.

"I had a miscarriage— *Alwan!*"

Lulu shrieked his name and pointed ahead to the car that had seemingly come from nowhere and merged in front of him. Arm flinging out to protect her, Alwan braked in time, bringing them to a screeching halt. There was a blaring of horns directly behind him, but no terrifying sound of metal crunching against metal.

Collision evaded, he whipped his head back to her and looked to where she was holding on to the arm he'd used to shield her.

Lulu stared back with wide, petrified eyes.

"You're not hurt?" he asked, feeling her hands squeeze his forearm and breathing in relief when she shook her head slowly. But the solace of knowing she was safe didn't last long.

How could he feel any comfort once he quickly remembered why he'd nearly rear-ended another vehicle?

Learning of her miscarriage had been such a shock that Alwan had taken his eyes off the road and almost sent them both to the hospital.

Though now it made sense. Why she'd run after he'd told her what Gisma had said about them having kids. Even though they both knew this relationship was a mere transactional exchange between them, it didn't mean that being reminded of children when she'd gone through such a loss wouldn't hurt.

"Lulu... I..." He didn't know what to say to her.

Didn't have the first clue as to whether his condolence was even acceptable at this point, or whether his sympathy would only cause more harm than good.

Throat clogged with emotion, Alwan clenched his jaw to hold back his useless words and just stared back at her, frozen with his helplessness.

"I don't want to talk about it, please. I just... I wanted you to know." She lowered her hands from his arm and looked out the window.

Registering the cacophony of car horns behind him,

Alwan stiffly turned his head back to the road and got the car moving again, figuring that it was the only way he could be of use to her right then.

Even if he wished that weren't the case.

Between planning a wedding and trying to get his business plans on track, Alwan should've had more than plenty on his plate.

He certainly shouldn't have been obsessing over Lulu like it was his full-time job. What she did outside their fake engagement pact wasn't any of his business, and he was wholly aware of that before she'd agreed to their deal.

Besides, she didn't seem to care what he was doing. Alwan hadn't seen her since he'd dropped her off at her home after their visit to the country estate venue.

That had been three days ago.

He tried reaching out to her on several occasions, but outside a succinct text or two, Lulu had made it clear that she'd wanted her personal space. And Alwan didn't mind giving it to her, but he wondered if she had needed the break from *him* specifically.

After all, she'd trusted him enough to tell him about her miscarriage. And though Lulu had said nothing more, Alwan was honored that she had offered up that vulnerable part of her. He didn't take her confidence in him lightly…even if he suspected that she was possibly regretting confiding in him.

That's probably why she shut down right after.

And why she was avoiding him now.

I don't want to talk about it, please, she'd requested. It was the sorrow radiating from her that had compelled him to leave well enough alone. She didn't want to discuss the very sad personal thing that happened to her, that was fine by him. He was totally unbothered. Completely. *Entirely.*

At least that was what he had kept repeating to himself unsuccessfully.

Because no matter how he fought it Lulu claimed a good portion of his thoughts lately. And Alwan might have had a smoother time of forgetting what had happened with her had his mother not reminded him of Lulu's absence at yet another one of their wedding planning get-togethers.

"Where is Luula?"

They were sitting at the dining table with his laptop opened between them and a plethora of different-colored and -sized card stock spread out over almost every inch of the tabletop. A self-professed DIY queen, his mother insisted on them making the save-the-dates for the wedding from scratch. It all just sounded like a lot more work for nuptials that weren't really even going to happen—not that he'd told his mother that. Instead, he'd just attempted to talk her out of her plan. But it had been like trying to get blood out of stone. She was adamant to do it her way and persuade him into lending a hand.

And she'd succeeded, no surprise there.

Though if he *had* refused her, then he'd have been spared his mother's version of a third degree now.

Biting back a sigh, Alwan stared at his laptop and said, "She's busy...again."

It was the same excuse from the day before, and any hope he had that his mother wouldn't notice was dashed when she clucked her tongue loudly at him.

She didn't need to say a word. He heard her suspicion-laced disapproval loud and clear.

Obviously, his mother thought *he* was the reason for Lulu's no-show streak. And he couldn't fault her, because he was starting to believe that too.

Not only that, with all this radio silence on Lulu's end,

Alwan had begun secretly worrying she wanted out of their deal. It wasn't a far stretch to believe that she'd changed her mind. He'd promised her a no-strings-attached arrangement, and now that it had gotten more personal than they'd planned, she might have decided to end it.

Despite understanding if Lulu had come to that decision, Alwan still scowled at the possibility. He couldn't recall the last time he'd felt so utterly exhausted and drained on every level and all because of someone else.

It was Hashim, a little voice chimed. His brother was the last person who had made him feel remotely close to what he was feeling now with Lulu. And though it was different, it felt too similar for his comfort.

So, Alwan told himself the only reason he cared was that he couldn't have Lulu backing out of the engagement now. Not when his legal practice was on the line, and not when the shock of the truth would probably destroy the look of bliss on his mother's face as they decorated the save-the-dates together by hand.

Although he and Lulu couldn't avoid the hurt that would inevitably follow when they announced the end of their engagement and wedding plans, they'd already decided how to gently let their families down when the time came.

Four months from now.

Until then she was his fiancée.

Mine.

The possessive claim startled him.

Whoa. Where did that *come from?*

Baffled to his core by that dangerous thought, Alwan hardened his jaw, his body tensing all over from the need to leave his parents' home and go clear his head someplace private. Because under *no* circumstances could he think of Lulu like that again.

She wasn't his.

She'd never be.

And that was how they both liked it.

Liar, the one word curled through his mind like black smoke warning of trouble.

He gritted his teeth and clenched his fists, one around his computer mouse and the other—

"Alwan!"

He startled and looked from his mother's deeply disapproving glare down to the card stock trapped in one of his hands. Loosening his fingers, he tried to smooth out the creases to no avail.

"Sorry," he mumbled, offering her a sheepish smile.

"Something's on your mind." She held up a hand, the irritation gone and stark concern for him creasing her brow. "And please don't say that you're fine. You always say that, and it always means the opposite. Does this have to do with Luula? Is it why she isn't here?"

The lie on his tongue evaporated at the sound of Lulu's name. Tightening his lips, he bowed his head, knowing that if he looked his mother in the eye he'd divulge far more than he wanted to her.

Taking his silence as an affirmative, he heard his mother's deep sigh.

"Whatever you've done—"

"I haven't done anything though," he groused, peeking up at her and grimacing when her glare quickly had him lowering his head again in deference.

"Then why are you sitting here with me, looking so miserable *and* ruining my card stock? Now, do you want my advice or not?"

Alwan knew that she'd be giving it whether he agreed to it or not, so he just nodded.

"Go to her. Talk. Apologize, if you have to, but don't sit here and do nothing. I know you care for her," she said with a pointed look that cautioned him about arguing with her.

Besides, he'd be lying if he didn't want any excuse to see Lulu.

"What about all of this?"

Smiling brightly, his mother stood, gathered the save-the-dates and slid them into his laptop bag. "Think of it as a good excuse to go see her."

Thirty minutes later he showed up at Lulu's childhood home. He hadn't told her he was coming over, uncertain whether his visit would be welcome.

Gripping the strap of his laptop bag, he rang the doorbell and anxiously smoothed a hand over his beard and down his knit sweater. While he waited for an answer, Alwan's gaze swept the unassuming but peaceful neighborhood, a warm smile lifting his cheeks at the memories he had of being there. Although he and Lulu were far from friends, their parents would often visit each other and he'd always liked hanging out with her younger brother, Liban.

This was the first time he was there to see Lulu.

But it was her younger sister, Ladna, who opened the front door.

"She's upstairs," she said to him after a quick, friendly greeting and inviting him in. "She hasn't been feeling well today and hasn't left her bedroom all that much."

He froze, one foot inside, the other on the threshold. He could hear Ladna call his name a couple times, but all that went through his mind was, *Lulu's sick. She's sick and I've been upset with her.* Picturing her lying in bed, delirious from pain and running a fever weakened his knees and unleashed a wave of nausea in him. *Ya Ilahi.* Alwan didn't know how he was still standing under the tremendous weight of guilt threatening to flatten him.

But he remained on his feet, and stepping inside now, barely acknowledged the concerned look on Ladna's face as he hurriedly set down his laptop bag and slipped off his shoes.

Without saying another word, he bounded up the staircase, two steps at a time.

Behind him he heard Ladna calling his name again.

He didn't need her help finding Lulu's room—there was only one with the door closed—and he knocked briskly.

"Luula, open up. It's me," he said, his hands squeezing the doorframe, his eyes lasered on the door as if he could see through the white-painted wood into her room. "Lu—"

The doorknob twisted and the door pulled open wide.

Wearing her pajamas, Lulu stepped back from the doorway, her hands clutching the fleece throw wrapped around her shoulders and her hair covered by a silk cap. She had no makeup on, and her feet were shod in fuzzy slippers with adorable cat ears. *Yet she's still beautiful.*

A vision of her like that in his home flashed through his mind.

"Why are you here?" she asked and snapped him back to focus.

Pushing out the image, Alwan lowered his hands off the doorframe and walked in, noticing that she slid back another couple steps as he did so. His heart twisted in his chest, but he kept the hurt off his face and out of his voice as he looked her over.

"Ladna told me you weren't feeling too hot. I was... I just wanted to check in on you."

Lulu rolled her eyes and sighed. "She shouldn't have worried you. I'm fine. Or I will be, after I take a nap."

A low yowl sounded from behind her. Alwan looked around her to where her cat watched him with those eerily bright blue eyes from the foot of her bed.

Her bed.

The rumpled bedsheets and distinct head print on her pillow fueled a different kind of fantasy, and it was one that had his body's core temperature running hotter. Blushing, Alwan backed out and stammered, "I—I'll just leave you to it, then. Hope you feel better. Have a good nap." And before he embarrassed himself further, he spun on his heels and sped away as fast as he arrived.

After telling him she'd be sleeping, Lulu didn't know what she expected Alwan to do other than to leave.

But his abrupt departure had her tiptoeing out into the hallway and listening in on his conversation with Ladna.

"I'm worried about her," her sister was saying.

"I am too," Alwan said.

Breathing slowly through her nose, Lulu rested her head on the wall, regretting that she'd eavesdropped on them. Because now their concern for her wrenched at her heart and almost made her go downstairs and reassure them she was all right.

But that would be a lie.

Lulu heard the front door close behind them, and as the silence of the house closed in, she wrapped her throw tighter around herself and shuffled in her fuzzy slippers back to her bedroom.

"Don't worry," she told Blue when he lifted his head and looked past her with a meow, like he'd expected Alwan to trail in behind her. Flopping down beside him on the bed, she rubbed between his ears. "He's not coming, if that's who you're looking for. He just left and I don't think he's coming back anytime soon."

Seeing Alwan at her home had shocked her.

Caught her off guard.

Particularly when he'd looked and sounded genuinely sincere about checking on her health.

"He wasn't really worried. He couldn't be," she said to Blue. "He's probably just worried I'd be too ill to parade around and play pretend couple with him. That's got to be it." But even as she spoke, Lulu wasn't fully convinced it was that black-and-white, that utterly clear-cut. It'd help if a part of her hadn't felt all warm and fuzzy when she fantasized about why Alwan might have visited. Had he really stopped by on a wellness check? Why would he do that?

Because maybe he cares what happens to me... Is that so hard to believe?

She didn't know what to think anymore. Her temples began to drum the now-familiar beat of a brewing headache, her lower body squeezing with the stirrings of pain again too. Popping a couple painkillers, she lay back down with the still-warm heating pad pressed below her stomach and smiled at Blue as he took his cue and moved out of the way to curl near her feet.

She closed her eyes and just before sleep overwhelmed her consciousness, Lulu's last thought was of Alwan.

When she awoke, it was exactly an hour later.

Lulu sat up, stretched and yawned, sniffing the air and rubbing her grumbling stomach. The pain medication had done its work, and coupled with the nap, she was feeling better. But now she had her hunger to solve. The mouthwatering scent wafting through from downstairs had her salivating.

Licking her lips, she shrugged at Blue as he hopped off the bed and trailed to the door, clearly enticed by the same delightful culinary aroma. "I guess Ladna's back." She knew it couldn't be her mom and dad; they had been so busy flitting about with Alwan's parents and wedding planning, they hadn't had as much focus on their business and were now playing catch-up with the tasks that had piled up.

Stuffing away the guilt to sulk over later, Lulu grabbed her fluffy bathrobe off the back of her computer chair and strolled out into the hall.

She and Blue followed the delicious scent down the staircase, past the small entrance hall through the open living and dining area, and into the kitchen beyond—where Lulu came to an abrupt halt.

Because rather than finding her sister cooking, Alwan was standing there stirring a pot on the stovetop.

She almost rubbed her eyes in disbelief. "Alwan?"

"Oh, good. You're awake." Casting a smile over his shoulder, he opened the cupboards above the counter and pulled down two bowls. "Your timing is perfect because the chicken soup's ready."

Lulu didn't know what was more shocking. That he was responsible for the delectable smell wafting through the whole house, or that he knew the kitchen well enough to know where her parents stashed their china. Not that any of that explained why he hadn't left like she'd assumed he had.

"What are you doing here?" It wasn't the first time that day she'd asked him that, but this time Lulu struggled for a reason to explain his presence. "And why are you wearing my mom's apron?"

Facing her, Alwan swept a hand down the heart-shaped top half of the frilly laced apron. "Are you saying it doesn't suit me? Because I really thought this sunny yellow brought out my eyes."

He grinned when she folded her arms and huffed.

"Okay, not in the mood for jokes, I see. I'm here because

Ladna suggested I should stay and keep an eye on you while she was out."

"I bet she did," Lulu grumbled, making a note to have a chat with her meddlesome younger sister.

"Don't be too harsh on her. She's just worried about you. Actually, we both are." Brows creased now and his smile dimmed, Alwan moved a step closer.

Still at her feet, Blue growled.

Shooting a nervous glance down at her snarling cat, he stopped.

"Why don't we sit down and have the soup before it gets cold?" he suggested, already spinning back to the pot on the stovetop. Acting like this homey scene that was playing out was the most normal thing ever, he stirred the chicken soup with a ladle, waving his hand over the curling steam and sighed. "Smells like it's ready. Want a bowl?"

Stunned by how all of this was unfolding, Lulu bobbed her head slowly and watched him place two bowls of soup onto one of her mother's silver serving trays.

Switching off the stovetop, he placed a lid on the pot and then hauling the tray up carefully, walked toward the dining table, but not before slinging her a sunny smile. "Food always tastes better sitting down. At least that's what my mom says."

Never had Lulu been more nonplussed in her life.

First, he dropped in for an unplanned visit. Then he cooked for her. *And now?* Now he was acting like a consummate gentleman.

Lulu looked down to Blue, who meowed up at her and lashed his puffed-up tail. Dropping to her haunches, she gave his back and tail a couple long strokes and whispered, "Should we trust him?" Her stomach gave a low answering rumble, reminding her that her hunger was at stake. "On second thought, I guess we have no choice," Lulu said, and Blue chirruped back with what she presumed was a warning to be cautious.

Though the dining table seated six, Alwan arranged two place mats beside each other. Not wanting to be rude, Lulu pulled out the chair by him and sat down. But she'd barely picked up the spoon by her bowl before Alwan sprang back up.

"Oops, forgot something. Where's your cat food?"

Confused, Lulu said, "In the pantry. Why?"

"I fed you. It's only fair that I feed the little beast too," he said, his charming grin drying up any urge she had to scold him for calling her cat a "beast."

Yowling, Blue kept a far distance from Alwan, but he didn't hesitate to creep up to his food bowl and dig into his favorite wet cat food the second Alwan stepped back.

"Maybe I was wrong about you, Beast?" Alwan stroked Blueberry's back but tugged his hand out of harm's way when her cat lifted his head and bared his fangs at him. "Or not…"

Lulu sucked in her lips to stifle her laughter, managing to suppress any trace of humor by the time Alwan rejoined her at the table. Feeling his warmth beside her again had her wanting to squirm, and needing something to do, Lulu feigned an inordinate interest in the soup before her.

But she paused with the spoon hovering in front of her mouth when she felt Alwan's unrelenting stare.

"This isn't poisoned, is it?"

His only response was a deep, sexy chuckle, but she took it as a positive sign when he dove into his own bowl.

They ate in silence for a while, but once their bowls were cleared, Alwan leaned closer to her, his features lined with anxiety. "Was it good?"

"I finished it, didn't I?"

"Good," he said murmured, exhaling and flashing her a relaxed smile. "I'm glad. I wasn't sure if chicken soup was the right way to go, but I assumed since you weren't feeling well, it might help. And hopefully it has." He rushed out the last part, his face tensing up again.

My opinion really matters to him. That knowledge had Lulu's heart fluttering just a bit faster. "It's only my period, Alwan. It's not that serious."

He rubbed a hand over his beard, what she now recognized was his nervous little tell. "Oh. Was the soup a bad choice, then?"

"No, it was a good choice. Thank you," she said, knowing he was blushing by the way he smiled shyly and ducked his head.

Again, it struck Lulu that her gratitude affected him so strongly. She'd never have believed it would, but she couldn't deny it either now that she could see it for herself. Of all the people she'd have thought would care about what she thought and how she felt, Alwan would be her last guess. He'd always come off as self-centered to her, so completely absorbed in his own world—it was hard to talk to him without his ego taking up breathing space. Sometimes, it'd even felt as if he'd done it on purpose. *Like he hadn't wanted anyone to get close.*

Lulu studied him while he had his head lowered, intrigued by who he'd turned out to be these last few weeks as her fake fiancé.

He was nothing like the bratty boy she'd thought he was once. Nothing like the man she'd written him off to be.

Whoever he was now had earned a level of trust from her that most people in her life didn't have. Not even her family. Because aside from her doctor, Alwan was one of only two people in the world who knew about her miscarriage.

The other person being her ex-husband.

There was no logic behind telling Alwan. No explanation as to why she'd done what she had, only that it had felt *right* sharing her loss with him.

That same feeling took hold of her now, and before she knew it, Lulu cleared her throat softly to grab his attention.

Alwan lifted his head.

"I didn't really expect you to still be here. I...haven't *exactly* been holding up my end of our contractual relationship lately, and, uh, well, I wouldn't be surprised if you wanted to back out of this—"

"That won't happen, ever."

Lulu pulled in a sharp breath at the vehement glint in Alwan's narrowed eyes and the gravel now roughening his deep voice.

"Unfortunately, you're stuck with me," he said, his stare intensifying with every one of her heartbeats. "At least until the end. Until we've both decided we're done."

A dragging beat of silence passed, and then he asked, "Are we done, Luula?"

Eyes wide and lips parted, she shook her head slowly.

"Good. Will you help me clear the table, then?"

Still having trouble finding her voice, Lulu gave him a nod and trailed him into the kitchen. They cleaned up quietly for the most part, but near the end, he looked over at her.

"You are feeling better, right?"

"I am." Wiping down the counter, Lulu hazarded a peek at him. "Just so you know, you don't have to be worried about me. None of this pain I'm going through is new."

"I figured it couldn't be. You seemed to be able to handle it at the restaurant," he reminded her.

"Yeah, I've gotten better at coping. Only because for as long as I remember, my body's been this way, so I'm pretty used to it. My official diagnosis is lean PCOS. The awful cramps, the bloating, nausea, dizziness, headaches and mood swings." Lulu stopped wiping, her fingers digging into the cloth in her grasp, her eyes glued to the now spotless counter. "The only part I've never been able to handle is the infertility issues…and the higher risk of miscarriage."

She heard Alwan's deep inhale right before he said, "We don't have to talk about this."

Stung that it felt like he was shutting her down, Lulu looked up, her brows knitted and a frown pulling down her mouth. "Is this about what happened in your car a few days ago? Because if you're upset—"

"God, no." Alwan pushed off the counter he'd been leaning on, walked over to her and, pulling the cleaning cloth fisted in her grasp free, tossed it aside. Then took her hand. Kneading her fingers softly with his, he gazed down into her eyes and said, "If you want to talk about it, then I'm all ears. But don't feel like you owe it to me. The only thing that happened in the car was that you were protecting yourself, as you should. Don't *ever* apologize for that. Not ever."

Lulu blinked, the heat creeping from the back of her eyes summoning tears.

He squeezed her hand, and she quietly gripped him back.

"I—I want to talk about it."

"Okay," he said and then stood there silently and patiently waiting for her to speak her mind.

It took her a moment, but she stoppered the waterworks and successfully cleared most of the hoarseness from her voice. "Losing the baby was always a strong possibility. But Mohamed and I, we still wanted to try."

"Mohamed's your ex, right?"

She nodded, quietly clocking how Alwan's dark eyes narrowed, his strong jaw stiffened and he jerked his head in understanding.

"We both knew that it wouldn't be easy or fast, and that we'd need to exercise a lot of patience. IUI and IVF weren't also options, not with our finances. And the publicly funded waitlist would've had us waiting years before getting a chance. Mohamed was hopeful we wouldn't need to go those routes, and I... I let his hope carry us both away.

"We waited three years and a handful of chemical pregnancies before, finally, it happened. A positive. A real one this time.

"We were both so happy," she said, looking down to where Alwan held her, his thumb drawing lazy circles on her hand, his fingers gently squeezing now and again.

"I let Mohamed talk me into shopping for the baby. Toys, clothes, we even started planning how to tell everyone. We were only seven weeks along. We should've known not to get carried away. Should've known to dial it down. It all just felt too good to be true. Too good to be *real*.

"A few days later, we lost the baby. And a little more than a month after that, Mohamed and I decided to file for our divorce."

"Luula," Alwan rasped her name, his fingers gripping hers. "I know no words in the world can convey my condolences, but I am sorry. Sorry that you couldn't be the mother you'd dreamed to be. Sorry that you had to endure a pain no one should go through. Sorry that you couldn't hold your child in your arms.

"I wish I could say I was sorry that your relationship ended, but no man—*no* life partner worthy of that title—would've let you go, not then, not when you needed support the most. I'm glad this Mohamed walked off when he did.

He didn't deserve you from the start." Alwan interlaced their fingers and stared down at her as fiercely and passionately as he stated his thoughts.

Lulu pushed the numbness back from taking complete hold of her and looked up at him with a weary smile.

"It's not his fault. It was just…too much for him to handle. I can't blame him for that."

Scowling, Alwan still appeared unconvinced.

As touched as she was that he was incensed on her behalf, she knew that it wouldn't change what had happened. And she hadn't told him any of this just to drag him down into the same dark headspace she'd felt trapped in for so long. It wasn't a place she would've wished on anyone, least of all him.

Lulu pressed the hand he wasn't holding to his warm, solid chest.

Alwan immediately lifted his free hand and clasped hers over his heart.

"Does your family know about your loss?"

She shook her head. "I don't want to worry them…"

Alwan's fingers massaged the back of her hand soothingly.

They didn't speak, just held on to each other for what felt like forever. If it weren't for Blue meowing loudly at their feet and redirecting their attention, Lulu didn't know if they would have moved apart anytime soon. She'd been too comfortable letting Alwan hold her—far too relaxed in touching him right back.

Don't confuse his kindness with something else.

Heeding her own warning, Lulu drew back. Alwan let her go.

"I should probably head back upstairs and rest," she said.

"Are you feeling unwell again?" he asked, his expression flipping to concern in the blink of an eye.

"I'm fine, I promise. Just a little sleepy. Nothing a nap won't cure."

"If you're sure…"

"I am," she said, flashing him a quick smile.

"Okay then, I'll take that as my cue to get out of your way now. And before I forget, here." He pulled her family's house key from his pocket and passed it to her. Seeing her questioning look, he explained, "Ladna gave me her spare, and I went grocery shopping for the ingredients to the soup. I let myself back in with it."

Somehow that knowledge only tugged at her heartstrings more… *If that's even possible.*

"I'll walk you out."

"Sure," he agreed, turning and heading for the front door.

At the entrance, he stopped suddenly and grabbed a slim messenger bag that was tucked between the coatrack and the shoe stand. "I almost forgot. My mom wanted you to have these." Opening the bag, he pulled out a small stack of decorative, delicate-looking cards. A cursory look told Lulu they were save-the-dates. As odd as it was to see her and Alwan's full names on the card, announcing a wedding they both knew would never happen, she had to admit that the cards were uniquely beautiful.

"These are really pretty."

Alwan smirked. "My mom will love hearing that because we made them."

"Sorry, *you* helped make these?" Lulu couldn't believe it. First he cooked, and now this. She wasn't used to complimenting him, figuring his ego never needed more stroking, but even she had to admit that she was in awe of his hidden skills.

"I'm a man of many talents," he preened.

She sighed and shook her head, but she struggled not to smile when Alwan laughed.

"So, take a look at the cards whenever you're ready and let us know what you think." He pulled his shoes on and backed up to the front door, his hand grasping the door handle. "Other than that, uh, I hope you feel better soon. So, um, bye." He gave her a little awkward wave, his smile bordering on bashful as he opened the door and walked out onto the porch.

"Alwan?" Lulu called after him just as he cleared the last step down the porch.

"Yeah?" he asked, lifting his hand to shield his squinting eyes from the sun and looking back up at her.

"Thanks for visiting. It was surprisingly nice."

"Surprisingly?" he laughed and lowered his hand.

Laughing too, she said, "Maybe we can meet up tomorrow and I can give you my thoughts on the cards."

"I'd like that."

Closing the door, and still smiling after their exchange, Lulu turned and looked down to where Blue was peering up at her curiously.

"Don't judge me. He did feed us both, so he can't be that bad, right?"

Meowing, Blue stalked over to her and rubbed against her leg.

Picking up her attention-seeking cat, Lulu carried him upstairs, back to their bedroom where she dropped him gently onto the unmade bed. Purring his satisfaction, Blue kneaded the bedsheets, settling himself down and looking at her as if wondering why she hadn't joined him yet.

Only there was one thing she wanted to do before lying down.

Lowering to her knees, she lifted up the bed skirt and,

searching in the darkness under her bed, found what she was looking for.

The small suitcase wasn't anything special on the outside. But it was what was inside that mattered to her.

Placing her hands atop it, Lulu pulled a deep breath in and out before she pinched the zipper and opened the luggage slowly. Her eyes stung as she pushed back the lid and stared down at the brand-new tiny clothes inside. There were even a couple toys, their packaging undisturbed. She counted to ten before her vision blurred and her hands groped at the lid to close the suitcase.

Pushing it back where she'd pulled it from, she climbed onto her bed and lay down, sniffling quietly.

Blue's wet nose brushed her cheek, his whiskers tickling her.

"It's all right," she said, tucking him beside her and petting him.

And it was. Those hadn't been empty words. She *did* feel better given what she'd just bravely done. Since packing those clothes and toys away a little more than a year ago, Lulu hadn't looked at them again.

But now, not only had she managed to do that, she wasn't spiraling into that awful darkness that had once taken hold of her life right after her loss. And though Lulu wouldn't attribute it to her conversation with Alwan completely, she had a feeling that it played a big role. Talking to him had been far more therapeutic than she could have ever imagined.

He really isn't so bad after all.

More than that, Lulu had to admit she was taking a strong liking to Alwan with every day that passed.

CHAPTER SEVEN

FOR A BIG CITY, Toronto had green spaces spread throughout the metropolis, and Lulu was immensely grateful for it now as she dropped onto her back and sprawled out her limbs on the picnic blanket beside Blueberry.

Her persnickety cat kneaded the spot beside her before settling his rump down and yawning.

She might have joined Blue in taking a nap if they weren't in the heart of busy High Park. Even if the constant foot traffic didn't keep her awake, or the possibility of being robbed, the knowledge that Alwan would be arriving any moment left her too wired to do anything else but wait out the time until he showed up.

It had been a little over a month since he'd stopped by her home to check in on her and ended up making soup for her. *Oh, and feeding Blue.* She couldn't forget that. All of it had been so uncharacteristic. So unlike what she'd expected him to do. His thoughtfulness was at odds with the vanity he'd always shown her.

In fact, Lulu was beginning to wonder if she'd even really *known* him at all.

Because over the past month he'd ramped up his generosity. Scheduling their meetings around her lunch breaks from work rather than his, letting her choose the places where they'd meet up and even treating her regularly to her favorite flavored iced latte. She didn't know what to make of his small shows of kindness. Was he being nice for some ulterior motive, or was it something else?

Something like how he feels sorry for you because of you-know-what...

Pressing her palms over her tightening chest, Lulu shut her eyes and breathed out deeply. She'd accepted that it was possible Alwan was handling her delicately now after everything she had shared with him. Overcompensating with his kindhearted acts because he didn't know what else to do. And if that was the case, she couldn't fault him for simply being considerate. It wasn't as if he'd signed up to be her therapist.

Just my fake fiancé, she thought dryly.

Opening her eyes, Lulu sighed long and deep, feeling the stony weight of it reverberate through her bones. She wanted to regret telling him all that she had, but just like being unable to be irritated with his overfriendliness, she couldn't find it in herself to do that. Because regardless of whether he felt sorry for her or not, Lulu felt better having confided in Alwan about losing her baby and how that led to her divorce. The emotional burden of carrying that baggage around wasn't so hefty now.

Which brought her to this point: as fake as their relationship was, it didn't lessen the very real comfort he'd given her by just listening.

For that, she owed him.

And not liking the weight of that debt, Lulu had devised a way to settle the score.

She pulled out her phone and searched his name. Just like all the other times she'd done this over the last several days, Lulu didn't have to scroll far to find the viral video of Alwan being assaulted by his former client. She'd watched the long clip several times, even seen shortened versions specifically focusing on the exact moment Alwan was hit in the chest by an array of lobbed pastries to the tune of funny circus music and laugh tracks.

Though he hadn't spoken too much about it, and had even acted like it hadn't bothered him, this video was what had inspired him to seek her out.

It was what started all of this for them both.

So, it couldn't be easy for Alwan to accept its existence. But now that he was on this path to a new venture, she presumed that he'd have to want closure, and to do that he'd have to talk about it.

That was where Lulu was hoping to return the favor.

This is how I can help him the way he helped me.

She paused the video on a clear frame of Alwan's shocked face just after he'd been attacked, and just stared and stared at him, her heart squeezing in sympathy and her thoughts carrying her away.

That was how she missed Alwan's arrival until his smooth, deep voice came out of nowhere.

"What are you looking at?"

She yelped, quickly shut off her phone, snapped upright to a seated position and whipped her head over to where he stood behind her. He had his shoulder propped against the large oak tree that she'd placed her outdoor blanket beneath, his laptop bag slung over the other shoulder, and he held a drink tray containing two cups.

Ready to defend her, Blue sprang to his paws, his tail bushy, back arched and fangs bared.

"Whoa, hey, I come in peace." Alwan pushed off the tree and despite his adorable grin, he eyed a hissing Blue warily. "Should I be worried he's going to attack?"

"Blue wouldn't hurt a soul, but it would serve you right if he did with the way you're sneaking around and jump-scaring us like that," Lulu said with a sniff, gathering her cat into her arms just in case she was wrong this one time.

He laughed. "You can't call it *sneaking* if you weren't paying attention to your surroundings. Now, what were you staring at on your phone that had you so interested you didn't hear me coming up behind you?"

"Nothing," Lulu squeaked, blushing. She wasn't about to confess that she'd been snooping on him online. *Nuh-uh. No way.*

"Really? It didn't look like nothing. But, okay, keep your secrets." His smile unbudging, he shrugged and passed her one of the drinks from the tray.

Lulu bundled Blue into one arm, accepted her iced coffee from him and murmured her gratitude. She drank a big gulp and sighed happily, the cold caffeine jolt already working its magic on her frayed nerves after Alwan nearly caught her spying on him.

"I'll take that as a sign I didn't mess up your order," he said, enjoying a sip from his own cup before he sat down beside her on the blanket, his thigh brushing up against hers. The scent of him, all toasted warmth and spiced earth, enveloped her and restoked the heat simmering under her skin. *Well, there goes my composure.* And so much for the coffee icing the fluttery feelings Alwan inspired in her more and more of late.

"So, what's up?" Lulu asked, sounding a little pitchy from her nerves. It was just that they weren't supposed to be meeting this early today. Instead, they'd had plans to see each other in the evening at his parents' home, where apparently his mother had some traditional Sudanese thobes she'd wanted Lulu to choose from for the nikah ceremony.

Not that a nikah would be happening. But they had pretenses to keep up, so Lulu had no choice but to show up.

None of that explained why Alwan had called to see her.

And it wasn't helping calm her when he scrubbed a hand over his bearded jaw and slung her an apologetic smile.

"Have I told you how much I appreciated you helping me find an office? Because I did, *and* I'm going to need your help again," he said.

"With?"

"A dinner."

Recalling how tasty his soup had been and how comfortable he'd appeared working in her parents' kitchen, Lulu frowned and tipped her head to the side. "You want me to help you make dinner?"

"Well, yes, I wouldn't mind the extra hands if you're offering. But that's not it. Do you remember how I told you that I'm trying to tap into my parents' network of contacts? They have friends and acquaintances within their business circles who could be potential clients for my practice."

Lulu nodded. "I haven't forgotten. It's the whole reason why *this*—" she gestured between them "—is even a thing."

"You mean you don't *actually* want to marry me?" Alwan touched a hand to his chest, his gorgeous features twisting into mock hurt. "Really hurting a guy here, Lu."

She blushed at the easy, affectionate way he'd used her nickname. It rolled off his tongue so naturally and softened her heart for him in a way it shouldn't have, but did anyway. Her body suddenly warmer, she pretended to be occupied trying to keep Blue away from sniffing curiously at her iced coffee. Juggling her cat and coffee, she asked, "What's dinner got to do with anything?"

"One of my parents' acquaintances reached out after they introduced us. He's the former Crown counsel for the Toronto Region, and now runs an internationally successful biotech start-up."

"Sounds like a man who should have a well-heeled litigator on retainer."

Alwan's twinkling eyes and laughter heated her up faster than any hot mid-June afternoon could ever. "You're on my wavelength. This dinner is my chance at pitching him, so everything has to be perfect."

"And when is this perfect dinner happening?"

"A few weeks from now. Though he's from the city and has a home here, he travels a lot for his business and is only going to be stopping by the city for a day or two. Only problem is that my one shot to meet with him is on the evening of Canada Day." He gave her a grimace before rushing to add, "I'll understand if you've already made plans to celebrate with your family or just want the day off to relax. It's not like our contract stipulates that I take up your holidays too. I'll just tell him that something came up and you couldn't make dinner because of it."

"He knows about me?"

"My parents told him about the engagement."

"Oh, of course," Lulu said, not certain why she was so disappointed by that news, or even why she'd leaped to the conclusion that Alwan had cared enough to mention her to this wealthy businessman he was trying to bag as a client. Smiling off the awkward pause, she asked, "Are your mom and dad going to join us?"

"No, the restaurant is open on Canada Day and it's one of their busiest times of the year. But my mom has offered to help me cook." He cocked his head to her with a smirk. "Also, did I just hear you say 'us'?"

"You did."

Lulu bit her lip to stifle laughter when Alwan pumped his fist and hooted his exuberance. A couple runners jogging past tossed them amused looks.

"People are staring at us," she observed, the laugh she was trying to hold in sparkling out. "Are you really that happy that I'm coming?"

"Of course I am! Listen, I didn't say this earlier because, well, my ego."

She snorted and he grinned.

"*But* now that you've said you're going to come through, I'll be honest and say that I'm a little nervous. Okay, fine, *a lot* nervous, but it'll feel good having someone else with me. You know, in case I choke or anything. Not that I mean I'll choke on dinner, hopefully. But you know—"

"Alwan?"

"Yeah?"

"You're rambling," she said with a kind smile at his obvious anxiety over this important business meeting. "It'll go smoothly, with or without me."

"For sure," he said with a nervous-sounding chuckle and a tug at his collar. "Gotta think positively, right? Right. Anyways, we're good for dinner on Canada Day at my place?"

Lulu was mid-sip her coffee and nearly spat it out in her hurry to blurt, "Your place?"

"Is that a problem?"

Yes!

"N-no, it's just, I thought it would be at your parents' home."

"Since they're working, I didn't want to bother them, and besides, I have a perfectly good place of my own to play host. Was that all, or is something else bothering you?"

Yes, the idea of us being together alone, in your home, definitely *bothers me.* Even if they had been alone together before, it was only that every time that happened they ended up getting close emotionally, physically... Then she always was left with these uncomfortable feelings she was clueless what to do about.

But seeing that Alwan was waiting on her, she offered him a reassuring smile. "Nope, I'm all good," she lied, hoping the little squeak at the end didn't give her away.

Appearing not to notice, Alwan beamed at her.

"We're solid, then. Dinner at mine."

From an early age, Lulu had always known there was a great disparity in wealth between her family and Alwan's. The gap in financial standing never kept their parents from being close friends though, and so Lulu liked to think of herself as being desensitized to the big houses, flashy cars and designer clothing labels.

And yet, even with all that said, she had a hard time picking her jaw up from where it landed on the gleaming terrazzo flooring when she stepped out of the private elevator and into Alwan's luxury condo for their Canada Day dinner.

Leaving her shoes in the built-in shoe cabinet by the elevator, she walked in slowly, turning her head every which way at the wealth oozing from the walls and furnishings.

The tall, elegantly coved ceilings, beautiful modern light fixtures, expensive-looking artwork and vases would've made this feel like a museum, but there were plenty of touches of greenery, the plant life adding warmth to the space along with several windows bringing in an abundance of sunlight. Lulu gawked at it all, feeling the affluence on a level she'd never anticipated.

It struck her that he lived on a totally different world.

Make that a different galaxy, she thought as she strolled past open French doors into the kitchen and was met by marble floors and walls, a bevy of state-of-the-art appliances, built-in closets and an impressive island with a dark wood base.

"Hey, you made it." Alwan came up behind her, giving

her a little startle that was instantly wiped away when he reached for the reusable grocery bags in both her hands.

"Here, let me get those for you," he said.

Though it was only a brief touch, his fingers skimming hers left a tingle with her long after he moved away and began unloading the bags on the island. There was milk, eggs, oil as well as all kinds of fruits and vegetables, seasoning, and finally small bags of rice and flour. Once her parents had learned about the business dinner Alwan was hosting, they'd insisted on chipping in with what they could.

He whistled, his eyes widening in awe. "Whoa. Your mom and dad really went above and beyond. Are you sure they're all right without me paying? Because I'd be more than happy to."

"They know," she said, smiling and walking to the other side of the island across him. "But they were adamant that I bring everything we *could* need for the dinner over here."

Scratching his head, Alwan looked around at the groceries overflowing his island counter. "There is no way we'll be using all of this though."

"I think that's what they were hoping. Knowing them, they're probably worried your fridge is empty, what with the bachelor lifestyle you live. You're just lucky I talked them out of emptying all their shelves and unloading most of their inventory on you."

He laughed before clapping and rubbing his hands together. "Well, then, I guess we better make this the best dinner ever. Don't want to disappoint anyone." Turning to the wall of pantry cabinets, Alwan pulled open one of the cabinet doors and fished out an apron. He passed it over to her and their fingers brushed again, that electric spark dancing through the light contact once more.

"Your dress is too beautiful to ruin," he said with another of his toe-curling, heart-racing smiles.

"What about you?"

He looked down at his plain long-sleeved shirt and light-wash jeans. "I dressed to make a mess. In other words, I should be good until I change for dinner later."

It struck her that it was the first time she'd seen him looking so casual. Usually he was stuck in one of his suits, and though he was dressed down, he still looked good. *Real good.* Had she ever noticed his biceps before? Because she was looking now and with every flex of his muscles, she felt her mouth grow drier, her breath quicken and her body tighten all over with longing.

Giving her head a shake, Lulu realized Alwan had asked her a question.

His small smirk told her that he'd caught her ogling him.

She steeled herself for his taunting, but instead of poking fun, he gestured to the groceries and asked, "Would you help me put some of this away in the fridge? It's not like many places are open today, and I don't want anything spoiling on us. This dinner has to go smoothly if not perfectly."

"Speaking of dinner, what are we making?" She placed her purse down on one of the sleek leather barstools along the island and, tying the apron around her long-sleeved light green maxi dress, looked around and raised an eyebrow at him. "Also are we waiting on your mom?"

"About that. She's not coming anymore." He then explained how the restaurant was even busier than his parents had been prepared for and that because one of their sous-chefs was out sick, his mother had no other recourse but to stay.

Letting it sink in that it was just going to be the two of them, alone, in his home, Lulu tried and failed to quell the little shivery excitement chasing up her spine.

"Is that okay with you? Or do we need to fetch your little beast to guard you from me?"

She placed her hands on her hips. "Blue is neither a beast nor my guard. Anyway, I don't need one. I've got my own claws."

"Feisty. Are you so sure about that?" Setting down a head of lettuce, he stalked around the counter to her, his long fingers trailing along the edge of the island, his dark brown eyes now hooded and fixed on her and his smile a slow, seductive pull of his thick brown lips.

"What are you doing?"

"What do you think that I'm doing?" He stopped before her, drumming his fingers on the granite countertop, that stupid, sexy grin of his making her weak in the knees.

"S-stop teasing me," she stammered and hugged her arms tighter to her chest.

He lowered his head, the space between them growing that much smaller as he whispered, "I'll stop when *you* stop making it so fun. Until then…" Trailing off purposefully, his gaze lowering to her mouth, Alwan moved in—his intent as clear as the day pouring in through the windows.

He's going to kiss me!

Breath hitching at the thought, she shut her eyes instead of shoving him away or running off.

But it wasn't a kiss she experienced.

It was the feel of air brushing along the side of her face. She snapped her eyes open and whirled around once she saw Alwan wasn't standing in front of her any longer. He was strolling toward the fridge, the lettuce back in his hand.

She sputtered quietly, her face heated, her irritation with him warring with her yearning for the kiss he'd denied her. That kiss he clearly never meant to give her, by the way he grinned mischievously at her from the open fridge doors.

"So, fiancée of mine, are you ready to cook with me?"

* * *

"I have to say that was the best dinner I've had in months. The downfall of globe-trotting, I'm afraid. But my compliments to the chef stand." Abdel, the Sudani businessman Alwan had invited into his home, now gestured to Lulu across the table from him.

His smile was as warm as his robust laugh when Lulu quickly corrected him. "As much as I'd love to take credit, Alwan made most of the food. I just contributed the sambusas."

"She's being modest," Alwan said, looking to her and taking in the heightened color in her glowing brown face. *Lovely* didn't begin to capture her attractive qualities to him, but it was a fair attempt. "She helped me out with quite a bit. In fact, I'd go as far to say that this dinner couldn't have happened without her."

Lulu's eyes flashed wide-open, her lips parting with her shock.

"It was a team effort, then," Abdel cut in, the older man nodding.

"A team effort," Alwan echoed before he turned back to regard their guest. "You said it best, sir."

Wagging a thick finger at him, Abdel said, "I thought I warned you not to call me 'sir.' Makes my already old bones feel older."

"With all due respect, sir, my parents would roll over if they heard me call you by your name. It's either sir, sayidi or ustadh."

Abdel barked another laugh and slapped his hand down over the dining table. "Very well. I'll acquiesce to the honorific, but only for the dessert I know you've both made."

"I'll get it," Lulu said cheerfully, standing before Alwan could. And when he tried to offer a hand to clear the table, she shook her head and gave him a surreptitious look complete with a little jerk of her chin toward Abdel. It dawned on him that she was trying to give him an opportunity to talk shop with the older businessman.

When Lulu left to fetch dessert, Alwan breathed deeply and, feeling braver, leaned forward.

Though threads of white coiled through his short, curly hair, Abdel's gaze was sharp as a blade as he assessed him quietly.

"I see it's come time to discuss business, then," he said, surprising Alwan when he raised a hand. "Before you rush and give me a long-winded speech extoling all your merits, I'd like to ask you something. Are you serious about opening your own legal practice?"

"Of course," Alwan replied quickly, the answer coming to him easily. Right now, right then, he wanted nothing more than for his private practice to take off and do well. It was why he was here. Why Lulu was by his side. Compelled by the thought of her, he flicked a glance over to where she worked in the kitchen. And just one look at her and his heart jolted faster, his cheeks warming up when he turned back to Abdel and found the older man looking back at him with a small knowing smirk.

"And that, right there, is why I'm asking." Abdel nudged his head to the kitchen with a hoarse chuckle. "I recognize that look because I've seen it on my own face whenever I'm near my wife.

"It's no wonder, then, that when I'm asked what I attribute my success to that I always answer with her name. Despite my late work nights, my overly filled schedule and the last-minute meetings interrupting our plans, she remains my main pillar of support even after almost fifty years of marriage. In fact when I told her about this dinner, she wanted to be here, but she's helping our daughter care for our first grandchild.

"Now, the reason I'm telling you this is because you remind me of myself when I was young, enterprising and so sure that I could juggle every aspect of my life smoothly. You're about to be married though, and from what I see, you care for your fiancée very much and she feels the same for you."

Alwan was stunned into silence. Was he being that obvious about his affection for Lulu? This baffling, bone-deep need to look at her, be around her and soak in all the attention she was willing to give him reading so clearly to everyone else but him.

And was what Abdel said about Lulu true?

Does she care for me too?

Alwan glanced over at her, the urge too strong to ignore or tamp down even as he looked back at Abdel and asked, "Are you saying all this because you're not interested in working with me?"

The older man shook his head. "What I'm saying is that I want you to seriously consider the sacrifices running your own business will require. Your parents have spoken highly of you…but also of your ambition. From personal experience, I wouldn't advise it's the best trait for a marriage." Abdel paused and looked over to the kitchen and Lulu again. "But in regard to business, I like that your practice, much like my own company's medical technology, intends to help those who our laws and society don't always empower. Yes, your parents told me that part too," he said with a benevolent smile. "Which is why, as a family man myself, I have no doubt that you'll be an asset and not a liability to me."

Understanding what he meant, Alwan had to fight not to jump up and shout out from sheer exhilaration. Hoping he looked calm and composed, he accepted Abdel's handshake and pumped the older man's fist.

"I'll still need to hear a full proposal, and bring you in to speak to my executives and board of directors, but I see a promising future partnership for us both." Abdel smiled toward Lulu as she walked over with a tray of smaller plates of basbousa in her hands. Made of ghee, yogurt and shredded coconut among many ingredients, the semolina cake was a favorite in many Middle Eastern and North African countries. It smelled as sweet as it tasted and Alwan wasn't alone in appreciating the traditional dessert.

Abdel rubbed his hands together and beamed happily. "My, I'm being treated like a king today. Fine food. Finer company. Careful, I might not want to leave."

They all shared in laughter.

Despite what he'd said, Abdel did eventually announce his departure, but he didn't leave empty-handed. Lulu persuaded him to take some of the cake they'd made. Seeing how happy her gesture made Abdel had Alwan wanting to hug her for her thoughtfulness. Resisting the instinct to take her in his arms was difficult, especially as it intensified when they were alone in his home again.

"What? Is there something on my face?" she asked when he trailed her from the elevator where they bid Abdel farewell back to the kitchen where she'd already started cleaning up. He'd been leaning against the island, watching her place the rest of the basbousa into a food storage container before walking it to the fridge.

She wiped at her cheeks when he didn't stop staring.

"Alwan, what is it? You're freaking me out."

He shook his head slowly, unsteadily, the need for her squeezing his lungs tight, fisting his throbbing heart and making him run hot and cold and all at once— Blinking out of his daze, he said, "I just...wanted to thank you for helping with everything. But most of all for showing up."

"You don't have to do that. At least for the time being, we're a team, so your wins are mine and vice versa."

Team.

There was that word again. Abdel had used it to describe them as well, and it'd sounded good then. *Just as it sounds good now*, he thought.

"Even so, my gratitude stands." He slid a step closer to her, then another.

She looked up at him, that tantalizing rush of blood just under her cheeks was back and her pouty mouth called to him on a primal level begging to be claimed.

Earlier he'd nearly tossed out all his doubts and kissed her. It would've been a mistake—a big one, he knew that. The kind of error that Alwan wouldn't be able to walk back easily. Not with Lulu, and certainly not with himself. Because kissing her would mean acting on his attraction and letting her know how he felt about her.

And since he shouldn't be feeling *anything* for her, a kiss was completely, totally, beyond forbidden territory.

Yet he still wanted to do it.

A muffled boom from someplace outside ripped away the moment.

"Fireworks," she murmured. "Guess the celebrations are starting."

"Did you want to go up to the terrace?"

Alwan led her upstairs to his private oasis, realizing that they'd been so busy cooking all afternoon and then entertaining through the evening that he hadn't had a chance to give her a full tour of his home yet. He promised himself he would another day, even if a little voice taunted, *Will you even have time for that?* It was true. The clock on their deadline was ticking closer with each day that passed, bringing them nearer to the reality that she'd probably never again have a reason to set foot in his home.

Shaking off the hurt that bloomed with that thought, Alwan smiled over at Lulu as she passed him and twirled in place with her arms stretched out, her delight in his rooftop terrace instantly cheering him up.

"This is where we should've had dinner," she exclaimed. "You have a whole kitchen up here!"

"What can I say? I love a good cookout, and it saves me from making trips up and down the stairs."

Lulu shook her head with a smile. Plopping onto the outdoor sectional sofa, she gently touched her fingertips to the pale yellow petals of the jasmines on a trellis and her gaze wandered up to the fairy lights strung above on the pergola. She gasped a soft, sweet sound, the whites of her eyes clearer in the dusk as the sky lit up with fireworks.

"I get some pretty good views up here." He sat down beside her, resting back on a couple cushions and tucking an arm behind his head as he divided his attention between the display lighting up the night sky and sneaking peeks at her.

For a short while they quietly watched together, but as soon as there was a lull between fireworks, Alwan looked over to her and said, "Abdel wants to work with me. It's not a done deal yet, but he's reassured me that he's strongly interested. Again, I couldn't have done that without you."

"You're giving me too much credit."

"No, don't do that whole humble thing. I was there, remember? I saw what you did, and you deserve every bit of credit."

Smiling and smoothing her hands over the long skirt of her billowy green dress, Lulu curled her legs up on the sofa and hugged a cushion to her chest. "Fine. But if anything, it was your cooking that sealed the deal. That...what did you call it? Bas-something?"

He chuckled. "Basbousa. It means 'small kiss.'"

"Oh, does it now? That's interesting." Lulu's eyes shifted ever so subtly to his mouth, but Alwan hadn't missed it or the way she lightly bit her lower lip and hummed softly, distractedly.

"A sweet meaning for a sweet dessert... Seems fitting to me."

Still staring at his mouth, Lulu murmured, "Yeah, me too."

Sheer willpower kept him from sliding over the small space between them on the sofa, taking her chin in hand and seeing for himself if she tasted as sweet as she smelled and looked.

The fireworks whooshing up, exploding and crackling overhead saved him from falling victim to temptation again.

And this time when the pyrotechnics took another intermission, Alwan stood to stretch his legs and walked to the edge of the terrace, his back to her now, the city with its carpet of bright lights spread out before him. His attempt to create distance didn't last long though. Her richly floral perfume reached him first, her voice following as she came to stand beside him.

"So, does everyone in your family know how to cook? Or did that gene skip your brother?"

Alwan thought desiring her and fighting his longing was tough, but then he hadn't anticipated that they'd be talking about Hashim. Even on a good day his brother was the last subject he wished to discuss. Lulu had no idea though, and he couldn't exactly tell her why, worried more about what questions she'd ask him then.

Because if she did, Alwan didn't trust himself not to spill

his family secrets to her. Just being near Lulu made him want to share more of his life with her than anybody else. But this was one thing that he wasn't prepared to tell her, so he aimed a small smile down at her and gave her what she sought: an answer.

"Genetics didn't really have anything to do with it. The reality was more that we were roped in to help out at the restaurant sometimes, so we just picked up the skills along the way."

"Still, that's sweet. I like that you all share a passion for making food. I guess it's true—a family that cooks together, stays together."

She didn't know how far off the mark she was with that comment. But he masked his grimace behind another forced smile, relieved to see that Lulu wasn't even looking at him any longer.

Resting her hands on the balcony railing, she was gazing ahead at the cityscape from his rooftop, her line of sight as far off as the CN Tower piercing the horizon like a lit-up needle. "I envy my parents and yours. That's what I would've wanted for my children, you know, if my...*circumstances* were different."

His heart pulsed for her, his hand already moving, covering hers on the railing, his fingers squeezing her comfortingly.

A moment later, he said, "I can't speak on your parents, but as for mine, let's just say that it's not as clear-cut."

Lulu turned her head up to him slowly.

Swallowing thickly, Alwan pushed himself to continue now that he'd started down this road. "Sometimes families look perfect on the outside, and that's just it. Assumptions. Perceptions. What they hold up to the world because reality... Reality is a lot less perfect." He gazed out at the city, the buildings and streets and trees all blurring to him. It took him a moment to realize why.

I'm crying.

Blinking fast, he coughed around the knot that formed in his throat, embarrassment heating him up from the inside out. But he couldn't stop now. She'd ask more questions, and that wouldn't make it easier on him. *No, I have to finish this.* Speak his mind and get through this as quick as possible. And hopefully, *just* hopefully it wouldn't be as painful as it felt now.

Alwan unclenched his jaw. "The reality is my…my family isn't so perfect."

"Alwan," Lulu whispered his name.

He wanted to look at her, but he kept his head dead straight, his vision still swimming with unshed tears.

"Hashim… We…"

Ya Rabbi.

This wasn't easy. The only thing helping was the feeling of her hand on his arm, her fingers pressing gently and anchoring his disjointed thoughts.

"The truth is Hashim isn't in Sudan. That was just a lie my parents told because we…we don't know where he is." Closing his eyes, he hurried through the rest. "We haven't known his whereabouts for a long time now. He's out there somewhere, or maybe he isn't anymore. All we know is that he's gone." *And probably never coming back.*

"Oh, I'm so sorry, Alwan."

"I am too," he said gruffly, eyes still closed and stinging from the tears he held back.

"I…don't know what to say."

Alwan understood how she felt. Even after all these years, it was still a lot for him to take in and accept too.

"Have you and your parents tried to look for him?"

He nodded, his head heavy. "My mom and dad hired private investigators, but any trail Hashim left led nowhere. And when my parents gave up searching, I tried, but my efforts were fruitless too."

"Do you want to talk about it?" Lulu asked, her sweet voice too alluring to ignore.

Opening his eyes, Alwan finally allowed himself to look at her and shook his head.

"Not really, no."

When she turned to him fully, he did the same. She touched his dress shirt, her hand over his slim tie, fingers scraping his buttons as she slid her palm up. The heated trail she left in her wake was a mixture of the same physical longing he felt for her and something else...

Something just as strong but nameless.

Lulu stopped her hand above his throbbing heart and, with a compassionate smile, said, "Then we don't talk about it."

He recalled what Abdel had said, how Alwan cared for Lulu and she for him. At the time he couldn't believe it, but now—*now*—looking down into her kind eyes, he wondered how he'd missed it. Because it was clear, on some level, that she did.

He already knew what he felt for her was a strong attraction and whatever that something else he was having trouble labeling was...

Affection, he thought after a little while, his hand curling atop Lulu's over his chest.

That was what he was feeling and hadn't been able to name but suspected all along.

I... I like her.

CHAPTER EIGHT

"Wow, the space has really come together."

Lulu made the remark softly to herself as she walked into Alwan's office. It'd been a while since she had last set foot there, and in the couple weeks of her absence, he and his newly hired staff had decorated the interior.

Potted ferns sat in a couple corners, adding spots of rich color to the sterile white walls and gray flooring. They had hung up large, framed, colorful photographs of various Toronto landmarks and brought in bookshelves that warmed the space, not that any of the legal texts sitting on the shelves were her idea of fun reading.

What she liked most though was the handwoven, vibrant Turkish rug filling the empty space at the center of the room. The reception desk sat atop it, the chair currently empty, but its smiling occupant walking toward her from one of the smaller offices.

"Hey, Luula. We weren't expecting you, but it's good to see you nonetheless." Uzoma's sunny grin was, as always, hard to resist. Freshly enrolled in a law practice program, and tech savvy like most early twentysomethings these days, Alwan's new office manager had been a choice hire. "Were you looking for Mr. Eltahir?"

Lulu smiled at the formal deference he was showing his new boss. "I am. Has he stepped out?" She looked over at his office, the glass walls making it easy to see the room was empty.

"He's in a meeting." Uzoma pointed over to the larger of the three offices, the room that Alwan had repurposed into a small conference room.

On arriving, she had noticed the drawn blinds, but hadn't assumed anyone was in there. *Weird.* Frowning, Lulu met Uzoma's curious eyes.

"Is he, um, doing okay?"

"Last I checked he was fine. A little busier than usual though."

Relief swept over her at that news.

"If it's important, I could interrupt," Uzoma offered. "I'm sure he wouldn't mind stepping out a moment for you."

"It can wait," she said just as Alwan's paralegal strolled over to them. Like Uzoma, Jagnoor was fairly young but smart as a whip on paper and fun to be around in person.

Greeting the other woman, Lulu laughed when Jagnoor gasped, "Is that what I think it is?"

She was goggling down at the brown paper bag Lulu was holding.

"It is. I passed the food truck on the way over, and I couldn't resist." Lulu placed the bag down on Uzoma's desk and stepped back, giving Jagnoor the honor of pulling out the boxes.

"I wasn't sure what everyone would like, so I bought one of each flavor."

Jagnoor opened a box with a happy little squeal. "You're now officially my bestie, Lulu."

Uzoma looked over her shoulder with a bemused laugh. "All this excitement for a cake on a stick?"

"Not just any old cake, but a *cheesecake*." Jagnoor gripped the end of the stick holding the confection and held it up to him. "Look at that caramel-on-chocolate combo and convince me you aren't drooling."

Uzoma shrugged, leaned in and took a bite. "Mmm, okay,

all right. I'll admit it's pretty good," he agreed with another laugh.

"Right? And you know what would make it better? Coffee."

"Let's grab some, then." Uzoma turned his bright smile from Jagnoor over to Lulu and extended the invite to join them.

"No, I'm fine, thanks. I'll just wait here for your boss," Lulu told them, looking over to the conference room.

They walked out together, chatting and laughing all the way.

She watched them go and already missed the diversion they offered with their humorous company. Because now she was back to worrying and hand-wringing, just as she had on the cab ride over.

It had all started when Alwan's parents had called her at work. They usually never reached out to her and only because it was easier for them to get Alwan to pass along messages. So, feeling a little uneasy, she had phoned them back during her lunch break. Whatever it was had to be serious. Strangely though, all his mother and father wanted to know was whether she and Alwan were free to stop by the restaurant later. When she'd asked if they had plans that Alwan forgot to mention to her, they hurriedly assured her that they only wanted to have dinner with them. They had then asked her to let Alwan know since they couldn't seem to reach him.

Lulu had tried calling him right after with the same result.

Alwan's phone had rung and rung and gone straight to his voicemail.

She'd then tried texting, but with no luck there too.

Before long an hour had passed with no word on his end, her texts and calls still unanswered. Now concerned for a different reason, Lulu had requested finishing up her work outside her office. "For personal matters," she'd reported to her boss. She'd then hailed a cab and headed straight for

Alwan's office building, stopping only for the cheesecake slices she'd brought.

Pacing the reception area, Lulu dropped down onto one of the comfy armchairs across from the conference room. She looked between the closed blinds and the glass door. It would be all too easy to sneak up and peek in on his meeting, but it didn't sit right with her to spy on him. Obviously whatever was being said was private. And given the sensitive nature of his job, it wasn't strange for him to be careful.

Still, it didn't mean she wasn't curious and worried.

Between that and his parents' out-of-the-blue invitation to dinner, her nerves were wound tight and a hair trigger away from exploding on her.

Lulu tapped her foot impatiently, crossing her legs—and then uncrossing them and springing up and pacing the distance between the desk and the small open waiting area. The cool, hushed atmosphere of the office amplified the loud rattling thoughts in her head and the thumping of her heartbeat in her ears. At one point the ducts above her head knocked loudly as the air-conditioning switched on and she startled at the jarring noise.

She did it again when the door to the conference room clicked open and voices filtered into the space, one was new to her, but the other—the other had her heart pitter-pattering. *Alwan.* By now she could recognize his smooth-as-melted-chocolate voice blindfolded.

The man he was talking to had a nervous catch to his speech as he said, "Th-thanks again for seeing me on such short notice. I didn't mean to drop this in your lap all over again, especially after how I reacted last time."

"Say no more, Kyle. It's forgiven and forgotten," Alwan replied with a lighthearted laugh, his tone friendly. "I'll reach out to you with a decision in the next day or so."

Thanking him once more, Alwan's visitor, a pale, dark-haired, bespectacled man stepped out of the conference room with Alwan closely on his heels.

Seeing her the moment they walked out, both men stopped immediately and stared at her.

Alwan spoke up first. "Luula? What are you doing here?"

Feeling her face growing hot from all the attention, she moved closer to him and, smiling at his familiar-looking guest, said, "I just wanted to surprise you."

Alwan looked from her to his visitor and back again, nodding. "Right," he drawled out the one word, a smile slowly drawing up his lips. "Of course, and what a pleasant surprise it is." He cleared his throat then. "Kyle, may I introduce you to my lovely and talented fiancée?"

"Brains and beauty," Kyle said, shaking her hand and pushing his glasses up the bridge of his nose. "I wish you both a happy marriage. Now, I'll leave you two alone. Thank you once again for squeezing me into your schedule, Alwan."

Lulu waited a full minute to ensure they were alone, before asking, "Was that the guy from the viral video? The one who…" She mimed a throw.

"That's him," he confirmed with an amused smile.

"What was he doing here, and why was he thanking you?"

Alwan nudged his head back to the conference room. "Let me explain in there."

Lulu walked ahead of him into the room and he closed the door behind them, then whisked open the blinds.

"Kyle was here because he wants me to handle his appeal and try and secure a retrial for his case."

"And is that why he was thanking you, because you said you're going to do it?"

"No." Tipping back his head, Alwan scrubbed both his hands down over his face and sighed heavily, his dark brows slashing together as his eyes locked on the long conference table before him. "I told him I'd think on it and call with my final decision."

"After everything he put you through, I'd understand why you wouldn't." Lulu pulled out a chair and sat down, sitting up straighter when Alwan sighed again and looked at her.

"That video circulating was, frankly, a nightmare. The public might have been casting their stones at me, but he's gotten plenty of backlash too. Kyle also has kids, and his family hasn't exactly been getting the privacy they need."

"Is that why the blinds were drawn?"

Alwan nodded. "He was uncomfortable. I don't think he even made eye contact with Uzoma when he walked in and asked to see me."

"You feel bad for him. That could be a reason to take the case."

"Or not. I can't risk getting too emotional this time, not with the practice still being new," he said and gripped the back of a chair, a helplessness twisting his handsome features. "What should I do, Lu?"

It was like when he'd asked for her opinion choosing his office. Lulu had resisted sharing her thoughts then, and she should now. Because as touched as she was that Alwan trusted her enough to ask her to weigh in on what was clearly a very important decision for him, the fact was he wouldn't do that unless he valued her greatly.

And if he valued her *that* much, then...

Then he probably cares for me too.

Something neither of them should be doing given they had promised not to complicate this unusual arrangement of theirs with feelings. It was easier for them both this way. *Safer even*, Lulu thought.

There wasn't room in her to love anyone again. The pain

of losing her baby and then watching her ex-husband pull away from her before their divorce was not an experience she wished to relive. Not that she thought Alwan loved her...

If Lulu had believed that, then she wouldn't have hesitated like she was now and would've walked out of the room right then and there.

And since that wasn't the case she stayed put right where she was and said, "Do you really want my help?"

He nodded quickly, eagerly.

"Okay. Tell me about Kyle first. Clearly his case matters to you, but why?"

Alwan then told Kyle's sad tale, starting with how the man lost his wife to a short battle with cancer, and then how one of their adopted children lived with a severe intellectual disability that required more hands-on support. The legal dispute between Kyle and his late wife's extremely wealthy family happened after his wife's dying will and testament requested that her inheritance from her parents be transferred to Kyle and their kids.

"Kyle and his wife had always relied on that inheritance to be a trust fund for their two children if anything were to happen to them. The worst part is that before lawyers were called and courts visited, when his wife was still alive, Kyle had had a good relationship with his in-laws. They'd even supported the adoption and never treated the children any differently. But now, all of a sudden, they've turned their backs on him. And family—family should be there for each other, no matter what." Alwan's jaw hardened visibly, his lips tightening into a thin, severe line and his brows slashing over his narrowed eyes.

Lulu admitted the story was upsetting, but Alwan's reaction felt...personal.

Like he's thinking about his brother.

Whatever had happened between him and Hashim had been painful enough for it to inspire the raw emotions now darkening his features.

Her heart lurched sharply for him, the ache prompting her to speak up and get his mind off his troubles.

"It sounds like you're invested already," she observed softly. "So, what's holding you back?"

"The fact that Kyle drained the last of his savings on his initial court battles and won't be able to pay any new legal fees anytime soon."

"I know finances and income are crucial for your practice at this stage, but since you've been doing all that volunteer work for that nonprofit anyway, couldn't you also take this on pro bono?"

"I did think of doing that," he said with a small smile, the sight of it promising.

"Then it's not money that's making you hesitate, is it? I watched that video, Alwan, and it would be natural if you were worried about that happening to you again. Most people would, myself included."

"Another viral video happening again is a fear, but the truth is I think I'm more scared of the disappointment."

"Letting down your client?" she asked.

"Yes, but also myself," he said, gritting his teeth and rubbing his hands over his face with a groan. "I just don't want anything to go wrong. With this case, with this business…" He lowered his hands, looked over at her then and left his thought incomplete, making her briefly wonder what else he'd been about to say.

Not wanting to delve into why he was staring at her so intensely and so suddenly, Lulu said, "You should do it, then."

He raised his brows. "Why?"

"Because I think even more than losing this case and disappointing yourself, you're really more worried about not doing anything to help."

"And that's because you know me so well?" he said with a wry lift of his lips.

"No, that's because you traveled thousands of kilometers to ask me to be your fake fiancée, and all because you were driven enough by *this* dream, this business of yours that I know will help people who need their voices and stories heard most."

Alwan clamped his lips together, and though his beard concealed his jawline, Lulu knew it was as sharp and hard as steel right now.

Had she crossed a line, some boundary that she shouldn't have? Before she could ask or even try to remedy whatever mistake she made, he cleared his throat and looked off to the side, almost as though he was embarrassed.

"I don't know what to say. Other than I'm grateful." Turning his head back to her slowly, their eyes met and Alwan smiled, his face far more relaxed and the pink undertone to his light brown cheeks brighter with his shyness as he rasped, "Thank you, Luula."

"Of course," she chirped, blushing now too.

"So, why did you stop by?" Alwan was rolling down the sleeves of his button-up shirt as he asked her.

"Your mom and dad called. They've invited us over to dinner at the restaurant."

Frowning, he pulled his suit jacket off the back of one of the conference chairs. "That's odd. Did they give you a reason why they called you instead of me?"

"Well, apparently they tried calling you, but you weren't picking up your phone."

Alwan genuinely looked surprised as he patted his trouser pockets and then checked inside his suit jacket before he snapped his fingers. "Right. I left it behind in my office.

Probably put it on silent too. I've been working out of this room for most of the day between meetings with some of my old clients and with Abdel and his team."

"How's it going with Abdel?"

"Good," he said with a big grin. "His people are sending over the contracts to make it official."

"That's great news!" Lulu didn't want to dampen his spirits but she needed to speak her mind, so she added, "I'm a little worried about what your parents might want. Do you think they know we aren't really…you know, *romantically involved*?"

He was silent for a moment, and then he shook his head. "I highly doubt it. If my parents knew, they wouldn't be sitting on the news without immediately giving me an earful about it. Literally. As in they'd be pulling on my ear and yelling at me."

"Are you so certain?"

"I mean, I'm hopeful," he chuckled. "But that isn't what you want to hear."

"Not one bit," she said with a sigh and a small tired smile.

"Don't worry. Even if they do know and want to ream us out, we're in this together."

After everything she'd just done to redraw the boundary line between them, Alwan had gone and blurred it again and with only one word. *Together*.

For Lulu's sake, Alwan had put on a brave face as they later drove to his parents' lakefront restaurant.

He knew she was nervous and used every opportunity to remind her that he was right by her side and wasn't going anywhere. When he parked his car, he reassured her again that he would be there with her every step of the way. When they walked up to the building, he held the door open for her and gave her an extra big smile. And when the hostess instructed them to go upstairs, and it was only him and Lulu in the elevator together, Alwan sidled closer to her, brushed the back of his hand against hers and looked down at her. Without saying a word, he tried to communicate that they would be all right.

Lulu must have gotten his message because she offered him a conciliatory smile right as the elevator pinged and the doors slid open.

"Surprise!"

The loud cheers and sound of confetti poppers had Alwan immediately covering Lulu with an arm, his instinct to protect her riding over his confusion as he assessed the unusual sight before him.

People. Dozens of people were standing in front of the elevator and staring back at him and Lulu. All people he knew. Family, friends, aunties and uncles from both the Somali and Sudani communities, and even neighbors who lived near his parents' home whom Alwan hadn't spoken to in a long while. But there were also faces he didn't recognize; faces he was starting to realize probably belonged to Lulu's friends and extended family.

Lulu squeezed the arm he had thrown in front of her and whispered, "Did we just walk into a party?"

"It seems so."

Before Alwan could answer, someone cried, "Let's get the party started!"

Of course it was Malek. Pushing his way to the front of the crowd, his cousin strode into the elevator and obnoxiously blew a kazoo in Alwan's face. "Come on, you two. As the guests of honor you can't leave everyone hanging." Waving at them to exit the lift, he made some sort of signal that had the music turning on.

As soon as they cleared the lift, Alwan was pulled one way and Lulu the other into embrace after embrace. Everybody was taking a turn congratulating them on their engagement.

By the time they were standing together again, it was under a beautiful, intricate balloon arch with his arm wrapped around Lulu's shoulders and a photographer snapping their pictures.

"Stand closer, lovebirds," Malek called out, laughing when his wife, Rima, gave him a censuring look, though even she appeared as amused as everyone else.

After what felt like forever, the photographer signaled for Lulu's parents and sister and his mother and father to join them in the pictures. Then other relatives jumped in and friends after that.

Taking it with stride, Alwan laughed along and smiled with everybody, all while inside his anxiety jangled louder with every second that passed. Because he hadn't had a moment alone with Lulu to gauge how she felt about all of this. Though she flashed pretty smiles for the camera and chatted contentedly enough with their family and friends, he knew better than to take her cheerfulness at face value.

She can't be happy.

It was his fault for not calling back his parents and grilling them until they confessed about the surprise party. He'd have to find a way to make it up to her, starting with a rescue. But it wasn't easy finding an opening.

After taking photos for what felt like a whole hour, they were pulled over to the cake table, where they took more pictures, and then he and Lulu were obliged to make a speech thanking everyone. Hoping that was all of it, Alwan bit back a groan when their well-wishers started making toasts blessing a marriage that he knew wouldn't ever be happening. It was tough sitting through that part, staring into the faces of all these people who cared for them and knowing he and Lulu were lying to them.

But I'm the one that wanted this.

Lulu hadn't approached him with the fake engagement,

and she'd only signed up because he had tempted her with the money she had needed for the repairs on her motor home.

Thinking on that only made him feel worse.

And if it wasn't easy for him, it had to be harder for Lulu, especially when some of the blessings mentioned children. Every time that happened, Alwan flicked a concerned look at her, but her beautiful smile and bright eyes gave nothing away.

Biding his time for a chance alone with her was a grueling test in patience.

The opportunity finally came when Lulu fanned a hand over her face at one point, pushed out of her chair and excused herself to get fresh air on the balcony.

"I'll go with you." Alwan stood quickly, his eagerness to escape the crowd and grab a moment with her not going unnoticed.

But other than laughing and flinging them knowing looks, their families didn't stop them.

As soon as it was just the two of them, he jokingly wiped at his brow and sighed. "Whew. Finally some peace and quiet. I thought we'd be in there, taking pictures, forever."

Lulu rewarded him with a smile. "It wasn't that bad. You're exaggerating."

"I wish I was. Look, it's already past eight. How did three hours fly by so quickly? Who takes photos for that long even?"

"Stop," Lulu said, snorting a giggle.

Hearing her laughter soothed his worry that she had been uncomfortable about the party this whole time. Feeling a little better, he still apologized. "Listen, I should've checked in with my parents. I honestly never thought they were planning anything like this, and if I'd known, I would've shut it down. I'll understand if you're upset with me."

"You think I'm angry at you?"

He stuffed his hands in his trouser pockets. "Aren't you?"

She shook her head. "I'm not mad. Surprised, yes, but that's kind of the whole point of the party."

"I guess it is," Alwan said with a chuckle.

Lulu smiled back. "Also, even if I was irritated, I still wouldn't have wanted you to say anything to your parents. They might have suspected something."

He nodded slowly, her reasoning clear to him.

"Besides, look at it this way, everyone's happy," she said, nudging her head behind them at the glass walls separating the balcony from the restaurant.

Alwan saw what she meant when he glanced back over his shoulder at their families and friends chatting and laughing inside. Turning his head forward again, he looked out at the reds and golds the setting sun painted the sky, the fading light of day rippling off the calm lake, and the breeze a couple degrees cooler as it swept over his face.

"You're right," he said. "Let's not take this moment from them just yet. I mean, we will have to eventually once we finish up our partnership here." Despite knowing this was always how it would end when he'd first asked Lulu to be his fake fiancée, Alwan hadn't given too much thought to how they'd break up. They had agreed early on to let their families know together that it had been a mutual decision. It would be their last act together before they moved on with their lives apart.

And now that it was on the horizon, it suddenly seemed to be the only thing on his mind.

The end of this.

No more reason for him and Lulu to talk or even see each other. Somehow the thought of that pained him physically. He swallowed with difficulty, his chest suddenly a little tighter and his eyes burning a little more. Telling himself that it was because he'd simply gotten used to her presence in his life, and that he'd only be mourning that loss, Alwan found his conviction swaying when he looked over at Lulu and was, as always, floored by his strong attraction to her.

He looked her over, from her springy curls down to her floral print blouse, long frilly skirt and cute strappy heels, and his breath sawed out and his suit suddenly felt too stuffy. Prying his fingers off the balcony railing, he unbuttoned his suit jacket and was in the middle of loosening his necktie when Lulu spoke up softly.

"We'll let them down as gently as we can. As long as they see that we're both on the same page with the breakup, your parents will understand and my family will too. I believe they'll just want what's best for us."

Lowering his hands off his tie, feeling no better, Alwan jerked a nod and forced a smile. "Of course. Same page. Right."

He wasn't surprised when her brows knitted together and she frowned. "Are you okay?"

Nodding again, he hooked his arms over the railing and stared ahead, finding it hard to look at her and breathe or think normally. "I'm fine. Just thinking…"

"About?"

Not ready to divulge the strong attachment he had to her, Alwan grasped for an excuse and landed on one. "Just the good news that we've scored two tickets to this star-studded charity gala. My parents go every year and try to get me to join them, but I haven't had a reason to until now."

Until you, he wanted to say, but instead he just stared at her for a beat, his attention lowering to her parted lips, his heart rate picking up.

Blinking, he snapped his gaze from her mouth back to her round eyes.

"What I mean is that it'd be a great place to network and build on referrals."

"I bet it'll be good for your practice." Lulu tipped her head to the side. "When will the gala be happening?"

"In two weeks, not that you should feel pressured to come with me or anything."

"Alwan, we're a couple."

His breath hitched.

Lulu seemed to have heard it too because she bashfully bowed her head and toyed with the dangling silver charm on her purse. "As in we're a couple for now and we have to present a united front, so I'm going with you." She peeked up at the end, her brown cheeks redder, her glossy lips twitching up.

"I… I'd be grateful for the support, thanks." Compelled by a gravitational pull stronger than him, Alwan drew nearer to her. First one step, then another. An outpouring of feverish warmth flared through his body that had nothing to do with the mid-July heat blanketing the city. He raised his hand, held it hovering near her cheek and vibrated with anxiety the second it took her to give him permission.

It was only a quick little jerk of her head, but it was plenty enough for him.

Electricity tingled out from where his fingers and palm cupped her wondrously soft cheek. Smiling, Alwan wasn't shocked at all by the chemistry sizzling between them. It'd been there from the start. From the very moment he clapped eyes on her again in the thick of the Albertan wilderness. And after the attraction came the affection. This strong urge to be near her all the time, to bask in her attention and…

And what?

He had a suspicion of what he wanted, but he couldn't afford to think on it too long. At least he could take comfort in the knowledge he wasn't unaffected alone.

Lulu's long black lashes fluttered, her warm breath teasing over his thumb when he stroked her bottom lip, her sigh floating up to his ears right before she shut her eyes, swayed forward and tipped her head up to him.

For a moment he had a flash of another time they'd been in a similar position.

Only then he had denied them both at the last second.

The self-restraint he'd shown that first time was nowhere to be had now. Not even the fact that they could clearly be seen from the restaurant registered in his head fully. None of it mattered. *Only her. Always her.*

Reading her invitation loud and clear, Alwan lowered his head tortuously slowly and focused his sights on her all-too-tempting mouth.

He was going to kiss her.

Another inch and their lips would connect.

Almost there...

"Alwan!" Malek appeared and they pulled back from each other quickly. "We're taking more group pictures, so if you guys can stop making googly eyes at each other long enough, we need you in here."

Alwan had never wanted to wring his cousin's neck more than in that moment.

Giving him a death glare, he growled, "We're coming," and Malek took the hint and left.

When he looked back at Lulu, she had her face covering her hands but peeped out at him from between her fingers.

"God. How are we even going to go back in there and look everyone in the eye?" she moaned.

Though embarrassed too, Alwan held out a hand to her, his heart thudding faster when she slipped hers into his. "Easy. We'll do it together."

CHAPTER NINE

"Okay, velvet or silk satin?"

Alwan held up two black bow ties, and from where Lulu sat perched in a highly comfortable armchair inside his luxuriously spacious walk-in closet, she could've sworn they looked the same, except for the subtle glossy sheen on the silk option.

"Is there a big difference?" she asked with squinty eyes before throwing her hands up and sighing in frustration. "I doubt anyone will notice or care."

He grinned and laughed lightly. "I will though, and I don't want to be distracted thinking I made the wrong choice and messed up this opportunity to rub elbows with Toronto's elite tonight. That's why I need your help."

Though he was smiling, Lulu sensed the undercurrent of uneasiness in his voice. He hadn't needed to spell it out that he was nervous about the charity gala and the networking he'd have to be doing all evening. She'd probably feel the same way if her business somewhat hinged on making the right connections with the right people. Sympathetic to his plight, she softly sighed and pointed to the bow tie she preferred.

"The silk, then. It matches the lapels of your dinner jacket."

Alwan's brown eyes sparkled at her, and his handsome smile delighted her probably more than it should.

"Silk satin it is." Turning up the collar of his dress shirt, he strolled over to one of two full-length mirrors at the back of the closet and tied the bow tie in a practiced, fluid motion. Whirling back to her, and sounding nervous again, he asked, "Does it look good?"

Her heart panged for him as she nodded reassuringly.

He's really worried, isn't he?

She bit the inside of her cheek, suddenly buffeted by the need to free him of his doubts. Like all her fluttery feelings around him, it confused her, but it didn't stop her from asking, "Are you nervous?"

"Is it that obvious?" Alwan said with a soft laugh, walking over to the glass-topped dark wood storage unit in the middle of the closet. Pulling open one of the drawers, he plucked out studs and a pair of round silver-and-onyx cuff links, and while he clasped them on his dress shirt, he told her, "I'm trying to think positively, really I am, but my mind keeps conjuring up the worst-case scenarios."

"Such as?" Gripping the chair's tufted armrests, Lulu sat forward when he frowned at her.

"Everyone laughs at me. Nobody wants to work with me. I have to close the doors on the practice." He tightened his lips, his hands curling into fists atop the dresser. "It sounds crazy when I say it aloud. Even so, I can't stop worrying that all of it will come true. That I'll fail at everything I try and disappoint the people around me, the ones I love most." Alwan was looking right at her as he said that last part.

Heat flushed through her, her face warmer from it, her toes wriggling under the voluminous skirt of her evening gown, and her fingers curling into the soft fabric of the armrests.

He's talking about his parents, his family. Not you.

As rational as it was, that thought did nothing to cool her body temperature.

What helped in the end was reminding herself that this moment wasn't about her. *It's about him.* Alwan was crying out for reassurance, even if he wasn't saying it out loud, and she just couldn't turn her back on him.

He needs you now.

Keeping that in mind, Lulu forced a calm into her voice she wasn't feeling at all and said gently, "That could happen, sure. But what if it doesn't? What if, instead, you make connections tonight that not only help your business but also prove you've chosen the right path?"

"I... I don't know." He looked away, his head bowed, shoulders sagging with the invisible burden he carried.

Her body took control and before she fully understood what she was doing, Lulu was out of her chair, the long skirt of her dress sweeping over the plush carpeting in his closet as she walked to where he stood dejectedly.

Taking a sharp breath, Alwan snapped his head up to her when she touched a hand to his fist, his eyes wide with the same surprise she was feeling.

She didn't know why she'd gone to him, or why she was holding his hand. Only that a pressing need to comfort him had pushed her into action and overridden everything else. But now that her brain had caught up with her limbs, rather than letting go of him Lulu kept her hand right where it was, and all because that need to support him and be by his side still overpowered rational thought.

Still took over her mind and body.

And the only way Lulu could see herself shaking it off was giving it what it demanded. *Help him.*

So, with her palm over his knuckles, she said, "I told you about my divorce, about my...miscarriage."

Without speaking a word, Alwan interlaced his fingers with hers. He squeezed her hand, offering solace through the contact.

A flood of gratitude pinched at her eyes, but blinking fast, Lulu held the tears at bay.

This wasn't about her. She was trying to help *him*.

"What I didn't tell you was that just before I left, right after I purchased the RV, I saw my ex and the subject of trying to restore our marriage came up. I—I almost considered doing it. Going back. Forgetting about my plans to hit the road. I wavered on what path was best for me," she said, her voice an octave above a whisper but cracking like a whip in the hush of his closet.

Seeing Alwan's eyes go soft with sorrow had her rushing through the rest before she lost the courage to continue.

"In the end I realized I had to move forward. That being nervous, even *scared* doesn't mean that you're making a wrong decision. Sometimes it's usually a sign that it's exactly the path you need to be on right now."

Alwan didn't speak immediately, his fingers gently squeezing hers, his gaze roving over her face. But then he unexpectedly tugged at her hand and pulled her into an embrace.

Lulu froze and let him hold her while her brain processed what was happening and why her heart was hammering against her ribs and her stomach churned from an explosion of butterflies. She didn't know how long they stood like that, but eventually Alwan drew back, his arms still holding her close to him, his warm eyes shining down over her as if she'd just hung the moon for him.

"Luula, I—I don't know what I'd do without you by my side."

His words and adorable stammer slowly melted her and

when he hugged her again, she lifted her arms and wrapped them around his middle and shyly pressed her heated face into his chest. For a moment she let herself exist nowhere else but in the cozy security of his embrace.

She knew she'd have to let go soon.

But that only made her want to cling to him even more.

Cling to this life they'd shared together for the past few months.

Being Alwan's fake fiancée wasn't at all what she'd imagined it would be like. And though this wavering in her heart and mind was exactly what she hadn't wanted happening—what she hadn't *ever* thought would happen, Lulu reminded herself that none of it was true. Her affection and attraction, perhaps. She *did* actually like him. But the rest of it was nothing more than a contract with a fast-approaching deadline.

The reality was Alwan could've had any other woman stand in her place right then. He'd pretty much said it himself. She was his first option because of her divorce and the unlikelihood that she'd want anything more from this charade of theirs.

He picked her solely for the reason that she *wouldn't* desire love from him.

That she wouldn't wish for their relationship to be real.

Deluding herself into thinking she was special would only end in the kind of trouble that had her picking up the pieces of her heart all on her own. *Again.*

Lulu was almost relieved then when a familiar pain radiated from her lower back as it was a reminder that she shouldn't be hugging him.

When she groaned softly, Alwan heard her and pulled back instantly, his hands on her upper arms softly kneading her tense muscles and his gorgeous face gripped with concern for her.

Before he could ask, she unclenched her teeth and said, "I'm all right. Just my time of the month, and nothing a pain reliever can't handle." Moving back from him then, she created much-needed space between them and walked over to where she'd left her chain clutch.

Alwan was her shadow, standing close at hand while she took the medicine from her purse.

"It seems like the pain is pretty awful. Do you always manage it this way?" he asked, now scowling and folding his arms.

Annoyance flared through her, hot and steady. It was a welcome change to the longing ache left behind after she'd pulled away from him. "Yes, not that it's any of your business. Because sometimes that's all that helps. Also, I'm very careful about the amount I take."

"I didn't mean to offend you," he said, sighing after and lowering his arms, hurt blooming over his face.

It was hard to stay angry with him looking at her that way.

Even harder when he explained, "Hashim had a sports injury, a severe one that had him relying on strong pain medication for a long time before we…we lost contact with him. I didn't mean to conflate your pain with my hang-ups on the subject."

If any upset lingered, it was obliterated with his apology. The urge to embrace him once again swept over her, but before it could pull her under, Lulu stumbled back to the large closet's exit with the excuse of needing water. Then she hurried away, sailing out of his bedroom and even considering heading straight for the private elevator to his condo and fleeing his home all together.

But she stopped herself from going that far.
Because I promised him.
And she intended to uphold her end of their deal. That meant the closest thing to sanctuary before they left for the charity gala was a moment of time alone in the kitchen.

Lulu pulled a bottle of chilled water from his fridge and perched herself on one of the stools at the kitchen island. She was looking around absently when she noticed one of the cabinet doors of the built-in pantry was slightly ajar, caught on something. Feeling nosy, she slid off the stool and walked over to pull the door open wider and jumped back when a closed bag of dry cat food landed on the kitchen floor.

She stared down at it, confused as to why Alwan had cat food of all things. As far as she knew he had no pets.
Unless it's for Blueberry...
"There's no way," she murmured with a shake of her head, already reaching down to lift the bag off the floor and place it back where she found it. But just as she set the bag back in the pantry, she startled at the sound of her name and swung around.

Alwan was walking into the kitchen, fully dressed to the nines now. His eyes landing on her, he stopped at the entrance and tucked his hands in the pockets of his tuxedo pants, his dinner jacket unbuttoned and his dress shirt now paired with a silky waistcoat. He looked beyond good. Like he was ready to conquer the night. *No, the world.*

She smiled, relieved that he seemed to be feeling more confident about the evening, but also pressing a hand to her pounding heart when he slowly moved closer to her.

"Are you feeling better?" he asked, his brow lined with the worry he was tempering from his tone.

Worry for her, she recognized.

Guilt slammed into her. First, for making him concerned

about her, but also at the way she'd walked off on him when he'd told her about his brother's plight with pain medication. She only felt worse when she nodded and Alwan smiled, some of the stress easing off his face.

"Are you still angry with me?" he whispered then.

Shaking her head, Lulu bit her lip when the feeling of tears burned at her eyes. It wasn't the first time he'd made her want to cry. And all it did was highlight the fact that despite what she kept telling herself, Alwan had sunken under her skin and burrowed deep into her in a way that she hadn't thought he ever would.

"I *am* sorry if I upset you."

"You didn't," she lied, then sighing, said, "*Fine*, maybe you did a little. But I'm not angry. Not anymore." Certainly not after the way he sweetly apologized and looked genuinely contrite.

His smile a bit wider, Alwan chuckled.

"I'm forgiven, then?"

She tapped her chin, beaming when he laughed a little louder. "I suppose," she said with a put-upon sigh and leaning back against the pantry door she'd forgotten to close. *Oops*.

Alwan was looking there now, but his reaction was unexpected. He glanced away shyly.

Lulu had fully decided to not bring up the cat food, but now that he was acting so strangely about it, she blurted, "Were you planning on getting a cat?"

He avoided her eyes and cleared his throat. "Ah. You found the cat food."

"I did," she said. Then realizing that she was admitting to snooping, hastily added, "I wasn't being nosy. The door was open and I saw it peeking out. I swear."

Alwan tossed her a quick smile. "I believe you. I might

have been thinking of looking into local shelters. My home's big but it can get lonely."

That actually made sense. *See. It had nothing to do with Blue or you.* Lulu wasn't sure why she was a little sad about it, but she couldn't pretend that it didn't motivate her when she said, "I could help you, if you want?"

"I'd like that," he replied, not leaving her hanging in suspense.

"Okay, then."

"Okay," he said huskily, only this time his smile had an edge of sexiness, his attention fully on her and her alone. The intensity of his stare had her blushing and walking back to the kitchen island to take a big swig from her water bottle.

Seeming well aware of his effect on her, he dialed up the heat on his seductive smirk before he turned and motioned for her to follow him.

She pointed toward the exit as they headed for his bedroom and walk-in closet again.

"Aren't we leaving?" Lulu asked, and Alwan suddenly spun back to her with that sinful smile and a pair of shoes in each hand.

"Sure. But right after you help me again. So, which will it be? Classic patent leather or crystal-embellished loafers?"

For all the years that Alwan had been dodging his parents' invitations to their parties, he could finally understand what the fuss was all about now that he was at one.

It seemed that all of Toronto's richest and most privileged had stepped out of their opulent homes and off their chartered planes to fete the night in style. And there wasn't a shortage of glitz and glam. From fashionable evening wear to the luxury vehicles the guests were all arriving in, everything oozed wealth in all the splendiferous ways that affluence could be flaunted. Even the venue that the charity gala was being hosted at set the sumptuous tone for the evening.

Situated in one of Toronto's oldest and most luxurious hotels, the ballroom harkened back to a time long past. Tall, vaulted ceilings decorated with oil paintings, gilded pilasters, arched windows and magnificent crystal chandeliers made the expansive ballroom a sight to behold and gave it an air of timelessness.

Like many other guests, Lulu was taking videos and photos with her phone, documenting everything and everyone she met. Alwan couldn't get enough of her glittering eyes winging over to him whenever she glimpsed a celebrity she recognized, and he loved that the noise forced her to lean into him frequently so she could communicate. Her sweet, warm breath teased his ear every single time, her peppery, resinous fragrance imprinting on his lungs, and her long painted nails secured on his arm as they navigated the packed ballroom to their table.

"I don't see your parents yet," Lulu said, her head craning this way and that, her glossy, natural curls even springier than usual and pinned up at her crown. Her beautiful hair bounced with her every step as they searched the ballroom for his mother and father.

Worried he'd lose her in the crowd between the dance floor and the rapidly filling tables, Alwan took hold of her hand and tucked it in the crook of his elbow. "Let's find our table first and then I'll message them."

He wasn't in any hurry to hunt for his parents.

Although he recognized and was grateful that they had helped him get this far with their professional and social connections, he had done plenty of work too. Besides, this was something they couldn't assist him with even if they wanted to. And he had Lulu there for support. Alwan couldn't think of anyone else he'd want by his side right then. He'd even already decided that if nothing else came of the night, at least he was able to share it with her.

It's not like we have a lot of moments like this left.

When that happened soon, in about a month, he'd miss her more than he ever conceived he would or thought possible. Had he known he'd feel this way about her, Alwan would never have proposed the fake engagement to her.

Not that he regretted it.

How could he when looking at her, touching her, breathing the same air as her made him so wholly, incomprehensibly, *deliriously* happy?

Alwan aimed a dopey smile down at her as she looked around and snapped more photos, seemingly oblivious to his powerful feelings for her. Meanwhile he wondered how any of this had transpired. After the lengths he'd gone to avoid it. The sudden trip to Alberta, the fake engagement, even his decision to choose her and not any other woman—none of it had stopped him from doing the very thing he'd planned would never happen to him.

I love her, don't I?

He knew the answer, and so did his heart as it skipped a beat every time Lulu so much as beamed up at him or clutched her fingers tighter around his arm.

I love her, he thought as they reached their table and greeted the other guests already seated.

He should've been happy about the arranged seating because there was a popular reality TV doctor, a pair of brand influencers with tens of millions of followers between them, an A-list actor and even a Grammy-award-winning rapper he often listened to on his commutes to work. Though they were all different, they all had three things Alwan needed for his legal practice: success, money and influence. Mingling with the metropolitan elite had been his goal all along, and here was his chance.

But instead of lauding and reaping his good luck, Alwan could barely focus, his attention diverting every other second to his very lovely—*very fake*—fiancée beside him and the fact that he loved Lulu so fiercely he could think of nothing else.

And he might have wasted the whole night doing just that had Lulu not intervened.

She made it look natural, lightly bumping her foot against his beneath the table, waiting until he looked at her before leaning in, her hand falling over his chest right above his thumping heart, her face drawing near until her lips hovered next to his ear.

"Are you okay?"

He jerked a nod, hyperfocused on every part of her. Her temptingly sweet perfume, her soft brown eyes, her glistening lips and her soft curls brushing his cheek as she moved in closer to whisper in his ear again.

"Just remember, believe in your dream," she said. "It's worth it, all right?"

Not knowing what to say, Alwan grasped her hand atop his chest and squeezed lightly, his thumb caressing the inexpensive but pretty ring she'd bought herself. It should've reminded him that their relationship was built on nothing more than lies they were using to fool the world into believing they were in love. But a yearning for her, *for this* to be real roared in him instead.

Keeping it from showing on his face when she searched his eyes was probably the toughest thing he'd done in a long while, but Alwan knew he succeeded when Lulu smiled beautifully and turned back to strike up a chat with their guests.

He followed her lead and started rubbing shoulders.

By the time the charity event officially kicked off, their hosts introducing themselves and the worthy cause that everybody had gathered to support and donate generously to, Alwan had traded contact details with half of their table and made promising connections with the rest.

The exquisite high-end dinner was worth the thousands his ticket and Lulu's had cost him. After six courses, each more decadent and elaborately plated than the rest, Alwan almost worried he'd pop the studs and buttons off his dress shirt. So when a chamber orchestra started up a lively waltz and other gala attendants moved to the dance floor, he held a hand out to Lulu.

But she shook her head and leaned in to whisper, "I've never danced to this kind of music."

He wasn't having it, and eventually she relented with a sigh, slid her hand in his and Alwan grinned so wide his facial muscles strained from the force. Having her in his arms made the world bleed away until only they existed, just the two of them on the dance floor, swaying and twirling to the music.

For all her doubt, Lulu naturally took to the steps, never once crushing his toes. She glided in his arms, resplendent in her gown. Her crimson dress was so tonally embellished, it glimmered with her movement, every swish of the skirt's hem whispering over the ballroom's highly polished hardwood floor. She'd added a waist-length, matching sequined cape for what he supposed was modesty, but his eyes zeroed in on the tantalizing hints of the dress's thin straps and her warm brown skin through the cape's sheer material.

A fantasy of him teasingly peeling the cape and dress off her flashed through his mind. So vivid was the daydream, Alwan almost stopped them mid-twirl, reached out and plucked open the clasp to the cape at the hollow of her throat.

Instead of falling to his primal urges, he spun her around a few more times, holding her closer to him with each graceful loop around the other dancing couples on the floor. It should've satisfied him to be this near to her. His hand on her back, her warm, soft body pressed to his, her glittering eyes, awed smiles and chiming laughter all directed at him.

All his.

Possessiveness drummed a beat in his head that matched his fast-marching heart rate, and it nearly drowned out the finishing chord of the waltz. At the last moment he dipped her in a flourish, pulling her back up slowly against him until their bodies were flush.

Until Alwan realized that not even that was enough for him.

As the orchestra moved on to a classical pop cover, he pulled down closer to her to be heard over the noise. "Do you want to head out?"

She gave him a nod, allowing him to lead her off the dance floor and back to their table to grab her sparkly clutch purse.

"Won't your parents worry about us?" she asked as they walked through the hotel foyer.

"My mom already texted," he said. "They're having fun with their friends, and knowing them, that means they won't be leaving anytime soon."

"And you're sure you want to leave without saying hello to them?"

He nodded vigorously, not even bothering to hide that he was eager to have Lulu all to himself right now. Nothing short of a fire in the ballroom would make him go back to see his parents and leave her.

Outside, the city's bright lights and loud hum greeted them and he welcomed the mild night breeze on his heated face.

"I'll admit that ballroom dancing was *way* more fun than I'd thought it would ever be," she exclaimed breathlessly, all smiles, her chest heaving from the exertion still.

"It usually gets easier with practice."

"Does it?"

"I'm no professional, and I've spent most my adult life dodging these kinds of events, but I picked up the skill anyway."

Lulu smiled at him before she closed her eyes and tipped her face up to the light breeze, a sigh drifting from her full, glossy red lips. "I can smell the lake from here."

"We're close to the Harbourfront, so that's not surprising. Why don't we take a walk down there?"

They strolled the streets, chatting easily about their jobs, their families and friends, the celebrities at the gala—everything but what his head and heart truly wanted to discuss. In the leisurely twenty-minute walk to the harbor, Alwan waged an internal battle between what he desired and what he'd always believed wasn't meant for him.

He didn't think he could lower his guard long enough to let love creep in.

Yet now that it had, he never wanted it to leave him...

But it had with Hashim, a cynical little voice whispered.

He'd loved his brother so much, and hadn't ever thought that helping him would lead to Hashim leaving him forever. That kind of betrayal left a mark. A wound. A valuable lesson that trusting others only increased his odds of being let down and catching hurt feelings.

With Lulu, the odds of him getting hurt were even higher

because their relationship hadn't been meant to last. They had both always known that there was an ending.

That the end was soon.

That they probably wouldn't have a reason to be in each other's lives again after this.

If he kept this up, Alwan was risking a broken heart again.

And yet all of that hadn't put enough fear in him to run away. Hadn't stopped him from touching a hand to her arm and calling out her name when they arrived at the lakefront.

"Luula, wait. As lovely as this all is," he said, sweeping a hand out to the city towering before them on one side and the dark, glittering water of the lake on the other. "Truthfully, there's a reason I wanted us out here, alone."

She laughed, the fluted sound nervous. "Maybe I've listened to too much true crime, but is this the part where you kill me by drowning me in the lake?"

He smiled and shook his head slowly.

"Then what? Because you look scarily serious."

Alwan unbuttoned his dinner jacket and tucked his hands in his trouser pockets. He then faced the water, finding it easier and faster to organize his helter-skelter thoughts when he wasn't looking at her. "There's something I've been meaning to tell you. Something I've kept from you."

"Okay, *now* you're freaking me out," she said with another anxious laugh.

Hearing the small thread of fear in her voice nearly had him reconsidering all of this. *There's still a chance to walk this back...*

To walk away for good.

As soon as he thought it though, Alwan knew he couldn't do that.

He'd been thinking about this moment with her all night.

Waited patiently for it through the gala and obsessed over every detail as he played out the steps he'd take. And now that he had his opportunity, the idea of letting it slip through his fingers didn't sit right with him.

I have to tell her.

But first he nudged his chin out at the obsidian lake to the now-dark islands. "Have you ever been to the Island?"

"No, but I've always wanted to go. Why?"

"No reason except that every time I look at it, I remember my brother. Hashim and I used to go out there all the time, especially during the summers. First with our parents, but then when we were old enough, they'd let us go on the ferry all on our own.

"We'd pretend we were pirates. The ferry our pirate ship and the island the perfect hideaway for all our treasure." Alwan clenched his jaw at the memories flooding back, the good and the bad times with Hashim melding in together.

"Life felt…easier then. Like we were in control of our destinies and nothing could hurt us."

He swallowed, the slow, convulsive pull of his throat giving him all of two seconds to put his brave face on and finish what he'd started. "But that wasn't true. Hashim was hurting quietly for years after his sports injury. His surgery was successful, but the doctors had only healed him on the outside. Inside, he wasn't the same. He was suffering and I… I didn't see it until it was too late.

"I was his brother. I should've known. Should have seen the signs."

"Alwan, I'm so sorry," she said, her soft voice closer than he realized.

"I am too. But that doesn't change anything. Because I let him slip through the cracks and didn't catch him. I failed him. Failed my brother."

Her hand alighted on his arm, her fingers squeezing him until he finally gave in and looked at her.

"You can't think that way. You'll only hurt yourself."

"I can't help it though." His heart twisted in his chest for Hashim and all that his brother was once and had lost to addiction. "This guilt, it's become a part of me."

"Alwan..." She gripped his arm with both hands now, her brows pinched together, lovely mouth downturned and eyes darker, rounder and glimmering with sorrow for him.

He didn't think it could happen, but in that moment, right then and there, it truly felt like Lulu was hurting and grieving almost as much as he was.

When her chin quivered, he cupped her face, smiling down sadly at her. A need to comfort her took hold of him, and not thinking, simply reacting, he leaned into her until his lips settled on her forehead.

She inhaled, tensing a heartbeat before she relaxed, her gentle sigh drifting up to him.

And she sighed again when Alwan wrapped his arms around her, touched his forehead to hers and gazed deeply into her eyes, feeling a serenity he hadn't in a long time.

"I love you."

The words fell from his lips far more easily than he imagined they would.

Though she was quiet after he uttered the confession, he knew she'd heard him because her eyes had gone wide.

"I can't tell you when it happened, and I know it goes completely against what this fake engagement was supposed to be, but...but I can't stop. I've tried. I really have. And apparently, it's not a faucet I can just shut off at will."

When she didn't speak, Alwan began worrying and urged, "Luula, say something...please."

She blinked, whatever shocked trance she was in wearing off, and even before she pushed her hands on his chest, he knew what was coming.

Letting her go, Alwan watched her carve distance between them and dropped his now-leaden arms and reminded himself to breathe through the thorny pain already vining around his throbbing heart. He'd prepared for this. Knew this was always a fifty-fifty possibility. Steeled himself for it happening.

And yet now that it was, now he was looking at her and seeing her guardedness against him, he realized he could've never protected himself from this.

Stupid, he thought. What had he been thinking? That the scenery alone would sway her mind when she'd made it *very* clear to him and *very* early on that she didn't want a relationship again?

Did he really think she would make an exception for him? *I'm so stupid.*

Alwan gritted his teeth and clenched and unclenched his fists, his fingers still burning with the memory of holding her a minute ago.

She still hadn't said a word. Hadn't even acknowledged his love for her.

He shook his head, but it did nothing to dislodge the hurt and humiliation now taking hold of him. The longer he stood out there, the more the reality of his rejection sank in, and the sharper the heartache became. "Let's head back," he said, hating the brusque tone he used but knowing that the anger masked the anguish quickly consuming him.

Arms now wrapped around herself, eyes ever-wide and alert and full of wariness, Lulu nodded silently.

It struck him that the walk back to the hotel was markedly different in tone this time around. Where before they were conversing contentedly about anything and everything, now the atmosphere between them was thickly oppressive with all that they'd left unsaid.

When they arrived back at the upscale historic hotel, Lulu finally ended her silence.

"I'm going to grab a cab." She was already walking in the direction of the taxi stand outside the hotel.

Her declaration caught him by surprise. They'd arrived together, so he had just assumed that she would catch a ride back with him.

Why would she want to be near you after everything that just happened?

Jaw clenched, Alwan stepped toward her, his offer to drive her home on the tip of his tongue.

But at the last moment he stopped himself. If this was what she desired—if she truly wanted the space apart from him, then he'd respect her wishes. Still, it took all his strength to remain on the curb while Lulu gathered the long skirt of her gorgeous dress and slid into the back of a taxi. He didn't breathe until the car drove away. Didn't turn his back and leave until the cab ferrying her from him had melded with downtown traffic.

Now, if only he could turn and walk away from this still-beating love he had for her.

CHAPTER TEN

Two weeks.

That was the first thought in Alwan's mind when he woke up to the bluish-gray light of dawn glowing through his bedroom windows.

It'd been a full fourteen days since that fateful night he confessed his love to Lulu. Two of the longest weeks of his life, not only because he hadn't seen, called or texted her and had taken her silence as a sign to give her all the space she needed, but also because he'd been debating on what it meant for their fake engagement.

Since they'd pushed their deadline up to Labour Day, they had a few weeks left on the clock.

Technically he could hold her to that date. But it hadn't felt right using it to force his company on her. Though if he was being honest, he'd considered the underhanded tactic. *If only to see her...*

In the end the better part of him had won out and Alwan had nixed the idea of manipulating her into spending time with him. He even told himself that the distance and time apart would lessen this hungering ache and persistent longing for her.

But he should've known that time didn't really heal wounds.

If it had that power, would he still feel shame and remorse every time he thought of Hashim?

More and more now, he'd been thinking of his runaway brother. He knew it was partly because of Lulu and her rejection, but the other part was finally understanding that a lot of his decisions of late had been influenced by what had happened in the end with Hashim.

Without realizing it, Alwan had allowed his choice to answer his brother's call and get him away from the addiction treatment center to shape much of his life. From feeling guilty for hiding his role in Hashim's escape from their parents, to feeling like he'd owed them happiness and giving in to their desire to see him married. All of which then led him to seeking out Lulu and proposing the fake engagement in the first place. Before finally, culminating in him falling hard for her, telling her that he loved her—

And getting my heart broken.

Really, it was all his fault. He couldn't do anything about Hashim anymore, not when he didn't even know if his brother was alive or long gone from this world. But he could help Lulu by ending this now.

It would go against their agreement to announce their breakup mutually and together, but he couldn't ask her to do that after he'd dumped his feelings on her. No, he'd shoulder the blame all on his own. By the time she learned what he had done, the truth will have already come out.

Anyway, it's not like I haven't broken any of our rules.

He'd touched and hugged her. Kissed her—albeit only on the forehead, yet still.

More than the physical intimacy they had promised to avoid was the emotional connection they'd made. At least on his part, it had felt like she'd opened up to him and let him get near to her vulnerabilities. And he'd done the same, even coming close to sharing his secret about how it'd been his fault that Hashim had run off and disappeared. He had confided in her. *Trusted* her.

Loved her.

It hadn't been enough to change her stance on relationships though.

As he showered, dressed and left his place to drive over to his parents' home, Alwan ruminated on that and hoped that she'd see ending their fake engagement as the olive branch it was. *Maybe this doesn't have to be the end...*

It was that small silver lining he'd clung to as he rang the doorbell and greeted his parents' housekeeper at the front door of the Tudor-style mansion.

Alwan found his mother and father in the drawing room, the gleaming cherry oak walls and coffered ceiling warmed by vintage-inspired brass wall sconces. His father sat in the lone armchair across the white marble fireplace, a double-wall glass mug full of tea in one hand and a newspaper in the other, his readers perched at the edge of his long, thick nose as usual. His mother sat on the sofa and leaned over the coffee table, peering through a photo album while stacks more were littered on the sofa cushions on either side of her.

They both looked up when he entered.

"Salaam Yumma, Abu," he said, squeezing his father's shoulder as he passed behind him and then bending down so his mother could kiss him on the cheek.

She made room for him on the sofa before giving him a curious look. "Although I love when you drop in unannounced, habibi, it also worries me. Is there anything wrong?"

His father lowered the paper he was reading, his bushy graying brows hiked up with intrigue.

Alwan gulped, realizing right then that his intention to tell them the truth might not be as simple as he thought.

"Alwan?" his mother called to him, her hand squeezing his leg, the gesture meant to be comforting but only heightening his guilt.

Choosing cowardice, he said, "No, nothing's wrong. I… I just wanted to see you both, that's all."

"Isn't that sweet?" his mother gushed, pinching his cheek. "How did we get to be such lucky parents?"

Alwan's father snorted lightly and was already lifting his paper up, but not before Alwan caught his warm smile.

Their praise swelled his chest with joy, momentarily numbing his guilt at the secrets he kept from them.

Wanting to hold on to the happiness a little longer, Alwan pointed to the photo album open on the glass coffee table. "What are you doing? Rearranging photos?" She had some of the pictures pulled out of the plastic pockets and spread out on the coffee table around a gold tray holding a tea set.

"I was, but then I became distracted," his mother said, nodding as she poured him a cup of shai.

"I haven't looked at some of these albums in so long. I almost forgot we took some of these pictures," she told him once she handed him a teacup.

Picking up one of the albums, Alwan flipped through a few pages and immediately understood what she felt as memories he'd forgotten came flooding back. He smiled and laughed at most of them, reliving the experiences in those frozen stills of his family's past. Although he should've known it was coming, it still gave him pause when he turned another page in the album and saw a younger Hashim staring back up at him.

In the photo he posed in his rugby jersey, the biggest grin on his face.

"He loved playing so much," his mother reminisced, surprising Alwan because his parents often didn't speak about Hashim.

And she continued to comment as Alwan looked through more of the album, smiling and sighing and even stroking some of the photos as if she could touch Hashim through them. Remorse constricted his chest, the chains tightening when his mother reached for a tissue and wiped her eyes at one point.

"Yumma," he quietly said, contrition squeezing his vocal cords.

"It's fine," his mother insisted with a sniffle. He might have believed her if her lips weren't trembling with the tears she was holding back.

His father lowered his newspaper swiftly and set his mug on the coffee table. "Stop looking at those if they're making you so sad. Put them away, Alwan. Put all of them away," he said firmly, his scowl fearsome.

Shaking her head, his mother pulled the album away from Alwan gently before he could even consider following his father's stern instruction.

"There's no reason to do that. He's still our son after all."

His father huffed and flung his hands out. "Son? What son abandons his parents and his younger brother?"

Alwan winced, not so much at his father's raised voice but the angry hurt in his tone as he hurled the words.

"Hashim is *our* son. No matter what happened, nothing will ever change that for me," his mother said, a fire in her teary eyes as she clutched the album to her chest, hugging the only connection to her other son that remained.

"Do what you want, but all of this—" his father stabbed his finger at the albums on the coffee table and the sofa "— all it does is bring us pain that I want no part of."

His mother covered her face with her hands and his father's pale brown cheeks were so red that Alwan worried he'd pop a vein.

"It's my fault," he whispered, the silence in the room amplifying his quiet voice and making his words crash as loud as thunder.

Both his mother and father snapped their heads to him.

Closer to him, his mother set the album aside and took his hands in her own. But Alwan pulled his hands away from her, unable to take her comfort without his culpability choking him completely. And before that happened, he needed to tell them everything—

All of it.

"I'm the one that you should blame. Not each other," he said.

"Alwan," his mother said, reaching for his hands again and holding on tighter this time, "your abu and I don't blame each other. And we would never blame you. What happened with Hashim, his sickness, it was not his fault either."

Alwan shook his head slowly, his eyes downcast and filling up. "It *is* my fault though. I'm the reason that Hashim is gone. I am why he isn't here with all of us now. I… I helped him escape. It was me. He called me and he asked if I could come to get him. I understand now why he had to go to the treatment center, but back then all I thought was that he needed me and I had to help him."

He then told them how he took the car, drove with only his learner's permit to the treatment center and picked his brother up after Hashim had snuck out of the building.

All these years and it just came pouring out of him, the dam completely broken, his vision swimming as he blinked free the first of his tears. At the end, having run completely dry of words, Alwan squeezed his eyes shut and covered them with a hand, crying quietly.

His mother embraced him, her warm bakhoor fragrance taking him back to all the times he'd skinned his knees and needed her comfort to ease the pain. Only this pain was burrowed so much deeper and had lived with him for so much longer.

Pulling him back by the shoulders eventually, his mother cupped his chin and forced him to look her in the eye.

"Alwan, we know," she said with a tender smile.

Shock swept away his shame and he stared wide-eyed back at her.

She lowered her hand from his chin and squeezed his shoulders. "We've always known, ya habibi."

Alwan looked between them, his father now sighing and resting back in his armchair.

"How?" he breathed.

"The treatment center caught you both on their security cameras. They told us the same night they reported that Hashim had left."

Alwan couldn't believe his ears. All this time he'd been hiding what he thought was some big, dark secret—all these years of worrying that he'd hurt them, and all he'd been doing was torturing himself. "W-why didn't you tell me?"

His mother gave him a pained look and patted his hands now. "We thought that it was for the best. That if we said anything, you'd blame and never forgive yourself. But it seems we inflicted the very harm we were trying to avoid." She hugged him again, squeezing him so tightly his ribs hurt but in a good way. "We're sorry, habibi. We should have said something from the beginning."

Alwan nodded and held still as his mother kissed him on the cheeks.

"Your yumma is right, Alwan," his father said, his expression softer now. "Put it out of your mind that it's your fault. It's no one's fault. Your brother simply made his decision to move on without us. If he ever chooses to return, then we'll welcome him. He is after all our son."

His mother beamed and squeezed Alwan's hands. "Now do you feel better?"

"I do," he said with a small smile. He did feel better without the weight of his secret about Hashim, but he was instantly reminded of the real reason he'd come over when his mother gave him a long look.

"And was that why you came over, or is something else bothering you? Because I had another reason for looking at these photo albums. I was seeing if there was room for more pictures once you and Luula get married."

Hearing Lulu's name had him tensing all over once more.

Especially when his mother said, "I haven't seen her in a while."

He opened his mouth, fully prepared to divulge his other secret. But before he could tell his parents that his and Lulu's engagement was a fabrication, his mother frowned at him.

"Alwan, have you done something to upset her again? Because if you have, I already told you that apologizing and communicating are very important to marriage."

If he knew that a simple apology would fix everything, Alwan would've already been down on his knees in front of Lulu a long while ago.

"She's just busy," he lied.

His mother didn't look like she believed him, but she slowly nodded. "Very well. But you bring her along with you next time, and tell her that we miss her."

I miss her too.

Two weeks without seeing and hearing from her was breaking him. After he left his parents, he sat in his car in their long, cobbled driveway and replayed that last night with her. Only now he realized that he hadn't given her a chance to talk. She'd been silent, yes, but he had jumped to the conclusion that she was rejecting him.

And maybe she wasn't, he thought, hope budding in him.

Maybe it'd be like with his parents, when he'd been so certain that they'd resent him for the role he'd played in Hashim's disappearance and the exact opposite was true.

Sitting up straighter, Alwan started his engine and sped off onto the busy city streets, already mapping out a game plan on how he'd try and shoot his shot with Lulu again.

And it either worked this time…

Or I let her go forever.

"Should I text him?" Lulu asked Blue, brushing a comb down his back in smooth, gentle strokes. They were sitting in the middle of her bedroom, her legs crossed and Blue dozing off in front of her. He opened his eyes and gave her a big yawn.

She sighed. "You're right. It's probably a bad idea." But even as she said it, Lulu's mind wandered over to Alwan, just as it had every day for the past two weeks. Not only had he become her waking thought, his face was the last thing she saw when she drifted off to sleep every night. And she wasn't even counting the dreams she'd been having of him lately. Dreams she wished she could say were pleasant, but were mostly variants of the same event: the night he confessed to her.

If that wasn't enough, Lulu had replayed that evening over and over in her head since then and still cringed at her reaction every single time.

When Alwan had told her he loved her, she'd just *frozen* up. There was no other way to describe it except that she had become a human statue. She didn't think she'd ever been that mortified in her life. Especially when Alwan asked her to say something and all she could do was stare at him like a deer trapped in headlights.

It's not like it's my fault. He surprised me.

She hadn't expected him to tell her that he loved her.

Sure, there had been the confusing electrical undercurrents of *something* that felt a lot like unbridled attraction and desire between them. But lust wasn't *love*. It wasn't the passion she heard in his voice as he'd said those three words to her, the reverence in his dark eyes as he looked at her, and it most definitely wasn't the heartbreak on his face when she hadn't given him a response.

Not even the barest reaction. No wonder he hasn't even messaged...

Lulu bit her lip, her frustration at the situation tangling up with her guilt. She was so caught up in her emotions, her brushstrokes snagged over Blue's fluffy white coat. No longer relaxed, he yowled at her immediately, batting his pink toe beans at the comb before bounding up onto all fours and prowling away from her, his tail raised indignantly.

"Sorry," she murmured after him, setting the comb aside and drawing her knees up to her chest.

She wasn't in the best control of her emotions as of late. It felt as if Alwan's confession had flung open the doors on the long-sealed part of her that had sworn off of romantic relationships and love in general. Because of him, now—after all this time—he had her wondering "what if?"

What if Lulu told him that she reciprocated his attraction?

What if she had said that these past few months faking an engagement with him had been the most thrilling of her life?

But most of all, she wondered what if she had said and done anything but the *nothing* she'd ended up doing.

Lulu's gaze drifted to her bed, knowing that the suitcase

underneath was a good part of the reason she had gone silent when Alwan had told her that he loved her. Before she knew it, she had moved there and pulled it back out.

Smoothing her hands over the hard shell, she remembered why she'd held on to the suitcase all this time.

First it was a symbol of her loss, but then it had become a reminder of why love was dangerous and why she shouldn't give herself the hope of ever trying for a family again.

But now, when Lulu looked at it, it just felt like it no longer belonged.

Picking up her phone, she pulled up to sit on the edge of the bed and rubbed between Blue's ears as she scrolled through to find the locations of the nearest donation bins. "I'm ready to let go," she told him when he nuzzled her hand with his face, his wet nose and rough tongue scraping over her fingers. The peace she felt was inexplicable...and also short-lived as a text from Alwan pinged in her inbox.

Need to talk. Will you meet me here?

He sent a location pin, and Lulu was intrigued to see it was Ward's Island, one of the Toronto Islands.

She already knew her response even before she sent it, but her excitement to see him melded with a trepidation over what he might have to say to her and how she'd react this time.

Figuring she could use a companion, Lulu peered down at Blue and asked, "Want to go on an adventure?"

Getting off the ferry, Lulu messaged Alwan and wasn't kept in suspense for long.

He texted her back with a live location, and she followed it all the way to him.

"You came," he said, standing in a break between trees at the sandy edge of the island. He looked nervous as he swiped his hands over his thighs and strolled up to her, wearing another of his handsome business suits. "I thought you might not, given how we left things last."

She wasn't surprised he'd said that. Just as Alwan hadn't believed she would show up, Lulu hadn't expected for him to text her, let alone with an invitation to meet up. Honestly, she wouldn't have been shocked if he'd just ended the fake engagement and moved on. The fact he hadn't and that he appeared happy to see her uplifted her mood and gave her some hope that, maybe, this wasn't the end after all...

From inside his carrier, Blue meowed loudly and insistently until she let him out and strapped him in his harness and leash.

Alwan chuckled softly.

"I should've known you two would come as a package," he rumbled above her, shocking her when he crouched down next to her. Though she didn't mind him being so close, Blueberry bared his fangs and hissed at him. "After all this time, he still doesn't like me. Is it because I didn't invite him?"

Stifling a grin at the adorable pout on Alwan's face, Lulu played along and shrugged. "Who knows? Maybe."

"Okay, fine, my ego's taken a hit. But one of these days, I'll win him over," he vowed, smirking at her.

It was the conviction in that promise that had her heart juddering faster. Because it sounded awfully like he was planning to see her cat again.

Which means he's planning to see me.

Hope washed through her as Alwan slowly rose up to full height and offered his hand to her. Grasping it gently,

Lulu blushed when his fingers squeezed hers and lingered after he'd helped her up.

When he did eventually let her go, he rubbed at his bearded jaw, the edginess she'd felt from him earlier rushing back.

"First, before I say anything, I want to apologize for my behavior on our last night together," he said with a frown, his brow lined with tension. "I… I should have been more understanding to you after I'd said what I said."

After he'd told her that he loved her, he meant.

The pressure over Lulu's chest pressed down harder, her guilt intertwining with the same pining she'd endured the last two weeks being apart from him. She opened her mouth to tell him that it wasn't his fault. That he'd shocked her with his confession, and that she'd been so confused, so unable to accept that he could care for her.

That he could love me.

But before she could utter a word, Alwan moved on.

"I should have let you understand what I was feeling and why. So, I'm going to fix my mistake and do that now. Starting with telling you the truth of what happened with my brother…and me. Because Hashim didn't just run away on his own. I helped him."

Lulu listened as Alwan told her about how his older brother had called him up and asked for a ride to leave the treatment center he was admitted to for his addiction. How after Alwan had shown up, Hashim had asked to be dropped off at the nearest train station.

"I didn't know that he'd buy a ticket to the next departing train and never look back. I sat there waiting in the car for almost an hour before I realized that he wasn't coming back, realized what he'd done and how he'd used me. I couldn't bring myself to tell my parents about the part I'd played once they found out that Hashim had left.

"I held on to that secret so long that I'd convinced myself they'd hate me if I ever revealed the truth, when all along my mom and dad knew what I'd done, and had chosen not to ask me about it as a way of protecting me. They worried that if they addressed it I would carry guilt and feel blame, not knowing that I did anyway."

Alwan sighed heavily. "What I'm trying to say is that I've only just realized in the last few days that I allowed what happened with Hashim to run my life. I convinced myself that I couldn't trust anyone, and that I was better off being on my own. And it worked…until you. Being with you these last four months has opened my eyes to just how lonely my life's become.

"Sure, I've got my career aspirations, but they aren't enough."

Lulu's breaths came out shallow, sawing through her lungs as he stepped in closer to her and lifted his hands, his fingers hovering by her cheeks.

"Being with you has made me want something I thought I'd never want. But I also know what you've been through, so after all this, I'll only say this one more time and respect your decision, whatever you choose." He paused meaningfully for a moment before he stopped her world again.

"Lulu, I love you."

Gazing into his eyes, she could see his yearning, adoration and the love he spoke of shining through clearly. Hear it catching deeply in his voice. It should've been enough to cast all her doubts away, but she still held on to one that kept her defensive. Clung to it like a lifeline as a little voice warned that they'd both end up being hurt if this continued.

"Why would you want to be with me?" she asked so

softly she barely heard herself. Shaking her head numbly, she said, "I have nothing to offer you. Not the kind of money or prestige you might want in a wife, not even the ability to…to give you a *family*. I'm sure something's long broken inside of me."

"Lulu—"

"It's true," she said, speaking over him, her eyes filling with tears. "I don't know if I could love again, and I don't know if I'm ready to risk being hurt by someone I care for deeply. Do you know what it feels like to watch someone you love look at you like a stranger? See their love for you eroding before your eyes?" She blinked and freed her tears, let them track down her cheeks as she tipped her head back to look at Alwan head-on. "I'm *broken*."

He framed her face with his hands, his gaze boring into her, his expression stern. "I don't believe that."

"You should," she whimpered. "Have I told you why I called my cat Blueberry? And, no, it's not because of his eye color.

"I got him the same week I found out I was pregnant. Seven weeks pregnant. My baby was just about the size of a blueberry…" Lulu let out a humorless laugh. "That's why you shouldn't want this. Want me. I can't give you what you want."

"What I want," Alwan began, lowering his head and leveling their eyes, "is right here."

"You don't mean that," she whispered.

"I do though," he argued gently.

"Well, what if you want a family? I'm sure your parents or mine want grandkids to spoil rotten someday and if I can't…"

"Then we don't," he said.

"Okay, but what if I decide I want to leave the city and travel some more?"

"Well, then I'd be willing to try a long-distance relationship."

"But—" She broke off with a muffled moan as Alwan kissed her for the first time, his lips coaxing hers to respond, the heat between them as electric and consuming as she'd always known it would be. When he broke off, he stayed close to her, their noses touching, hot breaths mingling, and his love staring back at her, his arms now holding, comforting and reassuring her.

"Are you sure?" she asked, breathless and still floating from his kiss.

Alwan's laugh melted her lingering doubt and stopped her tears.

"I'm certain that I love you, Lulu, and no matter how you think I feel or *should* feel, it doesn't change that fact. Doesn't change that I long for you. I. Love. You." He punctuated his declaration with little soft kisses to her parted lips.

"And you're sure you won't resent me later?"

"Resenting you would be like resenting myself, and I could never do that to me, and most definitely not to you." Then Alwan kissed her again, and Lulu felt it through her body, in her buzzing heart and head and right down to her soul.

"I can see why you like this place so much," Lulu said, looking from their tangled fingers and over her shoulder to him. She was sitting between his legs, her back pressed to his front, and her curly hair tickling his face. It was the only place Alwan wanted to be right then.

And forever, he thought happily.

He smiled at her. "It takes ahold of you, doesn't it?"

They looked out at the view of Toronto's skyline, the sun beginning to descend and lighting up the sky and the city in its wash of orange-golden light.

"Beautiful," Lulu said a little while later when the sun glowed behind the CN Tower, the fading light of day glittering in the lake.

Alwan saw exactly what she meant, but he found his stare tracking down to her at one point as he agreed, "Yeah, beautiful." He hugged her, wondering how he'd gotten so lucky.

She must have been thinking the same thing because she said, "I can't believe that a fake engagement did this." Lulu raised their clasped hands and shook her head in awe. "We only broke all our stipulations to get here."

He laughed and pressed a kiss to the heated tip of her ear. "Our little save-the-date charade turned out to be a big hit for us, so I can't complain if some rules were broken along the way."

"Incorrigible," she muttered, but her bright smile told him everything.

"I am, but you love it." He kissed her cheek, delighted when she turned her head to him and presented her soft, luscious mouth. They were both breathless by the time he lifted his head and panted, "Speaking of our charade, what ever happened to your RV repairs?"

"They're actually ready." Lulu looked away, confusing him by her sudden shyness until she explained, "They have been for a week now."

"A week? Why didn't you say so?"

"Because I kind of forgot to check my email with the update. I got so caught up in everything that was happening with us, that it escaped my mind."

Alwan grinned, understanding what she meant exactly. These last two weeks without her had stalled his life almost completely. He hadn't been able to focus on his practice or any work, for that matter. Though he imagined that would change now that Lulu had accepted his love.

"Did you want company to go pick up your motor home?" he asked, toying with the fake engagement ring she'd bought herself. "Alberta's a long way from here."

"I guess you can come. If you don't mind Blueberry coming along too?"

Alwan glanced over to where her cat lounged nearby on a Muskoka chair. "How could I mind it when he's so much a part of you?"

Lulu trapped his chin in her soft hand and slowly pulled up to touch her lips to his, whispering, "I think that's the sweetest thing you've ever said."

"Sweeter than telling you that I love you a whole lot?"

She scrunched her nose adorably. "Okay, maybe that *is* sweeter."

He chuckled and kissed her again, only this time longer and deeper, until her taste filled him, body and soul.

But they were both wrong, because there was something sweeter than their kisses.

"I love you," Lulu said when they took a break to catch their breaths.

It struck him that she hadn't spoken the words yet, but now that she had, Alwan couldn't believe it. And he asked her to say it again.

"I love you," she repeated with a bashful little smile.

"Say it again."

"I love you."

"Again," he breathed against her mouth, his heart leaping with joy.

And when she whispered, "I love you, Alwan," and kissed him, it left no doubt in his mind that she truly did.

EPILOGUE

"We really did it, didn't we?" Lulu touched the diamond platinum band on her finger, awe at its beauty filling her every time. The halo diamond ring was almost a perfect replica of the fake engagement ring she'd bought herself. Only these diamonds were very real and vividly bright in the hushed, cool darkness of Alwan's latest flashy car, an English white Rolls-Royce. She looked up at him as he took her hand and raised it to his lips, his mouth brushing the ring he'd given her, a symbol of their steady, eternal love.

"We did," he said, his slow, sinful smile stirring up those all-too-familiar butterflies in her stomach. "And now you're mine *for real*."

"Ditto." She gasped when his hand slid to her wrist and he gently tugged her across the back seat to him. Holding her to his chest, he kissed her with the hunger of a man that had kept his desires in check while they performed the nikah at the masjid.

Sure enough, he nipped her lip and pulled back, grinning wolfishly at her as he said, "I've been thinking of doing that all through the ceremony, and I might have if I wasn't positive that I'd have scandalized the imam and our families."

Lulu laughed when he smacked another kiss on her.

He cuddled her to him then, his hands wandering to the satin lacing of her corset bodice. She reached around and caught his wrists. "Not here," she whispered, flinging a look at the opaque privacy glass.

"Don't worry. The driver can't see us…or hear us, for that matter," he reassured her when she looked back at him.

"Hear us?" she echoed, confused.

At least she was until Alwan started tickling her, his hands running along her sides, finding all her secret sensitive spots. She wriggled against him, peals of laughter filling the back of the car. Soon her giggled pleas for mercy turned to soft moans when he kissed and nipped along her jawline to her collar and right above her heaving breasts.

She was so caught up in him that she hadn't noticed they had arrived at the venue.

It was Alwan who sat her up and helped smooth her dress of any evidence of their passion. Righting his tux next, he opened the car door, exited and guided her out with a hand before offering his arm to her.

As they walked up to the familiar castle-like mansion together, Lulu beamed up at Alwan, thrilled that he had surprised her by reserving their reception at the Casa Loma. She had fallen in love with the garden grounds and the darkly romantic, majestic stone building. They were supposed to meet their families and friends in the garden, at the glass pavilion she and Alwan had visited once before, but instead of heading down the path she knew would take them there, he steered her toward the parking lot.

"Where are we going?"

He grinned mischievously. "We're almost there, so why spoil the surprise?"

And he was right. After a short walk, Lulu saw what he was alluding to. Her motor home was there rather than where she'd parked it last.

"What's going on?" she asked warily, but still letting him lead her closer to the back of the RV to reveal the surprise.

Lulu covered her mouth with a hand when she saw it.

In big bold dark blue lettering was one word: *Blueberry*.

"Your RV needed a name, and this one felt appropriate." Alwan came up behind her, his arms circling her, his lips near her ear. "If you want to change it though, that's cool too."

Lulu blinked rapidly and sniffled, fanning at her face and crying out, "Alwan, really? My makeup doesn't need this right before our wedding reception." She turned around and hugged him, looking up only when she was sure she wasn't going to tear up. "I can't believe it's been a whole two years. That we started here," she said with a look back at the RV.

In those two years, a lot had happened. After they confessed their love to each other, they'd announced to their families that they wanted to take a step back and explore their relationship. Everyone had been more than happy to support them. And while they dated and got to know each other, Alwan's private practice went on to thrive, and Lulu had chosen to stay in the city with her family and had finally told them about her miscarriage. She and Alwan had even discussed their feelings and hopes about possibly one day having children, and he'd told her that he was happy trying for a family with her only if she wished for it.

Feeling a swell of appreciation and love for him, she sprang up on her toes and pecked his lips.

He stole his own kisses.

"My makeup," she reminded him as he kissed her cheeks and forehead.

Laughing, he took her hand and pulled her into the RV. Locking the door, he turned on her and swept her up into his arms and carried her to the bedroom, right past their two astonished cats. Blueberry and their latest addition Pea, a tiny, big-eared Cornish Rex who Alwan had adopted over a year ago.

"We're going to be late for the reception," she warned.

He shrugged and winked at her. "I'm okay with that. Besides, better late than not showing up."

"Alwan, don't you dare—" Lulu cut off with a squeal as he dropped her onto the bed.

He followed her, covering her body with his and making her forget her protests with his drugging kisses and rapturous caresses. At the end of it, her makeup wasn't the only thing she had to worry about.

As she lay in his arms, both their outfits rumpled, Lulu didn't think he could make her happier.

But then Alwan said, "I took three weeks off and I thought we could travel in the RV for our honeymoon."

She snapped up and looked down at him. "Do you mean it? What about your business? You can't close the office down for three weeks…"

"And I'm not going to. I trust my staff, and I've let my clients know that I'll be spending quality time with my once fake fiancée, now new wife."

"You did *not* tell them about our fake engagement," she griped, swatting his chest.

Alwan caught her hand and pulled her down to him, his thumb stroking over her engagement ring. "I didn't, but it wouldn't have mattered if I had because this is real now and will be always."

"I love you," she said, her heart never so full.

"I love you more."

Lulu rolled her eyes at his ever-present ego, but this time she let it go because his confidence proved that their love was as bright and hopeful as their future together.

* * * * *

*If you enjoyed this story, check out these
other great reads from Hana Sheik*

Another Shot at Forever
Falling for Her Forbidden Bodyguard
The Baby Swap that Bound Them
Forbidden Kisses with Her Millionaire Boss

All available now!

MILLS & BOON®

Coming next month

OFF GRID AND OFF LIMITS
Jenni Fletcher

'Why don't you come to the race this weekend and see what you think?' Dario suggested. 'I'll go as fast as I can. Just for you.'

He chuckled and held a hand out. 'What do you say, Ms. Thorne? Do we have a deal?'

'Livi.' She seemed to take a deep breath before wrapping her fingers around his. 'And yes, we have a deal.'

'Good.' He stiffened, surprised by a sudden buzz of heat, like electricity shooting up his arm. If he wasn't mistaken, her pupils flared at the same moment, as if she felt it too, before she yanked her hand away again.

'That's settled then.' She spun on her heel, practically running away from him toward the door. 'I'll go and find Camille.'

'Good idea.' He flexed his fingers. He had no idea what had just happened, but now it seemed he had two objectives for the weekend—to win the race and to convince her.

He wasn't sure which was going to be the bigger challenge.

Continue reading

OFF GRID AND OFF LIMITS
Jenni Fletcher

Available next month
millsandboon.co.uk

Copyright © 2026 Jenni Fletcher

COMING SOON!

We really hope you enjoyed reading this book. If you're looking for more romance be sure to head to the shops when new books are available on

Thursday 26th March

To see which titles are coming soon, please visit
millsandboon.co.uk/nextmonth

MILLS & BOON

TWO BRAND NEW BOOKS FROM
Love Always

Be prepared to be swept away to incredible worldwide destinations along with our strong, relatable heroines and intensely desirable heroes.

OUT NOW

Four Love Always stories published every month, find them all at:

millsandboon.co.uk

FOUR BRAND NEW BOOKS FROM
MILLS & BOON MODERN

Indulge in desire, drama, and breathtaking romance – where passion knows no bounds!

OUT NOW

Eight Modern stories published every month, find them all at:

millsandboon.co.uk

OUT NOW!

Available at
millsandboon.co.uk

MILLS & BOON

LET'S TALK
Romance

For exclusive extracts, competitions and special offers, find us online:

- MillsandBoon
- @MillsandBoon
- @MillsandBoonUK
- @MillsandBoonUK

Get in touch on 01413 063 232

For all the latest titles coming soon, visit
millsandboon.co.uk/nextmonth